Who Will Remember

Titles by C. S. Harris

What Angels Fear

When Gods Die

Why Mermaids Sing

Where Serpents Sleep

What Remains of Heaven

Where Shadows Dance

When Maidens Mourn

What Darkness Brings

Why Kings Confess

Who Buries the Dead

When Falcons Fall

Where the Dead Lie

Why Kill the Innocent

Who Slays the Wicked

Who Speaks for the Damned

What the Devil Knows

When Blood Lies

Who Cries for the Lost

What Cannot Be Said

Who Will Remember

Who Will Remember

A Sebastian St. Cyr Mystery

C. S. Harris

BERKLEY
New York

BERKLEY
An imprint of Penguin Random House LLC
1745 Broadway, New York, NY 10019
penguinrandomhouse.com

Library of Congress Cataloging-in-Publication Data

Names: Harris, C. S., author.
Title: Who will remember / C.S. Harris.
Description: New York : Berkley, 2025. | Series: A Sebastian St. Cyr mystery
Identifiers: LCCN 2024031506 | ISBN 9780593639214 (hardcover) |
ISBN 9780593639221 (ebook)
Subjects: LCGFT: Detective and mystery fiction. | Novels.
Classification: LCC PS3566.R5877 W47858 2025 | DDC
813/.54--dc23/eng/20240712
LC record available at https://lccn.loc.gov/2024031506

Printed in the United States of America
1st Printing

The authorized representative in the EU for product safety and compliance is Penguin Random House Ireland, Morrison Chambers, 32 Nassau Street, Dublin D02 YH68, Ireland, https://eu-contact.penguin.ie.

For Audrey.

Welcome to the world, little one.

Darkness

I had a dream, which was not all a dream.
The bright sun was extinguish'd, and the stars
Did wander darkling in the eternal space,
Rayless, and pathless, and the icy earth
Swung blind and blackening in the moonless air;
Morn came and went—and came, and brought no day,
And men forgot their passions in the dread
Of this their desolation; and all hearts
Were chill'd into a selfish prayer for light . . .

—LORD BYRON

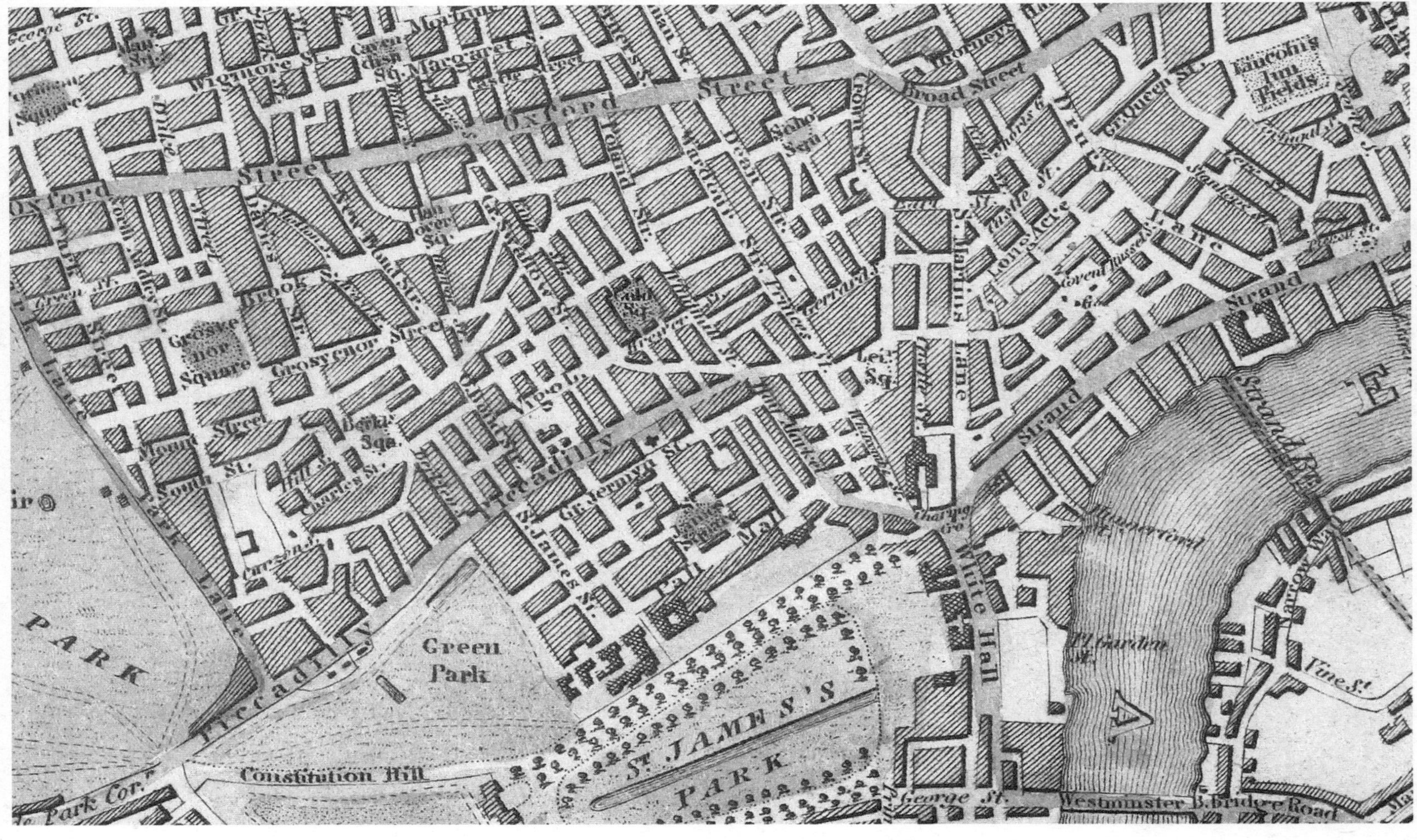

Wigmore St.
St. Margaret St.
Oxford Street
Broad Street
Lincolns Inn Fields
Gr. Queen St.
Drury Lane
Soho Squ.
Dean Str.
Princes St.
S. Martins Lane
Long Acre
Covent G.
Strand
Strand Br.
Hanover Sq.
Davies St.
Brook Str.
New Bond Str.
Grosvenor Square
Grosvenor Street
Mount Street
Berkley Sqr.
Charles St.
Curzon St.
Piccadilly
Gr. Jermyn St.
S. James St.
Hay Market
Charing Cro.
White Hall
Vine St.
A
E
Green Park
St. James's Park
Constitution Hill
Park Lane
Park
Park Cor.
George St.
Westminster B. Bridge Road

Who Will Remember

Chapter 1

London: Monday, 19 August 1816

The boy stood with his thin shoulders hunched against the cold, his hands shoved deep in the pockets of his ragged coat. Narrowing his eyes against the slanting rain, he studied the silent windows of a certain elegant town house on the far side of Brook Street, then shivered.

It was only midafternoon and yet already the sky was dark and gloomy, the wind icy enough to make it feel more like February or March than high summer. But then, they hadn't had anything like a summer that year. The crops in the fields were dying—or dead. People were already going hungry, and Father said he didn't know what the poor would do when winter came. Lots of folks were scared, saying the weather wasn't ever gonna get better, that the end of the world must be upon them and Jesus would be coming back soon to save the righteous and smite the wicked.

At the thought, the boy shivered again, for he sure enough

knew which category he belonged to—he and Father both. Then a flicker of movement jerked his attention back across the street, and he watched as a wavering light appeared in the room that lay to one side of that shiny black front door, as if someone there was lighting a brace of candles. A tall, lean man with dark hair and a slight limp crossed in front of the room's windows. It was the nobleman the boy was here to see: Viscount Devlin, he was called.

A trickle of rain ran down the boy's cheek to tickle his bare neck, and he swiped at his wet face with the back of one hand. He was afraid that what he was about to do was a mistake. But *something* needed to be done.

Sucking in a deep breath of the foul, coal smoke–scented air, the boy leapt the rushing gutter at his feet and crossed the street's wet granite paving. But at the base of the house's steps, he faltered. He had to force himself to march up the steps and grasp the door's shiny brass knocker. He brought it down so hard that he jumped back in surprise.

The door was opened almost at once by a grim-looking majordomo with a military air and a forbidding frown that darkened as he took in the ragged, undersized lad shifting nervously from one bare foot to the other. "The service entrance is—"

"Sure then, but 'tis his lordship I'm here to see—Lord Devlin, I mean," said the boy in a rush before the man could shut the door on him. "About a body, it is: a dead man. His face is all purple, ye see, and he's hanging—hangin' upside down."

"Ah," said the majordomo, some emotion Jamie couldn't quite decipher twitching the man's thin lips as he took a step back and opened the door wider. "Then, in that case, I suppose you'd better come in."

Chapter 2

Sebastian Alistair St. Cyr, Viscount Devlin, rested his hips against the edge of his desk and leaned back, taking the weight off a leg that still gave him more trouble than he liked to admit. He was a former cavalry captain, in his thirties, tall and lean, with dark hair and strange, wolflike yellow eyes. He was known to the world as the only surviving son and heir of the Earl of Hendon, although he was not, in truth, Hendon's son.

The black-haired boy who stood before him, blue eyes wide with fear as he nervously twisted his wet, ragged hat between his hands, looked to be perhaps fourteen or fifteen, although seriously underfed and scrawny. His features were even and surprisingly clean, but then, that might be the work of the rain.

"What's your name, lad?"

The boy had to swallow hard before he could answer, and even then his voice came out hushed and scratchy. "Gallagher, sir. Jamie Gallagher."

Jamie. It was a name that still had the power to twist at something deep inside Sebastian, even after three years, so that it was a moment before he trusted himself to speak. "Tell me about this dead man, Jamie. Where is he?"

"He's in the ruins of that old chapel, sir," said the boy in a soft Irish lilt. "Ye know the one? In the courtyard off Swallow Street where they're tearin' down everything to make way for the Regent's grand new avenue?"

"I've seen it. You say he's hanging upside down?"

Jamie nodded. "Hangin' by one foot, he is, sir. And someone done tied his hands behind his back, too—like this." The boy bent his arms, elbows spreading wide as he thrust both hands behind him.

So obviously not a suicide, thought Sebastian. Aloud he said, "Why come to me? Why not find a local bailiff or constable, or go to the nearest public office?"

The boy dug one mud-streaked bare big toe into the rug at his feet. "Faith, ye think they'd listen to the likes of me? Toss me in the watchhouse for making a disturbance, that's what they'd do—if they didn't go decidin' it musta been me who done for the nob and hang me."

The nob. This was a new detail. "The dead man is a gentleman?"

The boy sniffed. "Sure then, but he must be, wearin' clothes that fine."

Pushing away from the desk, Sebastian walked to the library door. He spoke for a moment with his majordomo, then glanced over at the boy. "Morey here will take you down to the kitchens for a bite to eat while the horses are put to."

At the mention of food, something leapt in the boy's eyes, something painful to see. But he wasn't about to be distracted from his original purpose. "So you'll be comin', then? You'll be lookin' into it?"

"I'll come," said Sebastian.

"It might be a trap," said Hero some minutes later as she watched Sebastian move about his dressing room. She stood in the doorway from the bedroom, the Honorable Miss Guinevere Annabelle Sophia St. Cyr, their nine-month-old daughter, balanced on one fashionably gowned hip. The baby was chewing on a chubby fist, her brilliant blue eyes narrowed with the seriousness of her task, and Sebastian paused for a moment to tousle with a gentle hand the child's silken fair hair before turning away again.

"It might be," he acknowledged, reaching for his greatcoat. "But I doubt it."

"You will be careful."

"I'm always careful."

His wife made a scoffing sound deep in her throat and shifted the baby to her other hip. "No, you're not."

"Well, more careful than I used to be," he acknowledged, looking up with a smile as he slipped a small double-barreled pistol into the pocket of his coat.

Chapter 3

The rain had eased off by the time they left, although the air was still cool and damp against their faces, the sky above heavy gray, the city's cobblestones and granite setts glistening with wet. Sebastian had decided to take his curricle, both because the chestnuts needed exercising and because after months and months of endless rain he was sick and tired of riding in a closed carriage.

The boy, Jamie, sat hunched on the high seat beside him, his shoulders rounded and his hands clasped between his knees so tightly the knuckles showed white. He was obviously frightened. But then, reasoned Sebastian, what lad wouldn't be after stumbling upon such a gruesome corpse?

"What made you think to come to me with what you'd found?" asked Sebastian as he turned the chestnuts down Bond Street toward Piccadilly.

Jamie cast him a quick sideways glance, then looked away again. "Heard about ye from Father, ye see. He told me about how ye solve murders, sometimes even when the other nobs don't want ye to be solvin' 'em."

"And where is your father now?"

A quiver passed over the boy's features, then was gone. "Dead. These past two years and more."

"And your mother?"

"I don't even remember her."

I'm sorry, thought Sebastian. But he didn't say it, because the rigid set of the boy's shoulders told him any expression of sympathy would not be welcome.

He was aware of the boy tensing up tighter and tighter as they threaded their way through the sodden traffic on Piccadilly and then turned in to the deserted remnants of Swallow Street. Once, this had been a thriving if somewhat aged neighborhood of small shops, workshops, modest houses, livery stables, blacksmiths, and pubs. Most were now reduced to rubble, with only rain-soaked stacks of salvaged timbers or piles of old bricks and stones standing here and there. The Regent had an ambitious scheme to push a broad, architecturally consistent avenue through the western end of London, all the way from Carlton House in Pall Mall to what they were now calling Regent's Park, and the longest stretch of it was slated to run right through here. Little had as yet actually been built, largely because of the economic woes that had beset the country since the ending of the French wars. But the wholesale destruction of everything in the project's path was well underway.

"In there, he is," said Jamie, nodding to a crumbling stone archway that still stood midway up the street. As Sebastian turned in to the ancient courtyard, he could see what had once been a private chapel tucked into one corner. Built of the same golden sandstone as the ancient archway, the chapel—like the arch—was the relic of a decrepit, now half-demolished Tudor-era mansion. The chapel's door was already gone, part of the roof appeared to have caved in, and the facade's single lancet window gaped blankly, its delicate stone tracery empty and broken. Sebastian had been here once before, although for an entirely different reason.

"Do you live around here?" asked Sebastian, reining in before the ruin.

The boy kept his gaze fixed straight ahead. "I do not."

Sebastian waited for him to say more, but he didn't. "So what were you doing here, in the chapel?"

"Ducked in there to get out of the rain, I did. If I had the doin' of it again, I reckon I'd just get wet." A quiver passed over the boy's features as he glanced at the chapel's dark, ominously yawning doorway. "I don't need t' be goin' in there again, do I?"

"Yes."

The boy's nostrils flared on a quickly indrawn breath. Then he gave a jerky nod, braced one hand on the edge of the seat, and jumped down.

For a moment, Sebastian thought he might run, but he didn't.

"Walk them out on Swallow Street," Sebastian told his young groom, Tom, as the tiger scrambled forward to take the reins. "And be ready to get out of here fast and head for Bow Street if this is a trap."

Tom glanced over to where Jamie now stood, his hands tucked up under his armpits, his solemn gaze on the doorway before him. "Ye reckon it might be, gov'nor?"

"No." Sebastian leapt lightly down to the broken cobbles of the ancient, shattered courtyard. "But I could be wrong."

Sebastian saw the hanging body's menacing, swaying shadow first, its arms akimbo and one leg bent up so that it appeared to be dancing a bizarre pirouette over the crumbling, rain-streaked altar.

He glanced at the boy beside him. "You all right?"

Jamie nodded, his face pale and grim. Sebastian had expected him to try to hang back, but he didn't.

Due to the orientation of the old Tudor house, the door from the courtyard entered the chapel's southern wall, up near the altar, with the columned nave stretching away into shadow to their left. Debris from the partially collapsed groin-vaulted ceiling filled the dark, musty interior, so that they had to pick their way carefully over rain-soaked segments of broken, age-darkened timbers and shattered stones. Whatever pews might once have been here were long gone, doubtless carried off by the area's impoverished residents for firewood. But through the scattered rain puddles and bird droppings at his feet, Sebastian could catch glimpses of half-obliterated inscriptions on the worn paving stones. BELOVED DAUGHTER OF . . . HERE LYETH THE BODY . . . BURIED THIS DAY . . .

"You'll be findin' him just there, sir. At the back," said the boy softly.

"I see him," said Sebastian as they came abreast of one of the chapel's slender columns and the dead man himself came into full view. *"Damn."*

The man had been hung by one ankle from an old wooden beam exposed by the collapsed stone vaulting above. Blood from the gory mess someone had made of his head had dripped down to pool on the worn paving stones beneath him and congealed there. A piece of white cloth Sebastian suspected was the dead man's own cravat lashed the foot of his bent right leg to his straight left knee. His elbows were also bent, his hands hidden behind his back. As the body swayed again in a gust of wind that whistled through a gaping hole in the chapel's rear wall, Sebastian could see that the same white cloth had been used to bind together the dead man's wrists.

"Ye know who he is?" whispered Jamie, taking a step back.

Sebastian studied the hanging man's blood-streaked, distorted features, now a ghastly reddish purple thanks to what was known as the "darkening of death." He'd been in his late forties, big and stocky, with a full face and dark hair. His clothing was that of a prosperous gentleman who patronized London's best tailors without falling victim to the lures of extreme dandyism; his only jewelry was a macabre and highly distinctive gold watch that dangled from the pocket of his pantaloons, with a single fob attached to the end of its chain.

His heart beating heavily in his chest, Sebastian hunkered down to take a closer look at that watch. Exquisitely rendered in the shape of a skull decorated all around with reliefs of Adam and Eve and the Grim Reaper, the watch was hinged at the back of the cranium so that the lower jaw dropped down to reveal its elaborate dial. It was a kind of memento mori, carried by its somber-minded owner as a reminder of human mortality and the brevity of life. And even if he hadn't recognized the dead man's discolored features, Sebastian would have recognized that watch.

"I know him," said Sebastian, his voice flat.

He was aware of the rain starting up again, pounding on what was left of the roof and slanting in through the holes in the walls and ceiling. "When exactly did you find him?" Sebastian asked—or rather started to ask. Except he knew even before he twisted around to be certain that he was now alone in the chapel.

Jamie Gallagher was gone.

Chapter 4

Bit gruesome, isn't it?" said Sir Henry Lovejoy, his knees popping in protest as he squatted down beside the gently swaying cadaver to peer at the dead man's bloated, discolored face. The rain had died shortly after Sebastian sent Tom off to Bow Street, but it had begun again with a vengeance, drumming loudly overhead and billowing in through the chapel's open doorway and gaping window.

Sir Henry was one of Bow Street's three stipendiary magistrates, a small, sparse man with a high-pitched voice, a balding head, and an intense dedication to such undervalued principles as truth and fairness. In his late fifties now, he had once been a successful merchant. But the murder of his wife and young daughter fifteen years earlier had forced him to reevaluate his choices in life. After undergoing a severe spiritual crisis, he decided to dedicate himself to public service and had been a magistrate ever since.

Sebastian had known the taciturn magistrate for over five years, ever since that dark time in Sebastian's life when he'd been accused of murder and Lovejoy the man tasked with seeing him captured.

Since then, the two men had forged a rare friendship, based on mutual respect and a shared passion for seeing justice done in a woefully unjust world.

"Was he alive when he was hung up like this, do you think?" asked Lovejoy, squinting up at the worn rope that had been used to fasten the dead man's straight left leg to an aged, exposed beam barely visible through the rubble of the collapsed stone vaulting overhead.

"I doubt it. The wound above his ear wouldn't have killed him, but the blow to the back of his head caved in his skull."

"That would be a mercy if it meant his death came quickly," said Lovejoy. Shifting position, he leaned forward to take a closer look at the dead man's head. "Yes, that wound is quite ghastly. He must have been beaten about the face, as well, for it to be so badly bruised."

"Possibly. Although that could simply be due to gravity."

Lovejoy looked up at him. "Gravity?"

"Once the heart stops pumping, a body's blood tends to settle into whatever parts are the lowest—in this case, the head and face—so it becomes . . . discolored."

"Lovely," said the magistrate, bracing a hand flat on the floor so he could push to his feet. "Are we quite certain this is indeed Lord Preston Farnsworth? I met him once, but it's been several years, and with his face like this . . ."

"It's Farnsworth. Look at his watch."

Lovejoy stared at the distinctive timepiece in silence for a moment, then said, "Oh, dear."

Oh, dear, indeed, thought Sebastian. Lord Preston Farnsworth was the younger son of the late Third Duke of Eversfield and brother to the current holder of the title, Archibald Douglas Farnsworth, the Fourth Duke. Lord Preston himself had a reputation as a charming, witty, but determinedly upright and moral man who'd dedicated his life to such worthy causes as ending the slave trade and advocating before Parliament in favor of the creation of a centralized, uniformed police force to control the upsurge of crime in London. But his brother, the Duke, was a very different sort of man, addicted to games of chance of every description, notorious for keeping a string of wildly expensive mistresses, and rarely seen abroad when he wasn't the worse for drink. Unsurprisingly, the Duke was one of the Prince Regent's boon companions. And that meant the Palace was going to insist on seeing someone caught and punished for this. Quickly.

"How long do you suppose he's been hanging here?" said Lovejoy, hunching his shoulders against the unseasonable cold. "A day?"

"At least. He's quite stiff."

"That would fit with when he disappeared. His sister reported him missing yesterday afternoon, but he was last seen Saturday night. I gather she lives with him?"

Sebastian nodded. "In St. James's Square." A dedicated spinster, Lady Hester Farnsworth had moved in with her brother shortly after Lord Preston's lovely young wife ran off with a dashing cavalry officer named Major Hugh Chandler. That salacious scandal had rocked the ton—and earned Lord Preston the enduring sympathy of Society's outraged matrons. "I don't recall seeing anything about him being missing in the papers."

"That was at Lady Hester's request. She didn't want a fuss made in case there was an innocent explanation for his absence. It seems Lord Preston went out walking Saturday evening sometime around half past seven. Lady Hester herself retired to her rooms shortly afterward, so she didn't realize her brother hadn't returned until she learned of it from the servants shortly after noon the following day."

"Does she know where he went?"

"She says she does not." Lovejoy paused for a moment. "Did you know Lord Preston well?"

"Not well, no."

Lovejoy let out his breath in a long, pained sigh. "I met him when we were both called upon to testify before one of the parliamentary committees investigating crime in the city. How ironic that a man who campaigned so tirelessly for the creation of a centralized police force should himself fall victim to such a vicious crime."

"That it is."

His brows drawing together in a faint frown, Lovejoy let his gaze drift over the shadowy, cobweb-draped walls of the chapel's once elegant interior. "Do you think he was killed elsewhere and then brought here for some reason?"

"That's what I thought, at first. But I looked around after I sent Tom off to Bow Street, and there's a two-foot length of blood-stained old timber up near the altar that looks as if someone used it as a club, and a patch of relatively fresh blood on the paving stones nearby. I think he was killed here."

"Yes, I see it now," said Lovejoy, going to study the pool of dried blood beside the altar. He looked up thoughtfully. "Whatever could have brought Farnsworth here, of all places? It's hardly the sort of destination one is likely to choose when simply out for an evening stroll."

"He could have come here to meet someone."

"Someone unsavory, from all appearances."

"Very."

Lovejoy's features hardened. "It's unfortunate the boy who discovered him ran off like that. The least he could have done was wait around and save us the bother of now having to find him."

"He was frightened."

"Understandably so, I suppose. Frankly, I'm surprised he didn't simply help himself to the dead man's watch and fob and take off. But then, perhaps he was afraid to touch the body. You say he's Irish? They do tend to be a superstitious lot." Lovejoy turned to stare again at the upside-down corpse now swaying macabrely back and forth as a cold, damp blast of wind gusted in through the collapsed section of the back wall. "What a very odd way for the killer to have posed the body."

"It's *Le Pendu,*" said Sebastian.

Lovejoy glanced over at him. "What do you mean?"

"In the version of the tarot that's popular in southern France, there's a card called *Le Pendu*, the Hanged Man. It depicts a man hanging exactly like this—upside down by one foot, with his hands behind his back."

Lovejoy looked troubled. "A coincidence, surely?"

"Possibly."

"Hopefully." Lovejoy thrust his own hands deep into the pockets of his greatcoat as the silence between them filled with sounds of the rain splashing on the worn paving stones of the courtyard, the wind whistling through the broken wall, and the murmur of distant voices. Then one of the constables he'd left waiting outside appeared in the doorway to say, "The men from the deadhouse are here with the shell, Sir Henry. You want we should let them in now?"

"Yes, tell them to come in, Constable Sutton." To Sebastian, Lovejoy said quietly, "This card . . . what is it supposed to mean?"

Sebastian shook his head. "I have no idea. But I doubt it's anything good."

Chapter 5

Sebastian returned to Brook Street to find his baby daughter asleep under the watchful eye of their French-born nurse, Claire, and Hero out walking with the two boys. He changed into dry clothes, poured himself a glass of brandy, and went to stand for a time at the library window, his gaze on the gray sky pressing low on the city, his thoughts drifting painfully to the past, to a time before Hugh Chandler had run off with Lord Preston's wife, when Hugh had still been a captain and Sebastian only a lieutenant, and they'd both endured a grueling winter retreat that no one who'd survived it would ever forget . . .

Pushing aside the memories, Sebastian turned abruptly from the window. Opening the bottom drawer of his desk, he withdrew the deck of tarot cards he'd acquired the previous summer—back when England had actually *had* a summer—when he'd encountered a mysterious, deadly woman who called herself Sibil Wilde.

Removing the deck from its case, he began turning the cards over one by one, beginning with an image of a man dressed in the multicolored habiliments of a medieval court jester. The card bore no number but was entitled *LE MAT*: the Vagabond, the Fool. Then came the numbered cards: *LE BATELEUR*, the Magician or Mountebank, with the tools of his trade spread across a table before him, followed by *JUNON*, *L'IMPERATRICE*, *L'EMPEREUR*, and *JUPITER*. He laid the six cards in a neat row, then started a second row and kept going until he came to XII: *LE PENDU*, the Hanged Man.

In this deck's interpretation of the card, the man wore a green coat with a red collar and yellow braiding down the front. His pantaloons were red, his one visible boot brown and tied by a rope to a wooden beam resting between two trees. The trees were leafless and looked dead, their branches broken off in a way that reminded Sebastian of a forest shattered by intense artillery fire. Or was that simply because the man's clothing looked vaguely like a military uniform and because Sebastian had once, after a particularly brutal engagement in Spain, come across some two dozen French soldiers hanging like this, upside down—except by both feet and with their bodies hideously mutilated by the Spanish peasants into whose hands they had fallen?

He pushed the memory aside and forced himself to focus on the image depicted on the card. The man's eyes were closed, his forehead furrowed as if with age or a frown, although his features were not otherwise distorted. Despite those two shattered dead trees, a stretch of bright green grass grew beneath him. The man was hanging so low that his head touched the grass, tilting it slightly to one side.

What did it all mean? And for what possible reason had Farnsworth's killer posed his victim's body like this? Was it simply, as Lovejoy had suggested, a coincidence? Or was the killer sending them a message?

What message?

The sound of a young child's voice, followed by laughter, drew Sebastian's attention to the street outside. He heard the quick patter of little boys' feet on the front steps as Morey moved to open the front door.

"I see Papa's hat!" shouted Simon. "He's home?"

"He is, but—Master Simon! Master Patrick—"

Two small boys came hurtling through the open doorway to the library, one after the other, the straw hats in their hands streaming grimy wet ribbons and their nankeens liberally splashed with mud. "Papa!" cried Simon. "We've been for a walk along the Serpentine, and you wouldn't *believe* how full it is! Everything is *wet*!"

"And so are you, from the looks of things," said Sebastian, laughing as he caught the grubby three-year-old boy around the waist to hold him at arm's length.

"Simon fell," said Patrick, coming to stand beside his brother. "Not in the Serpentine, but almost." There'd been a time when the older boy's accent had been that of a Bishopsgate barmaid, but no longer. The two boys looked enough alike that, except for the slight difference in their heights, they might have been twins. But only the younger, Simon, was Sebastian's own son; Patrick was an orphan, the son of a man who'd looked enough like Sebastian to have been his brother, although the connection between the two men had never been explained. His name had been Jamie Knox, and it was because of Knox's resemblance to Sebastian that Knox had died and Sebastian lived. . . .

"It's slippery!" said Simon.

"One of the park-keepers told Mama they think it's gonna flood," said Patrick.

Simon nodded solemnly. "Betsy says it's 'cause the sun is dying and the world is gonna end!"

"Who is Betsy?" asked Sebastian, his gaze meeting Hero's as she followed the boys into the library.

"The new nursery maid," she said, taking off her own sodden

hat and going to work on the buttons of her wet pelisse. She was an extraordinarily tall woman, nearly as tall as Sebastian himself, with a Junoesque build, dark hair, and an aquiline nose she had inherited from her father, Lord Jarvis, the formidable, ruthless man known as the real power behind the Prince of Wales's fragile regency. "From the sound of things, she and I need to have a little talk."

"*Alors,*" said the children's nurse, hurrying down the stairs toward them. "Look how wet you two are!"

"Claire!" said Simon, running toward her. "I fell!"

"I see you did," said the Frenchwoman, scooping him up and holding out her hand to Patrick. "*Venez, mes enfants.*"

"I thought you had an interview scheduled for this afternoon," Sebastian said to Hero as Claire and the two boys disappeared up the stairs.

"I did," said Hero, easing off her wet pelisse. For several years now she had been writing a series of articles on the poor of London for the *Morning Chronicle.* It was a project that enraged her father, but Hero was one of the few people in the Kingdom whom Jarvis had never been able to intimidate. Her current article was on the hundreds of thousands of destitute ex-soldiers and sailors who had been discharged since the ending of the decades-long wars with France, and Sebastian knew she was finding the research for this article particularly troubling.

"The man I was supposed to talk to died during the night. I knew he wasn't well, but . . ."

"I'm sorry."

She tossed her pelisse aside. "Was it all a hum, then, your hanging man? No dead body?"

"Oh, there was a body, all right: Lord Preston Farnsworth's." Sebastian reached for the card labeled *Le Pendu* and held it up. "He was hanging upside down, posed exactly like this."

"Good heavens." Hero came to take the card from him and study it. "Why would someone do that?"

"Revenge, perhaps?"

She set the card back in its place on the desktop but continued to stare at it, her features pinched with worry that mirrored his own. "Farnsworth is well known for his work with Wilberforce and Clarkson to end the slave trade. And while it's been eight or nine years since the bill successfully made it through Parliament, slave traders and plantation owners are dangerous enemies to make, and some people can hold a gr—" She broke off as if suddenly realizing her reasoning was leading her exactly where she didn't want to go.

"A grudge? They can indeed. And who is more likely to hold a grudge than a man forced by a vindictive husband to pay twenty thousand pounds for the sin of falling in love with another man's wife?"

Hero looked up, her features strained. "You can't think Hugh did this. Not Hugh."

Sebastian drained his brandy, then set the glass aside and went to stand again at the library's front window, his gaze on the wet, rain-lashed street. It was a long moment before he said, "Honestly? I'm afraid he might have."

Chapter 6

How do you accuse a friend of murder?

The question ate at Sebastian as he ordered his curricle brought round. Driving out of London, toward Chelsea, he found his thoughts drifting again to the past, to that long, brutal British retreat across northern Spain in the winter of 1808–9. At that point, Wellesley—not yet the feted Duke of Wellington—had been recalled to London over the scandal surrounding the Convention of Sintra, and the ambitious British assault on the Peninsula handed over to Sir John Moore. Then Napoléon decided to personally take command of the French forces in Spain, and what began as a confident expedition turned first into a prudent withdrawal, then into a desperate race for the coast and the transport ships thought to be awaiting them at Corunna. As the British troops slogged through freezing rain and snowy mountain passes, thousands of men were lost to the relentlessly pursuing French; discipline collapsed, Spanish villages were plundered, and drunken or wounded troops were simply abandoned to their fates.

With the cavalry assigned to cover the Army's retreat, Sebastian was out one miserably cold December day riding reconnaissance through the mountains when he came upon Hugh and a small band of men who had been caught by a detachment of French dragoons on the wrong side of a defile crossed by a single narrow stone bridge. Sebastian checked for only an instant to evaluate the situation, then rode straight into the fray with enough noise and élan to convince the French that he was at the vanguard of a rescue party.

The French drew off, giving Hugh's men time to collect their wounded and beat a hasty retreat across the bridge. Sebastian was guarding their rear when a well-placed musket ball crumpled his horse beneath him. The horse fell with a groan, trapping Sebastian's leg beneath it and smashing his head against the bridge's stone abutment.

By that time, the French had caught on to Sebastian's ruse. A dozen howling, jeering dragoons turned back to descend on him, the weak winter sun dancing on their bronze helmets, their neo-Greek manes and red plumes billowing in the wind. Unable to free his leg, Sebastian yanked his pistol from its holder, determined to stop as many of them as he could before they killed him. Then he saw Hugh rein in, his mouth opening in a roar, his angry shout lost in the thunder of hooves as he wheeled his mare and charged back.

"No!" shouted Sebastian. Then one of the French dragoons loomed over him, his straight saber raised to strike. Sebastian shot him point-blank in the chest.

A second green-coated soldier took the first dragoon's place, but Hugh rode the man down, his blade slashing through the air. Then, kicking his feet from the stirrups, Hugh landed in a crouch and came up with his saber still in his hand to ram the point through the chest of a third man and turn to smash a fourth in the face with the hilt of his saber.

"Leave me!" shouted Sebastian. "Get your men out of here!"

Hugh snarled and sent his sword whistling through the air to practically decapitate another dragoon. "Like hell I will!"

Crouching down, he helped Sebastian drag himself out from under his dead horse and stagger to his feet. Half-senseless, Sebastian could only hang on to the coping stones of the bridge, gasping, while Hugh lunged to snag the reins of a wild-eyed, riderless mare trotting by. Somehow, Hugh got him up in the saddle and jammed the reins into his hands. By then Hugh's own men had rallied and were riding down on them with a roar.

The remaining French dragoons regrouped, then galloped away.

"You should have left me," panted Sebastian, so weak and dizzy he had to grasp handfuls of the mare's mane to keep from sliding out of the saddle.

"Nah. You still owe me a beer, remember?" said Hugh, and then laughed.

It had been just two years later that Hugh was badly wounded in a skirmish and sent home to England to recuperate. He was nursed back to health by his sister Anne and her dear friend, Lady Theresa—Tess to her friends. The only daughter of James Haywood, the Third Earl of Whitcombe, Tess had been married to Lord Preston Farnsworth at that point for seven years. The marriage was generally thought to be happy, although childless. And yet one night, when Hugh's arm was still in a sling, Tess fled her husband's comfortable London home for her soldier-lover's embrace.

And she never went back.

Most men who found themselves in Lord Preston's position were too mortified to publicly brand themselves cuckolds and drag their affairs through the mud by suing their wives' lovers for criminal conversation—or crim. con., as it was popularly known. But the normally congenial Farnsworth's rage was matched only by his desire for revenge. He sought and obtained an ecclesiastical separation from his wife but refused to divorce her. And then he sued Hugh for twenty thousand pounds.

And won.

How do you accuse a friend of murder? A friend who once saved your life?

Sebastian found himself still unsettled by the question as he neared the gates of the small, isolated manor on the outskirts of Chelsea that had once belonged to Lady Tess's great-aunt and now provided the disgraced couple with something of a refuge.

Hugh's family might be ancient, but it had never been particularly wealthy, and the small estate he'd inherited from his grandfather—a general famous for his exploits in the Seven Years' War—had been sold to pay Farnsworth's judgment. In addition to virtually bankrupting Hugh, that long-ago elopement—and the scandal it provoked—had also wreaked havoc on his military career. It was only after several frustrating years of being sidelined to the Horse Guards that he was finally called back to active duty to help Wellington push the French over the Pyrenees. His brilliant performance at Waterloo had even made him something of a hero.

Given an old, respectable family name, a decent interval of time, and success on the battlefield, a man could eventually weather such a storm. On his return from Belgium, Hugh found himself once again invited to the dinner parties, balls, and routs held by all except the ton's highest sticklers—but only if he left his disgraced lover at home. For Lady Tess, there would be no forgiveness, no welcoming back to Society. Ever. The one time she dared appear at the theater, she had been loudly hissed.

She never went again.

"Reckon ye ought t' know that I heard some o' Sir 'Enry's constables talkin' while we was in Swallow Street," said Tom as Sebastian turned in through the simple gates.

Sebastian glanced back at his small, sharp-faced tiger. The boy had been with him for over five years now, ever since those desperate days when Sebastian had been on the run for murder. "What were they saying?"

"They think it's obvious Lord Preston's wife musta been the one done fer 'im—well, her and the major, workin' together. Every last one of 'em said the same thing."

"That's not good," said Sebastian.

"No. I didn't think so, neither."

Sebastian was reining in on the gravel court before the small redbrick house when he heard his name called and turned to see Lady Tess crossing the wind-tossed gardens toward him. Now in her early thirties, she was built small and slender, with fair hair, dark eyes, and a chin too determinedly square for Society to have ever christened her a true Beauty. She wore a plain broad-brimmed straw hat and had an apron pinned to her simple muslin gown, and carried a basket in which a pair of secateurs rested atop a bed of rose clippings.

"Devlin," she said again as she drew nearer. She was paler than normal, he noticed, and her smile of welcome had a bit of a tremble about the edges. "How are you? Hugh has gone off to the stables to see to one of the carriage horses, but he should be back directly." She paused for a moment, then drew a deep breath and said, "I can guess why you're here."

"You know about Lord Preston?"

She nodded. "One of our neighbors heard the news and came

to tell us. We've been expecting a visit from Bow Street. Please tell me you're not here as their representative."

"No; I'm here as a friend," said Sebastian, the gravel crunching beneath his bootheels as he hopped down from the curricle's high seat.

"Thank heavens." She handed her basket to a maidservant who hurried out to take it, then waited until the woman was out of earshot before saying, "Is it true what we're hearing? That whoever killed Preston hanged him upside down?"

"Yes," said Sebastian, watching her face as they turned to walk together along a path that wound through untidy, wet gardens. She had lived with Farnsworth as his wife for over seven years—was still married to him in the eyes of the law. So what did she feel, Sebastian found himself wondering, on hearing of his brutal murder? Shock? Sorrow? Worry?

Vindictive delight?

He supposed it all depended on the part she—and Hugh—had played in the events of last Saturday night.

"We didn't kill him, you know," she said bluntly, as if following the train of his thoughts.

"Do you have any idea who did?"

She was silent for a moment, obviously choosing her words carefully. "Preston Farnsworth was known to the world as a good-natured, deeply religious, witty man who selflessly devoted himself to noble causes. It was an image he deliberately cultivated, and he did it very well. But that's all it was: an image." She glanced over at him. "I suppose you don't believe me."

"No, I believe you." *To a certain extent,* thought Sebastian. "A genuinely good-natured, unselfish man doesn't sue his wife's lover for twenty thousand pounds and then refuse to divorce her, so that she can never remarry."

She drew up and swung to face him. "And yet you are here."

Just because I don't believe Lord Preston was as much of a saint as he chose to appear doesn't mean I think Hugh couldn't have killed him, thought Sebastian. But all he said was, "Believe me when I say that if Hugh is innocent, I will—"

"'*If*'?" She brought up a hand to her forehead as she turned half away from him. "I can't believe— Even you think—" She broke off and swallowed hard. "I beg your pardon," she somehow managed to choke out. "But you must excuse me." And with that she fisted her hands in the skirt of her gown and fled back toward the house.

She met Hugh halfway across the lawn, coming toward them. Hugh was in his late thirties now, of average height and build, with brown hair and light brown eyes and strong, rugged features, and he reached out to snag her arm as she passed him. She said something to him under her breath that Sebastian couldn't quite catch, then jerked her arm away and ran on.

Hugh hesitated a moment, looking after her, then continued on toward Sebastian. "Devlin," he said, his features set in troubled lines as he drew closer. "I was going to say it's good to see you. Except Tess tells me you think I killed that damned husband of hers."

"Not exactly," said Sebastian as his friend paused before him. "But you must admit I'd need to be a fool not to admit it as a possibility."

"*God damn it.* I didn't kill Farnsworth!"

Sebastian studied his friend's tense, angry face. "Then I hope to God you have a damned good alibi for Saturday night."

Most officers learned quickly to keep their features schooled in a stoic mask, lest their own fears and worries panic those under their command. Hugh was no exception. But Sebastian saw his friend's eyes narrow, saw his chest jerk on a quickly indrawn breath. "Is that when Farnsworth was killed? Saturday night?"

"It seems likely."

Hugh sucked in another breath, his throat working as he swallowed. "Well, hell."

"I don't like the sound of that."

They turned to walk together toward a white-fenced paddock that lay beyond the garden's low hedge. After a moment, Hugh said, "Tess and I had a spat that night over—well, it doesn't matter over what, does it? The thing is, I felt the need to be alone, so I went for a ride." He paused. "A very long ride. I was gone for hours."

"Can anyone verify where you went?"

"No. Like I said, I wanted to be alone." A gleam of wry amusement showed in his eyes, then was gone. "Lousy timing, wasn't it?"

"Yes."

They paused beside the paddock's fence, Hugh resting his elbows on the top rail, his gaze following a bay mare and her black foal as they cantered around the enclosure. After a moment he said, "I had no reason to kill the bastard. Not now."

"Most people would consider having been forced to virtually bankrupt yourself in order to cough up twenty thousand pounds a fairly powerful motive for murder."

"Maybe—if I'd killed him six years ago. But why wait until now?"

"Sometimes resentment . . . festers."

Hugh made a huffing sound deep in his throat. "Well, I won't deny that."

The two men stood side by side watching the mare nuzzle her colt. Then Sebastian said, "You do realize you could also be accused of having a second motive."

Hugh looked over at him. "What?"

"Farnsworth's death makes Tess a widow. She's now free to marry you."

Hugh was silent for a moment. "I realize it's probably an odd thing to say, but after all these years it feels almost . . . irrelevant. There was a time I was desperate to be able to marry Tess, to give her the protection of my name and 'make an honest woman of her' in the eyes of the world, as they say. But now . . ." He shrugged. "At this point we've been 'living in sin' for six years. I suppose if we'd had children it might be different, but that hasn't happened. And after a while you begin to realize what's important—that the real strength of your relationship comes from what's inside you and from the promises you make to each other. Not from whatever laws God or your society have decided to impose on you." He glanced over at Sebastian. "Do you consider that blasphemy?"

"No."

Hugh smiled, then looked away again. "The sad truth is, we could be married tomorrow by the Archbishop of Canterbury himself and the ton would still never accept Tess. You know why? Because she dared to do what so many of the grand lords and ladies of our world will never have the courage to do: She turned her back on the dictates of 'propriety' and walked—no, *ran*—away from a miserable marriage. She dared to grasp at happiness, basically telling them all to go to hell in the process. And that's why they will never, ever forgive her. If she'd stayed with Farnsworth, she might have taken a dozen lovers and still been received everywhere—as long as she was relatively discreet, of course. As long as she stayed in her loveless marriage and lived the same lie so many of them are living. I've seen noblewomen pass Tess on Bond Street and actually lift their skirts away from her as if she were somehow contaminated. I'm talking about women everyone *knows* have been endlessly unfaithful to their own husbands. But that doesn't stop them from feigning moral indignation and outrage over what Tess did. They've made her the scapegoat for all their own sins, and it's a role they will never, ever allow her to stop playing."

Sebastian felt a weight of sadness pressing in on him—sadness and something else he suspected was alarm. "You do realize that's why you're in danger, don't you? You and Tess both. Society has already made her their scapegoat, and if they can hang her for this, they will. Hell, if they could burn her at the stake, they'd do it." There was a time not so long ago when the penalty in England for a woman killing her husband was to be burned alive. "And if they can't hang her, I suspect they'll be more than willing to make do with you."

Hugh nodded, his lips pressed into a hard, tight line, his gaze still on the mare and her colt.

"Where was Lady Tess that night?" said Sebastian. "Here?"

"Yes."

"You're quite certain?"

Hugh opened his mouth as if to say, *Of course I'm certain,* then closed it. Because if he hadn't been home that night himself, then he could not, in truth, claim to know for certain.

Sebastian said, "Bow Street is going to ask, you know."

"I know. *Bloody hell,*" whispered Hugh, bringing both hands up together to scrub them down over his eyes and nose. "I've faced death more times than I can count—we both have. But I don't think I've ever been this afraid. Not like this."

Sebastian said, "Who do you think killed Farnsworth? Do you have any idea at all?"

Hugh shook his head. "He was a strange, complicated man. I never understood him and I don't think Tess did, either—at least, not entirely. People always say their marriage was happy until she met me, but it's not true. She was miserable. He made her miserable—in a thousand different, subtle ways."

"Did he keep a mistress?"

"Not that she was aware."

"Do you know if he had any enemies?" *Besides you,* thought Sebastian.

"He must have, surely. But I couldn't name them, and I can't tell you who would be able to."

"If you think of anything—anything at all—that might help make sense of this, you'll tell me?"

"Yes, of course."

But Sebastian saw the hesitation in his eyes and knew his friend did not entirely trust him.

Chapter 7

George Augustus Frederick, His Royal Highness the Prince Regent of the United Kingdom of Great Britain and Ireland, was in the sort of petulant mood that worried his physicians and alarmed everyone from his servants to his cabinet ministers.

"You've heard what people are saying, haven't you?" the Prince demanded, the corset he wore hidden beneath his exquisitely tailored evening clothes creaking as he paced up and down one of Carlton House's vast gilded chambers. "That if not even the brother of a duke is safe walking the streets of our city, then no one is!"

The Prince might be only fifty-four, but between the heat of the room and his several hundred pounds of excess weight, His Highness was puffing and red in the face when he swung back around. "How could something like this have been allowed to happen?"

Of the two gentlemen to whom these remarks were addressed, only one—the Prince's cousin and most powerful advisor, Charles, Lord Jarvis—ventured to reply. Personally, Jarvis thought that any gentleman unwise enough to take an evening stroll down Swallow Street was asking for trouble, but all he said was, "It's beyond shocking, sir. I knew you'd be interested in hearing directly from Sir Nathaniel himself."

The Prince turned his rather protuberant blue-gray eyes toward the second gentleman in the room. "Well?"

Sir Nathaniel Conant, Chief Magistrate of Bow Street Public Office, cleared his throat and bowed low with the subtle obsequiousness that helped explain how a man who'd begun his career at sixteen as a bookseller's apprentice had somehow managed to rise to his present exalted position. He was more than ten years the Prince's senior but looked younger, his hair a thick, dark gray, his body stout but still strong and agile. "I would like to assure you, sir, that we are moving quickly to apprehend the fiend responsible for this appalling outrage. My colleague Sir Henry Lovejoy has personally taken charge of the investigation and is already making great progress. Yet one can't help but reflect upon the unfortunate fact that if Parliament had created the centralized municipal police force for which Lord Preston and I have long advocated, this might never have happened."

He paused long enough to allow his listeners to remember that it was Sir Nathaniel himself who had drafted the bill that became the 1792 Middlesex Justices Act, establishing the seven London public offices that came after Bow Street. Then he said, "Rest assured that we already have a prime suspect and anticipate being able to have him remanded into custody within days."

"Good," said the Prince, tugging a silk handkerchief from his pocket to dab at the sweat beginning to trickle down his plump cheeks. "See that you do." To Jarvis, he said, "What with harvests failing all over the Kingdom, riots in East Anglia, naval mutinies in

Newcastle and Lyme Regis, and rumblings in every part of London from Rotherhithe to Clerkenwell, this is the last thing we need. Liverpool confided to me just this morning that he thinks the realm is in greater danger of revolution now than at any time since 1792."

"Lord Liverpool has always had an unfortunate tendency toward alarmism," said Jarvis dryly, making a mental note to warn the troublesome prime minister to watch his bloody tongue.

The Prince pressed the handkerchief to his damp forehead. "You don't agree?"

Jarvis gave a careless shrug. "Crime always rises when soldiers and sailors are released from service at the end of a war, just as wages always fall and people complain. There is no doubt the next year or two will be painful as the government works to reduce spending and retire the debt run up during the wars with France and the United States. But I see no dire threat to the realm."

"Yes, of course." The Prince tucked away his handkerchief. "You relieve my mind, Jarvis."

Jarvis bowed his head and signaled to the magistrate to withdraw with him.

"You truly believe that?" said Sir Nathaniel quietly as their footsteps echoed down the vast marble-floored corridor.

"Of course not. We're in a worse place now than we've been in our lifetimes. But what the devil was Liverpool thinking, blurting out something like that in front of Prinny?" He nodded to a bowing liveried footman as they passed, then said, "I trust you have enough informants in place?"

"Almost, my lord. We're working on it."

"Work harder," snapped Jarvis as they turned the corner. "And the other matter?"

Sir Nathaniel allowed himself a tight smile. "That is progressing nicely."

"Good." Jarvis paused before the doors to the chambers reserved exclusively for his own personal use in the palace. "As for this Farnsworth business, I don't care who you hang for it; just make certain you don't let it drag out too long."

"Yes, my lord," said Sir Nathaniel with another low bow.

But Jarvis was already gone.

Chapter 8

That night, shortly before midnight, the cloud cover broke up and for one brief, glorious moment, a full moon appeared to ride high in the sky and cast its silvery light over the huddled wet rooftops and sodden streets of the city. Sebastian stood at his open bedroom window, his outstretched hands braced against the sill, the air cool against his bare skin. He could hear the rattle of a night soil–man's cart and a dog barking somewhere in the distance. Then he caught the rustle of bedclothes and a light step on the floor, and Hero came to stand beside him.

"Something's troubling you," she said, resting a hand on his hip. "What is it?"

"You mean besides the fact that one of my old friends is in danger of being hanged for a murder even I'm not convinced he didn't commit?"

She leaned into him. "Yes. Besides that."

He looped his arms around her, drawing her close. She was warm and soft and still vaguely languid from their recent lovemaking, and he pressed his forehead against her hair and said, "Imagine you're a fourteen-year-old orphan alone on the streets of London. You're cold, you're hungry, you're wet. You duck into a ruined, abandoned chapel to get out of the rain and see a dead man hanging upside down with his gold watch and fob dangling from his pocket in plain sight. No one knows he's there—well, no one except whoever killed him, I suppose, but that person is presumably long gone. And, more important, no one knows *you're* there. It would be the simplest thing to snatch that watch and run.

"But you don't do that. Instead, you travel halfway across London to knock on the door of some 'nob' you've never met and ask him to come deal with the murder of a man who is nothing to you." Sebastian paused. "Why would you do that?"

"Well . . . what if I'm poor and desperate but I'm not a thief, so I don't know a fence I can sell the watch and fob to—at least, not someone I think I can trust. And I'm afraid that if I try to pawn something so distinctive, I'll get caught and end up being hanged for the murder."

"That sounds reasonable. So why not take the plump purse from the man's pocket? Throw away the purse itself but keep the money."

"Do you know for certain it was still there?"

"It was. I checked while I was waiting for Lovejoy."

"Ah." She was silent for a moment, considering this, then shook her head. "The only explanation I have is that I'm a good Catholic who promised my mother on her deathbed that I'd never steal or—" She broke off. "No; I give up. Why didn't Jamie steal the purse? He's cold, hungry, and alone. It makes no sense."

"No, it doesn't." Sebastian rested the side of his head against hers and breathed in the sweet fragrance of her hair. "Lovejoy suggested the boy was too afraid to touch the body, but I have a hard time believing that. The Irish wake their dead. Not only that, but when you're poor, you and your family live all together in one room—maybe even with another family or two in there with you. People you know die all the time, and until they're buried, their bodies are kept in that crowded room, too, because there's no place else. Boys like Jamie grow up with dead bodies. I can't believe he was too afraid to reach his hand into a dead man's pocket in search of a purse, even if the dead man was looking more than a bit gruesome."

"So how do you explain it?"

"I can't. And if I hadn't been so focused on Hugh and what Farnsworth's murder was going to mean for him, it would have occurred to me to question it all sooner. I need to talk to that boy again."

Tuesday, 20 August

A light drizzle started up again shortly before dawn the following morning and was still falling when Sebastian drove through the dreary, wet streets of London toward the Tower Hill surgery of the anatomist Paul Gibson.

Traveling east into the humbler sections of the city, it was impossible to miss the devastation wrought on the nation's poor by both the ending of the wars and the strange, deadly weather no one could explain. The streets were filled with wretched, pinch-faced children; worn, skeletal women willing to do anything—anything at all—for a couple of pennies; and ragged clumps of hollow-eyed ex-soldiers and sailors missing arms and legs or rendered hideous by scars.

By the time he drew up before the row of ancient sandstone houses that dated back nearly to the first days of the old Norman castle that loomed over them, Sebastian was in a grim mood. "Best walk 'em," he told his tiger. "I'll never understand how it can be this bloody cold when it's the middle of bloody August, but here we are."

"Reckon we just ain't gonna have us a summer this year," said Tom, scrambling forward to take the reins.

Sebastian grunted and hopped down to the worn cobbles of the lane.

Cutting through a narrow passage that ran along one of the low-slung houses, he reached the weathered wooden gate that led to a walled rear yard, at the base of which stood the high-windowed stone outbuilding where Gibson conducted his official postmortems. It was also where Gibson surreptitiously practiced new surgery techniques and expanded his knowledge of anatomy by performing illicit dissections on cadavers filched from London's overflowing churchyards by body snatchers, or Resurrection Men, as they were sometimes called. But Bow Street carefully turned a blind eye to those activities.

"Thought I'd be seeing you bright and early this morning," said Gibson, setting aside his knife as Sebastian walked toward the building's open door.

The surgeon was a slim man, Irish by birth, with a jaunty dimpled smile and eyes as green as a Donegal glen. He was only a couple of years older than Sebastian, in his mid-thirties now, although he looked much older, his dark hair heavily laced with gray, the lines on his thin face dug deep by years of pain. His friendship with Sebastian dated back to the days when Gibson had been a regimental surgeon, when he and Sebastian had fought and bled, laughed and cried together from Italy and the West Indies to the high mountain passes of the Peninsula. Then a French cannonball tore off the lower part of Gibson's left leg, and though he tried to keep going, the endless pain—and the opium he used to control it—eventually forced him to come here, to London, to open this small surgery near the Tower and teach anatomy at hospitals such as St. Thomas's and St. Bartholomew's. With the help of Alexi Sauvage, the mysterious Frenchwoman who'd become his lover, he'd recently managed to get the better of the phantom pains from his missing limb that had bedeviled him for so long. But his dark love affair with opium was proving brutally difficult to overcome.

Sebastian paused in the doorway to the crude, single-roomed building, his gaze on the mottled, naked body of the half-eviscerated middle-aged duke's son who lay on Gibson's stone slab. "Can you tell me yet what killed him?"

"Aye, that's easy," said Gibson, tossing aside the rag he'd been using to wipe his hands. "Someone did a commendable job of bashing in his lordship's head. From the looks of things, I'd say this"—he broke off to point to the wound on the right side of Farnsworth's head—"was the first try. It wouldn't have come close to killing him, but it probably knocked him down. One assumes he must've fallen on his face. And then your killer—whoever he was—hit him again on the back of his head. And that was that." Gibson looked up. "I can roll him over and show you that mess if you've a fancy to study it."

"That's quite all right; I saw it before."

Gibson nodded. "Figured you would've. Pretty much caved in his skull, that blow. Death must have been virtually instantaneous."

"Any other marks on him?"

"Well, you can see where the rope was pressing his boot into his ankle, and where the strips of cravat he was tied with were digging into his wrists and his knee. But by then he was already dead."

"He was dead when the killer tied him up and hanged him?"

"Oh, yes; no doubt about that."

"How long would you say he's been dead?"

"Roughly? At least a couple of days at this point. We're lucky the weather kept the bluebottle fly eggs from hatching, otherwise he'd have been crawling with maggots."

"Lovely," mustered Sebastian. "So since Saturday night?"

"That would fit."

"It's when he was last seen." Sebastian brought his gaze back to the dead man's bloated, discolored face. "Can you tell me anything—anything at all—about the man who killed him?"

Gibson crossed his arms at his chest and blew out a long, thoughtful breath. "Well, he's probably right-handed—that is, if he first hit your duke's son from behind and landed his first swing. Of course, if he missed the first time and only managed to hit him on the backswing, he could be left-handed. But if he hit him from the front and landed the first blow, then I'd say he's likely left-handed."

"Unless he missed and only landed his backswing?"

"That's about it."

"Well, that narrows things down."

Gibson huffed a soft laugh and rocked back on his heels. "Other than that, let's see . . ." He shook his head. "Nothing. Beyond that, I have nothing."

"Have you ever heard of anyone being hanged the way he was? Upside down, I mean."

All trace of amusement went out of the surgeon's eyes. "Not since Spain."

"I was thinking of that, too."

Both men were silent for a moment. Then Gibson said, "You can't think Major Chandler—"

"No. No, I don't think it." *Don't want to think it.*

Gibson sucked in his cheeks and nodded. "But this is him, isn't it? The man whose wife the Major ran off with?"

Sebastian looked up to meet his friend's worried gaze. "Yes. Yes, it is."

Sebastian's next stop was a row of aging Stuart-era buildings on the south side of Golden Square.

Once, this area had been the height of fashion, home to noblemen, ambassadors, and High Churchmen. But it had already been fading for some time, and now that it was located on the wrong side of the Regent's New Street, that decline would surely accelerate.

The woman Sebastian was here to see was a French cartomancer who kept rooms on an upper floor of one of the houses in the row, and as he climbed the flights of stairs, he found himself remembering the things she had told him—and not told him—when he'd first met her several years before. By the time he reached her floor, he was heartily regretting his decision to come and might have turned around and simply left if her door hadn't opened to reveal a fine-boned woman dressed in an elegant, old-fashioned gown of dusky blue satin with a fitted bodice and a skirt draped à la polonaise.

"Ah, you're here," said Madame Blanchette in her soft Parisian accent, and stepped back to allow him to enter.

She was a small, olive-skinned woman somewhere in her fifties or early sixties, with dark eyes and graying hair and a determinedly straight back despite the pronounced limp that was said to date from the earliest days of the French Revolution. "Expecting me, were you?" he said as she closed the door behind them and led the way to her small parlor.

"One assumes that since the death of Sibil Wilde, the number of cartomancers of your acquaintance is now somewhat limited."

He managed to stop himself from asking how the hell she knew he needed a cartomancer. But then a faint gleam of amusement shone in her eyes and she said, "It's in all the newspapers, you know—the manner in which he was found hanging, I mean."

"Ah." Sir Henry wasn't going to like that.

Her parlor was as strange as he remembered it, filled with a variety of crystals, brass bells, ancient leather-bound books, and dark, fantastically carved furniture that looked as if it belonged to another time and another place.

A distant time and place.

He sat on the tapestry-covered settee she indicated and waited while she settled in the chair opposite, a medieval-looking, high-backed thing carved with an assortment of winged mythical creatures and writhing, naked men. She said, "The cards I read are of my own creation, you know. I don't use the tarot."

"I know. But you are familiar with it."

She inclined her head but said nothing.

Reaching into the pocket of his coat, he drew forth the card he had brought with him and laid it on the Syrian-looking inlaid table between them.

She stared at it a moment, then reached to pick it up, her lips pursing as she fingered it thoughtfully. "He was found exactly like this?"

Sebastian nodded. "Hanging by one foot from a rope tied to a beam in the chapel's roof, with the knee of his other leg bent and his hands tied behind his back."

She kept her gaze on the card. "I'm told it can take over a day for a man to die when hanged upside down. He's fortunate he was dead first."

"That wasn't in the papers."

"No, it wasn't." She looked over at him. "Not all tarot decks show the hanged man upside down, you know. In the Tarocco Siciliano, he hangs right side up, by his neck, from a tree limb. And I've seen a Spanish deck that shows him hanging upside down, naked, from both feet."

"But this version is typical of the decks popular in the south of France, isn't it?"

She nodded. "Those and others." He waited, and after a long silence she said, "As to what the card means . . . it varies, of course, depending upon the reading and the other cards that surround it. I have heard that this method of hanging—by one foot, upside down—was used long ago in Italy for traitors."

"Is that what it symbolizes? Betrayal?"

"It can. But there are other, more subtle meanings. Some see it as a warning of the need to reevaluate a situation, to pause and perhaps look at things from a new perspective. Others consider it a card of sacrifice, of the acceptance of one's fate, or even of redemption."

"So which meaning did Farnsworth's killer intend?"

"Perhaps all of them." She handed the card back to him. "Or none of them. You are assuming that whoever killed the man and left him hanging this way knew the meaning of the card he was imitating."

"How well-known is the tarot?"

She shrugged. "Interest in the cards for divination has been growing here in England, particularly since the well-publicized deaths of the Weird Sisters last summer. And you must remember that the deck was originally designed as a card game." She kept her gaze on his face. "Why do *you* think he was left like this?"

"I don't know. Hanging upside down is used as a form of degradation. So perhaps it was done in revenge."

She seemed to consider this, although he had the impression the idea was not new to her. "That's what worries you, isn't it?" She paused. "Have you spoken to him yet? Your friend, I mean."

Sebastian knew a spurt of alarm mingled with anger he made no effort to disguise. "Didn't you see that in your cards?"

To his surprise, her eyes sparkled with silent laughter. "You still don't believe in them, I take it?"

Sebastian pushed to his feet. "I believe in very little."

"But you do believe in some things," she said, walking with him to her front door. "You believe in honor and friendship, justice and truth. And those beliefs make you vulnerable."

He paused with the door open to look back at her. "Is that supposed to be a warning?"

The amusement was back in her eyes. "What makes you think it's not simply an observation?"

He studied her enigmatic face. "You know something you're not telling me."

"Perhaps. But I don't think you're ready to hear it yet."

Chapter 9

Lean, sun-darkened, and tough as shoe leather, the soldier said his name was Billy Callaghan and that he was twenty-eight years old, although he looked far, far older. He agreed to talk to Hero in exchange for ten shillings and a couple of hot sausages from a nearby street vendor.

Still dressed in his tattered uniform and broken-down boots, he leaned against the edge of a worn, flat-topped tomb in St. Andrew's churchyard and talked to her while he ate. In between bites, he said he'd been looking for work ever since he'd been shipped back from France in June. But he hadn't found anything yet beyond a few odd jobs every now and then.

"Faith, once I realized how bad things were, I tried to reenlist," he said in a husky voice that still carried the soft lilt of County Clare. "But they wouldn't take me. Got no use for men like me these days, ye see. And the sad truth is, the only thing I know how to do is fight."

"You said you were in the Peninsula with Wellington?"

"That I was. Haven't got a pension, though. I was a seven-year-man, ye see." Most men who took the King's shilling enlisted for twenty-one years, but some committed to only seven or fourteen.

"Were you at Waterloo?"

"I was not. If I had been, at least I'd have me a medal I could sell. The thing is, ye see, right after Boney abdicated the first time, they loaded our battalion on a transport. Thought we were going home, we did—fools that we were. I'd only a few weeks left of me enlistment and I remember thinking, 'That's it, Billy; ye survived yer seven years and now it's good-bye to grapeshot and musket fire, bugles and night marches and all that rot.' 'Cept then I started noticin' we'd been at sea for days and days with a good wind behind us, and I knew we should've been seeing land when there weren't nothin' out there but endless blue waves. That's when the officers finally told us the truth, that we was on our way to America."

Hero looked up from scribbling her notes. "What a nasty trick to play on you."

"Sure then, but I thought so, and that's the truth. Sent us to some godforsaken place called Florida, they did, and then we was supposed to take New Orleans. Should've been able to do it, too, if it weren't for General Pakenham. He was Wellington's brother-in-law, ye know, and a right arrogant idiot he was, too. I know folks like to snicker at us, sayin' all we was fightin' was squirrel hunters, Indians, free Black men, and pirates. But it was their artillery that ripped us to pieces, not their muskets, and Pakenham was a bleedin' fool to attack the way he did. If ever a man deserved to get hisself killed, it was that blotter. Just wish he hadn't taken a couple thousand of our lads with him."

Billy gave a ragged cough, turned his head, and spat up what looked to Hero like blood. "And then what do we hear but that the government had already signed a peace treaty with the Americans! Reckon it was all for naught, but me, I'm thinking, 'Well, Billy, ye made it through *another* war and now yer gonna get t' go home.'"

He readjusted his battered shako hat and gave a harsh laugh. "We was maybe halfway back across the Atlantic when we run into this French naval ship—one of ole King Louis's, it was, and fit to be tied they were on account of they'd just heard Boney was back in Paris. So instead of headin' to Portsmouth like we was supposed to, what do we do but get sent to Belgium! And me, I'm thinkin' I might've survived two wars, but I ain't gonna survive a third."

Hero said, "But you weren't at Waterloo?"

He shook his head. "Got real sick on the ship, ye see, so that by the time we landed I was fit only for hospital." He gave her a strange look. "Y'ever been on a ship, ma'am?"

"Unfortunately, no."

He nodded. "A fine lady like yerself, I reckon it might be a different experience altogether for ye. But there's few things worse'n a crowded troop transport. Don't think I'll ever get the smell of it outta me nose. Bilgewater, tar, hemp, and rum, all mixed up with the stink of men bein' seasick. The sailors, ye know, they get to sleep in hammocks, but us soldiers, we had to bed down on deck—hundreds of us, squeezed together so tight we couldn't hardly move. In some ways it's better 'cause at least ye've got the fresh air. But when it's cold, or it's raining, or the sea's runnin' rough so everybody's rollin' all over the place . . . I don't reckon I've ever been so miserable. I sorta been thinkin' about maybe goin' down to South America—know lots of lads who've gone there to fight in their revolutions, and officers, too. But whenever I think o' crossin' that ocean again . . ." His voice trailed away as he stared into the distance and swallowed hard. "I don't think I could do it."

It was the last thing she'd expected to hear him say. "Do you miss the Army so much?"

"I miss me messmates. But the Army?" He laughed. "No, ma'am."

"And yet you're thinking of going to fight in South America?"

"What else am I t' do? Been a soldier most me life; like I said, it's the only thing I know how t' do. Seems like South America might be better'n staying here and starvin' . . . if only it weren't so blasted far away."

"Have you thought about going home to Ireland?"

A sad, faraway light crept into his eyes. "Think about Ireland all the time, I do. But I'm never going back there. From what I hear, they're all starvin' to death over there, too—or dead already. They don't need me back there. Me girl got tired of waiting and married somebody else; m' mother and da are both dead, and me sister's got troubles enough of her own without me adding to 'em."

He was still holding the last of his sausages, and he stuffed it in his mouth and swallowed before saying, "I've heard tell that one out of every three soldiers in King George's Army is an Irishman. Did ye know that?"

"No, I didn't."

He nodded. "Guess there ain't much else for a likely lad from Tipperary or Kilkenny or Dublin Town to do, now, is there? He can go off t' fight in France or America and get himself shot, or stay home and get shot by some bloody constable don't like the look on his face. Sometimes I think, *What would old King George and his bloody cousin Lord Jarvis do without us?* Wouldn't be winning so many wars, that's fer sure. 'Course, maybe they wouldn't be startin' so many, neither."

Hero smiled faintly and said, "If you don't go to South America or back to Ireland, what will you do?"

He fell silent, his head tipping back as he watched the heavy white clouds shifting overhead. She was beginning to think he wasn't going to answer when he said, "Ask meself that all the time, I do. But the truth is, I don't know."

He paused, then said more quietly, "I just don't."

Chapter 10

Sebastian returned to Brook Street to find an ornate gentleman's carriage with four well-matched, cream-colored horses drawn up before his house and the ponderous figure of Archibald Douglas Farnsworth, Fourth Duke of Eversfield and brother to the late Lord Preston Farnsworth, descending the front steps.

The Duke was taller than his dead brother and considerably heavier. He might be only in his fifties, but his hair was already white and wispy, his eyes bloodshot, his face bloated and blotchy. There were few vices in which His Grace did not indulge with gusto, and it showed. He weighed some fourteen or fifteen stone, had lost a high percentage of his teeth, and suffered from a tendency to both gout and dropsy. But he was as always impeccably dressed, wearing pale yellow pantaloons, a well-tailored navy coat, and an elaborately tied cravat.

"Ah, there you are," said the Duke, drawing up halfway down the steps at the sight of Sebastian. "Devilish glad you caught me." He hesitated. "That is, you do have a moment, don't you?"

"Yes, of course," said Sebastian, handing the reins to Tom and jumping down. "Come in, please. Brandy?" he offered, leading the way to the library.

Eversfield swiped the back of one meaty fist across his lips. "I'll take Scotch if you've got it."

"I have, indeed." Sebastian poured a generous measure of Scotch in one of the crystal glasses kept on a table near the hearth and handed it to his guest.

"Thank you kindly," said the Duke, taking a deep drink. "Ah, excellent. I'm here because Bow Street is being bloody close-lipped about everything, and I hoped I could count on you to give it to me straight: Is it true what the papers are saying? That Preston was found hanging upside down by one foot, with his hands tied behind his back?"

Sebastian poured himself a brandy, then carefully replaced the carafe's stopper. "It is true, yes. But he didn't die that way. He was killed by a blow to the back of his head, so he didn't suffer."

"Thank God for that. But . . . you're saying someone strung him up like that after he was dead? Why would anyone do that?"

"I have no idea. Do you?"

The Duke's eyes widened. "Me? No. We weren't close, Preston and I; never were. There's nearly ten years between us, y'know, so I suppose that's probably part of it, although I'll be the first to admit it's not the whole story. The thing is, whatever our differences are now, I dearly loved the little boy he once was and it's hard—damned hard—to think of him dying like that."

"Do you know if your brother ever had anything to do with the tarot?"

"*Preston?* Good God, no. He hated fortune-tellers—said they did the devil's work for him." Eversfield grimaced. "He talked like that, you know; always going on and on about sin and sloth and all manner of other pious claptrap. Can't imagine who he got it from. M' father was never a churchgoing man, and the only Bible verse our mother ever quoted was something about bridling tongues and deceiving hearts."

Sebastian took a slow sip of his brandy. "Who do you think killed him?"

The Duke shook his head slowly back and forth. "Damned if I know. Like I said, we weren't close. Preston disapproved of me and my ways." Eversfield drew the word out, so that it sounded more like *disapproooved*. "It was one of his favorite expressions; he *disapproooved* of so many things, my brother. The last time I saw him, he called me a godless, immoral heathen. So is it any wonder I avoided him as much as possible?"

"I take it he got on well with your sister, though?"

"Hester?" Eversfield rolled his eyes. "Oh, Lord, yes. Two of a kind, they are—or were, I suppose I should say. Last time I was crazy enough to accept one of Hester's invites to dinner, they did their damnedest to convince me that this crazy weather we've been having means the world is coming to an end."

"They aren't alone in that belief."

The Duke stared at him. "Don't tell me you think it, too?"

"Me? No."

"Thank God for that." The Duke took another deep swallow of his Scotch.

"Was that the last time you saw your brother?" said Sebastian. "At this dinner?"

Eversfield looked thoughtful. "Well, it's the last time I *spoke* to him. I did see him briefly last Saturday, in the Strand, but I didn't talk to him—only nodded in passing, on account of him being deep in what looked like a pretty intense conversation with that French priest."

"What French priest?"

"Father Anselm, I think his name is." The Duke frowned. "No, that's not it. Abbott? No. Ambrose? Yes, that's it: Father Ambrose. He ministers to that appalling colony of Irish immigrants in Southwark—them and whatever French Catholics down there haven't scurried back across the Channel now that old King Louis is sitting on his throne all right and tight again. Came here as a refugee from the Revolution himself, I'm told. One of those nonjuring priests. Guess he didn't want to wait around and get his head chopped off along with all the others—not that I can say I blame him for that."

"What time was this? That you saw your brother with this priest, I mean."

"Musta been shortly before noon. I'm not normally abroad at that hour, but I had the devil of a toothache and was on my way to the dentist."

"Do you know what this French priest had to do with your brother?"

"No idea at all. Preston couldn't abide Catholics, y'know. In another age he'd have given old Richard Topcliffe a run for his money."

"But you know this priest?"

"Yes, but only because he tutors the son of one of m' friends."

"In French?"

"French, maths, history, natural science, what have you. M' friend's son needs all the help he can get. Boy takes after his mother, I'm afraid. She's as pretty as all get-out, but a sillier widgeon never made her curtsy at Almack's—and that's truly saying something."

"You never married yourself?"

"Me?" The Duke's eyes bulged. "Good Lord, no. Almost got

caught once. It was a close-run thing, I can tell you. But after that I learned to be more careful."

"So Lord Preston was your heir?"

"He was, yes." Eversfield froze with his Scotch raised halfway to his lips. His hand shook, and he lowered the glass without taking a sip. "You can't . . . you can't think *that's* why Preston was killed."

"No. But I don't see how we can ignore it as a possibility, either. Who is next in line?"

Eversfield's features contorted with the effort of thought. "It's a cousin of some sort . . . second or third, I believe, although there could be a remove in there somewhere. Always expected Preston to step into my shoes when the time came, so I can't say I ever paid too much attention to m' relatives—there's too damned many of 'em to begin with, and they're all as boring as hell. It's one of 'em, obviously, but I'll be damned if I could tell you which one. Hester would know. That's the sort of thing she keeps track of."

"Your brother's death must be hard on her."

"Truth be told, I haven't seen her yet, although I suppose I should mosey on over there." He sighed. "God help me." He polished off his drink with a flourish and set the empty glass aside. "Thank you for your time, your Scotch, and your honesty, Devlin. I suppose there'll be an inquest?"

"There will be," said Sebastian, walking with him to the front door. "But I haven't heard the time or place yet."

The Duke paused in the doorway, his hat in his hands, his head shaking sadly back and forth. "I still can't believe Preston is dead. *Dead.*" Then he settled his hat on his head, nodded to Morey, and said, "Do give my best to Lady Devlin."

"Yes, of course."

Sebastian watched as one of the Duke's footmen leapt forward to help hoist His Grace up into the waiting carriage. Then he turned and climbed the stairs to where Hero sat beside the drawing room's bowed front window, half her attention on the notes she was organizing from that morning's interview, the other half keeping an eye on little Miss Guinevere, who was sitting on a rug nearby and babbling a steady string of utterly incomprehensible nonsense as she placed a collection of colorfully painted wooden blocks one by one into a bucket and then took them out again.

"Learn anything?" asked Hero, setting aside her notebook.

Sebastian went to settle on the rug beside their daughter. "Maybe. Maybe not. I gather Lord Preston and his brother the Duke were not what you might call close." He accepted a block handed to him by Guinevere, said, "Thank you," then looked over at Hero. "You wouldn't happen to be familiar with a French priest named Ambrose—or something similar—would you? I'm told he works with the poor Irish and French immigrants in Southwark and tutors gentlemen's sons in French and maths on the side."

"You mean Father Ambrose de Sancerre? What could he possibly have to do with a man like Lord Preston?"

Sebastian dropped the block into the bucket, then said to Hero, "The Duke tells me he saw his brother talking to this priest last Saturday, which strikes me as . . . strange. What do you know of him?"

"Not a great deal. I've only met him once, but he's a memorable man, very wise and kind and . . ." She paused, as if searching for the right words. "I don't quite know how to describe it, but the closest I can come up with is 'intense.' He's very passionate about the work he does with the poor. It's his life. As I understand it, he supported the Revolution in its early days but eventually turned against it because of its excesses. I gather he lost virtually his entire family, and at one point was arrested and condemned to death for hearing confessions and saying Mass clandestinely."

Guinevere chose that moment to dump out her blocks all at once, then babbled a string of nonsense at her father and handed him the empty bucket. "My turn, is it?" He reached for one of the blocks. "Shall we start with the yellow one?" To Hero, he said, "Interesting. How did he get out of that?"

"I didn't hear that part. But I think he went to Spain first and then came to England."

"And yet he chooses to remain here rather than return to France now that the Bourbons have been restored to their ancestral throne?"

A faint gleam of amusement showed in her brilliant gray eyes. "I had the distinct impression he's not what you might call an admirer of monarchy. After all, he has dedicated his life to working with the poor and oppressed. And he did support the Revolution at first, remember?"

"Ah. So how does an anti-monarchist French Catholic priest who ministers to the poor come to know the wealthy and fervently anti-Catholic brother of an English duke?"

"That I can't begin to imagine."

Sebastian fell silent, his attention seemingly all focused on his daughter, who was now handing him the blocks one at a time so that he could put them in the bucket. He was aware of Hero watching him, and after a moment she said, "What is it, Devlin?"

He looked up, his fist tightening around the block in his hand. "After I spoke to Gibson this morning, I went to see Madame Blanchette. She tells me *Le Pendu* can symbolize treachery and betrayal but also sacrifice, the need to view things from a different perspective, the acceptance of one's fate, or even redemption."

"So much?"

"Evidently. Although of course it's always possible that whoever killed Farnsworth has no idea what the card means and simply posed his victim's body that way for some other reason entirely."

"But you don't think so?"

Sebastian dropped the last block in the bucket, kissed his daughter on the top of her head, and pushed to his feet. "No. No, I don't."

Chapter 11

Sebastian traced the French priest to Deadman's Place, a miserable, grimy lane of wretched shops and crumbling tenements that curved away from the river to the east of London Bridge. Lying on the south bank of the Thames, the part of London known as Southwark had long ago acquired a well-deserved reputation as a refuge for debtors, thieves, prostitutes, immigrants, and the desperately poor.

He found the street thronged with rattling carts and drays, ragged street sellers, and muddy, underfed children. The smell of fermenting beer from a nearby brewery hung heavily in the air, mixing with the stench of rotting garbage, effluent, and damp decay. Following directions elicited from a stooped, toothless old woman in a ratty shawl who was selling potatoes near one of the brewery's soot-stained brick walls, Sebastian ducked down a dark, foul-smelling passage that led to a small, irregularly shaped stone-and-brick-walled court that looked as if it might once have been part of some ancient, long-forgotten monastic establishment. What had been an elegant oriel window was now bricked up, and an intricately carved sandstone cornice over the recessed arched doorway in the far corner was crumbling and blackened with centuries of soot. But the worn cobbles underfoot were well swept, and in a row of earth-filled old stone horse troughs lined up against one wall, a carefully tended assortment of herbs and vegetables struggled to survive in a slice of pale slanting light.

Hunkered down beside the stone troughs, a trowel still held loosely in one hand as if he'd been tending his herbs, was an aged man in a threadbare black cassock, with shaggy dark gray hair and a neatly trimmed salt-and-pepper beard. He was deep in earnest conversation with a thin, dark-haired girl in rags who looked to be perhaps five or six. She had her head bowed, her gaze fixed firmly on the cobbles at her bare feet, and as Sebastian entered the courtyard he heard the priest say softly, "*Alors*. Now, don't worry about it anymore, you hear, Mary?"

The little girl nodded solemnly.

"Go on, then, my child," said the priest, pushing awkwardly to his feet. "And remember what I said!"

The little girl took off at a run, swerving around Sebastian on her way to the passage. The priest watched her go, then turned his gaze to the gentleman in the caped driving coat, top hat, and gleaming Hessians who now stood before him. "You're looking decidedly out of place, young man. Do I take it you're searching for someone?"

"You're Father Ambrose?"

"*Oui, je suis lui*," said the priest, pivoting to thrust his trowel into the dirt of the trough before wiping his hands on the skirts of his cassock. He was a solidly built man of above-average height, with a weathered, craggy face, heavy gray brows, and deeply etched smile lines that radiated out from lively brown eyes. "How may I help you?"

"My name is Devlin."

The priest nodded. "I have heard of you, *monsieur.* But I must confess I can't begin to imagine what the son and heir of the grand Earl of Hendon would be wanting with a simple old French priest."

"I'm told you were seen speaking to Lord Preston Farnsworth last Saturday, in the Strand."

"Ah." The lines beside the old priest's eyes deepened as he tilted his head and brought up a sturdy, blunt-fingered hand to pull at one earlobe. "Well, to be honest, I don't know if I'd say we were exactly 'speaking.' 'Having a shouting match' might be a better description of our brief encounter."

"I hadn't heard that part."

The priest gave a soft chuckle. "No? Then forget I mentioned it."

Sebastian had to stop himself from smiling back. "What was the shouting about?"

The priest turned to his plants, his work-worn fingers plucking the yellowing leaves from a bunch of parsley. "I assume you know Lord Preston was an enthusiastic member of the Society for the Suppression of Vice?"

"No, I didn't know. But I can't say it surprises me." The Society for the Suppression of Vice was a collection of self-righteous busybodies dedicated to an aggressive crusade against what they saw as the dangerous national slide into sin and degradation. They pursued their vendetta against wickedness by coercing those of the "lower orders" they considered "morally deficient" into behaving, and one of the best ways they'd found to do that was by using archaic, half-forgotten laws to go after any and all transgressions against what they considered proper conduct. To this end they eagerly pursued prosecutions for everything from street brawling to swearing, "profaning" the Lord's Day, publishing radical pamphlets, and selling what they considered "licentious" books.

"Three weeks ago," the priest was saying, his attention seemingly all for the task of tidying his herbs, "a boy was caught trying to steal a ham. His name was Cian; Cian Donahue. He was just ten years old, small for his age and frail, and the constable who nabbed him wanted the shopkeeper to let the lad go with just a warning. But the Society—well, Lord Preston Farnsworth, to be specific—pressed the shopkeeper to prosecute. They do that, you know: help fund prosecutions and secure rewards for successful suits."

Sebastian nodded. It was one of the peculiarities of English common law that except in cases such as murder, manslaughter, treason, and uttering, the Crown itself did not prosecute lawbreakers. It was up to the victims of everything from theft to rape and assault to bring charges and prosecute their cases in a court of law. If the victim declined to prosecute—which was a costly exercise—then the thief or assailant went free. But if the prosecutor was successful, the Crown granted him a hefty reward of forty pounds—a practice that inevitably led to some serious miscarriages of justice. "And were Lord Preston and this shopkeeper successful?"

"They succeeded in having Cian remanded into custody to await trial. But they've had jail fever in Newgate, you know. When I went to visit the boy last Saturday, I was told he'd died during the night. It was right after that I chanced to run into Farnsworth and . . . well, I suppose you could say I lost my temper."

"And shouted at him?"

"Yes. Rather vociferously, I'm afraid."

"How did you come to know him?"

"Lord Preston?" Father Ambrose's lips tightened. "I do my best to teach the poor boys and girls around here to read and write, and it seems as if one or the other of them is always falling afoul of that damnable Society—either the children, or their siblings, or one or the other of their parents . . . particularly their mothers, if they've been widowed or abandoned."

"You know this Cian's parents?"

"I did. They're both dead now—which is why Cian was stealing hams." The priest moved on to an unhappy-looking basil. "I'll never understand how the Lord Prestons of this world think London's orphans are supposed to keep themselves from starving to death. It isn't as if they can go into a workhouse—not unless they were born in one of the local parishes. And to be honest, most of them think they have a better chance of surviving on the streets. And they're probably right."

Sebastian wasn't about to argue with that. "And that's all you spoke of? The dead boy?"

The priest nodded. "I was still raging on about it when Farnsworth simply turned and walked off."

"Did you happen to see where he went when he left you?"

"I assume he kept going, toward Temple Bar. But to be honest, it isn't as if I were paying attention." He threw a thoughtful glance at Sebastian over his shoulder, then said, "Why do you ask? When do you think he was killed?"

"Probably sometime that evening."

"Ah. The papers didn't say that. Any idea as to who killed him?"

"Not at this point, no."

Father Ambrose was quiet for a moment, his gaze on the lavender he was now tidying. When he did speak, the words came out slowly, as if he were choosing them with care. "The part Farnsworth played in helping bring about the end of the slave trade was unquestionably admirable, and I will forever respect him for that. But he was an arrogant, bigoted man, self-righteous and inflexible to the point of being merciless and cruel. A man like that can make any number of enemies."

"Are you thinking of anyone in particular?"

"Me? No." The priest dropped the handful of dead leaves he'd been collecting into an old market basket at his feet. Then he hesitated, his eyes narrowing as he studied Sebastian and said, "You aren't by chance related to the McClellans, are you?"

Sebastian felt his breath catch, but he was careful to keep all trace of emotion off his face. "I believe there is some connection. Why do you ask?"

"I knew Maréchal Alexandre McClellan. It was long ago, of course, before I left France, so he wasn't even a general then. In fact, he was about the age you are now. And the thing is, you look startlingly like him."

"So I've been told."

Father Ambrose bent to pick up his basket. "You've heard the Bourbons are trying to kill him?"

"McClellan?" Sebastian's voice sounded leaden, even to his own ears. "No; I hadn't heard."

The priest nodded. "Any general who served under Napoléon and hasn't rushed to fawn over the Bourbons is basically fair game."

"Except that McClellan didn't rally to Napoléon during the Hundred Days; he stayed in Vienna."

"He did. But since when did the Bourbons allow technicalities to stop them? McClellan's name might not be on the list of those to be prosecuted, but he isn't the only such one they've targeted in secret."

Sebastian had heard whispers about the vicious wave of revenge sweeping France ever since Waterloo: about the countless hundreds of Bonapartists, Protestants, Jews, and Muslims who'd been slaughtered; the villages looted and burned; the women stripped naked, whipped, raped, and tortured. But details were hard to come by. And the British government and their army of occupation were resolutely turning a blind eye to the activities of the monarchy they themselves had put back in place by force. Twice. "How many of Napoléon's generals have been killed?"

"So far? Well, let's see. Besides Marshal Ney, they've now officially executed at least four generals: Chartrand, the twins César and Constantin Faucher, and the comte de la Bédoyère. Marshal Guillaume Brune they simply murdered—as they did General Jean-Pierre Ramel. And Ramel wasn't even a Bonapartist."

"This attack on McClellan—when did it occur?"

"I'm told the last known attempt was something like a month ago, but he hasn't been seen since. No one knows if they've succeeded in killing him or if he's simply lying low—or has gone elsewhere."

Sebastian found himself studying the old priest's weathered, inscrutable features. "You seem remarkably well-informed."

If he expected the man to be discomfited, he was not. "For a simple priest living in exile in some wretched Southwark rookery, you mean?" Father Ambrose shrugged. "It's worrisome, what's happening in France. Violence begets violence, and atrocities committed in revenge for past atrocities lay the seeds for future acts of vengeance. I don't see this chaos ending anytime soon, and that hurts my heart."

"Do you have family left in France?"

"Some, but not much. Truth be told, I don't have much family left, period."

Sebastian nodded and touched his hand to his hat. "Thank you for your time."

"Of course," said the priest, still holding his basket of dead leaves. "I hope I have been of some help."

It wasn't until Sebastian had reached Deadman's Place and was turning toward his waiting curricle that he realized the priest had never actually explained how he came to know so much about what was happening across the Channel.

Jamie Gallagher waited until he heard the Viscount's footsteps retreating back down the passage. Then he made himself keep waiting, counting slowly to one hundred before he crept from behind the worn old arched door.

"You didn't tell him," said the boy, going to where the priest still stood in the center of the courtyard, his gaze on the now empty passage. "Why didn't you tell him?"

Father Ambrose shook his head. "The timing wasn't right. I think it's best he discovers a few things for himself first."

"But what if he doesn't?"

Father smiled and turned back to his small garden. "Don't worry. He will."

Chapter 12

Later that afternoon, Hero drove out to Moss Grove, the modest eighteenth-century house that served as the refuge of Lady Tess Farnsworth and her lover.

Hero had been only casually acquainted with Tess at the time her scandalous escape from her unhappy marriage led to her banishment from Society. Thanks to their husbands' friendship, the two women had come to know each other better in recent years. But Hero was still uncertain as to how Tess would react to her visit.

She found her in a corner of the old stone barn, seated cross-legged in a bed of hay with a litter of three gray-and-white kittens nestled in her lap. She wore a pale blue muslin gown with long sleeves and a simple high neck, and even as she looked up from the kittens with a smile, the expression in her eyes remained wary.

"I hope you won't mind if I don't disturb them by getting up," she said as the housemaid who had showed Hero out to her mistress curtsied and withdrew. "Their mother disappeared a few days ago, so I've been bottle-feeding them. But the little hussy reappeared this morning acting for all the world as if she'd only been out for an extended stroll, so hopefully they'll be all right now."

"How old are they?" said Hero, coming to sit on a nearby three-legged milking stool as one of the kittens lifted its head and yawned.

"Five weeks, I think."

An awkward silence fell as the two women watched the kittens. Then Hero said, "I came because I thought you might like some moral support. I don't want you to think I'm here as Devlin's emissary."

"No?"

"No."

The wakeful kitten scrambled off Tess's lap and scampered toward Hero, who smiled and held out her hand. Tess said, "So tell me, has all of London decided that Hugh and I must be guilty?"

"Not quite all."

"But most?"

Hero reached to pick up the kitten and cradle him in her arms. "The papers aren't helping."

Tess pressed her lips together, her nostrils flaring as she drew a deep breath. "We had Sir Nathaniel Conant out here this morning, you know. He insisted on speaking to Hugh first, alone, then me."

Hero looked up from the kitten in her arms. "I thought Sir Henry Lovejoy was handling the investigation."

"He is. But Sir Nathaniel said that as Chief Magistrate he felt it his duty to conduct the 'most important' interviews personally." Tess's jaw hardened. "In other words, so that he can take credit when he has Hugh arrested."

"What a beastly man he is."

Tess nodded. "He actually said he was shocked—*deeply* shocked—

to find me not wearing mourning for Preston. As if I would drape myself in black crepe for a husband I loathed and from whom I've been officially separated for six years. I told him I'm not such a hypocrite, and I think that shocked him even more."

"That I can believe."

"Ironically, my brother said the same thing when he drove out here yesterday evening."

"You mean Whitcombe?" Jasper James Haywood, the Fourth Earl of Whitcombe, had succeeded his father to the title shortly after Tess's marriage to Farnsworth. The new Earl had always been inclined to be dull and stuffy, but since Tess's fall from grace he'd become insufferably priggish and straitlaced, as if to counteract the opprobrium of his sister's shameful conduct.

Tess nodded. "Julius is still in France with his regiment, but if he were here, I've no doubt he'd wholeheartedly agree with Whitcombe's mission. They both completely disowned me after I left Preston—told me I could starve to death naked in a ditch as far as they were concerned. Neither one had spoken to me since."

"So why did Whitcombe come?"

"To suggest—no, *insist*—that Hugh and I leave the country at once. Preferably by immigrating to America, but, failing that, then at least to take up residence in some out-of-the-way corner of the Continent where we would be unlikely to encounter any stray British tourists. He was quite enraged when Hugh said we were determined to stay and defend ourselves against whatever accusations might come our way. To hear Whitcombe talk, you'd think I've made it my sole mission in life to dishonor the Great House of Haywood."

To Hero's surprise, a tear welled up to trickle down Tess's cheek, but she dashed at it angrily with one fist. "Sorry. I didn't think my family still had the power to hurt me, but in that I was wrong. He even had the nerve to throw Aunt Jane up at me."

"Aunt Jane?"

A ghost of a smile touched her lips. "My great-aunt, Jane Haywood. She wasn't received by Society any more than I am, you know. At the age of twenty-eight, when everyone assumed she must have long ago resigned herself to the dull life of an old maid, she up and ran off with a *most* unsuitable lover and lived with him 'in sin' until the day he died. Moss Grove was his home, you see. He left it to her, and then she left it to me when she died. It was shortly after Preston had secured his separation of goods and successfully sued Hugh for all that money, and I don't know what we'd have done otherwise. He'd had to sell everything, including the small estate he'd inherited from his grandfather, to pay Preston, so we were utterly destitute. I never could understand why Whitcombe simply assumed Aunt Jane would leave Moss Grove to him—I mean, it's not as if he needed what is really little more than a farm. But he'd always taken it for granted that she would, so he was doubly furious when she left it to me."

"Because in one fell swoop she deprived him of both the land's income and the pleasure of seeing you starve to death in a ditch?"

"Basically, yes." She fell silent, her attention all for the two remaining kittens in her lap, who were now stirring. Then she said, "It looks bad, doesn't it? Tell me honestly."

Hero could only nod. "You can't think of anything—anything at all—that might explain why someone would hang Lord Preston upside down like that?"

"No. But whoever did it must have hated him, don't you think? Which suggests it was an act of revenge."

"Who could have hated him that much?"

"Besides Hugh and me?" said Tess, looking up with a soft laugh.

Then she drew a ragged breath and looked away again, swallowing hard. "I'm frightened, Hero. I try not to let Hugh see it, but he's no fool; he knows. And while he's far better at hiding his thoughts and feelings than I am, the truth is, he's frightened, too. That's one of the dangers of 'counting the world well lost for love,' isn't it? The world—or at any rate our own rarified corner of it—will never forgive you for the sin of scorning them. And that means that if an opportunity to make you pay comes along, they'll seize it."

Hero nuzzled the soft fur of the purring kitten in her arms, wishing she could reassure Tess; tell her she was wrong.

But they both knew their world.

Chapter 13

For reasons he couldn't have explained, Sebastian found himself back in the old cobbled courtyard off Swallow Street, standing in the doorway of the abandoned chapel as a new rush of rain fell gently around him.

Over the past twenty-four hours, Lovejoy's men had thoroughly scoured both the chapel and the surrounding area, looking for something—anything—that might help explain what had happened here.

They'd found nothing.

So why here? Sebastian wondered. Why had Lord Preston Farnsworth's killer chosen this place for the site of the man's death? Because it was a chapel? Because of some personal significance of which Sebastian was unaware? Or simply because it was deserted and out of the way? Had Farnsworth set off that evening for a routine walk, only to be snatched and brought here to be killed? Or had he come here willingly to meet his killer?

Why would he do that?

"Why, why, why," said Sebastian aloud, his words falling into the hush of the ruined chapel. And he found his attention caught, as before, by the worn engravings on the paving stones at his feet. HERE LYETH THE BODY OF JOSEPH JENNINGS, ESQ, BURIED THIS 6TH DAY OF APRIL ANO 1626 . . .

Who had owned the ancient house of which this chapel had once been a part? he wondered. Did that explain its choice as the site for murder? Was there some connection between the house, the Farnsworths, and the family of the man who had killed him? A vendetta, perhaps, that stretched back centuries?

A ridiculous thought?

Or not?

Sebastian had come to the ruins of this old Tudor house once before, a year ago, to see a young half-Scottish, half-African fencing master who sometimes used the courtyard as a convenient open space for giving lessons. And found himself wondering, *Could there be some connection there?*

Another ridiculous thought?

Or not?

Swearing softly to himself, Sebastian turned and was about to leave when he became aware of the sounds of a carriage drawing up in the street outside. He heard a gentlewoman's voice giving instructions to her coachman, followed by quick footfalls crossing the wet courtyard toward him. Then the figure of a woman elegantly dressed in black appeared in the doorway, her step faltering at the sight of Sebastian, her hand coming up to her mouth as she let out a soft mew of surprise.

"I beg your pardon, Lady Hester," said Sebastian, touching his hand to his hat. "I didn't mean to frighten you."

A faint flush of annoyance showed high on her ladyship's cheekbones. She shook her head, her back stiffening, her hand falling to her side. "Don't be absurd; I was merely startled. How do you do, Lord Devlin?"

She had been born the daughter of a duke, and the arrogance and sense of superiority that had engendered in her showed in every movement, every utterance, every fiber of her being. Whereas the current Duke of Eversfield was an affable and unpretentious man and Lord Preston had had a reputation for being charming and likable, most people found Lady Hester proud and stiff. She was relatively tall for a woman, even taller than her dead brother but built thin and bony, with angular features, pale grayish blue eyes, and dark blond hair she wore scraped back in an austere style. In honor of his death, she was dressed in brutally severe but inescapably expensive mourning, from her demure black hat and short veil to her somber black pelisse, black gloves, black reticule, and dulled black shoes. "Bow Street has told us you are assisting them in their efforts to catch my brother's murderer," she said. "Have you found the evidence necessary to have him remanded into custody?"

Not "someone" or "the killer," Sebastian noticed, but *him*, as if Lord Preston's killer had already been identified and it was simply a matter of proving the case against him. "Not yet," he said. "Please accept my condolences on the loss of your brother."

"Thank you." She tightened her jaw against a threatened upsurge of emotion, her nostrils flaring on a deep breath as she let her gaze drift over the broken altar and rubble of fallen stones. "I came because I wanted to see for myself where my brother died." She paused. "What a wretched place for Preston to have breathed his last."

"Do you have any idea why your brother would come here?"

"No. I can't begin to imagine."

"This chapel was once part of a nobleman's house from the sixteenth or seventeenth century. Did the Farnsworths perhaps have some connection to either the house or the family that owned it?"

"Was there a nobleman's house here in the past? If so, I wasn't aware of it. Surely you can't think that might somehow be relevant to my brother's death?"

"It seems worth exploring. Do you know if Lord Preston had received any threats recently? Perhaps from someone he encountered in his work with the Society for the Suppression of Vice?"

Something glittered in her ladyship's hard eyes. "My dear Lord Devlin, I trust you don't intend to fritter away valuable time by searching amongst the city's criminal classes for the perpetrator of this outrage. The identity of my brother's killer is more than obvious to everyone."

"It is?"

"Of course it is. Six years ago Hugh Chandler ran off with my brother's wife, then turned more than ugly when forced to pay for his sinful crime. And he never forgave my brother for it."

Sebastian had to work to keep his voice even. "And how precisely did Major Chandler 'turn ugly'?"

"Ask anyone who saw the man's face when the verdict was returned and he heard the sum awarded. If looks could kill, Preston would have been dead six years ago." Her lip curled. "Oh, I know he's considered something of a hero now since Waterloo, but I've no doubt his character is the same as it has always been: devious, deceitful, and utterly devoid of any of the qualities one expects of a gentleman."

Sebastian found he was unconsciously clenching his fists and had to deliberately relax them. "Do you have any idea why your brother went out Saturday evening?"

"Yes, of course; as I've already informed Bow Street, my brother always took a walk after dinner. We've never kept fashionable hours, you know. With the exceptions of Tuesdays and Sundays, when we typically attend evensong at St. George's, Preston believed in dining at six." She said it smugly, as if it had long been a matter of pride for both brother and sister. "And he was not one to linger over his port. 'A walk after the consumption of sustenance cleanses the humors and strengthens the constitution,' he always liked to say."

"And did he make a habit of walking to Swallow Street?"

"As to that, I have no idea, although I shouldn't think so. I myself typically take two turns around St. James's Square and then retire to my rooms to read."

"But you did see him before he went out that evening?"

"Oh, yes."

"Did he seem upset in any way? Distracted? Afraid, perhaps?"

"Preston? Afraid? I can't think of anything short of the wrath of God that would have frightened my brother."

"So there was nothing unusual about that evening?"

"Nothing. As I told Bow Street, he did receive a note shortly before dinner, but I doubt it was important."

Sebastian knew a quickening of interest. "Do you still have it? The note, I mean."

"No. If I remember correctly, he slipped it into the pocket of his coat after reading it." She frowned. "Are you suggesting the note might have come from his murderer?"

"It's possible, is it not? Did Lord Preston say anything about this note? Anything that might indicate who it was from?"

"No, nothing. We were having a glass of wine in the drawing room before dinner and discussing the prosecution of a Radical newspaper editor Preston had recently undertaken, when Dunstan—our butler—brought up the note. Preston thanked him, read through it quickly, then tucked the note in his pocket and continued our conversation."

"Did he seem upset by the note in any way?"

"No, not at all. I assumed it had something to do with a report he was preparing to submit to the Select Committee on the police of the metropolis. My brother worked tirelessly to rid our streets of every sort of vermin, from loose women and unruly public houses to the dangerous, shameless atheists and radicals who seem to be proliferating more and more each day. If it hadn't been for certain misguided individuals, this city would have had a disciplined, effective police force years ago, and my brother might well be alive today."

"Was there a specific 'misguided individual' you had in mind?"

Her nose twitched. "I was referring to Lord Quinton-Thomas, of course. If you ask me, he has my brother's blood on his hands."

"Because Quinton-Thomas opposed the creation of a centralized police force, you mean?"

"No one has worked harder to defeat every proposal Preston advanced." She was growing impatient. "But I fail to see how any of this can help convict my brother's killer."

"Perhaps not," said Sebastian.

He had the sense Lady Hester was no longer listening to him. He watched her gaze drift again around the ruined chapel, her features pinched. "I'm told the inquest is scheduled for Wednesday afternoon."

"Is it? I hadn't heard."

She nodded. "Let us hope the jurors reach a swift, sensible conclusion. It's my understanding the coroner has the power to commit a case for trial to the Old Bailey directly without needing an indictment from the Grand Jury, does he not?"

"He does, yes. But I doubt that will happen in this case."

Her lips pressed into a tight line. "In that, I trust you will be proven wrong." She inclined her head in a gracious manner. "Good day, Lord Devlin."

Sebastian touched his hand to his hat. "Lady Hester."

She turned and walked away, her head held high, the muscles

of her neck rigid with the effort required to keep every manifestation of her inner pain determinedly repressed. Impossible not to feel sorry for this lonely, grieving woman who had lost not only her brother but the daily rhythm of the life they had shared together for years. And yet Sebastian found himself wondering how well she had truly known her brother; how much she had known about the entirety of his life.

Sebastian himself had a widowed sister living in St. James's Square. Amanda was his only surviving sibling, but they had never been close, even as children. Now they barely spoke to each other, and when he thought about it, Sebastian realized how very little he knew about the ways in which she spent her days.

Of course, Lady Hester had actually lived with her brother; she not only managed his household but, from the sound of things, also shared his enthusiasm for squashing the pleasures and exuberant excesses of the so-called lower orders. Was it really so hard to believe that one of the despised denizens of that reviled teeming multitude had decided to strike back at those who considered themselves his "betters"?

Sebastian didn't think so.

Chapter 14

In Sebastian's experience, a man's enemies could often tell you more about him than either his friends or his family. And Mallory, Lord Quinton-Thomas, was definitely one of Lord Preston's enemies. He was also one of the few truly Radical noblemen sitting in the House of Lords. Of an old but not particularly distinguished or wealthy Hampshire family, he was in his forties now, determinedly single, and notorious for his blunt, outspoken opposition to the Society for the Suppression of Vice.

"Farnsworth wasn't just a member," said Quinton-Thomas when Sebastian met with him later in a public house across the street from Westminster. "He was the driving force behind much of what they did."

A big bear of a man with full cheeks, a ruddy complexion, and fiery auburn hair, Quinton-Thomas had written a stream of articles attacking the Society and criticizing the various ambitious plans for the establishment of a centralized, uniformed London police force.

"He wasn't as visible in the Society as the likes of Wilberforce or Bowles," said the Baron, hunching forward to wrap both hands around the tankard of ale that rested on the battered old table between them, "but he sits—or I suppose I should say *sat*—on the Society's General Committee. They have three subcommittees, you know. The first is essentially dedicated to making the poor hate Sundays by digging up old Jacobean laws against doing anything on the Lord's Day besides going to church or sitting inside your house in gloomy silence. If you're rich, you can go on picnics or promenade in Hyde Park or whatever. But God forbid one of the self-anointed saints should be offended on their way to church by the sight of the poor playing skittles, or buying meat, or maybe getting a badly needed haircut because they work hard the other six days of the week and Sunday is the only day they have off."

Quinton-Thomas took a long, deep drink of his ale, and Sebastian signaled the barmaid for two more tankards.

"And the second subcommittee?"

"Ah," said the Baron, setting aside his empty tankard. "That's dedicated to eradicating what they consider blasphemous or lewd books. Of course, they don't touch the kind of elite bookstores that sell leather-bound copies of the Marquis de Sade to the ton. Much easier to go after some poor hawker with a cartful of cheap romances that might—just might—inflame the imaginations or corrupt the impressionable minds of young schoolgirls. That subcommittee doesn't like circulating libraries, either, and woe betide the street balladeer who dares sing some flash song about a highwayman or a drunken whore in their saintly presence. But it's the third subcommittee that was truly dear to Lord Preston's own heart."

"What's that one?"

"Theoretically, they go after pickpockets, thieves, whores, and beggars. But in practice they tend to focus more than anything on whores and beggars. They have this idea that all sin and crime can be traced back either to the foolish, kind souls who allow themselves to be tricked into misplaced philanthropy or to lewd women tempting innocent young men into debauchery."

Sebastian took a slow sip of his beer. "You're suggesting it can't?"

Quinton-Thomas leaned back in his chair as he laughed, then hunched forward again and winked. "One has to wonder how these men spent their youths, aye?"

"Why exactly is giving to beggars misplaced philanthropy?"

"Ah, that's because these worthy souls have convinced themselves that all beggars are frauds. So you see, they aren't actually sick or blind or missing a limb here and there, or starving because they can't get work. And if you accept that premise, it naturally follows that indiscriminate almsgiving is a sin because it contributes to sloth and corruption."

"How?"

"Because if people didn't give money to beggars, they would quit trying to beg and start working."

"At what jobs?"

Quinton-Thomas waved one meaty hand through the air. "Oh, somewhere. If you ask me, I think the good members of the Society hate beggars largely because they're a constant reminder of some of the less admirable things Britain has done that they don't want to be reminded of—everything from the slave trade and Ireland to the Highland Clearances and Enclosure Acts. And now we have a couple hundred thousand ragged ex-soldiers and sailors turned loose with no money and no way to earn it—not to mention the widows and orphans of the men who'll never come home. It's a hell of a lot easier to haul all the beggars off to gaol than to confront—or even admit to—the problems that created them in the first place."

Sebastian took a slow sip of his ale. "I can see how being a victim of that kind of a crusade might inspire someone to want to kill Farnsworth. But I have a hard time imagining a beggar or a thief—or a prostitute—bashing in Farnsworth's head and then hanging him upside down, rather than stealing his purse and watch and running."

The Baron set down his tankard with a heavy thump. "Are you saying he still had his watch and purse on him?"

"He did."

"Well, hell." Quinton-Thomas leaned back in his seat again. "There goes my theory. I was thinking it musta been Half-Hanged Harry who got him."

"Half-Hanged Harry?"

Quinton-Thomas chuckled. "Half-Hanged Harry McGregor. He was a notorious horse thief who operated on the outskirts of the city around the end of the last century. But no one would bring charges against him until Lord Preston stepped forward and supported two of the man's victims in prosecuting him. The scoundrel was duly found guilty, sentenced to death, and strung up on the gallows. But while it doesn't happen often, occasionally when they cut down a hanged man, they discover that somehow or another he's still alive."

"And this Half-Hanged Harry survived? I was under the impression that in such cases the poor bastard is typically hanged again on the next execution day."

"Typically, yes. But ole King George must've been in an unusually benevolent mood when McGregor's case came up for royal review because His Majesty took pity on the miscreant and commuted his sentence to transportation for fourteen years. Not even for life."

"And now he's back?"

The Baron nodded. "I heard just last week that Lord Preston was going around complaining that the fellow was following him."

"Interesting. So where would I find this Half-Hanged Harry?"

Quinton-Thomas took a deep drink and swiped the back of one hand across his lips. "Well, I believe he was originally from Lambeth. But as to whether he's returned to his old haunts, I don't know."

"Do you have any idea what Lord Preston might have been doing in Swallow Street last Saturday evening?"

"Not a clue. Seems a queer place for him to take a walk after dinner, although I suppose he could have gone there to meet someone he was supporting in a prosecution. He didn't only work through the Society, you know. I've heard he sometimes financed prosecutions all by himself. And since he took a percentage of the reward a successful prosecutor received from the Crown, he usually came out ahead."

"Clever."

Quinton-Thomas met his gaze, and Sebastian saw that all trace of amusement had vanished from those troubled hazel eyes. "That's one word for it. The cost of just one of those prosecutions would feed half a dozen poor families for the better part of a year. But that would require Lord Preston and that damnable society to admit that people might—just might—not be poor by choice. And once they did that, they'd lose their excuse for bullying everyone they disapprove of. If you ask me, that's what it's really all about: punishing anyone who's different from them. Punishing the people they hate."

Chapter 15

Paul Gibson was standing with his hands on his hips, his gaze thoughtful as he stared down at the waterlogged, days-old corpse of a woman laid out on the slab before him, when Sebastian walked up to the stone outbuilding's open doorway.

"Good God," said Sebastian, cupping a hand over his nose and taking a quick step back when the smell hit him. "Where did that come from?"

"Rotherhithe, via Old Father Thames." The surgeon sighed. "At one time this was a young woman, perhaps comely, surely bursting with enough hopes and dreams to fill a long lifetime. Now she's just . . . rotting flesh."

Sebastian cast one swift glance at the gruesome cadaver, then looked pointedly away. "Who was she?"

"No idea, and unfortunately no way of finding out. Most young women pulled from the river are considered suicides and simply consigned to the oblivion of the local parish's poor hole after a cursory inquest. But this one was found by a certain civic-minded Quaker who's had the misfortune over the past couple of years to find two other such young women washed up on a property he owns. He said he was tired of seeing them buried anonymously and wanted to try to identify this one, which is how she ended up here." Gibson reached for a sheet and spread it over the body with the tenderness of someone tucking a loved one in for the night. "All for naught, of course." He looked up. "What are you doing here, anyway? Please tell me there hasn't been another murder."

Sebastian shook his head. "I'm wondering if you found a piece of paper in one of Lord Preston's pockets."

"I had a message from Bow Street a bit ago, asking the same question, and I can tell you the same thing I told them: No." Gibson nodded toward a chipped enameled bowl that rested with the pile of Farnsworth's neatly folded clothes on a wooden shelf beside the door. "That's the contents of his pockets there."

The bowl contained only a few items, most of them predictable: Farnsworth's macabre pocket watch and fob, his coin purse, a fine silk handkerchief, a leather case of calling cards, a delicately carved wooden pipe and bag of tobacco, an ivory toothpick in its case, and a supple, fine leather pouch that opened to reveal several neatly folded segments of cured sheep's intestines.

The Italians called them *guantos*, gloves, while the French referred to them as "English riding jackets." And because young men on the Grand Tour had once tucked examples of such curiosities into their letters home from France, the English tended to call them "French letters."

"Well," said Sebastian after staring at the condoms in silence for a moment. "This tells us something interesting about the morally upright Lord Preston Farnsworth."

"It does indeed. Except that I'm afraid he obviously didn't always use them."

Sebastian looked up to meet his friend's gaze.

"It's the only other thing I noticed in finishing his postmortem," said Gibson, "and the Chief Magistrate of Bow Street has made it quite clear that I'm not to make any reference to it at tomorrow's inquest. It was an old infection, and he'd obviously received treatment. But mercury does its own lasting damage, and the disease rarely actually goes away, of course."

What was it about sex, Sebastian wondered, that caused nations to name its more embarrassing aspects after their enemies? The English called it the French pox, while the French called it the Italian disease and the Turks called it the Christian disease. He said, "Farnsworth had syphilis?"

Gibson nodded. "For a good ten years or more."

"So he carried these"—Sebastian held up the leather envelope—"to protect someone else. A mistress, perhaps?"

"Perhaps. Or perhaps he thought he was cured and was afraid of catching it again. Either way, it doesn't exactly fit the saintly image he liked to project, does it?"

"No. No, it doesn't."

"Do you think Tess knew?" Hero said later that evening when they were having a quiet glass of wine in the drawing room before dinner.

"That her husband had syphilis, you mean?" said Sebastian. He thought about Hugh saying wistfully, *I suppose if we'd had children*, and felt an aching sadness settle over him. "Probably. I think Lovejoy was planning to spend the day interviewing Farnsworth's servants; it will be interesting to hear what his valet had to say."

Hero went to stand by the window, her gaze on the rain-drenched street below. "You think he'll tell the truth?"

Sebastian considered this. "Maybe not—at least, not if he's hoping for a nice severance bonus from Lady Hester." He went to stand beside her, his gaze, like hers, on a sodden costermonger in a red kerchief, his shoulders hunched against the rain as he pushed his barrow down the street. It had been raining hard for the last several hours, and the man looked cold, tired, and miserable.

"Was it raining last Saturday evening?" he asked. "I can't recall."

"It was, yes. It started shortly before dinner."

"So around eight?"

"Something like that. Why?"

"Just wondering." Sebastian was silent as they watched the costermonger turn his cart onto Davies Street, where a man stood at the corner: a tall, well-dressed man in a light gray driving coat with a fashionable profusion of shoulder capes, highly polished French-style riding boots, and a broad-brimmed hat he wore tipped low over his eyes. A scarf hid the rest of his face from view.

"What is it?" asked Hero when Sebastian's eyes narrowed.

"There's a man across the street, near the corner of Davies. I noticed him standing there when I first came down from dressing for dinner."

"He could be waiting for someone."

"In the rain?"

"Uncomfortable, but certainly possible."

"Maybe." Sebastian pushed away from the window and turned toward the door. "But I think I'll just go ask him."

Sebastian slammed out of the house, the wind blowing the fine misty rain in his face, his right hand resting significantly in the pocket of his coat. He had made it to the base of the steps and was about to start across the wet street when the man near the corner turned and ran.

"Bloody hell," swore Sebastian under his breath and took off after him.

Chapter 16

Sebastian careened around the corner into Davies Street in time see the unknown man in the pale gray greatcoat race past the arched opening to Davies Mews and keep going. Sebastian pelted after him, their bootheels clattering on the pavement to echo down the narrow, rain-washed street. One after the other they streamed past the entrance to a stableyard, past the mouth of a dark, noisome alley. But with every passing second, Sebastian was aware that he was gradually falling behind. The man might be roughly Sebastian's age and size, but Sebastian was already gritting his teeth against the pain that shot up from the old wound in his thigh with every jarring step.

Putting on a burst of speed, the man swerved in front of an oncoming brewer's wagon to dash across the street, heading toward St. George's Market. As he leapt up onto the far pavement, he hesitated long enough to throw a quick glance back at Sebastian. And in that instant the man's hawklike profile was silhouetted against the pale Portland stone of the building behind him. Then he darted around the corner.

Cursing silently to himself, Sebastian dodged the brewer's wagon and sprinted after him, the wet pavement slippery beneath his leather soles, his thigh a howling agony. He exploded into the market square—

And found it empty, its stalls shuttered, the cold wind blowing a ragged playbill across the worn cobblestones.

The man in the caped greatcoat and polished French boots had disappeared.

Sebastian returned to Brook Street to find Hero waiting at the top of the front steps.

"What was that about?" she asked.

The rain was coming down hard again, and he swiped one crooked elbow across his wet face as he turned to look back at the now deserted street. "I have no idea."

Wednesday, 21 August

The next morning, Sebastian met with Sir Henry Lovejoy in a coffeehouse tucked away beneath the old stone arcade that stretched along the south side of Covent Garden Market. Normally at this hour the piazza would be a raucous, confusing bustle of shouting stallholders, peddlers hawking wares from battered trays slung from their necks, haggling buyers, barking dogs, braying donkeys, cracking whips, creaking cartwheels, and hordes of laughing, screaming, running children. But today the wet plaza was half-empty, both buyers and sellers abnormally subdued. The problem wasn't simply that morning's rain. The repeated, unprecedented late frosts and constantly soggy fields had hit the market gardens around London hard. That—combined with the endless months of disappearing jobs and depressed wages since Waterloo—was taking its toll. Even the coffeehouse was quieter than normal, the air thick with the smell of freshly ground coffee and wet wool, the few scattered patrons sitting with their hands wrapped around their hot drinks, their shoulders hunched and faces set in grim lines.

No one was laughing.

"We're working with the Society for the Suppression of Vice to come up with a list of those who might have held Lord Preston responsible for their prosecutions," said Lovejoy, taking a cautious sip of his hot chocolate. "Unfortunately, it looks as if it's liable to be a long list. He was an industrious man, Lord Preston. Before the Society for the Suppression of Vice was formed, he was active with the Proclamation Society that preceded it. This Half-Hanged Harry McGregor you told us about was actually prosecuted by the Proclamation Society."

"Any luck finding him?" said Sebastian, wrapping his hands around his hot coffee.

Lovejoy shook his head. "Not yet, but from all accounts he's a decidedly unpleasant fellow. If he is our killer, we might be lucky enough to end all this quickly." He paused, then added in a dry voice, "That would make the Palace—and Sir Nathaniel—happy."

"Breathing down your necks, are they?"

Lovejoy sighed. "Heavily. It's unfortunate the details of how Lord Preston was found hanging leaked to the newspapers. Sir Nathaniel was at first inclined to disbelieve that Lord Preston was deliberately posed in a way that echoed some tarot card. But now that the idea has taken hold in the popular imagination, we've started arresting every gypsy and fortune-teller we can get our hands on."

"Lovely," said Sebastian. Sir Nathaniel Conant had been Bow Street's Chief Magistrate for several years now, ever since he'd flattered the Prince Regent by taking part in Prinny's "delicate investigation" of his estranged wife, Caroline, the Princess of Wales. The plum position at Bow Street—and a knighthood—had been his reward. Sebastian raised his coffee to his lips. "Wasn't Sir Nathaniel active in the Proclamation Society?"

"He was, yes. Like Lord Preston, he believes the prevention of crime is linked to the control of immorality."

"So is he also a member of the Society for the Suppression of Vice?"

"I don't believe so, no. As much as he admires their work, he believes membership to be inappropriate for magistrates. He was at the Great Marlborough Street office, you know, before moving to Bow Street."

Sebastian took another sip of his coffee. "Did Farnsworth's servants have anything interesting to say?"

"Not really. Both his valet and the butler confirmed that his lordship went out that evening for his usual after-dinner walk. The servants all describe their master as a morally upright, devout Christian who was invariably cheerful and polite, and none of them have any idea of anything that could have led to his murder."

"You might want to talk to the valet again," said Sebastian, giving the magistrate a succinct description of what he and Gibson had discovered. "It might not have anything to do with what happened to Farnsworth, but I find it doubtful his valet was unaware of his master's active sex life. And that means he might not be being exactly truthful about other things."

"Indeed," said Lovejoy, looking troubled. "The note his lordship received before dinner is proving to be a bit of a puzzle. The butler,

Dunstan, says it was delivered shortly before six by a lad who claimed to come from Viscount Sidmouth. But we've checked with the Home Secretary, and he knows nothing of it."

"Interesting. I wouldn't put it past Sidmouth to lie, but in this instance I can't think of a reason he would. He could simply claim it was something innocuous and let it go at that."

"Yes, well . . ." Lovejoy cleared his throat and looked away. There was a strong link between Sidmouth and all of the city's public offices, but especially with Bow Street and Sir Nathaniel Conant. Not only did the Home Secretary appoint all of the offices' stipendiary magistrates, but he also controlled an officious little man by the name of John Stafford. Officially, Stafford was simply Bow Street's head clerk, but his true function was to recruit and direct the legion of informants and agents provocateurs the government used to spy on reformers, Radicals, dissidents, and basically anyone critical of the monarchy or Parliament.

Sebastian said, "What does Farnsworth's butler remember about this lad?"

"He describes him as about sixteen or seventeen, tall and fair and decently dressed, although not in livery—which Dunstan concedes in retrospect he should have found odd."

"So it obviously wasn't Jamie Gallagher," said Sebastian, setting his empty coffee mug aside.

Lovejoy looked surprised. "Did you think it might be?"

"No, not really. That would have been a bit too neat. Any luck finding the boy?"

"Jamie? No. Which is rather disturbing, given that he will need to testify at the inquest . . . although I doubt there's much he could add at this point."

"Probably not," said Sebastian, and left it at that.

"It might help if this endless rain would stop," said Lovejoy, his face bleak and strained with worry as he stared out at the sad, half-deserted marketplace.

It was still raining some fifteen minutes later when Sebastian left the coffeehouse. He paused at the edge of the arcade's drip line to button his greatcoat, his breath forming a vague white cloud of exhalation around him, his attention seemingly all for the desultory activity in the sodden marketplace before him. Some fifteen feet to his right, a tall, slender man in a light gray greatcoat and highly polished boots leaned casually against one of the arcade's row of worn stone pillars, his face turned half away as he, too, stared out at the rain.

It was a profile Sebastian recognized.

Adjusting the tilt of his high-crowned hat, Sebastian turned to walk toward his unknown shadow. He expected the man to take off, losing himself quickly in the plaza's crush of people and carts.

He didn't.

"You didn't run this time," said Sebastian, halting before him.

The man turned his head to look directly at him. "Why should I?" he said in French. It was the French of the Vendée, Sebastian noticed; of Eleanor of Aquitaine's ancient Poitou, a fervently Catholic region of France famous for having risen up against the revolutionary government in a bloody revolt that left over a quarter of a million people dead.

"You did before," said Sebastian, answering him in the same language.

The man shrugged.

Sebastian studied the Frenchman's narrow, aquiline nose, the deep-set charcoal-gray eyes, the jutting cheekbones and thin lips.

As far as he knew, he'd never seen the man before last night. "Why are you watching me?"

Slowly, provocatively, those thin lips curled into a smile. "I'm looking for Maréchal Alexandre McClellan."

Sebastian knew a jolt of jumbled emotions he was careful to keep off his face. "I've never met the man."

"Perhaps. But the connection is there."

"Who sent you? The Bourbons?"

The smile lingered as the man turned his head to gaze in silence at a donkey cart rattling past toward Bow Street.

Sebastian said, "I heard the Bourbons already had him killed."

"No. Still trying." The Frenchman brought up one hand to touch his hat in a mocking salute. *"Bonjour, monsieur,"* he said, and walked away, his open greatcoat flaring in the wind, the heels of his highly polished boots going *tap-tap* on the old cobblestones.

Sebastian was aware of a choking rush of rage that swept through him. He had an urge to reach out and grab the man by his shoulder to jerk him around and—

And what? thought Sebastian. It would be a satisfying but basically primitive gesture ultimately accomplishing nothing. He took a deep, steadying breath.

There was a better way.

Chapter 17

Charles, Lord Jarvis, was seated at the elegant French desk in his private chambers at Carlton House, writing a letter to Wellington, when he heard an exclamation of alarm from his clerk in the anteroom, followed by the sound of a chair being pushed back as the useless man scrambled to his feet.

"But you can't—" bleated the clerk. "His lordship left strict instruction he was not to be disturbed!"

Jarvis laid aside his pen and folded his hands together atop his letter as his son-in-law strode into the room, Jarvis's clerk at his heels.

"Leave us," Jarvis told the clerk. To Devlin he said, "I take it this isn't what one might term a friendly familial visit."

The Viscount came at him, bracing his hands against the far side of the desk and leaning into them. And so intense was the flare of menace in the younger man's eyes that it took all of Jarvis's self-control to remain calmly seated. Then Devlin uttered a smothered oath and pushed away to go stand at the windows overlooking Pall

Mall. "I just had an interesting conversation with the Bourbons' new assassin in London," he said, swinging around again to face Jarvis. "Is this one working for you, too?"

Jarvis drew an enameled snuffbox from his coat pocket and casually flipped it open. "I don't know what you're talking about."

"Oh, you know," said the Viscount, his unnatural, wolflike eyes narrowed down to lethal yellow slits. "I can handle the bastard following me. And if it comes to it, hopefully I can also handle him trying to kill me. But I'll be damned if I'll put up with him lurking outside my house like he was last night. Tell him to stay the hell away from my family or I'll kill him. It's as simple as that. Give my regards to Lady Jarvis."

He was halfway across the room, headed toward the door, when Jarvis said, "Do you know where Maréchal McClellan is?"

Devlin paused, his expression unreadable. "What difference is it to you?"

Jarvis raised a delicate pinch of snuff to one nostril and sniffed. "He's a dangerous man."

Devlin's head jerked in denial. "Dangerous to whom? The war is over. The French are our allies now, remember? McClellan took an oath of allegiance to the Bourbons after Napoléon's first abdication and he stayed faithful to that oath throughout the Hundred Days. Why the hell are the Bourbons trying to kill him?"

"His ideas are dangerous."

A gleam of understanding showed in those nasty eyes. "By which I take it you mean he's less than enthusiastic about the Bourbons' determination to yank France back to the days of eighteenth-century royal absolutism? Interesting."

"You didn't know?"

"No. I've never met him. But the truth is, men like McClellan should be the least of your worries. This restoration is not going to end well, and if you weren't so blinded by your own bloody prejudices and smug assumptions, you'd know it."

Jarvis felt an icy flare of rare, pure rage. He prided himself on being a man who indulged in few vanities. But his one overriding conceit was his unshakable confidence in the superiority of his intellect and the acuity of his analysis and understanding.

Devlin was at the door when Jarvis stopped him again by saying, "I hear you're looking into the murder of Lord Preston Farnsworth. I wonder, are you familiar with a man named Plimsoll? Lancelot Plimsoll."

Devlin looked back at him. "He's a natural scientist. What could he possibly have to do with Farnsworth's death?"

Jarvis reached for his pen and allowed himself the faintest hint of a smile. "I think you might be surprised."

Chapter 18

Although now a successful, widely respected natural scientist famous for his expertise on everything from surveying to the classification of fossils, Mr. Lancelot Arnold Plimsoll had begun life as the son of a humble Lyme Regis fisherman.

Because he suffered badly from seasickness, the boy spent much of his childhood clambering over the area's limestone and shale cliffs, collecting fossils he sold to tourists and collectors and learning to understand the world around him in ways few did. Given a rudimentary education by a local schoolmaster, he became a voracious reader and autodidact. But it was the chance purchase of a secondhand copy of Daniel Fenning's *The Art of Measuring* that changed his life. Talking his way into a position as a surveyor's assistant, he quickly rose to prominence in his new profession, with clients ranging from coal mines and canal builders to estate managers and "improving farmers." Yet even as he became more and more prosperous, his true passion remained fossils, minerals, and what was rapidly becoming known as the science of geology.

Sebastian had first met Plimsoll several years before, when he hired the man to manage the drainage of some newly acquired boggy fields. He admired the man's uncanny knowledge of what he called the hidden "strata" of the earth as well as his willingness to voice ideas about the earth's history that many considered blasphemous. But Sebastian couldn't begin to fathom what might possibly connect a humbly born natural history enthusiast like Plimsoll to an arrogant, morally crusading duke's son like Lord Preston.

Or what game Jarvis was playing when he sent Sebastian after the man.

If Lancelot Plimsoll had one weakness, it was his desire to be accepted by the wellborn, well-educated gentlemen of leisure who collected fossils and had recently banded together to form what they called the Geological Society. To this end, he frequented all the "right" tailors, diligently worked at improving his diction, and had recently purchased a small town house in Bloomsbury, not far from the British Museum. It was there that Sebastian found him, a puzzled frown knitting his brow as he stared down at a tray containing various examples of ammonites.

A short, energetic, solidly built man in his forties, the geologist had a large, prominent nose and rugged face weathered by years spent scrambling around Britain's mountains and valleys with a small pick and a knapsack full of specimens. He looked up sharply at his middle-aged housekeeper's timid knock, his frown disappearing at the sight of Sebastian.

"Lord Devlin, what a pleasant surprise! Margaret, some hot tea, if you will," he said to the housekeeper. Then he set aside his tray, muttered, "Oh, dear," under his breath, and rushed to remove the pile of books that spilled from one of the pair of overstuffed brown leather chairs drawn up before the crackling fire. "Please, have a seat, my lord. This is indeed an honor. Are you planning to begin a new project on your estate?"

"I have been considering purchasing some more fields badly in need of new drainage," said Sebastian, settling into the recently cleared chair and leaning forward to stretch his cold hands out to the blaze. "But the truth is, that's not why I'm here."

The geologist looked up from redepositing his armload of books. "Oh?"

"I'm wondering if you ever did any work for the Duke of Eversfield or his brother, Lord Preston."

"I haven't, no." Plimsoll came to sink slowly into the opposite chair, his nostrils flaring on a deeply indrawn breath. "I take it you're looking into Farnsworth's odd death, and you've heard he and I had a bit of a run-in?"

Sebastian settled back in his chair. "Actually, I hadn't heard that. How did you come to know him?"

"I didn't know him—at least, not in any meaningful way. But he'd somehow heard about a presentation I'd given to some colleagues of mine, and he confronted me about it."

"When was this?"

"I don't recall precisely, but it must have been several weeks ago now." He paused. "Are you by chance familiar with Thomas Raffles?"

"If you mean the lieutenant-governor of Java, I have met him, yes. Why?"

"He's quite interested in everything from biology to geology, you know, which is how we came to meet. It was from Raffles that I learned of a massive series of volcanic eruptions that occurred in April of last year on an island called Sumbawa, in the Dutch East

Indies near Java." He paused. "I say 'near,' but it's actually something like eight hundred miles away. And yet the explosions were so loud Raffles initially thought it was cannon fire."

Sebastian nodded. "I remember hearing something about it from a naval captain who was in the area at the time. Mt. Tam-something, wasn't it?"

"Yes, Mt. Tambora. The eruptions went on for days, emitting a massive, mushroom-shaped ash cloud that spread out to turn the sky as black as night and inundate a wide area with ash falls as deep in some places as over three feet. Raffles says they estimate that the mountain lost three thousand or more feet from its summit." Plimsoll cleared his throat. "It was after my discussion with Raffles that I developed a theory that it is the eruption of Mt. Tambora that is causing our current weather abnormalities. I believe the explosion threw so much material so high into the air that it has been unable to fall back to earth. As a result, over the last sixteen months, the trade winds have dispersed this massive ash cloud around the world, and now it's simply hanging there, shielding us from the warmth of the sun's rays and disrupting our normal weather patterns."

"Is that possible?"

"Well, I think it is . . . Although I fear my colleagues did not agree."

"But there have been countless other volcanic eruptions throughout history—including several quite recently. Why would the effects of this one be so different?"

"Because of its incredible force—that, combined with the enormous amount of material it sent so high into the sky."

Sebastian was silent for a moment, his gaze on the flickering dance of the fire before them. "It does sound plausible—or at any rate, as much if not more so than many of the other explanations I've heard. I take it Lord Preston did not agree?"

"No, not at all. In fact, he threatened to have me prosecuted for blasphemy."

"I've been told Lord Preston was becoming more and more convinced the end of the world is upon us."

"Indeed he was. It was after I suggested—somewhat facetiously, I'll admit—that perhaps the Good Lord had decided to end the world with ice rather than fire and brimstone that he accused me of sacrilege."

"Sacrilege?"

"Lord Preston was not fond of geology, you see. As far as he was concerned, any discussion of natural forces—or at any rate, any suggestion that those forces have been reshaping our earth for hundreds of millions of years—is blasphemy. And my theory did rely on a rather blunt discussion of the history of those forces."

"Ah. Yes, I can see that. But what I don't understand is what any of this has to do with Jarvis."

"Lord Jarvis?" Plimsoll gave a slight shake of his head. "I don't understand."

"Was this confrontation over your theory about Mt. Tambora your only interaction with Lord Preston?"

"Yes, yes."

"Where did it take place?"

"Unfortunately, we were at the British Museum. I was there to inspect some fossils recently donated to them by an Oxfordshire vicar and ran into Lord Preston by chance as he was exiting the Reading Room. Our encounter was not in any sense private, but Lord Jarvis was not there. I'm almost certain of it."

"Perhaps not, although I've no doubt he would have heard of it." Sebastian paused, his gaze on the geologist's sunbrowned, tensely held features. "What I don't understand is why it would interest him."

"That I can't explain," said Plimsoll, looking both faintly puzzled and afraid.

Sebastian could understand the man's fear, given that the simple mention of Jarvis's name was enough to alarm most people. But as he thanked the geologist for his time and rose to take his leave, he couldn't shake the impression that Plimsoll was leaving something out of the narrative of his encounter with Lord Preston.

Something important.

Chapter 19

Sebastian walked out of Plimsoll's small but respectable town house and paused for a moment on the top step, his head falling back as he stared up at the heavy gray clouds pressing down low on the city.

Was it possible? he found himself wondering. Was it possible that a massive volcanic explosion on the far side of the world could be doing . . . *this*? Could be causing this unseasonably bitter cold and rain? Ruining grain and hay harvests from Turkey to Ireland and probably beyond? Sending endless rains to flood the low-lying fields of the Netherlands and the high mountain valleys of Switzerland alike? Killing people—killing untold tens of thousands of people—who'd never heard of Mt. Tambora?

Who probably didn't even know what a volcano was?

Before taking his final leave of Lancelot Plimsoll, he had asked the geologist if he thought all that volcanic dust and ash—if it really was stuck up there high in the sky—would eventually fall back to earth, allowing the world's weather patterns to return to normal.

But the geologist had simply shaken his head and said, "Only time will tell."

The rain was still falling half an hour later when Sebastian pulled up before the sprawling Park Lane home of the Dowager Duchess of Claiborne.

She'd been born Lady Henrietta St. Cyr, the elder sister of Alistair St. Cyr, the current Earl of Hendon. She was a large woman, built much like her brother, with a stout body, broad, plain face, and the famous intensely blue St. Cyr eyes. Although she had never been beautiful, even when young, she possessed an exquisite sense of style and had long reigned as one of the grandes dames of Society. She also had a knack for hearing—and remembering—every scandal and on-dit that had rocked the ton for the last sixty or more years. She would always be one of Sebastian's favorite people and he still called her "Aunt" even though he now knew that Hendon was not in fact his father. It was a technicality that neither of them heeded.

Now, splendidly gowned in purple satin with a fine paisley shawl draped over her shoulders, she was seated at her breakfast table, a piece of toast half-forgotten on her plate as she studied the copy of the *Morning Chronicle* spread open before her. "Viscount Devlin," intoned Her Grace's butler in a colorless voice that nevertheless managed to effectively convey the weight of his disapproval.

She looked up.

"Good morning, Aunt," said Sebastian, going to kiss her cheek. "This is a surprise. It's barely eleven o'clock and you're down already?"

"That's your fault, you unnatural child," she told him, leaning back in her chair. "The night soil men woke me at dawn, and I was so convinced I was going to be the recipient of one of your ungodly early-morning visits that I couldn't get back to sleep."

"I was being considerate," he said, pouring himself a cup of tea before going to sit in one of the chairs beside her.

"Gammon. If you were truly intent on letting me sleep, you wouldn't have come before one."

He laughed and took a sip of his tea.

Her eyes lightened with a smile that faded as she folded her newspaper and set it aside. "I'll confess I never cared for Lord Preston Farnsworth, but this murder is beyond nasty."

"That it is," said Sebastian. "Why do you think someone did that—posed him hanging upside down in a posture from the tarot, I mean?"

"Good heavens, I couldn't begin to imagine."

"So tell me why you didn't care for him. Most people considered him a paragon."

"True. But then, as you know, I've never had much patience for paragons." She paused. "Of course, there's more to it than that."

She paused again, and he waited while she smoothed the crease of her newspaper and then folded it once more into a neat rectangle. "Lord Preston was well-liked partially because he was a Farnsworth but also because he came across as an amiable, good-natured man with a dry, self-deprecating wit. And even though he was known to be religious, he somehow managed to cultivate a reputation for being devout without embarrassing anyone with his pious excesses the way so many of that sort do."

That was important in Society, Sebastian knew; most members of the ton found excessive displays of religiosity embarrassingly gauche—although he'd noticed that had begun to change.

"But . . ." she began.

"But?" he prompted.

"Let's just say that while I don't in any way condone what Lady Tess did, I still find Farnsworth's reaction to it appalling."

"Which aspect of his reaction?"

"All of it, frankly, but particularly the crim. con. case. And yes, I know Henry Wellesley did essentially the same thing, and I found that beyond distasteful, as well."

The Wellesley-Paget case was one with which Sebastian was very familiar. Henry Paget, a decorated British cavalry officer who was now a marquis but until recently had been the Earl of Uxbridge, had in 1809 eloped with Lady Charlotte Wellesley, wife of Henry Wellesley—who was of course the brother of Paget's commanding officer, the Duke of Wellington. Refusing to ever let her see their children again, Wellesley divorced Charlotte by an act of Parliament on the grounds of adultery, then sued Paget for criminal conversation and was awarded the staggering sum of twenty-four thousand pounds. After several years of disgrace, Paget had been brought back to serve as Wellington's second-in-command at Waterloo—although the relationship between the two commanders remained decidedly chilly.

"And then, on top of it all," Aunt Henrietta was saying, "Farnsworth refused to divorce Tess, which in my mind was simply being petty. If he was spiteful enough to want to keep her from marrying Chandler, he could have had the prohibition inserted in the divorce decree. But by refusing to divorce her, he prevented her from ever marrying anyone. At least now—" She broke off, her troubled gaze meeting Sebastian's.

"Just so," he said, and let it go at that. "Tell me this: Did Lord Preston keep a mistress?"

"I've never heard even a hint of rumor to that effect, but I wouldn't be surprised."

"Any particular reason?"

"Partially, I suppose, because he was still a relatively young man and, since he refused to divorce Tess, he couldn't remarry, either. But also because . . ." Once again she hesitated, and he waited. She was not normally so circumspect. "There is a certain aura that some men have about them. Don't ask me to explain it any more than that. I know it sounds fanciful, but that doesn't mean it isn't real. Lord Preston always struck me as being unpleasantly . . . shall we say *aware* of any attractive young woman in his company."

"Who do you think killed him?"

"I have no idea, but I suspect whoever did it had a very good reason."

Caught in the act of sipping his tea, Sebastian choked and fell to coughing. When he could, he said, "Do you know anything else about him that might explain why someone would want to see him dead?"

She frowned. "Well, I assume you know about the breach of promise case?"

He stared at her. "No. He sued someone for breach of promise?"

"Technically, *he* didn't; he simply assisted Lady Hester in her suit." The Duchess frowned in thought. "It was years ago, probably when you were up at Oxford. Hester was about twenty-five at the time. By that point it was largely taken for granted that she would be left on the shelf, which some considered surprising given that she wasn't unattractive and old Eversfield had left her a handsome portion. But she never 'took,' for obvious reasons."

"What obvious reasons?"

The Duchess looked at him. "You have met her, haven't you?"

"Yes."

"Well, she was exactly the same then, at age twenty-five, as she is now in her forties. Not in looks, of course; she was much prettier before her disposition began showing on her face. But in every other respect. I could never understand what possessed the man to offer for her in the first place, but in the end he obviously thought better of it and cried off. A *most* ungentlemanly thing to do, but one can nevertheless sympathize."

"And Lady Hester sued him for breach of promise?" It was one of the rare legal advantages of being a woman: A jilted woman could sue for breach of promise, but a jilted man could not. Of course, any woman who broke her betrothal would severely damage her reputation, usually irreparably. But women were nevertheless afforded the privilege—legally, at least—of changing their minds.

"She not only sued him," said Henrietta, "she won ten thousand pounds. The suit asked for fifteen, so they didn't get quite as much as they wanted out of him. But his family has never been particularly plump in the pocket, so it was a massive financial blow. It's obvious he's still bitter about it."

"Who? Who was the man?"

"Didn't I say? It was Quinton-Thomas."

"*Mallory?*"

"That surprises you?"

"It does, yes. A great deal."

Chapter 20

Lord Quinton-Thomas was striding across Old Palace Yard toward Westminster, his head down and a sheaf of papers tucked up under one arm, his slightly rumpled greatcoat open and billowing behind him in the wind, when Sebastian fell into step beside him. "We need to talk."

"Yes, yes; of course," said the Baron without breaking stride, his bootheels clattering on the ancient yard's paving stones, his gaze fixed firmly on the old medieval palace before them. "But now is not a good time. I've a meeting with Brougham in less than half an hour and first I need to—"

"You didn't tell me you were once betrothed to Lord Preston's sister. Or that they sued you for ten thousand pounds. And won."

Quinton-Thomas drew up abruptly, his features going slack as he swung to face Sebastian. "That was a long time ago," he said, leaning forward and keeping his voice low.

"How long ago?"

"Sixteen years."

"Ten thousand pounds is a lot of money."

"Not for some, perhaps," muttered the Baron, casting a quick glance around the largely deserted space. "But for me, yes. I won't pretend it didn't hurt, because it did. Had to sell off every piece of land that wasn't entailed, just to pay the bloodsuckers. But then, that was the point, wasn't it? They wanted to ruin me. I was lucky; they asked for fifteen thousand. That truly would have broken me."

"Why did you cry off?"

"Why?" Quinton-Thomas huffed a low, bitter laugh. "What's the proper expression? Ah, yes: 'We didn't suit.' Isn't that it? We didn't suit. And the reason we didn't suit is because I finally realized Hester has the soul of a Spanish Inquisitor and I didn't want to spend the rest of my life in hell—which is what marriage to her would have been."

Sebastian found himself trying to envision the neat, exquisitely dressed, repressively conservative Lady Hester agreeing to marry this big, untidy, passionately radical man, and could not. "So why did you offer for her in the first place?"

"Why?" A wistful, faraway look crept into the Baron's hazel eyes. "You might not think it to look at her today, but she was beautiful when she was younger. Oh, she was serious and a bit on the joyless side, but I thought she was simply reserved. Shy." He gave a disbelieving shake of his head. "Except of course she wasn't shy. Women who are shy feel awkward around people, maybe worry that others are evaluating them poorly. But no one has a higher opinion of herself than Lady Hester. No one."

"You asked her to marry you because she was beautiful and serious?"

Quinton-Thomas puffed out his cheeks and blew out a long, slow breath. "I wasn't the same man sixteen years ago that I am today. I *liked* the fact that she was serious. I saw myself as serious. I was terrified that what had happened in France was going to happen here, and I thought the only way to stop it was not to reform things but to suppress any and every suggestion of reform. I not only agreed with Burke and Reeves; I thought the Seditious Meetings and Treason Acts didn't go far enough—that the only thing standing between civilization and chaos was 'right-thinking people,' and we were the right-thinking people."

"So what changed your mind?"

"About reform? Careful thought and maturity, I suppose. About Hester . . ." He was silent for a moment, the misty wind blowing his wild hair around his face as he turned his head to stare toward the river, now as gray as the sky above. "Honestly? I think it was a cascade of little things that just kept piling up, one after another, until I couldn't ignore the implications of it all any longer. She and Preston both genuinely believed that they were wealthy not because they were lucky but because God loved them more than he did other people. And when you convince yourself of that, it follows naturally that poor people must be poor because God hates them. And because God hates them, he's obviously punishing them—that's why they're suffering, because they deserve it. As if a tiny orphan starving to death in a workhouse could possibly be guilty of anything that would justify that. We actually had that argument one day. That's when I realized I couldn't go through with the wedding and walked out." He paused. "I suppose it should have occurred to me that they'd sue me, but somehow it didn't. I still hadn't realized just what nasty, insufferably self-righteous hypocrites they were. It was a revelation to me."

"When did you last see Lord Preston?"

"I don't remember exactly. I've generally tried to avoid the two of them as much as possible."

"Except when arguing against Lord Preston's proposals in the House of Lords?"

"Well, yeah; except for then."

"Do you know if Lord Preston had anything to do with Lancelot Plimsoll?"

Quinton-Thomas looked vaguely surprised by the abrupt change in topic. "You mean that canal builder who's always going on and on about fossils and stratigraphy?"

"Yes."

Quinton-Thomas frowned. "I vaguely recall hearing about some sort of dustup between them, but I couldn't begin to tell you what it was about. Lord Preston argued with a lot of people. He was an arrogant, opinionated—" He broke off as the bells in the Abbey began to toll, sounding the hour.

"I must go," he said quickly, shifting his hold on his papers as they started to slip.

"One more question. Where were you last Saturday evening around seven or eight?"

Quinton-Thomas stared at him, his mouth going slack. "I was at my club, damn you. And then I went home. You can't think I killed the bastard! Because he milked me out of ten thousand pounds sixteen years ago?"

"No," lied Sebastian. "But you must realize that the question will come up."

The Baron's tongue darted out to lick his suddenly dry lips as his gaze drifted sideways. And Sebastian thought, *Oh, hell; he wasn't at his club that night.*

Or at least, not the entire time.

Chapter 21

The sailor's name was Eli Dawson, and Hero interviewed him that afternoon near the Grand Surrey Docks in Rotherhithe.

He was a tall man with sun-bronzed, weathered features and thick dark hair he still wore in a seafaring man's pigtails. But his tattered blue jacket and long trousers hung on his frame in a way that suggested he'd recently lost considerable weight, and he was missing most of his left arm.

"They impressed me off a merchant ship," he told Hero, his face expressionless as he stared out over the forest of masts beside them. "Back in 1805, it was. I'll never be able t' understand how ole John Bull can pride himself on being a 'free man' when any one of us can be kidnapped and forced to serve in the bloody Navy whether we want to or not. If I'd wanted to join the bloody Navy, I'd 'ave joined the bloody Navy—beggin' yer pardon, ma'am, fer the language. But nobody in his right mind joins the bloody Navy. They feed ye rotten food, if ye look at an officer sideways they peel the hide off yer back with a cat-o'-nine-tails, and even if ye want to, ye can't quit. If ye ask me, a naval ship's a floating prison, that's what it is. Prison, with the chance of drowning."

"Do you receive a pension?"

He huffed a laugh. "Me? No, ma'am. Ye'd be hard-pressed t' find a sailor who does. They say we don't need one—that, unlike soldiers, we have what they like t' call 'marketable skills.' Me, I say, Where's this danged market? Half the Navy's ships are in ordinary—if not more—and a goodly chunk of the ones that are left are set to be broken up. Built in too much of a hurry, ye know, with green wood, so they're falling apart. The East India Company's sending a bunch of their ships to the breakers, too, on account of what Parliament's done. And trade's down just about everywhere, what with all the pirates drivin' insurance rates up so high."

Hero looked up from scribbling her notes. "Have the pirates truly become so bad?"

"Oh, aye. A bunch of 'em used to be privateers, so they're just doin' what they was doin' before, only it ain't legal no more so they're sailin' under a black flag and goin' after any ship they can get. But there's discharged sailors with 'em, too. They can't find work on ships or in port, so they take their 'marketable skills' and use 'em the only way they can."

"I've heard some British sailors are joining various South American navies."

"Aye, I know more 'n a few who've done that. There's all sorts of recruiters around here, signing up lads and hiring ships to transport 'em down there. That wouldn't be for me, though—even if I still had both me arms. I've seen all the fighting and godforsaken parts of the world I care to, thank ye very much."

"Why weren't you awarded a pension?" Hero asked quietly. Men who'd been left badly maimed were typically given something, even if it was only a pittance.

"I was listed as a runner in the muster books of one of me ships. I tried t' tell the board I only left t' go t' me da's funeral and that I'd come back right away. But I'd left without permission—that captain was a real prick, if ye'll pardon me language, ma'am. Anyway, it was enough to queer things for me with the board. One of me messmates got turned down the same day, and you know why? Because he's American! They impressed him off an American ship, and all he wanted was enough money to get back to Boston. But they wouldn't give him even that."

"Do you find you miss the service in any way?"

"Miss it? Nah. I miss the sea and me messmates. But the Navy?" He turned his head and spat. "Never. And I sure as hell don't miss the war. I remember when we was gettin' ready t' come back from America, after they signed that peace treaty, the officers was all glum because they reckoned that with the wars over they was all goin' home to be put on half pay and would probably never get another ship. Then we found out Boney'd come back, and ye should've heard those officers. They was all whoopin' and cheerin' like they'd just won the lottery or somethin'. Officers *like* war, ye see. For them it means full pay, promotions, prizes, and honors. But for men like me, all it means is another chance to die." He lifted the stump of his left arm. "Or maybe lose an arm or a leg or somethin' else a man really don't want t' lose. We just wanted to go home."

"Where is home?" asked Hero.

"Penzance."

"Have you thought about going back there?"

He was silent for a moment, his eyes narrowing as he watched a wherryman ship his oars. "I reckon I've thought about it; I won't deny that. But . . . what would I do there?"

What are you going to do here? thought Hero. But somehow she couldn't quite bring herself to ask.

Chapter 22

The inquest into the death of Lord Preston Farnsworth was scheduled to begin at four o'clock that afternoon at the Golden Dog Inn on Piccadilly, chosen as the site of the proceedings simply because it was the largest venue near the murder site.

"One would think," said Sir Henry Lovejoy, a handkerchief held discreetly to his nostrils as he stared out over the taproom's raucous, shoving, malodorous crowd of curious onlookers, "that a city the size of London would erect a building specifically dedicated to inquests. The very idea of holding an official inquiry of this sort in a bar—complete with the dead son of a duke displayed naked for all to gawk at—is surely . . ." He hesitated as if searching for the right word and finally settled on "unseemly."

"The lack of beer might also help reduce the size of the audience," said Sebastian, trying not to breathe too deeply. The room stank of wet wool, unwashed bodies, cooked cabbage, spilled beer, and the inescapable sour-milk odor of the four-day-old corpse.

"One could hope," muttered the magistrate, his words muffled by his handkerchief.

Under English law, any sudden, violent, or unnatural death required an inquest. Legal rather than medical in nature, inquests were presided over by the local coroner, who impaneled a jury of between twelve and twenty-four "good, honest men" to inquire on behalf of the King into "how and by what means" a victim had come to his death. To this end the jurors would be required to view the body of the deceased and hear the testimony of witnesses; they could also ask questions themselves, if so inclined. And because the viewing of the victim's corpse was considered such an important part of the proceedings, Lord Preston himself was present, laid out naked on a table in the center of the room with a cloth draped strategically over his bare buttocks. Due to the fact that the fatal blow had been struck to the back of his head, he had been positioned—unusually—face down, so that the jurors could study the extent of the gory damage themselves. But anyone who wanted could wander in off the street and have a look, too.

As the person who had originally summoned Bow Street to the murder scene, Sebastian would be one of the first witnesses called. Sir Henry was here to testify as to the location of the various bloodstains found at the site as well as their recovery of the presumed murder weapon, now on display beside the corpse. He would also outline for the jury the steps the authorities had taken thus far in their attempts to identify the killer. The inquest would then expect to hear from the surgeon who had performed the official postmortem, although Gibson had yet to arrive and Sebastian was beginning to wonder what was keeping him.

Nor was Gibson the only important witness missing.

"I understand the coroner is decidedly annoyed by our inability to produce the boy who first found the body," said Lovejoy, now using his handkerchief to clean his wire-framed spectacles. The testimony of the person who first discovered a murder victim should have been a vital part of such proceedings.

"Still no trace of Jamie?" said Sebastian as a familiar lean figure in high black boots and a dark blue coat with a decidedly military cut began to push his way in through the crowd milling around the door from the street.

Lovejoy shook his head. "We can't find anyone who's even heard of the lad. I'm beginning to suspect he gave you a false name."

"Perhaps." *Or perhaps his friends dislike talking to constables,* thought Sebastian.

"Who is that?" said Lovejoy, refitting his spectacles as the man with the military bearing paused beside the rough table displaying the corpse, his arms crossed at his chest, a muscle jumping along his clenched jaw as he stared down at the dead man before him.

"That's Major Hugh Chandler."

"Ah, yes; the cavalry officer who was forced to pay twenty thousand pounds for the privilege of running off with Lord Preston's wife. Sir Nathaniel is becoming more and more convinced he's our man. He personally interviewed the Major and discovered he has no alibi for that evening." Lovejoy was silent for a moment, watching the major intently. Then something about his companion's silence must have struck him because he looked over at Sebastian. "You don't agree?"

"No," said Sebastian, his throat painfully tight as they watched Hugh turn on his heel and leave. "But then, I served with Chandler in the Peninsula and consider him a friend."

"Ah. That I did not know."

An eddy of movement near a door at the rear of the taproom

heralded the entrance of Lady Hester Farnsworth. Her back was rigid, her shoulders tense, her chin held high as the motley crowd parted respectfully before her. Sebastian had no doubt this was the first time the Duke of Eversfield's sister had ever been called upon to set foot in such an establishment, and from the looks of things, she would vehemently agree with Lovejoy that a bar was not the proper venue for an inquiry of this sort.

"I fear the Palace is not going to be happy when the jury returns a verdict of willful murder against a person or persons unknown," said Lovejoy.

"No," agreed Sebastian as Lady Hester took her place in a chair that had been reserved for her. *And I know someone else who is not going to be happy.*

She was dressed for the occasion in a severe high-waisted gown of black bombast topped by a plain black spencer; the veil of her modest black hat was long, heavy, and full, effectively obscuring her features from the scrutiny of the vulgar. Her older brother, the Duke of Eversfield, had yet to put in an appearance, so the chair beside her was empty and she was thus alone except for an elderly man hovering at her elbow whom Sebastian suspected was her solicitor.

"Unfortunately," Lovejoy was saying, "they found another Frenchman dead this morning."

Sebastian turned his head to look at him. "Another one?" He vaguely remembered hearing something about an aged Parisian who'd been fished out of the Thames after supposedly slipping and falling into the river in a bad storm a week or so ago.

Lovejoy nodded. "This one's a man by the name of Jean-Louis Ouvrard. He was discovered early this morning, although it took some time to identify him. Fortunately, it wasn't a spectacular murder—a quiet stabbing in the back in an alley off Fleet Street, so it can conceivably be construed as the work of footpads. But there is concern in certain quarters that the Bourbons may have sent a new assassin to do away with their enemies here—or at least those they consider their enemies."

"Oh, they have," said Sebastian. "I met him this morning in Covent Garden. He seems to think I can lead him to someone the Bourbons are anxious to kill. But in that he is wrong."

"Good heavens. Do you know the Frenchman's name?"

"Not yet." *Although I've no doubt Jarvis could supply it.*

Lovejoy was silent as they watched a large, untidy gentleman in a badly tied cravat and rumpled olive green coat push his way through the crowd to stand beside Lord Preston's bloated, discolored body. The wet day combined with the heat of the crowded taproom was turning the man's curly, overlong hair into a fuzzy halo.

"He looks familiar," said Lovejoy.

"That's Lord Quinton-Thomas."

"Ah, yes. I gather he has made it his mission to oppose virtually every suggestion Lord Preston put forward for dealing with crime in the city."

"Every single one," said Sebastian. "Partially because he intensely dislikes the Society for the Suppression of Vice and everything they do, but I suspect it also has something to do with the fact that the Farnsworths successfully sued him for breach of promise after he broke off his betrothal to Lady Hester."

"Oh? For how much?"

"Ten thousand pounds."

Lovejoy frowned thoughtfully as they watched a nasty smile curl Quinton-Thomas's lips. "How many people have the Farnsworths sued?"

"I don't know, but it might be worth looking into." Sebastian paused as his lordship, still smiling, turned on his heel and left. A tall, thin man with the face of an ascetic took his place. "Who's he?"

"That's Mr. Crispin Carmichael, the rector of St. George's, Hanover Square. We're told he and Farnsworth were good friends, and he's offered to assign one of his clerks to assist Bow Street in compiling a list of the various criminal cases Lord Preston helped prosecute."

Sebastian studied the vicar's thin, handsome face, the long aristocratic nose and sensitive mouth, the deeply set pale blue eyes framed by straight, light blond hair. Instead of a cassock he wore fashionable pantaloons and a well-tailored coat; a high-crowned hat dangled from one hand. "Is the Reverend also a member of the Society for the Suppression of Vice?"

"He is, yes."

As if aware of their scrutiny, Mr. Carmichael looked up, his gaze meeting Sebastian's from across the noisy, crowded room. Then another swirl of movement at the back of the taproom jerked the churchman's attention away.

"Ah, here comes the coroner now," said Lovejoy, just as Paul Gibson, his cheeks shadowed by a day's growth of beard, his waistcoat and cravat splattered with fresh blood from some patient, pushed his way through the crowd clustered around the street entrance. "The coroner does not look pleased, does he?"

Frowning fiercely, a wizened old man in tattered robes stood in the taproom's rear doorway, one hand coming up to adjust his crooked wig as a constable with a booming voice shouted, "Oyez, oyez, oyez: Ye good men of this parish are summoned to appear this day in the presence of Lord Preston Farnsworth, lying dead here before you . . ."

Sliding into the seat Sebastian had saved for him, Gibson caught his friend's eye and winked.

The proceedings dragged on until the shadows were lengthening in the street outside and the crowd of spectators had thinned considerably. But once the last witness was finally heard, the jury didn't even need to leave the room to decide to return a verdict of homicide by party or parties unknown. The coroner signed a warrant allowing the body to be lawfully buried and reminded the various witnesses that they were required to stay and sign their depositions before they could leave. The inquest was then adjourned.

As the coroner pushed to his feet, Sebastian looked across the room to where Lady Hester still sat in rigid silence in her straight-backed wooden chair, her black-gloved hands clenched together in her lap. At some point she had pushed back her veil, allowing Sebastian to see her tense, flushed face.

And she was glaring at him from across the room as if the inconclusive nature of the proceedings were entirely his fault.

Chapter 23

Dusk was falling by the time Sebastian made it back to Brook Street. At some point in the late afternoon the rain had finally eased off, but the air was still cool and full of a mist that haloed the rows of streetlamps and clung eerily to the chimneys and rooftops of the city. As he paid off the hackney, he was aware of a roughly dressed man with a misshapen hat pulled low over his eyes watching from the shadows of a nearby house's area steps.

The hackney was still pulling away when Sebastian tightened his fist around the handle of the sword stick he carried and turned to walk straight toward the lurking man. "Who the hell are you?"

To his surprise, the man stood his ground. He was small and wiry, with lively blue eyes, lank, filthy brown hair heavily threaded with gray, and a week's growth of dark beard shadowing his cheeks. When he spoke, his voice was a harsh, torn whisper. "The name's McGregor. Henry Otis McGregor. The Third."

Whatever Sebastian had been expecting, it wasn't that. "You're Half-Hanged Harry?"

The man sniffed. "That's what they call me." He was so short the top of his head barely reached Sebastian's shoulder. In age he could have been anywhere between forty-five and seventy, his nose crooked, his face dark and weathered by his years of toiling beneath the hot sun of New South Wales. Botany Bay was hard on a man; few convicts survived their fourteen—or even seven—years of transportation. Fewer still ever found a way to return.

"Why are you here?" said Sebastian.

"Why? *Why?*" The man's chin jutted out pugnaciously. "Because I don't like what I'm hearing, that's why."

"Oh? And exactly what are you hearing?"

"That they're tryin' t' pin that bloody nob's murder on me, that's what I'm hearin'. As if the nasty bugger weren't a big enough pain in me arse when he was alive, now he's dead and he's *still* messin' wit me."

"You're saying you didn't kill him?"

"Of course I didn't kill him! Think I'd be standin' here if I'd killed him? I didn't have nothin' t' do wit whatever happened t' the bleedin' mutton-shunter—although if ye ask me, the fine people of this here city ought t' get together and hand whoever did do it a reward, rather than trying to string up an old coffin dodger like me. Because if ever there was a rum character, it was that blotter."

Sebastian studied the man's angry, animated features. "If you didn't kill him, then why were you following him?"

McGregor flashed a wide, largely toothless grin. "Jist wanted t' rile him up a bit—that and maybe scare him some while I was at it. Make him look over his shoulder and wonder what was gonna happen t' him. That's all."

"That's all?"

"Aye. How else is a man like me gonna get back at somebody like him?"

By killing him, thought Sebastian, although all he said was, "So where were you last Saturday evening?"

Half-Hanged Harry's gaze slid sideways. "I was around."

"'Around'?"

"Aye. Around."

"That sounds less than conclusive."

McGregor's eyes narrowed as if he didn't quite understand but still suspected he was not being complimented.

"You're brave," said Sebastian, "waylaying me outside my own house."

"I ain't waylayin' nobody. Ain't no law agin talking t' a man, now, is there?"

"What made you so certain I wouldn't call the watch on you?"

McGregor tapped the side of his forehead and grinned. "Watch ain't come on yet. Ye think I don't know such things?"

It was one of the criticisms frequently leveled by those trying to establish a centralized London police force to replace the traditional parish-based system of night watchmen—that the men were not only too old and too few and far between, but that they slowly walked set rounds, shouting the time and weather, so that any enterprising lawbreaker could easily avoid them.

Sebastian said, "I'm not entirely clear on what you think I can do for you."

"Y'er in thick wit Bow Street, ain't ye? Ye can tell 'em I didn't have nothin' t' do wit what happened t' that bloody duke's son. Ye hear me? Nothin'!"

"You could always try telling them yourself."

McGregor's eyes widened until the whites showed clearly around their dark blue centers. "Think I'm addlepated, do ye?" He began backing away. "Well, I ain't."

Sebastian suspected that no man who'd suffered through what

this one had experienced in the last fourteen or fifteen years could still be entirely sane, but he kept that opinion to himself. "So who do you think killed Farnsworth?"

Half-Hanged Harry stopped backing. "How would I know?"

"Because you were following him."

His expression slid from fearful to sly and knowing. "Did I say that?" His eyes danced with silent amusement. "I don't remember sayin' that."

"You do realize that the easiest way to save your neck is to tell Bow Street what you know?"

The amusement fled as Harry's hand crept up to touch his throat. "I don't like talkin' about me neck."

"You might even be eligible for a reward if your information proves useful."

"I ain't no squeaker. Ask anybody, they'll tell ye: Harry McGregor was never a squeaker. It's enough t' make a body wish he'd stayed in Sydney Town, it is—that and this endless infernal rain. I swear, I'm half tempted to go back, I am."

"Why did you come back to England?"

"I don't know." The animation had drained from the man's face, leaving him looking bleak, sad, and lost. "Seems like I ask myself that all the time, and I jist don't know the answer anymore."

Chapter 24

That night, long after the house had grown quiet around him, Sebastian stood in the doorway of the darkened drawing room, a glass of brandy in one hand, his gaze on the eighteenth-century portrait of a young woman that hung above the hearth.

A thick band of clouds had obscured the waning moon, so that the only light came from the banked, dying fire. Taking a sip of his drink, Sebastian went to stand with one hand braced against the mantel; he did not light the candles. But then, he didn't need them.

He'd been perhaps eight or nine when he realized that most people's perception of the world differed subtly from his. That most people couldn't see well enough to move at ease through a darkened landscape, couldn't see clearly over great distances, couldn't hear whispered conversations from another room. He remembered the time his mother found him absorbed in a book in the summerhouse long after sunset. "Oh, Sebastian," she'd said with a laugh. "You can't possibly see well enough to read anymore." He'd looked up in surprise and said, "Of course I can."

He still remembered the strange, faraway expression that leapt into her eyes, the catch in her voice when she said, "Ah. Then it's a gift." It wasn't until much, much later that he'd realized she *knew*. She knew his strangely acute eyesight and hearing had come to him from his father—from his *real* father, who wasn't the Earl of Hendon at all.

It was something Sebastian wouldn't discover himself for another twenty years. Instead he'd grown up wondering—wondering so many things. Why his eyes were yellow instead of the famously intense St. Cyr blue. Why his relationship with the man he called Father was so strained and troubled. Why he was tall and lean rather than large and heavy boned like his father and brothers. Why the acute eyesight and quick reflexes that helped Hendon's third son excel at things like shooting and fencing seemed to trouble the Earl as much as they made him proud.

It wasn't until both of Sebastian's older brothers were dead and he had been Hendon's heir for many years that Sebastian finally discovered the truth: that the beautiful, wild, wayward Countess of Hendon had played her lord false, presenting him with a bastard who had no legitimate claim to the titles and estates that the deaths of his two elder brothers meant he would someday inherit.

Draining his glass, Sebastian let his head fall back, his gaze once more on the portrait hanging above him. She'd been so young when Gainsborough painted her, her face flushed with laughter, her unpowdered golden hair cascading loose around her shoulders. And he felt choked by such a swirl of fierce, conflicting emotions—love and fury, longing and resentment, all tangled up with a piercing, breath-catching grief so intense that he shuddered.

For years he had thought her dead, only to learn she'd actually run off with one of her lovers, leaving the eleven-year-old child Sebastian had been then behind. As a father now himself, he couldn't begin to understand how she could have done such a thing. Hendon had told him once that she'd thought it for the best, for all of them. An easy excuse? Or a painful reality?

He set his glass aside, his gaze still on his mother's hauntingly beautiful face. She had died over a year ago, in Paris, on a cold, dark night on an island in the middle of the Seine. It had been a painful, violent death, and he still ached when he thought of what her last moments must have been like. She had died without telling him the name of his father, and because some things didn't quite line up or make sense, Sebastian still wasn't entirely certain of the man's identity. But Sebastian's resemblance to the Napoleonic general Alexandre McClellan was impossible to deny.

Descended from a family of Scottish Jacobites who'd fled to France in the bloody aftermath of the Forty-Five, Maréchal McClellan was a man famous for his brilliance on the battlefield. A man known for his unnaturally acute hearing and his ability to see great distances and in the dark. A man with strange yellow eyes.

A man the Bourbons were trying to kill.

"Where is he now?" Sebastian said aloud to the silent woman who stared at him from out of the past. Was the Bourbons' assassin right? Had McClellan fled France for England?

It was a thought that brought with it a rush of exhilarating hope and anticipation mingled with something else. Something it took Sebastian a moment to realize was fear.

Thursday, 22 August

"You're doing it again, aren't you?" said Alistair St. Cyr, the Fifth Earl of Hendon, as he and Sebastian trotted their horses along the Row in Hyde Park. It was just past seven in the morning and the two men had met for an early-morning ride, as they often did when both were in London. Sebastian's relationship with the gruff, demanding man who'd raised him as a son had never been easy and it never would be. But they'd gradually found a way to move past the painful revelations of the last few years to a new understanding.

"Doing what again?" asked Sebastian, glancing over at him.

Hendon grunted in disgust. "You've involved yourself in this damned murder inquiry." His heir's commitment to investigating murders had long been a source of aggravation for Hendon.

Sebastian kept his voice light. "I didn't exactly involve myself in this one; the boy who found the body came to me."

"God help us," muttered the Earl.

In his early seventies now, Hendon was a large, barrel-chested man with a plain, slablike face, heavy brows, and the characteristically intense blue eyes of the St. Cyrs. Once his hair had been almost as dark as Sebastian's, but it had long ago turned completely white and was now beginning to thin. In addition to the careful management of his estates, the Earl had dedicated his life to statesmanship, serving under a succession of prime ministers in various capacities. For some years now he had been Chancellor of the Exchequer and was known as one of the few people in Britain with the courage to stand up to the King's powerful cousin Lord Jarvis.

"I was under the impression you've been focusing on improving your estate," said Hendon. There'd been a time when Sebastian's possession of a small estate in Hampshire—a legacy from a maiden great-aunt—had been a source of endless irritation to Hendon. But at some point he'd become reconciled to his heir's economic independence. "I hear you've been expanding it."

"We have, yes."

"And experimenting with some of these damned newfangled farming techniques."

Sebastian smiled. He and Hero had taken to spending more and more of their time in Hampshire, expanding their holdings, coordinating the draining of boggy fields, mixing soils, experimenting with new breeds of cattle, sheep, and pigs, and in general exploring various innovations—most of which Hendon had long disapproved. "Yes." He looked over at the Earl. "What would you have me do instead?"

"Go into government."

At that Sebastian laughed out loud. "So I can agitate for Catholic emancipation and universal suffrage? I don't think you'd like that."

"God help us," Hendon muttered again.

"Never mind all that," said Sebastian, his gaze on the wisps of mist drifting through the treetops. The day had dawned cool and cloudy but blessedly dry—at least, so far. "Tell me what you're hearing from the Continent. Is the French harvest as bad as ours?"

"If anything, it's worse. They've had the same damnable late freezes and even more rains. And the problem is, the weather's been crazy all over—Spain, Italy, the United States and Canada, even Russia and Turkey. With harvests bad everywhere, no one can import grain." Hendon sighed. "Bringing a twenty-five-year war to an end would have been difficult enough without a bloody famine to go along with it. The only way King Louis has been able to keep the peace in Paris is by stripping the grain from the provinces and shipping it to the capital. But while that might stop the people of Paris from revolting, it's causing widespread discontent in the parts of the country that have traditionally stayed loyal to the monarchy."

Sebastian looked over at him. "Any danger of France disintegrating into civil war?"

"Honestly? It's a very real possibility. The only thing that will probably stop it is the fact that so many of their young men are already dead. That and our massive army of occupation—although that causes its own problems, since the French have to feed and billet them. Things aren't as ugly as they were at first, when there were royalist bands roaming the countryside, looting and burning and killing at will. But Louis has basically given his brother Artois and his damned heir, Angoulême, free rein do their worst, and they've realized they can do whatever they want because they have our army of occupation backing them up. So they're doing it."

Hendon was silent for a moment, his jaw working back and forth in that way he had when he was thoughtful or quietly agitated. "The fools think they're making their hold on the throne more secure. But they're not. They're not."

His words both surprised and troubled Sebastian, for Hendon's fears of revolution and republicanism had long made him an uncompromising champion of the Bourbons. "I thought they were finally starting to move away from the widespread arbitrary arrests and executions we've been hearing about."

"They are, but only because they've now shifted to what is basically a legal terror. They've set up these new provost courts they're using to try anyone deemed an enemy of the state. No jury, no appeal; just summary judgments. They've executed thousands and deported God knows how many more to their wretched penal colonies in the tropics."

"In other words," said Sebastian, "they've brought back the revolutionary tribunals."

"Basically, although they don't like the comparison. It's being called the White Terror to distinguish it from the Red Terror of revolutionary days. Hopefully, it won't end up being as bloody—although it won't be for lack of trying."

Sebastian kept his gaze on the track ahead and chose his words carefully. "I'm told they're killing some prominent officers who fought under Napoléon—even when their names aren't on the proscribed list. Is that true?"

Hendon let out a low growl. "It is. Mouton-Duvernet is the latest; I heard just yesterday that they've shot him. And there've been at least two attempts to quietly assassinate McClellan."

Sebastian had to work to keep his voice level. Calm. "He's dead?"

"No one knows exactly what's happened to him, but he's disappeared. Rumor has it he may have gone to America."

"Any chance he could have come here, to Britain?"

Hendon looked over at him, his brows drawn together in a frown. "Not if he's smart."

Later that morning, Sebastian and Hero were sitting down to breakfast when someone rang a peal at the front door.

"Expecting anyone?" said Hero, looking up from pouring the tea.

"No."

They heard the booming voice of one of Lovejoy's constables in the entry hall; then the man himself appeared at the doorway to the breakfast parlor, hat in hand.

"Beggin' your pardon for intruding on you like this, ma'am," he said to Hero with a bow. "But Sir Henry thought his lordship would like to know they've just found Half-Hanged Harry McGregor dead. In Swallow Street, my lord."

Sebastian stared at him. "Not in the same chapel?"

The constable nodded, his nostrils flaring as he sucked in a quick breath. "Same exact place, my lord."

Chapter 25

As if pushed by an unseen hand, the dead man's ragged, limp body swayed gently back and forth in the chapel's dank air. Sir Henry Lovejoy stood beside the dangling corpse, his head tilted back as he followed the rope's taut line up to the dark beam above. The killer had hanged Harry McGregor in almost exactly the same spot as Lord Preston, near the chapel's broken rear wall. Except this time he'd fastened the rope around his victim's neck rather than the dead man's foot.

"Unbelievable, isn't it?" said the magistrate as Sebastian walked up to him.

"Yes." Sebastian breathed in the odor of damp old stone tinged with the coppery smell of fresh blood. "Who found him?"

"An ex-soldier. Says he crawled in here just after midnight looking for a place to sleep and didn't notice the body until he awoke this morning at first light."

"Well, that gives us a pretty narrow time of death, then," said

Sebastian. "I saw McGregor myself just before nine last night. He was waiting for me when I arrived home from the inquest."

Lovejoy stared at him. "Whatever for?"

"He'd heard Bow Street was considering him a suspect in Lord Preston's murder and he was afraid you might hang him again."

"How bizarre. He must have left Brook Street and then for some reason come here. The question is . . . *Why?*"

Sebastian shook his head, his gaze on the former convict's sun-darkened features, now slack-jawed and oddly calm. This was not the bloated, contorted face of a man who'd strangled to death at the end of a rope. Then the wind caught the body again, spinning it around in a way that flapped open the dead man's ragged coat, and Sebastian saw the bloody, torn mess of his chest. "He was shot?"

"So it appears," said Lovejoy. "I suppose it's possible the two deaths—his and Lord Preston's—aren't related in any way beyond their location. Men like McGregor do tend to keep dangerous company."

Sebastian looked over at him. "Except that if the two murders aren't related, then why hang him here?"

"As some sort of a sick joke, perhaps?"

Sebastian found himself remembering the stricken look on the former convict's face and the way his hand crept up to touch his throat simply at the mention of the word "neck." "Hanging the man was a sick joke."

Lovejoy let out a long, pained breath. "Indeed. Hopefully, he was already dead by then."

"Hopefully."

Lovejoy turned to let his gaze drift around the abandoned chapel. "What I'm having difficulty comprehending is why someone who killed a duke's son would also want to kill a simple thief like McGregor."

"Given that Harry was following Farnsworth, the killer probably thought McGregor could identify him." Sebastian fell silent, his gaze on the worn paving stones beneath the dead man's dangling feet. He could see a few splatters and smears of blood amidst the debris, doubtless the result of the body resting there briefly before it was strung up. But there wasn't enough blood to suggest that McGregor had been killed at this spot. "Any idea exactly where he was shot?"

Lovejoy nodded. "There's a fresh spill of blood up near the altar."

"Again?"

"Again."

Sebastian was examining the paving stones at the front of the chapel when the sound of raised voices drew their attention to the courtyard, where Lovejoy had stationed one of his constables to keep back any curious onlookers while his partner went off to the deadhouse to fetch a shell and some men to carry the corpse to Tower Hill.

"Oi, hold on!" Constable Jones was shouting. "You can't go in there!"

"But I'm his sister!" cried a woman. "Ye gotta let me see him. Don't ye understand? I gotta know if it's really Harry they're sayin' is dead. *Please.*"

Moving to the open doorway, Sebastian could see her now: a short, stout woman with a large shelflike bosom and the heavily muscled arms of someone who worked hard for her living. She looked to be somewhere in her late forties or fifties, her hair pewter gray, the plain features that were so similar to Harry's contorted with fear and grief. She wore a ragged but clean gown of brown fustian and was frantically twisting her red, work-worn hands in the cloth of the apron she had pinned to her dress.

"Please," she said again.

"Calm yourself, my good woman," said Lovejoy as he and Sebastian walked toward her. "Who are you?"

The woman swung to face them. "I'm Sally—Sally McGregor." She raised one shaky finger to point toward the ruined chapel behind them. "They're sayin' me baby brother, Harry, is hangin' in there. I just want t' see if it's really him." Her voice broke, her features crumpling. "Please tell me it ain't him."

Lovejoy cleared his throat awkwardly. "Miss—er, Mrs. McGregor, you must understand that you cannot be allowed to enter the chapel at this time. But I can assure you the dead man is indeed Harry McGregor, and I'm—"

"No!" Her unearthly wail cut him off as she swung away to double over in grief, her arms wrapping around her waist as if to hold herself together. "*Oh, no. Oh, no.* Not me Harry. Oh, *Harry*."

"Sir Henry," whispered Constable Jones under his breath as Constable Sutton, now escorting two men from the deadhouse, started to turn in through the arch and then drew up abruptly at the scene before them. "You want I should show—"

"No, I'll deal with the men from the deadhouse," said Lovejoy hastily. "You stay here, Constable Jones, and keep an eye on the woman." To the men he said, "This way."

As Lovejoy disappeared into the chapel with the men at his heels, Constable Jones planted himself in the doorway, his arms crossed at his chest and his expression grim, as if to convey his determination to block Sally McGregor should she try to force her way into the chapel again.

But all belligerence seemed to have leached out of the woman. "Here," said Sebastian, walking over to where she now stood slumped against an old mounting block, her entire body heaving with her sobs.

"Thank you," she whispered, groping almost blindly for the handkerchief he was holding out.

He waited patiently while she cried for some minutes, the handkerchief simply clutched in one clenched fist. Then she sucked in a deep, shaky breath, shuddered, and brought up the handkerchief to dab at her wet face. "Poor Harry," she said, her eyes pinched with anguish as she raised her head to look at Sebastian. "They're sayin' somebody hanged him. Please tell me it ain't true. He was so, so afraid of being hanged again."

"His body is hanging," Sebastian said as gently as he could. "But whoever did it shot him first, so it's likely he was dead by then. I don't think he knew what was done to him."

She began to cry again, but silently now, the tears running freely down her cheeks. "Oh, my poor Harry. Who'd want t' do somethin' like that to 'im? Who?"

"You don't have any idea?"

"*No.*" Her voice cracked.

"Had he quarreled with anyone recently?"

She shook her head. "Harry wasn't what you'd call real quarrelsome—at least, not anymore. I ain't denyin' he was a scrapper when he was a lad, but Botany Bay . . ." She swallowed hard. "It changed him."

"When did he arrive back in London?"

"Last month—or maybe it was the month before. He did fourteen years as a convict in Botany Bay, and then when he's finally able to earn enough money to buy his passage home again, what does somebody do but up and hang him for good this time! How can that be?" Her lips pressed into a tight line. "It ain't right."

"What has he been doing since he came back?"

Her gaze slid away from Sebastian in a way that reminded him of her brother. "Oh, this and that," she said vaguely. "You know."

Sebastian suspected he knew only too well. "Do you know if Harry had anything to do with Lord Preston recently?"

She nodded. "Harry was watchin' him. Swore he was gonna get his own back at the bugger; it was pret' near all he talked about. I think maybe it was a big part of why he came back—that and because gettin' home again was all wrapped up in his head with survivin' the hell of being transported. I told him not to be daft, that if he went after Farnsworth he was gonna get himself hanged again, and there was no way he was gonna get lucky twice. But he just got mad and told me t' shut up. He didn't like hearing folk talk about hanging. Didn't like the way people was always callin' him Half-Hanged Harry."

"Do you think he killed Farnsworth?"

She stared at him. "Harry? Nah. I ain't saying he didn't want to, mind you. But Sarah and me—she's my granddaughter, ye see—we was with him when we heard about his lordship bein' found hanging upside down, and Harry, he just laughed and laughed. Said he wished he'd had the chance to kill the bugger himself, but since he hadn't, he was glad t' know somebody'd done it right."

She fell silent for a moment, her face stark as she let her gaze drift over the broken tracery of the chapel's window, the gaping black maw of the ancient arched doorway. "This is where he was killed, too, ain't it? Lord Preston, I mean."

"It is, yes."

"Why would somebody do that? Kill Harry here, in the same place—*hang* him here, in the same place they killed that duke's son?"

"You said Harry was watching Lord Preston. Did he by chance mention seeing Farnsworth quarrel with anyone?"

"Well . . ." She paused, thoughtful. "There was some priest. A Frenchie, Harry thought he was."

Father Ambrose, thought Sebastian. "Anyone else?"

Sally was silent for a moment, her mouth screwed up with the effort of memory. "And there was that other cove."

"What other cove?"

"Don't know his name. But Harry told me he saw the two of 'em lightin' into each other somethin' fierce."

"Lord Preston and this other cove, you mean?"

She nodded. "One day late last week, it was. Harry said Lord Preston was carryin' on like he was dicked in the nob—shoutin' about the Bible and some dead usher and layers of cake."

"Cake?"

Sally pulled a face and shrugged her shoulders. "Aye. Damned if I know what 'twas about."

Layers, thought Sebastian as he watched Lovejoy reappear in the chapel doorway, his head turned as he looked back to say something to the men behind him. *Layers and the Bible and a dead usher. Usher. Usher. . . .* Enlightenment dawned. "Do you mean Lancelot Plimsoll?"

She stared at him blankly. "What's that? I ain't never heard of it."

"It's a man's name: Mr. Lancelot Plimsoll. He's a geologist."

"Don't know nothin' 'bout him," said Sally, just as Constable Jones stepped to one side and the men from the deadhouse emerged, carrying Harry on a shell between them.

"Oh, no. It *is* Harry!" she cried, throwing herself forward so fast that Lovejoy's constable barely managed to snag her arm and haul her back. "What ye doin' with him?" she demanded. "Where ye takin' him?"

"There will need to be a postmortem, obviously," said Lovejoy, stiff with all the painful embarrassment of a rigidly controlled, unemotional man confronting a frantic, grief-stricken female. "But I can assure you the body will be returned to you after the in—"

"You're gonna cut him?" screamed Sally, struggling against the constable's grip. "You bloody bastards! First ye try to hang him, then ye send him off to a living hell on the other side o' the world, and

now ye're gonna slit 'im open like he was a pig? Fifteen years ago, when he was sentenced t' hang, he couldn't hardly sleep, knowing that once he was dead the surgeons was gonna be cuttin' him open for everybody to gawk at. It ain't right, you doin' it to him now. Ye hear me? It ain't right!"

It was part of the punishment meted out to those sentenced to hang—that after their deaths, their bodies were delivered to the surgeons to be publicly dissected. "Calm yourself, my good woman. This won't be a public dissection—" Lovejoy started to say, just as Sally squirmed out of the constable's grip and threw herself on her brother's body.

"Oi!" shouted Constable Jones, hauling her back again. But she'd managed to grab one of Harry's arms, dragging him half off the edge of the shell in a way that dislodged from somewhere a thin rectangular piece of cardboard that fluttered down to lie on the cobbles at their feet. It looked like a playing card, its back decorated with a green, white, and red geometric pattern that seemed oddly garish against the worn old stones.

"What's that?" said Sally, going suddenly limp in the constable's grasp.

Reaching down, Sebastian picked up the card and turned it over, his throat dry as he stared at the strange, brilliantly colored image on its face. "Do you know if your brother ever had anything to do with the tarot?" he asked Sally, looking up at her.

"What? No," she said, her features pinched with confusion as Sebastian held up the exquisitely rendered image of a man plunging headfirst from the crumbling battlements of a burning medieval tower.

Chapter 26

Most of the British Museum's fossil holdings, donated to it over the years by gentlemen collectors, were kept tucked away in a bank of drawers and cabinets deep in the bowels of the building. It was there Sebastian found Lancelot Plimsoll, bent over a drawer of fossilized nautiloids.

"We need to talk," said Sebastian, keeping his voice low. "In private."

The geologist straightened. "But I—" he began. Then whatever he saw in Sebastian's face caused him to quietly slide the drawer closed and reach for his hat.

Outside, they found the wind brisk and smelling strongly of coming rain. "Tell me this," said Sebastian as they passed through the museum's monumental sandstone gateway and turned toward Bloomsbury Square. "Did you have one confrontation with Lord Preston, or two? Because you were seen arguing with him near the end of last week—and I should warn you that I've just spent more hours than I had to spare talking to various members of the Geological Society, and I'm hearing from them that your recent attempts to be accepted into the Society were stymied by Farnsworth. And, as one of them put it, you flew into a towering rage over it."

Plimsoll snorted. "Of course I flew into a rage! Who wouldn't? The cretin wasn't even a member of the Geological Society; he got some of his friends to blackball me. *Me.* Apart from William Smith himself, there isn't anyone in Britain who knows more about this country's stratigraphical makeup than I do."

"And the Geological Society hasn't allowed Smith to become a member, either, have they?" William Smith, the man who'd single-handedly just produced a detailed geological map of Britain—the first of its kind in the world—was scorned by the likes of Lord Preston because his father had been a simple blacksmith.

"No, they haven't," Plimsoll said, more calmly now. He drew a deep breath and let it out slowly, his gaze on the leafy green tops of the plane trees in the distant square billowing in the wind. "You're right: I wasn't being exactly truthful with you before. I did have a second confrontation with Farnsworth, last Friday. But for God's sake, what are you thinking? That *I* killed the man? Over my society membership? What good would that do me?"

Sebastian supposed the answer to that would depend on how many members of the Geological Society agreed with Farnsworth that Plimsoll's humble birth should preclude his ever being admitted to their learned association. But all he said was, "What did Archbishop Ussher have to do with it?"

Plimsoll looked confused. "Who?"

"Archbishop James Ussher, the seventeenth-century prelate who concluded that Creation occurred at six o'clock in the evening of the twenty-second of October 4004 BC."

"Ah, yes; *him*. Farnsworth actually threw that ridiculous calculation up at me as 'proof' that my theories on the great age of the earth must be incorrect. It wasn't only my humble birth he objected to, you see; he thought my 'sacrilegious' theories should in and of themselves preclude my ever being admitted as a member of any respectable society. In fact, he said that if it were up to him, he'd have me burnt as a heretic!"

"You're fortunate you weren't born two hundred years ago."

"As are we all."

"True," said Sebastian. "So tell me this: How familiar are you with the tarot?"

Plimsoll stopped and turned to stare at him. "You can't be serious."

"I am, actually."

"I read the earth below us, not cards, or the stars, or whatever they do."

"Why do you think Lord Preston's killer posed him in the posture of a figure from the tarot?"

"I have no idea. But Lord Preston Farnsworth was a pompous, self-congratulatory piece of shit, and men like that tend to make any number of enemies." The geologist's accent and careful diction were both beginning to slip. "Right before I lit into him that day, he was talking to one of his mates about some woman named Angelique. To hear him talk, you'd think she was the greatest threat to civilization since Salome—or maybe it was Jezebel; I tend to get them mixed up, I'm afraid. The Church of England and I parted ways long ago."

"Angelique? Who is she?"

"Someone he wanted to find—and have executed, from the sound of things. But beyond that, I couldn't tell you. It's not as if I was deliberately listening to the conversation, you understand; I was simply waiting for the two men to finish talking and the other fellow to walk away."

"And to whom was Lord Preston saying this?"

"Some rarefied prelate—tall, thin fellow dressed up as fine as a Bond Street Beau. I gathered he and Farnsworth considered themselves comrades-in-arms in the war against atheists, whores, blasphemers, republicans, and any number of other undesirables."

Crispin Carmichael, thought Sebastian. Aloud, he said, "Is there anything else you're not telling me?"

"No, I swear it!" insisted Plimsoll, just as the heavy gray clouds above opened up and it began to pour.

Adjusting his hat against the windblown rain, Sebastian went back to the wasteland that had once been Swallow Street. His conversation with Lancelot Plimsoll had—perhaps—answered one question. But not the others.

There were two obvious explanations for the murder of Half-Hanged Harry McGregor: Either whoever killed Farnsworth had then killed Harry because they believed the ex-convict could identify them, or else McGregor himself had killed Lord Preston, and then someone had killed McGregor in revenge, choosing the same site and leaving a tarot card because—

Because why? And why the hell would someone like Harry McGregor stage his victim's body in such an elaborate pose? He wouldn't. Which left only the first explanation—that McGregor had been murdered because he could identify Farnsworth's killer.

So why hadn't Harry told Sebastian what he knew? Because he'd thought he might be able to blackmail the killer? Was he really that stupid?

Probably.

Pausing at the base of the street, Sebastian let his gaze drift over the forlorn remnants of so many unknown, broken lives: a crumbling flight of stairs that disappeared into rubble; a stray dog that ran off when he called to it; the crushed husk of a child's old tin drum. There was nothing he could see here that might explain why the killer—or killers—had chosen to use this place, twice, as the site of their murders.

One might argue that the chapel had been selected simply because the area was deserted; there was no one near to hear a startled cry of alarm, no one to wonder about the isolated report of a pistol shot. But there were other such places around the metropolis, so why had this one been chosen? For something as simple as proximity? Or for a different reason entirely?

Turning to look back up the street, Sebastian found himself remembering something Quinton-Thomas had said: that Lord Preston Farnsworth might have gone to Swallow Street to meet someone in connection with his work with the Society for the Suppression of Vice.

It was past time, Sebastian realized, to talk to one of those self-anointed saints.

Chapter 27

The Reverend Crispin Carmichael, Lord Preston's good friend and fellow crusader against whores, drunks, blasphemers, and sellers of lewd books, was no humble churchman.

The soaring, classically fronted church of St. George's, Hanover Square, was the parish church for the wealthy, exclusive section of West London known as Mayfair. The men appointed as its rector were traditionally of the same background as their more distinguished parishioners, and Crispin Carmichael was no exception, being the younger son of Lord Carmichael of Plumbury Castle and a grandson through his mother of the Earl of Bathurst. As was to be expected for someone with such glittering connections, Carmichael had enjoyed rapid preferment. After taking bachelor's, master's, and doctoral degrees at Cambridge, he spent just one year at a parish in Kent and as the second prebendal stall in Rochester Cathedral before being appointed to the rectory of St. George's. It was fully expected that he would be made a bishop in a few more years.

The actual, tedious work of the parish was naturally delegated to less exalted underlings, which allowed Mr. Carmichael himself to spend the bulk of his time in the library of his elegant little house on Conduit Street producing a stream of erudite, improving tracts. And it was there that Sebastian found him, seated at a graceful mahogany desk, a pen balanced in his long, aristocratic fingers as he stared down at his latest composition.

"Lord Devlin, come in, come in," said the Reverend, setting aside his pen and rising from his chair to come around from behind his desk as his housekeeper quietly curtsied herself out. Today Mr. Carmichael was dressed in a long black cassock of fine wool exquisitely tailored to his tall, thin form, with silk tassels that shimmered in the light of the branches of beeswax candles he had lit against the gloom. "May I offer you something to drink? Tea, perhaps? Or would you prefer brandy?"

Sebastian had left his rain-soaked hat and greatcoat in the entry hall, but he was still damnably wet and cold. "I'll take brandy, thank you."

"Excellent choice for such a wretched day," said the Reverend, going to pour two drinks. "I fear it's becoming increasingly difficult to doubt those who say something has gone seriously wrong with our world." He glanced over at Sebastian. "You've heard the theory that this strange weather we're experiencing is caused by the unusually large sunspot that has recently appeared? Some even speculate that the massive spot is weakening the sun's rays in a way that will permanently cool our earth. Either that, or the sun may in time become so wholly encrusted with such spots as to plunge us forever into darkness."

"I've heard the theories. But I don't personally know enough about sunspots to have an educated opinion," said Sebastian, taking the glass handed to him.

Mr. Carmichael gave a soft laugh and turned to pour himself a drink. "Does anyone, really? I've seen speculation they could be anything from volcanoes on the surface of the sun to chasms in its atmosphere caused by currents of gas. But I don't see how we'll ever be able to know for certain." He extended a hand toward one of the leather chairs drawn up to the fire. "Please, have a seat."

"Thank you."

"I'm glad to have the opportunity to speak to you," said Mr. Carmichael, his brandy cupped gracefully in one hand as he settled in the chair opposite Sebastian. "I found your testimony at yesterday's inquest troubling, given that the boy who claimed to have found Lord Preston's body has now disappeared. Why do you think he has done that?"

"It's understandable, isn't it?" said Sebastian. "What poor lad off the streets is going to want to find himself tangled up in the investigation of a nobleman's murder?"

"I suppose," said the Reverend, although he sounded less than convinced.

Sebastian took a slow sip of his brandy. "I understand you and Lord Preston were friends."

Mr. Carmichael expelled his breath in a long sigh. "Yes, good friends, from the time we were boys. First at Eton, then at Cambridge, although of course Preston stopped with his bachelor's. He always liked to say knowledge is found in books, but a true understanding of the world we live in can only be learned when one goes out into the world itself." A faint smile touched the cleric's thin, sensitive lips, then was gone, and he brought up a splayed hand to rub his eyes before continuing. "I still can't believe he's been murdered, and in such a hideous, bizarre fashion."

"You were both members of the Society for the Suppression of Vice?"

"We were, yes. It was Preston's passion, you know. He wanted to see London become a place where women and children could walk freely without fear of having their ears assaulted by obscenities or encountering drunken men or lewd, immoral women."

"Do you have any idea what might have taken him to Swallow Street last Saturday night?"

"No; I can't imagine."

"He hadn't involved himself in some prosecution in the area?"

"Not to my knowledge, no. But then, he was always far more active in such things than I. You might try asking Lady Hester. She has worked with him quite closely for years now."

"I hadn't realized that."

"Oh, yes; the Society has always encouraged women to take an active role in its campaigns."

"Can you think of anyone who might have wanted to kill him?"

Mr. Carmichael held his brandy up so that the amber liquid captured the light of the fire within its depths. He stared at its warm, golden glow for a moment, his thin, scholarly face drawn and troubled. Then he gave a slight shake of his head. "Not really. Bow Street has asked for the Society's help in compiling a list of those from the lower orders in whose prosecutions Lord Preston played a part, so one assumes they have reason to suspect his killer of being from the criminal classes."

"But you don't?"

"There's no denying that Preston's dedication to finding a way to control London's crime must have brought him into conflict with any number of rough, dangerous individuals. But the manner of his death suggests to me that his killer is someone more sophisticated. More . . . educated."

"What makes you say that?"

Setting aside his drink, the rector leaned forward, his hands coming up together as if in prayer. "Are you familiar with the tradition of *pitture infamanti*?"

"No."

The Reverend nodded as if he had expected such ignorance. "It was basically a form of punishment in effigy once popular in the Italian city-states, mainly during the thirteenth and fourteenth centuries, although it didn't completely disappear for another two hundred or so years. In those days, men of wealth and position valued their reputations above almost all else, and the paintings were designed to humiliate them. Hence the name *pitture infamanti*—defaming portraits or shame paintings. When the authorities wanted to punish someone who'd managed to evade capture, they paid an artist to paint the man hanging upside down. Since men of the upper classes were typically beheaded, being hanged was shameful enough, but to be hanged upside down was particularly dishonorable."

Madame Blanchette had mentioned an Italian connection, Sebastian remembered, when he'd asked her about the meaning of *Le Pendu*. He took another sip of his brandy and felt its warmth spread slowly throughout his chilled body. "I don't believe I've ever seen an example of such a painting."

"That's because they were frescoes—life-size portraits painted on the outside of the cities' public buildings. So they weathered and eventually disappeared, or else they were whitewashed over when the authorities had some new miscreant they wanted to humiliate. It's a pity, because, since the authorities wanted these portraits to be instantly recognizable, the artists they hired to paint them were amongst the best—Andrea del Castagno, Botticelli . . . even Leonardo da Vinci is believed to have been forced to do at least one. Painters were often reluctant to do them, for obvious reasons." The Reverend thrust himself up from his chair. "I'll show you."

Tilting his head to one side, he ran a finger along the spines of the leather-bound books in a nearby case before pulling a heavy tome from one shelf and leafing through its pages. "Here," he said, turning the open book around as he handed it to Sebastian. "This is a reproduction of a preliminary sketch for one that was done by Andrea del Sarto in red chalk on white paper."

Taking the book, Sebastian found himself staring at an exquisitely rendered drawing of a man suspended upside down by a rope tied to one ankle. He was clothed in the doublet, full sleeves, and slashed and padded breeches of the early sixteenth century, his arms dangling below his head, the features of his face frozen in a hideous grimace for some three hundred years. This figure was caught in a wild, dynamic pose, whereas the hanged man shown in *Le Pendu* was static, almost dead. But the connection between the two images was easy to see.

"So who were the men punished in this way?" asked Sebastian.

"Sometimes they were murderers, frauds, or thieves. But most often they were traitors, men who were believed to have betrayed their fellow citizens or the ruling family. Those guilty of the worst treachery, particularly condottieri who switched sides, were typically shown hanging by one foot." Carmichael pointed to the image. "Like that."

"Can you think of a reason why someone would want to do this to Lord Preston?"

A bleak, troubled expression crept over the Reverend's features. "Preston was a wonderful man, fiercely faithful to God, King, friends, and family. He dedicated his life to making London—and the world—a better place to live. His killer's only purpose can have been to shame him."

Sebastian handed the book back to the Reverend. "Did you know a man named Half-Hanged Harry McGregor?"

Mr. Carmichael closed the book and turned to slide it back

into place. "The ex-convict who was bothering Preston, you mean? I know Bow Street was looking for him. Have they caught him?"

"He was found dead this morning, hanging in the same chapel on Swallow Street, although the rope was around his neck rather than one of his feet."

The Reverend swung back around to stare at Sebastian, the skirts of his expensive cassock swirling around him. "Oh, goodness. How . . . bizarre."

"You knew McGregor was following Lord Preston?"

"I did, yes; he mentioned it to me several times. It was a source of considerable aggravation to him, although I don't believe he saw the fellow as a serious threat."

"What about a woman named Angelique? Did Lord Preston ever talk to you about her?"

The Reverend nodded. "Yes. In fact, he was telling me about her just last . . . Friday, I believe it was."

"Who is she?"

"Some Radical, from the sound of things. I gathered Lord Preston considered her quite dangerous. But beyond that I'm afraid I can't tell you much."

"Do you know why he considered her dangerous?"

"As I understand it, she is both wellborn and educated but has dedicated herself to working with the poor and, in the guise of 'educating' them, fills their heads with all sorts of inappropriate ideas and aspirations. That kind can be quite dangerous."

"Yes, I can see that," said Sebastian. "Do you know if Lord Preston ever had anything to do with the tarot?"

"The tarot? Only in his attempts to suppress the charlatans who prey upon the gullible."

"He prosecuted fortune-tellers?"

"Oh, yes. Particularly cartomancers."

"Another dangerous lot."

"Indeed," said Mr. Carmichael, his tongue darting out to wet his dry lips. "Tell me this: Do you think . . . that is to say, is there a chance that the other members of the Society might be in danger?"

"I suppose it's possible," said Sebastian, pushing to his feet. "It probably wouldn't hurt to be careful."

"Oh, goodness," said Mr. Carmichael, rising with him. "Yes, indeed. I appreciate your blunt honesty. I'm sorry I couldn't have been of more help."

"Actually," said Sebastian, "you've given me a great deal to think about."

Chapter 28

Sebastian had to knock twice at the door of Madame Blanchette's apartment before it was answered, not by Madame herself but by a thin, pale slip of a girl whose eyes widened at the sight of him.

"Pardon, monsieur, mais madame n'est pas ici," she whispered in a rush, and would have closed the door on him if Sebastian hadn't thrust out his hand, stopping her.

"I'll wait for her return," he said, then paused at the sound of the street door opening and closing below.

He heard a woman's halting step as she limped across the entry hall and began to slowly mount the stairs. Madame Blanchette's voice drifted up to them. "Do not manhandle my young maid, *monsieur le vicomte.* I shall be there directly."

He waited until she came into view, her body swaying awkwardly back and forth as she maneuvered her shattered leg up the stairs one step at a time. He said, "I wasn't manhandling her."

A gleam of amusement showed in the cartomancer's eyes, but

she didn't say anything until she reached her floor and handed her shopping basket to her maid. The girl took the basket and disappeared into the depths of the apartment.

"You didn't tell me Lord Preston was going after the city's fortune-tellers," he said, following the Frenchwoman into her apartment. "Were you one of those he targeted?"

She shut the door behind him, her eyes widening as she turned to face him. "*Alors.* Am I a suspect now? If so, I would be interested to hear how you think I managed to bash in the man's skull and then hoist him up into the air."

"You could have had help."

She pursed her lips and tilted her head back and forth as if considering this, then wrinkled her nose. "Unlikely. I have many customers here in London, but few friends. And none of such a nature."

"So why not return to France?" he surprised himself by asking. "You could now."

A sad, faraway look crept into her eyes. "The friends and family I once had there are all dead now. And the France I once knew and loved no longer exists." She shrugged. "So I am here."

"But it is true that Lord Preston was prosecuting fortune-tellers?"

"He was, yes. But surely you don't expect me to give you their names, do you? To save myself?"

"No."

She sucked in a deep breath that flared her nostrils. "Farnsworth's kind go after anyone in the 'lower orders' who doesn't keep to what those worthies consider his 'place'—or who even dares to try to have fun. The poor are supposed to work hard for their 'betters,' eat a meager and humble diet, pray, and die. Anything else isn't simply an outrage; it's a sin—and therefore must be punished."

There was something about the vehemence of her words that told Sebastian she knew at least one person—and probably more—

who'd been the victims of the Society for the Suppression of Vice. He said, "Did you know an ex-convict named Harry McGregor?"

She gave him such a blank look that he found it difficult to believe it was assumed. "*Non*. Who is he?"

"He was found dead this morning in the same chapel where Farnsworth was murdered, except this time the killer hanged his victim by his neck instead of from an ankle. And he left this." Sebastian drew the green, white, and red patterned tarot card from his pocket and held it up.

She reached to take the card and stared at it a moment before saying abruptly, "Follow me."

She led him to a small room he'd seen before, her *cabinet d'études*. Yards and yards of deep red cloth draped the walls for a tentlike effect; there was no window, only an inlaid table in the center flanked by two stools and illuminated by a pierced brass Moroccan lantern that hung overhead and was already lit. The air was thick with the scents of frankincense and myrrh and something else he'd never been able to identify. An articulated skeleton leered at him from one corner; a large carved wooden chest stood against the far wall. But the owl that had once blinked at him from its perch here was gone.

"She had an injured wing," said Madame Blanchette. "When she recovered, I let her go."

Sebastian caught his breath. He'd been around the cartomancer enough that her perspicacity shouldn't still have this effect on him. But it always did.

She set the card in the center of the table so that it faced him, then raised her gaze to his. "Are you familiar with this particular tarot deck?"

"No."

"It comes from the printing press of a man named Ferdinando Gumppenberg. He is German by birth but moved to Milan some six or seven years ago, taking with him the German tradition of publishers commissioning tarot decks from well-known illustrators and engravers."

"I didn't know the Germans used the tarot."

"Oh, yes." Turning, she lifted the lid of the chest that stood behind her chair and withdrew from it two decks she set face down on the table before her. The green, white, and red pattern on the back of one deck matched the pattern of the card from the chapel; the other deck was unknown to him. Picking up the first deck again, she fanned it open, selected a card, and laid it face up beside the one he had brought.

They were identical.

"It's a beautiful deck, *oui*? The artist, Giorgio Bassano, uses copper plates to produce exquisite engravings that are then delicately colored."

Setting aside the first deck, she picked up the second deck and withdrew from it a single card she set beside the other two cards on the table. She said, "This is the same card from a typical deck from Marseille. You see the ways in which the two cards are similar and the ways in which they differ?"

He nodded. The card from the Marseille deck was much cruder than that from Milan, a cheap wood-block print colored in roughly after it was printed. Rather than being smashed by a bolt of lightning, the top of the tower on the Marseille deck looked as if it were being sheared off by a thunderbolt so stylized it might have been a plume of red and yellow feathers billowing down from heaven. And rather than crumbling, the top of this tower was falling essentially intact, so that its crenellations made it look like a tumbling crown.

The figures falling from the tower were also markedly different. In the card from the Marseille deck, the most prominent man, falling with his arms outstretched before him, wore an oddly serene expression and was so close to the ground that he might have been an acrobat walking on his hands. Rather than lying dead on the ground, the second man on this card appeared to be reaching from inside the tower as if to pluck something from the ground outside. And whereas the Milanese deck showed bricks and pieces of stone from the crumbling tower filling the air around the falling man, the sky in the Marseille deck's card was filled with an odd cascade of red, blue, and yellow balls that might have been colored hailstones but could just as easily have been dozens of jesters' balls.

The card was even labeled differently: *LA MAISON DIEU* rather than *LA TORRE*: "The House of God" rather than "The Tower."

"Why are they so different?" he asked, looking up at her.

She shrugged. "Many cards have such differences. I have seen a deck from sixteenth-century Florence in which this card shows two naked people fleeing a burning building, and there is one from Belgium that has a shepherd beneath a tree being struck by lightning. That one was labeled *LA FOUDRE*, lightning. This deck from Marseille essentially merges the earlier traditions, while the Milanese one . . . shifts it."

"Where does the imagery of the tower come from?"

"Ah, that surely originated in Italy. I've heard it said that in the Middle Ages such towers were a common status symbol amongst the wealthy of Italy's city-states. The nobles competed with one another to see who could build the tallest tower. At one time Florence had some two or three hundred such towers, but they were so high they were constantly being struck by lightning and crumbling. It's the perfect metaphor for the kind of pride that brings about one's downfall, yes?"

"Is that what the card symbolizes?"

"Different people see it differently. But it's all mostly about the same thing: pride, ruin, people bringing about their own destruction."

Sebastian thought about Half-Hanged Harry McGregor, with his misshapen hat and ragged coat; he doubted anyone would call the ex-convict a prideful man. But if he had made the mistake of identifying himself to Lord Preston's killer, one could say he had brought about his own destruction. . . .

He was aware of the Frenchwoman watching him silently, as if she were once again somehow divining the direction of his thoughts. "When exactly was this deck printed?" he said, reaching out to retrieve the card left by Harry McGregor's killer. "Do you know?"

"Two years ago, I believe."

"So it's relatively new."

"Yes."

He tucked the card back into his pocket. "Thank you."

"Of course."

She walked with him to the door. But before she opened it for him, she paused with her hand on the knob and looked back at him. "You are aware, of course, that your sister was close to Lord Preston?"

He wondered how she came to know he even had a sister, let alone that Amanda was close to the Farnsworths. He said, "Yes. Her house is on the same square, and she is friends with his sister, Lady Hester."

"There's more to it than that."

"What is that supposed to mean?"

She shrugged and opened the door.

This time he was the one who hesitated. "The Bourbons have sent a new assassin to London. Do you know anything about him?"

Rather than answer his question, she said, "I did warn you that you were . . . vulnerable." Which he supposed was an answer, of a sort.

Sebastian said, "You know the reason for his interest in me?"

She met his gaze and said simply, "I know."

Chapter 29

Distraction can be a dangerous thing.

Perhaps if he'd been less preoccupied with his thoughts, Sebastian would have sensed the atmosphere of tense anticipation that now permeated the storm-darkened staircase, or heeded the faint warning sounds of cloth brushing against cloth and the quick, nervous intake of breath. But his thoughts were on the past, on a deeply buried private pain that had nothing to do with hanged men or self-congratulatory saints or ancient cards of divination.

He had descended the first set of stairs and was turning toward the next flight when they came at him, two roughly dressed men who charged up the staircase in a headlong rush. The man in the lead was lean and quick, with flashing dark eyes and olive skin and a knife held in a practiced grip at his side. His companion was larger, slower, and armed with a stout cudgel, his lips pulling back from his crooked yellow teeth in a rictus of determination as he lumbered up the stairs in his partner's wake.

"Bloody hell," swore Sebastian as the first man lunged at him.

Wrapping his hands around the banister, Sebastian levered his weight up and kicked out with both feet, catching the lead man in the chest to send him tumbling end over end back down the stairs.

Dropping to a crouch, Sebastian yanked his dagger from its sheath in his boot and came up just as the big man swung his cudgel. Sebastian jerked his head to one side, but not quite fast enough, the jagged wood of the club scraping the flesh beside his ear. With a guttural growl, the big man swung again, the hunk of wood whistling through empty air as Sebastian ducked. This time when Sebastian came up, he stepped in toward his attacker, the dagger flashing up to drive the blade deep into the big man's chest. Sebastian saw the man's eyes widen in surprise, his mouth sag to spill a rush of blood.

"Pots!" shouted the man's companion, staggering up from where he'd landed at the base of the stairs to charge back up again.

Sebastian tried to yank his dagger from the big man's chest, only to have it catch on the cloth of the man's stained fustian waistcoat. With a grimace Sebastian kicked out, his bootheel thudding against the big man's stomach, the cloth of the waistcoat tearing as the knife came free and the dying man hurtled backward.

Still only halfway up the flight of stairs, the lean man tried to catch his friend, but the big man's momentum sent him tumbling past.

His breath coming hard and fast, the lean man stared up at Sebastian and froze.

"Come on, you bastard," swore Sebastian, dropping to a fighter's stance, his knife dripping blood as he held it at the ready. "What are you waiting for?"

The man's gaze flicked from Sebastian to his companion, now lying motionless in an ungainly sprawl on the tiles of the entryway below. Then he turned and bolted back down the stairs, his bootheels clattering on the uncarpeted treads, the hinges of the street door creaking as he threw it open wide and disappeared into the swirling rain.

Swiping one raised shoulder against the bloody side of his face, Sebastian walked slowly down the stairs, his knife still in his hand.

The big man lay on his back, one leg crumpled beneath him, his neck twisted at an unnatural angle, his chest a sheen of dark wetness as he stared up at Sebastian with unseeing eyes.

"Bloody hell," said Sebastian again.

The sound of a door opening above jerked his gaze up to where Madame Blanchette appeared, leaning over the second-floor banister. She stared at him in silence for a moment, then shifted her gaze to the dead man at his feet.

Sebastian bent to wipe the dagger's bloody blade on the dead man's coat, then slipped it back into his boot. "Do you recognize him?"

"He's not French," she said.

Which was not, he noticed, exactly the same as saying she did not recognize him.

❧

"Interesting," said Sir Henry Lovejoy, his gaze on the dead man sprawled at his feet. "I wonder which killed him? The broken neck, or the knife wound?"

Sebastian swiped again at his stinging, still-bleeding face. "Does it matter?"

"Probably not." The magistrate bent over, tipping his head first one way, then the other as he studied the dead man's face. "I don't recognize him. You say his companion called him Pots? Had you ever seen either man before?"

"No."

"Any idea as to who might have sent them?"

"None."

Lovejoy put a splayed hand on the small of his back as he straightened with a quickly concealed grimace. "Someone must feel threatened by whatever you've learned about the Swallow Street hangings."

"I haven't learned a bloody thing."

Lovejoy looked over at him. "Perhaps you've discovered more than you realize."

Sebastian was pouring a pitcher of hot water into the washbasin in his dressing room when Hero came to stand in the doorway.

"Please tell me that's not all your blood."

"Not all of it. My face looks worse than it actually is."

"You always say that."

He laughed and set to work stripping off his waistcoat, cravat, and shirt while he provided her with a quick rundown of what he'd learned.

"It sounds as if Lady Hester might know something about who her brother was in the process of prosecuting," he said, rinsing his face. "But since she's decided Hugh is the killer and I'm somehow personally responsible for Bow Street's failure to arrest him, I can't see her volunteering the information I need. In fact, I wouldn't be surprised if she simply refused to see me."

"I suspect she'll see me," said Hero.

He looked over at her in surprise. "You know her?"

"Not well. But she's had a tendre for Jarvis for decades. Evidently, no one ever told her he likes his women small and very pretty."

Sebastian dried his face. Carefully. "You can't be serious."

"I wish I weren't. Watch her around him sometime. She becomes all fluttery. And simpers."

Sebastian reached for a clean shirt. "I find that profoundly disturbing and yet somehow, at the same time, oddly endearing."

"Endearing?"

"It makes her seem unexpectedly vulnerable. More human." But not exactly likable.

Hero made an inelegant sound deep in her throat. "When my mother was alive, she used to say that if she were ever found murdered, we should consider Lady Hester the primary suspect."

"Someone ought to warn the new Lady Jarvis," said Sebastian as he finished buttoning his shirt and reached for a fresh cravat.

Hero gave a rude snort. "I think Cousin Victoria is more than capable of taking care of herself."

Lady Hester Farnsworth sat enthroned in a delicately carved Louis XV–style chair positioned beside one of her drawing room's massive fireplaces. Even by Mayfair standards, the pastel-toned room was immense, its twin fireplaces faced with Carrara marble, the sparkling crystal chandeliers overhead from Vienna, the figured carpets from Persia. In accordance with the household's state of mourning, black crepe draped every window, door, mirror, and gilt-framed oil painting. Lord Preston's grieving sister wore an elegant long-sleeved afternoon gown of black silk crepe over black sarcenet made high at the neck with a collar of deep Vandykes. Her shoes were Spanish slippers of black queen silk with jet clasps; the cap of fine black Belgian lace pinned to her fair hair heightened the aura of delicate tragedy. She kept her eyes downcast as she listened to Hero's polite expressions of condolence, her attention seemingly all for the task of pouring tea from a heavy silver pot into two delicate Sèvres cups.

"Your words are very kind," she said, looking up with a faint smile when Hero had finished. She handed Hero one of the cups, then took her own and leaned back in her chair to fix her guest with a steady gaze. "But you do realize I am not so naive as to be unaware of the fact that you are here today as your husband's emissary."

"That doesn't mean my condolences are insincere," said Hero.

"No, of course not." Lady Hester took a sip of her tea, then settled the cup and saucer on the inlaid Italian table at her side. "And while I am still firmly of the belief that Major Hugh Chandler is the person responsible for my brother's death, I had an interesting visit earlier today from Mr. Carmichael, the rector of St. George's, Hanover Square. He convinced me that the best way to expedite Bow Street's investigation is by humoring this ridiculous determination to collect the names of those from the criminal classes who might conceivably have harbored ill feelings toward my brother. I am therefore in the process of compiling just such a list."

Hero took a slow sip of her tea. "And is there anyone on this list who might be considered dangerous?"

"I suppose one might say there are several, in particular a former publican named Lionel Sykes and a lewd woman who calls herself Letitia Lamont, although one assumes that is a nom de guerre. Of course, it's possible that one or even both of these individuals are still in prison; Lord Devlin would need to speak to Sir Windle."

"Sir Windle?"

"Sir Windle Barr, Chief Magistrate at Great Marlborough Street. He handled both cases."

Hero studied Lady Hester's thin, aristocratic features, the delicately arched brows, pale blue-gray eyes, and thin lips. But the woman was giving nothing away. "Did Lord Preston consider either Sykes or Lamont a threat?"

"Hardly. My brother was not the type to give credence to the blusterings of rogues and miscreants." She reached for her cup and took another sip. "I hope Lord Devlin is not such a fool as to be taken in by all the nonsense we're hearing about this 'Half-Hanged Harry.'"

"You think it unlikely that McGregor could have been involved in what happened?"

Lady Hester's lip curled in disdain. "Harry McGregor was a pathetic excuse for a man, filled with malice, perhaps, but fundamentally weak and stupid. Such a cretin could never have managed to get the better of my brother."

"Did you know McGregor had recently been following him?"

"I did, yes; Preston mentioned it to me a week or so ago. He was annoyed but not unduly concerned—as I told Bow Street." She set her cup down on its saucer with enough force that the china clinked together. "And yet this magistrate—not Sir Nathaniel, of course, but his subordinate, Sir Henry Lovejoy—seems determined to chase every will-o'-the-wisp that might possibly lead him away from the true perpetrator of this outrage. I actually had him here yesterday wanting to know who is now the heir presumptive to the dukedom. As if a Farnsworth could be so *common* as to stoop to murder for financial gain."

"Who is the new heir?"

"Captain Michael Farnsworth, a second cousin once removed, currently serving with the army of occupation in the south of France." Her nose crinkled. "Not precisely the caliber of man one might have wished to see step into my father's shoes someday, I fear, but we should be able to bring him up to snuff."

"No doubt," said Hero, sparing a moment of pity for the unknown captain. "I wonder, do you know anything about a woman named Angelique?"

"Angelique?" Lady Hester frowned. "Is she a gypsy?"

"Possibly. What makes you think she might be?"

"Only that Preston was determined to remove them from the streets. Why precisely do you ask?"

"Her name came up."

"If I ever heard him mention her, I do not recall it." Lady Hester took another sip of her tea, then set it aside and rose to her feet. "And now I fear you must excuse me, Lady Devlin. My abigail was kind enough to offer to spell me by staying with Lord Preston for the last several hours, but I am determined to sit with him myself until dinner."

"Of course," said Hero, rising with her. "Thank you for agreeing to see me. And please accept my sincere condolences again on the loss of your brother."

The Duke's sister gave a regal incline of her head. "Thank you. He's lying in the library, so I shall walk down with you."

As they descended the broad, sweeping flight of stairs to the entry hall, Hero noticed that the door to the library now stood open. The heavy crimson velvet drapes at the room's windows were drawn close and festooned with more black crepe, casting the room into a deep gloom relieved only by the banks of beeswax candles arranged at each end of a fine coffin. The coffin was, thankfully, closed, its surface piled high with mounds of heavily scented lilies and roses. And yet the stench of death was still inescapable.

"When is the funeral?" asked Hero.

"Saturday evening," said Lady Hester, pausing at the foot of the stairs as if struck by a sudden thought. "Actually, it occurs to me that there is someone who threatened Preston quite recently—no more than a week or so ago."

"Threatened him in what way?"

"She said that if it were up to her, his head would be on a pike."

That sounded to Hero more like an insult than a threat, but all she said was, "Lord Preston was threatened by a woman?"

"A notorious woman. Calhoun is her name; Grace Calhoun. She owns a public house in Smithfield and another in Stepney. Both are of the sort vulgarly known as 'flash houses.' Have you heard of her?"

"I have, actually," said Hero, and left it at that.

"Good. You'll be certain to tell Lord Devlin, won't you?" An unmistakable gleam of malicious amusement narrowed her ladyship's eyes as her stately butler moved to open the front door for Hero. "And do give my regards to your dear father."

"You think she knows Grace Calhoun's son is my valet?" said Devlin a short time later, when Hero told him of her conversation with the dead man's sister.

"Oh, she knows, all right," said Hero, stripping off her hat and tossing it onto a nearby chair. "I suspect it's the only reason she said it."

"Maybe," said Devlin, thoughtful. "Or maybe not."

Chapter 30

The Public Office on Great Marlborough Street, Westminster, lacked the power and prestige of the better-known Bow Street, but its neighborhood was considerably more refined.

Or at least, much of it was.

One of seven such establishments created by the Middlesex Justices Act of 1792, the Great Marlborough Street Public Office was situated just below Oxford Street in what had previously been an impressive nobleman's house. Its current Chief Magistrate, Sir Windle Barr, was a well-fed, graying widower somewhere in his late fifties with a self-satisfied air of authority and such impressive jowls that his small eyes, nose, and mouth seemed scrunched together in the center of his face. A firm believer in the superiority of the ways of the past, he still favored the style of frock coat that had been fashionable in his youth, with a modest fall of lace at his throat and a powdered wig he sometimes wore even when not on the bench.

The magistrate was in his chambers, seated behind a broad, somewhat messy desk, when a harried clerk ushered Sebastian into

His Honor's presence. Looking up, he set aside his pen, his padded leather desk chair creaking as he leaned back. "Thought you'd probably make it here sooner or later."

It was said in a way that reminded Sebastian that Swallow Street lay within Great Marlborough Street's jurisdiction. And while the murder of such an important aristocrat as Lord Preston Farnsworth would inevitably have resulted in the Home Office passing control of the investigation to Bow Street, it obviously rankled with Sir Windle that Sebastian had gone directly to Lovejoy rather than having the courtesy to contact the Great Marlborough Street office first.

"Thank you for taking the time to see me."

"Of course." Sir Windle folded his hands together and rested them atop the rounded mound of his belly while looking at Sebastian expectantly. "So what can I do for you today, my lord?"

"I understand you handled some of the cases Lord Preston helped prosecute."

"I did, yes." He waved a soft, pudgy hand toward the papers on his desk. "In fact, I'm currently in the process of preparing a list of the individuals involved for Bow Street."

Another list, thought Sebastian; Bow Street was going to be inundated with lists of potential suspects. "Is there anyone in particular on that list whom you suspect?"

Since the magistrate had not invited him to sit, Sebastian simply prowled the room, pausing to study first the ormolu clock on the mantel, then the titles of the books on the shelves in a way that brought an annoyed frown to the magistrate's features. But it was too late by then for Sir Windle to correct what he obviously realized had been an ill-judged attempt to emphasize his authority and power.

The magistrate tightened his jaw. "Anyone in particular? Not really, although I do believe we could possibly be dealing with a killer from the criminal classes. I know Lord Preston's sister does not agree with me in that, but, well, let's just say Lady Hester sometimes allows her emotions to run away with her."

Sebastian thought he'd seldom met a less emotional female than the dead man's formidable sister, but all he said was, "What can you tell me about a publican named Lionel Sykes and a woman who calls herself Letitia Lamont?"

Sir Windle's frown deepened. "Why those two?"

"Their names came up."

"I don't see why they would. Lionel Sykes is a failed former publican who had a habit of selling outside of hours and made some unwise decisions that eventually led to him losing his license. I have no idea what he's been up to since then or if he's even still alive. He certainly hasn't been seen around here. As for Letitia Lamont, she's currently locked up in the Bridewell and has been these last five months and more."

"She's a thief?"

"Amongst other things—'other things' basically translating into running a succession of nasty bawdy houses, the latest of which specialized in preying on ignorant, vulnerable girls fresh up from the country."

"Where was that?"

"Her last house? Oxford Street, damn her hide."

"And you say she's now in the Bridewell?"

"She is." Barr thrust out his lower lip in thought. "But women of her kind are frequently allied with henchmen who do their dirty work for them—'bully men,' they call them. So if you've good reason to suspect her, I wouldn't let the fact that she's in the Bridewell rule her out."

"What about Harry McGregor? Were you familiar with him?"

"Half-Hanged Harry? I had some dealings with him long ago, but fortunately he tended to confine his activities to Southwark after his return from Botany Bay." Sir Windle sighed. "Far be it for me to question the King's judgment, but I'll never understand why, if His Majesty was determined to save the devil from a second hanging, he didn't order the man transported for life rather than a mere fourteen years. But," he said, tipping his chair forward suddenly to rest his forearms on the surface of his desk, "at least someone's taken care of *that* problem for us. I just wish they'd done it in a less spectacular fashion."

"You don't think McGregor's death is related to Lord Preston's murder?"

"No, I don't. Just the work of someone with a sick sense of humor. And no, I don't think Half-Hanged Harry killed Farnsworth, either. Why would someone like Harry take the time to pose his victim's body in such an outlandish fashion—even if he knew something about the tarot, which I sincerely doubt. Can't see it at all." The magistrate sighed again. "Lord Preston was a good, selfless man who dedicated his life to fighting the forces of darkness and chaos that have threatened this city for far too long. In a sense you could say he was a victim of his own goodness."

"Are you also a member of the Society for the Suppression of Vice?"

"Me? No. As magistrate I have a different role to play in the struggle to make our capital a safe place. But I appreciate what they do, and I've been working with Robert Peel, Sir Nathaniel, and Lord Preston to craft a new police bill. Ironic, isn't it, that his murder should serve as such a profound illustration of just how badly this city needs an organized, centralized police force."

Sebastian wasn't convinced that a uniformed police force modeled on the one Robert Peel was envisioning could have prevented

Farnsworth's death. He said, "What about a woman named Angelique? Did you ever hear Lord Preston mention her?"

"I don't believe so, no. Who is she?"

"I've no idea. Do you know if Lord Preston had any enemies beyond those from what he considered the 'criminal classes'?"

"Can't think of anyone, really, except those such as Quinton-Thomas who were opposed to his proposals. And I can't see even Quinton-Thomas bashing in Lord Preston's head." He hesitated, then frowned. "Of course, there is that fellow who ran off with Lady Theresa a few years ago. Chandler was his name; Hugh Chandler. And while I'm not quite as single-minded about it as Lady Hester, the truth is that Bow Street could do worse than focusing on him. The fellow had to pay through the nose for what he did; that must surely rankle. And if I remember correctly, he was in the 25th Hussars, so it's not like he's a stranger either to killing or to—" Sir Windle broke off as if he had only just remembered something, although Sebastian knew it was all for show. "But then, you were in the 25th, too, weren't you?"

"Yes," said Sebastian. "Yes, I was."

Chapter 31

Jamie didn't like being this close to magistrates, constables, bailiffs, and their kind.

Standing across the street and down a ways from the Great Marlborough Street Public Office, he shifted nervously from one foot to the other as he waited for Viscount Devlin to emerge. He didn't want to think about what Father would say if he knew Jamie was here, following the Viscount. Watching him. But Jamie couldn't just wait; he had to *know*. He didn't understand how Father could be so—so "accepting" was the word Father used. "Cold-blooded" was more like it, Jamie'd always thought. But then he supposed watching your mother, father, and brother all get their heads chopped off would make anyone's blood run cold.

"I don't understand," Jamie had said to him once. "Why'd ye go and watch?"

"Because I owed it to them, to be there for them."

"Weren't ye afraid? Afraid somebody'd recognize ye? Afraid they'd be cuttin' off yer head, too?"

"Yes."

Whenever he was afraid, Jamie would try to imagine he was like young Father Ambrose, brave enough to stand in the rain watching that blade rise and fall, rise and fall. Except of course there was a big difference between being there for your doomed family and doing what Jamie was doing now.

He realized he had let his attention wander and sucked in a deep, frightened breath when he discovered the Viscount had appeared on the front steps of the public office. And instead of looking to where he'd left his tiger with his curricle, Devlin was staring down the street, straight at Jamie.

"Jesus, Mary, and Joseph," whispered Jamie. Pushing against the brick wall at his back, he took off at a run.

He heard Devlin shout, heard the clatter of the Viscount's bootheels behind him, but kept going. Dodging a stout water carrier and a shaggy brown dog nosing something smelly on the pavement, he careened around the corner into an older, quieter street of smaller houses and shops that stretched out before him like a long, empty shooting gallery.

"Dia," he breathed in dismay, clamping one hand to the crown of his hat as a cold wind gusted up the length of street. The mouth of a narrow lane opened up to his left and he darted down it. *Please don't let this be a dead end, please don't let this be a dead end,* he prayed.

His heart singing with joyous thanks, Jamie erupted into the colorful, motley turmoil of a small market square filled with vegetable and fruit sellers, butcher shops and fish stalls, their tattered striped awnings flapping in the wind. The air was thick with the pungent smells of raw meat, earth-encrusted carrots and turnips, and fish. Dogs barked; a donkey brayed; someone shouted as Jamie tore across the square, leaping over the outstretched long handles of a half-empty barrow and swerving around a fruit seller who was beginning to pack up. His feet slipping and sliding on a mush of fresh manure, pungent cabbage leaves, and rotten tomatoes, Jamie didn't dare take the time to look back. But he knew the Viscount was still behind him, could hear the vendors calling out to him, recognized the clatter of his vaguely uneven gait on the square's worn old cobblestones.

It wasn't until Jamie reached the entrance to the lane that opened up on the far side of the market that he risked throwing a quick glance back over his shoulder. He felt his breath catch in his throat when he saw that, if anything, the Viscount had gained on him. For one frozen moment, Devlin's intense, furious gaze caught Jamie's, and Jamie found his step faltering. Then a stall-keeper staggering beneath a heavy bin swung around without looking, knocking the Viscount off-balance to send him careening into the rickety fish stall behind him. The stand collapsed with a crack of splintering wood and an outraged howl from the infuriated fishwife.

"*Sweet and merciful Jesus,*" whispered Jamie, and took off.

Half an hour later, Sebastian drew up before his Brook Street house. He was sorely out of temper, bruised, and smelling strongly of fish.

"See to the chestnuts," he told Tom. "Then I want you to do what you can to find that damned boy, Jamie Gallagher. But I want you to be careful," he added as the tiger scrambled forward to take the reins.

Tom looked vaguely insulted. "Careful of a *boy*?"

"Yes, of a boy," said Sebastian, grunting when he hopped down from the curricle's high seat and landed with most of his weight on his bad leg. "I'm not entirely convinced his part in all this is as innocent as he would have us believe."

Chapter 32

Jules Calhoun picked up the slime-smeared coat with one crooked finger, his nose crinkling as he held it out at arm's length. A lean, lithe man with straight fair hair and even features, the valet had been with Sebastian nearly five years now and had never yet complained about the havoc the pursuit of murderers tended to wreak on Devlin's wardrobe. But then, that could be because he had started life in one of London's most infamous flash houses.

"And to think you've only worn it twice," he said with a sigh. "But I'll try, my lord."

"You'll never get the smell out of it," said Sebastian, stripping off his cravat and dropping it on top of his muck-stained white silk waistcoat. "Tell me this: Is your mother likely to be at the Blue Anchor or the Red Lion tonight?"

Calhoun looked over at him. "The Red Lion, I should think, my lord. Shall I ready the new Bath superfine?"

"For dinner, yes." Sebastian peeled off his grimy shirt and

tossed it atop the growing pile. "But after that I'll be needing something a little different."

Several hours later, inconspicuously clad in a black cravat, worn shirt, stained breeches, and battered brown corduroy coat—all culled from the secondhand stalls of Rosemary Lane—Sebastian trolled a string of cheap public houses and gin shops that stretched from Soho to Covent Garden and beyond. These were the kinds of establishments favored by dockers and drovers; bricklayers, costermongers, and navvies; thieves, fences, prostitutes, and various others stigmatized by the likes of Lady Hester and the Reverend Crispin Carmichael as the "lower orders."

Sebastian slipped easily through the rough, boisterous crowds, for he'd learned long ago that an effective disguise involves more than a simple change of clothing; it requires a man to alter his entire way of walking and standing, of holding his head and looking at the world. Gone was the proud, confident Earl's heir; in his place was a slump-shouldered man who knew what it was like to go to bed cold and hungry night after night; who knew the fear of Newgate and the hangman's noose and the threat of transportation to Botany Bay. He bought endless foaming tankards of beer and shots of Blue Ruin, none of which he ever got around to drinking; he listened to men's jokes and tirades, asked a few carefully worded, strategic questions, and eventually ended up at the Red Lion.

Tucked away on an ancient side street not far from the death-haunted expanse of Smithfield, the Red Lion was a ramshackle, Tudor-era inn notorious as the haunt of housebreakers, footpads, highwaymen, and whores. He found the taproom crowded with a motley collection of its usual clientele, its heavy-beamed low ceiling and ancient walnut wainscoting dark with the smoke of centuries and the worn flagstone paving underfoot strewn with sawdust. Buying a pint from the brawny, stony-faced ex-prizefighter behind the bar, Sebastian retreated to an empty table near the cold hearth and waited.

Slowly sipping his beer, Sebastian watched the former pugilist disappear through a doorway behind the bar, then reappear a moment later. A couple of highwaymen who'd been sitting at a nearby corner table slipped away; a tattered, aging streetwalker in a torn red dress came in, quickly drank a tankard of ale while still standing at the bar, and left again. Then a tall, upright woman with thick black hair only beginning to be touched by gray appeared from behind the bar to walk up to Sebastian's table. Now somewhere in her fifties, she was still a handsome woman, with fine bone structure, a graceful carriage, and dark, knowing eyes.

"I know you're not here for the beer," said Grace Calhoun, settling in the seat opposite Sebastian to fix him with a steady stare.

He raised his tankard and took a deep swallow. "Not exactly, although I'll admit it's welcome."

She leaned back in her chair, her eyes hooded, her face giving nothing away. She was a formidable woman, uneducated but brilliant and shrewd and more than a bit ruthless—as one would expect of someone who ran two of the most notorious flash houses in all of London. "Jules tells us you're lookin' into the murders on Swallow Street."

"You know anything about them?"

"Why would I?"

He took another sip of his drink. "Did you know Harry McGregor?"

She huffed a soft, muffled laugh. "I hear Bow Street's thinkin' about pinnin' Farnsworth's killing on Harry and then trying to claim he shot and hanged himself." She pressed her lips together and gave a disbelieving shake of her head. "Poor Harry, he wasn't just half-hanged; he was half-crazy. I ain't sayin' he wasn't capable of killing Farnsworth, but there's no way he would have bothered to string the bastard up in some fancy pose like that. And he sure as hell wouldn't hang himself."

"That was pretty much my thinking." Sebastian swiped the pad of one thumb at a line of foam trailing down the side of his tankard. "I hear you told Farnsworth you'd like to put his head on a pike."

"No; what I said was I'd like to *see* his head on a pike." She tipped her head to one side, studying him thoughtfully for a moment. "Where did you get that from, anyway?"

"Does it matter?"

"It might." A faint smile played about the corners of her lips. "I must have scared him more than I'd realized."

"So what did he do to you to inspire you with such a bloodthirsty ambition?"

"He didn't do anything to me; his kind know better than to go after anyone who's liable to fight back—and fight back dirty. It's what he did to another publican I know."

"Lionel Sykes?"

Her eyes narrowed. "Where'd you hear about him?"

"From the same source."

She was thoughtful a moment. "I can't see why someone would be tryin' to stick these killings on Lionel. It's true that Farnsworth ruined him, but then, Farnsworth ruined a lot of people. And Lionel, he's a gentle soul."

"How well do you know him?"

"Well enough." She rested her forearms on the table and leaned into them, her features unreadable. "It's a nasty trick that damned Society plays on the publicans they've decided to target. They send a young woman to pretend to faint outside his house on a

Sunday, and then when the publican kindly offers the woman something to drink, the bastards haul the poor sucker up before the magistrates for trading on the Sabbath."

"But the fine isn't exactly ruinous, is it?"

"No, because the law they have to use is so old. But they have other tricks, too, and they played them all on Lionel. Poor man had just lost one of his daughters, but Farnsworth didn't care. He eventually convinced the Home Secretary that Lionel's pub had become a hotbed of Radicals, so they yanked his license."

"Was it? A hotbed of Radicals, I mean."

Again that faint smile. "Maybe. There's lots of hungry, out-of-work men around these days."

"Where would I find Sykes now?"

The smile was gone. "Even if I knew, you think I'd tell you?"

"I mean him no harm."

"That don't mean no harm would come to him, and you know it."

Sebastian wasn't going to deny it. He said, "Who do you think killed Farnsworth?"

She flattened her hands on the battered old tabletop and stood up. "I neither know nor care. That man hid a dark, nasty soul behind a show of canting holiness. He obviously messed with the wrong person and paid for it, and the world is better off because of it." She started to turn away, then paused, her gaze on his face. "Why do you even care? Why waste your time tryin' to figure out who killed him?"

"Because the authorities are going to blame someone for this murder, and if I can't find the real killer, then they'll hang some innocent like your friend Lionel Sykes." *Or Hugh,* he thought, but didn't say. He drained his tankard and set it aside. "You wouldn't happen to know a young Irish lad named Jamie Gallagher, would you? An orphan, maybe fourteen or fifteen, but looks younger?"

"Never heard of him. What's he have to do with any of this?"

"He claims to have found Lord Preston's body."

"'Claims'? You thinkin' he didn't?"

"Honestly?" Sebastian pushed back his chair and rose to his feet. "I don't know what to think at this point."

"So did you learn anything?" Hero asked, later, as she lay in Sebastian's arms.

He ran his hand up and down her side. "Not really. I learned that the 'morally deficient orders' of this city despised Lord Preston every bit as much as he despised them—and with good reason. From what I was hearing tonight, he ruined a lot of people's lives—or at least increased the burdens on lives that were already difficult enough. But that's not exactly a surprise, is it? If he'd been hit over the head and left to bleed to death in some dark alley, then we'd be looking at hundreds of suspects—if not more."

"But that's not what happened."

"No." He drew her closer. "And I'll be damned if I can figure out why."

Chapter 33

Friday, 23 *August*

Early the next morning, Paul Gibson was washing his hands in a basin of pink-tinged water when Sebastian came to stand in the open doorway of the surgeon's stone outbuilding. What was left of Half-Hanged Harry still lay on the stone slab in the center of the room, eviscerated and pale in the early-morning light.

"Finished?"

Gibson nodded and reached for a ragged towel to dry his hands. "Just now. But if you're looking for answers, I don't have any. He was shot, then hanged. That's all I can tell you."

"Was he dead before he was hanged?"

"I'd say so. The bullet severed one of the arteries to his lungs; he would have drowned in his own blood within minutes."

"Hopefully that was quick enough." Sebastian remembered Sanson, Paris's longtime public executioner, telling him once that the human brain remains aware for at least one to two minutes after death. And who should know better than a man who had chopped the heads off literally thousands of people?

He forced himself to look again at what was left of Harry McGregor, at the thick purple wheal-like scar left around his neck by the rope the Crown had used to try to hang him fifteen years before; at the shackle scars on his wrists and ankles cut deep by his years as a convict in Botany Bay; at an old knife scar on his side. "He lived a hard life."

"That he did. His back is nothing but scar tissue on scar tissue. I wouldn't want to try to guess how many times he was flogged."

Sebastian moved over to study the chipped enameled bowl containing the contents of the dead man's pockets: a simple clay pipe, a few coins, a broken comb. "Nothing interesting?"

"Nothing."

He turned to meet his friend's worried gaze.

"You've no idea who's doing this?" said Gibson, his arms hanging loose at his sides as he leaned back against the wooden shelf behind him.

Shaking his head, Sebastian went to stand in the open doorway and draw the cool, damp air of the morning deep into his lungs.

That same gray morning, Hero paid a call on the Tothill Fields Bridewell.

The original Bridewell lay in London, in a cluster of decrepit brick buildings that had once formed part of an early sixteenth-century palace of Henry VIII. The palace had taken its name from the nearby St. Bride's Church and its ancient holy well, and when Henry's son, Edward VI, handed the palace over to the City of London for the incarceration of vagrants, beggars, petty criminals, and "wayward women," the name Bridewell went with it. There were now well over a hundred such institutions, all called Bridewells, scattered across England. They were considered "houses of correction" rather than prisons, for their purpose was not simply to imprison those guilty of disorderly behavior but to "correct" it through the use of hard labor, rigid discipline, and liberal use of the whip.

The Westminster Bridewell lay near Vincent Square in the wretched southwestern part of the city known as Tothill Fields. When Hero's yellow-bodied carriage and snorting team of fine blacks drew up before the Bridewell's forbidding stone doorway, a troop of soldiers in the nearby artillery ground, a gang of schoolboys, and a passing farmer all turned to stare. She sent one of her liveried footmen to warn the keeper of her imminent arrival and was still descending the carriage steps at a leisurely pace when the man came hurrying out to greet her. It wasn't often that someone like Mr. Horace Bottomley received a visit from such an important personage as the daughter of the Regent's most formidable cousin.

"Lady Devlin—*dear* Lady Devlin!" he exclaimed, bowing low. "Welcome! Such an honor. Such a great honor." A small, plump-faced man in his middle years with a balding head, round belly, and pasty complexion, he clasped his hands together and brought them up to hold them tucked beneath his chin as he straightened. He had a determined smile plastered on his face, but his small, watery eyes were tense and wary. There was a growing campaign initiated by Quakers such as Elizabeth Fry to improve the brutal, inhumane conditions that existed in British prisons, and it was obvious that Mr. Bottomley feared his Bridewell was about to become the social reformers' next target. He cleared his throat. "How very kind of you to pay us a visit."

Keeping her expression solemn, Hero ran a critical eye over the miserable huddle of ancient buildings. "When was this Bridewell built?"

"In 1618, my lady," he said proudly with another bow. "Then expanded in 1675."

"So it's nearly two hundred years old. I must say, it does look it, doesn't it?"

Mr. Bottomley swallowed. "If you've come for a tour of the facility—"

Hero brought her gaze back to his face. "Yes, I would like to arrange an inspection, perhaps for sometime next week. But today I'm interested in speaking to one of your inmates, a woman named Letitia Lamont."

The frozen smile slid off Mr. Bottomley's face as his eyes bulged. "Letitia Lamont? You want to see Letitia Lamont?"

"Yes. She is here, is she not?"

Bottomley cleared his throat again. "Oh, yes; she's here."

It was decided that the best place for Hero to interview the woman was in what Horace Bottomley called the "passroom." It turned out to be a long, narrow hall lined on each side with a row of crude low wooden boxes, each with a thin layer of dirty straw. It took Hero a moment to realize they were beds—of a sort. The Bridewells were the only prisons in London that provided their inmates with any bedding at all. The Bridewells were also one of the few such institutions that regularly kept their female inmates separate from the men or provided the women with female matrons rather than predatory male guards.

The passroom was empty, for the women who slept in these crude wooden boxes were in the workroom engaged in the mindless, painful task of picking oakum. While she waited for Letitia to be brought to her, Hero went to stand at the small barred window cut high into the room's end wall. It was so high that most of the inmates were probably unable to see out of it, and its view of the foggy, soot-stained brick courtyard beyond was wretched. As she watched the rivulets of rain chase each other down the dirty glass, Hero felt a chill crawl up her spine and found she had to take a deep breath.

The sound of approaching footsteps brought her back around.

"Here she is, Lady Devlin," announced the matron, a stout, middle-aged woman in a brown stuff gown topped by a bulky knitted shawl. "Go on, get in there—and mind yer manners, ye hear?" she hissed to the woman beside her.

In the course of her research for various projects, Hero had met dozens of prostitutes of all ages. A few were gay and saucy, but most were either bitter and defiant or frightened and ashamed. And all of those interviews had left her with a deep and abiding loathing for women such as Letitia Lamont who preyed upon and exploited their more vulnerable sisters. Abbesses, they were called, or procuresses, madams, whoremistresses, bawds, panderers, and nymphkeepers. They were almost without exception vicious, predatory, and utterly amoral. Brutal, merciless, and pitiless, they preyed on the young, the weak, the helpless, the innocent and ignorant. Most such women were old crones, and that was what Hero had been expecting.

But the woman who called herself Letitia Lamont was probably no more than thirty-five or forty and not unattractive, with a narrow face and pale hair that would have been beautiful if it weren't so lank and dirty. In defiance of her surroundings, her carriage was proud, although her cheap, worn uniform hung on her thin frame in a way that suggested she had lost weight during her months in the house of correction. But then, Bridewells were not known for feeding their charges well, and one of their favorite forms of punishment was withholding food from troublesome inmates.

The woman paused just inside the doorway, her hands on her hips, an insolent smile curling her lips as she regarded Hero across the width of the room. "Well, well, well; look at the fine lady who wants to talk to me."

"You're Letitia Lamont?" said Hero.

The woman pursed her lips and struck a pose. "If that's who you want me to be."

"She's Letitia," growled the matron, giving the abbess a nudge. "And remember what I told ye."

The look the abbess flashed the woman was fierce enough to make even that hardened matron take a step back.

"Thank you, Matron," said Hero. "You may wait outside the door. I'll call you when we're finished."

The matron hesitated a moment, then withdrew.

"Not afraid to be alone with me?" said Letitia, turning her cold pale blue eyes on Hero.

"No."

The abbess's accent was not what Hero had expected. Not East End London, but what sounded more like Kent. Her diction was also surprisingly good. Either she had been born into a different social stratum than the one she now occupied, or she had worked very hard to elevate her speech. Impossible not to wonder about this woman's life, about what had brought her to . . . this.

As if sizing Hero up as a candidate for one of her houses, the abbess let her gaze rove over Hero, taking in her fine green wool carriage gown, the dashing hat with its two nodding cream plumes. "Bit of a Long Meg, aren't you?" she said at last. "You'd have a hard time if you ever had to make a living on the streets. Men don't like tupping a woman who towers over them when they take her up against an alley wall."

It was said to shock, but Hero had dealt with her kind before. She shrugged. "Understandable, I suppose."

Something that might have been disappointment flickered behind the woman's wintry eyes. She took a step closer and tried again, letting her accent become broader, more common, until Hero was left wondering which was real and which assumed. "Hard t' do it standin' up when ye're so mismatched. A fellow'd need a step stool to take ye like that, wouldn't he?" She leaned in even closer. "Ye ever done it standin' up?"

"Actually, yes."

"Huh." The woman met Hero's gaze and held it. "I think perhaps you have." Letitia shrugged and swung away, her more careful diction returning. "Why do you want to talk to me, anyway?"

"I'd like to ask you some questions about Lord Preston Farnsworth."

Whatever the woman had been expecting, it wasn't that. She turned back around. "Oh, you would, would you? And why the bloody hell should I answer these questions of yours?"

"Because I'll pay you a pound."

"Make it three, and I'll consider it."

Hero drew a pound from her reticule and held it out. "One now, one afterward—*if* you're cooperative, and if I'm satisfied as to the veracity of your answers."

Letitia plucked the money from Hero's hand. "Deal." Tucking the coin into the bodice of her gown, she wandered the room, fiddling absently with this and that.

Hero stayed where she was, watching her. "How long have you been here, in the Tothill Fields Bridewell?"

"What time is it?"

"Just past ten."

Letitia paused, her head falling back as she stared up at the ancient, heavily beamed ceiling. "Let's see . . . five months, twenty-nine days, and eighteen hours."

"You were given six months?"

"It's the usual sentence."

"From what I hear, you were lucky to be sent here rather than to Newgate."

"Lucky? You think so?" The woman turned to face her again, holding out red, swollen hands with torn nails and open, weeping sores. "They don't make you pick oakum till your hands bleed in Newgate. In Newgate, I could've worn my own clothes and bought myself a real bed—along with real food and water to wash with."

Anyone else, Hero might have felt sorry for. But not this woman; not someone who'd earned the money to buy such comforts by luring innocent, ignorant girls fresh up from the country into a brutal life of exploitation, degradation, shame, and early death.

Hero had to work to tamp down her revulsion and keep her voice even, unemotional. "I'm told Lord Preston Farnsworth was responsible for your arrest and conviction. Is that true?"

The abbess's brows drew together in a quick frown. "And if he was?"

"You know he's dead?"

A tight, fierce smile curled the woman's lips. "Not only dead, but hung upside down like a gutted pig. That must've been a fine sight to see." Her eyes narrowed. "Is that why you're here? You thinkin' I killed him?" Her accent was slipping again as she waved one hand through the air in a gesture that took in the grim narrow room, the dirty barred window, the stout matron waiting outside the open door. "And how ye reckon I managed that from in here?"

"With the help of your bully boys. A woman like you must have them."

Letitia laughed. "Oh? And what's a fine lady such as yourself know about bully boys?"

"Not a great deal, but enough."

The laughter went out of the woman's face instantly in a way that sent another chill down Hero's spine. There was something palpably evil about this woman; evil and dangerous. Hero had the unshakable conviction when she looked into the abbess's eyes that she was staring into a yawning abyss; that there was no soul within, only grasping selfishness and unbridled desire.

Letitia shrugged her thin shoulders. "I didn't kill him. I'm not denying I'd like to have—I might even have been planning on it. But someone beat me to it."

"So who do you think did kill him?"

"How the hell would I know? There must be a hundred or more people out there who'd have stood in line for the chance to do in the bugger, and hundreds more who'd cheer 'em on." She paused, her expression becoming shrewd, speculative. "Why you care, anyway? What was he to you?"

"Absolutely nothing."

"Then why you here, askin' me all these questions? *Paying* me so's you can ask them?"

"Does it matter?"

"It might." She walked back to Hero, not stopping until she was right in front of her. "Tell me this: Has Bow Street found his rooms yet?"

Whatever Hero had been expecting, it wasn't that. "What rooms?"

The saucy smile was back on the woman's face. "He kept them, you know."

"For what purpose?" As soon as she'd said it, Hero realized the answer was obvious.

Letitia leaned forward, her eyes going wide as she said in a husky, suggestive whisper, "Use yer imagination, yer ladyship."

Hero had to force herself to stand still and not take a step back. "And precisely where are these rooms supposed to be located?"

Letitia straightened. "Now? I've no idea. Six months ago, they were in Jermyn, but I doubt they're still there. He changed them regularly, you know."

Hero studied the woman's hard, mocking face. "You can't say where these rooms are, and yet you expect me to believe they exist?"

"Oh, they exist, all right." Letitia held out her hand, palm upward, fingers curled. "And you owe me another pound."

Chapter 34

"Do you think she had him killed?" Devlin asked later, when Hero told him of her encounter with the abbess.

"I wouldn't put it past her," said Hero, more troubled by her visit to the Bridewell than she was willing to admit even to herself. "I don't think I'd put anything past that woman. Do you think she could be telling the truth about Farnsworth's 'rooms'?"

"Well, it would fit with the French letters Gibson found in his pocket, wouldn't it?"

"It would. So whom did he entertain there? A mistress? Or women he acquired more . . ." She hesitated, searching for the right word, and finally settled on "casually."

Devlin met her gaze. "If a woman like Letitia Lamont knows about them, I'd say it was probably the latter. Wouldn't you?"

She nodded. "That's what I was thinking."

Sebastian was at his desk, writing a quick note to Lovejoy, when he heard the sounds of a carriage drawing up before the house. He caught the imperious tone of a woman's familiar voice addressing her coachman and set aside his pen. He listened as Morey moved to open the front door; heard the woman's curt reply to the majordomo's polite greetings.

"He's in the library, is he?" she said. "Don't bother; I'll announce myself."

Sebastian pushed to his feet just as a woman in a somber black hat and exquisitely cut carriage gown of black-trimmed, fine gray bombazine appeared in the library doorway. Her late husband, Martin, Lord Wilcox, had been dead for over five years, but she still wore half mourning for him in a display of affection and devotion that was utterly, almost offensively false. She had despised Martin for years and was heartily glad he was dead.

"Good morning, Amanda," said Sebastian, coming around from behind his desk. "What brings you here today?"

His sister drew up just inside the doorway. Now in her mid-forties, she had inherited their mother's golden hair and thin, elegant form, but her blunt features were all Hendon's. With twelve years between them, the siblings had never been close, even when young. She had hated Sebastian from the day of his birth, and though it puzzled him growing up, he now understood it only too well. "To what do we owe this . . . pleasure?"

She stared at him long enough to make him remember that the side of his face still bore a yellowing bruise and half-healed abrasion from his would-be assassin's cudgel. She said, "You are doing it again, aren't you? Involving yourself in Bow Street's investigation of Lord Preston's murder."

It had always enraged her that the man known to the world as her father's son and heir should involve himself in such a plebeian activity. But unlike Hendon, who worried about the dangers Sebastian might encounter, Amanda was concerned only with herself and the effect her brother's unseemly conduct might have on her own social standing.

"That's right," said Sebastian. "But given that Stephanie is now happily married, and with Bayard unlikely to enter into any matrimonial ventures in the near future—" He broke off. "At least, I assume that's unlikely?"

"As it happens, you could not be more wrong." She said it frigidly, for they both knew there was something not quite right with her only surviving son, the new Lord Wilcox. "Indeed, the betrothal should be announced next week."

"Interesting. Congratulations. So that's why my activities have brought you here today to badger me, is it?"

"I am not here to 'badger' you," she said crossly, yanking off her gloves as she went to hold her hands out to the small fire he had kindled on the hearth.

"May I offer you some wine?" he said, going to where a collection of carafes and glasses rested on a tray.

"No, thank you."

"I hope you won't mind if I do." He reached for one of the carafes and lifted the stopper before looking over at her again. "So, then, why exactly are you here, Amanda?"

"I am here because, despite all the experience you've had dealing with these things over the last five years, you seem to be making a ridiculous muddle of this. One would think you'd be better at it."

He was getting confused. "Better at what?"

"Catching Preston's murderer, of course!"

Not "Lord Preston," he noticed, but simply "Preston."

"Ah. I was forgetting you were friends with both Lady Hester and her brother."

"Yes, good friends," she said stiffly. "He was such a worthy, admirable man. I still can't believe this happened to him."

Sebastian studied her half-averted face. "When did you last see him?"

She brought up a hand to shade her eyes for a moment before letting it fall to her side. "It must have been last Friday. Yes, Friday."

"Did he seem nervous to you in any way? Troubled? Preoccupied?"

"No, not at all. I don't believe he had any premonition or warning of what was about to befall him. Who would have expected it, after all these years?"

"After all what years?"

She stiffened. "Are you being deliberately obtuse? Or are you so blinded by your friendship with the man that you refuse to see what is obvious to everyone else?"

Sebastian took a long, deep drink of his wine. "Hugh Chandler—at least, I assume you're referring to Hugh—had nothing to do with what happened to Farnsworth. He had no motive to kill the man."

She stared at him. "No motive? How can you say that? He was forced to pay twenty thousand pounds for his shameful, disgusting behavior. *Twenty thousand pounds.*"

"That happened six years ago."

"So the man was cold and calculating enough to allow some time to pass before he struck. Apart from which, you forget that with Lady Theresa a widow, he will now be free to marry the trollop."

"They've been living together quite happily without benefit of clergy for years. I don't think making it legal is as important to them as you evidently think it should be."

"Really, Devlin? Really? You forget that, with Preston dead, Lady Theresa will now recover her dowry. It was quite substantial, you know, and I think you'll find that your friend Major Chandler is very much in need of an infusion of cash."

Sebastian took another long, slow sip of his wine. Perhaps because of his unwillingness to believe Hugh guilty of murder, this was one aspect of Farnsworth's death that he had failed to consider. By law, a man retained control of his wife's property in the event of a separation of goods or even a divorce. Or at least, he retained control of her property until his death, at which point it reverted to the estranged wife. And Sebastian knew only too well that Hugh was hurting financially; the reversion of Tess's dowry would be an enormous relief to them.

"*Quite* a substantial sum," Amanda said again, oblivious to the effect her words had had on him.

"Anything else, Amanda?" He kept his voice bland. Bored. "Can you think of anything else that might shed light on what happened to Farnsworth?"

She stared at him. "At this point, don't you have enough?"

"No."

"Well," she said, drawing on her gloves again with quick, angry jerks. "Let us hope that Bow Street has the sense not to allow this willful blindness of yours to prevent them from bringing that vile miscreant to justice." She gave a regal inclination of her head, said, "Devlin," and swept from the room.

Draining his wineglass, Sebastian went to stand at the window, his gaze on the raindrops pockmarking the puddles in the street as his sister waited, one foot tapping with impatience, while her carriage steps were let down.

"Damn," he said softly. *Damn, damn, damn.*

Chapter 35

With Tom off chasing down Jamie Gallagher and the sky above the city heavy with the threat of more rain, Sebastian ordered his carriage brought round. As they set off for Chelsea, he settled back against the plush squabs and crossed his arms at his chest, his thoughts in a dark place.

It had been—what? Three days? No, four, he realized, since he'd found Lord Preston Farnsworth dangling upside down in the dank ruins of that chapel off Swallow Street. And he felt no closer now to understanding what had happened to the man than he had on that first day.

Lord Preston had been a man liked and respected by such worthies as the Rector of St. George's and the Chief Magistrates of both Bow Street and Great Marlborough Street. And yet he'd been heartily despised by everyone from his own estranged wife to the various members of the "lower orders" who had suffered from his determination to rid London of those he considered "undesirable elements." So where lay the truth? Sebastian wondered. Had Farnsworth been an admirable man who dedicated his life to such worthy causes as ending the slave trade and making his city a safer place for women and children? Or was he a sanctimonious hypocrite who had made his wife's life miserable and kept rooms where he secretly indulged his lust for the very kind of women he claimed to despise?

Sebastian was inclined to believe the latter. But was that because he had a constitutional dislike of crusading, self-anointed saints, or because he was desperate to ignore the evidence that pointed to his old friend as the obvious killer?

No, Sebastian finally decided; he wasn't exactly ignoring it, but he couldn't deny that he had discounted Hugh's potential culpability more than he probably should have. For many men in Hugh's precarious financial position, Tess's dowry would be motivation enough for murder. Add to that a desire for revenge and the chance to finally marry the woman he'd long loved, and if Hugh were to be indicted, he'd have precious little chance of convincing any jury that he was innocent.

Bloody fool, thought Sebastian. Bloody, bloody fool.

As the carriage turned in through the manor's modest gateway, Sebastian could see Hugh standing at the edge of his shrubbery, deep in conversation with an aged man in a broad hat and farmer's smock. But at the sound of the approaching carriage, Hugh turned his head, his eyes narrowing as he recognized the horses. For a moment he hesitated; then he said something to the farmer and walked forward to meet the carriage as it drew up before the small brick house.

"Why do I get the feeling I'm not going to like what you're here to tell me?" he said as Sebastian opened the carriage door and hopped out without bothering to let down the steps.

"A guilty conscience, perhaps?"

Hugh's nostrils flared on a quick, angry intake of air. "What the hell is that supposed to mean?"

Sebastian turned to issue instructions to his coachman, then said to Hugh, "Let's go for a walk."

They followed a narrow country lane that wound through trees still dripping from the recent rain.

Sebastian waited until they were out of earshot of the house before saying bluntly, "I've just been reminded that in addition to allowing Tess to remarry, Farnsworth's death means she'll now be able to recover her dowry—and I'm told her dowry was substantial. Why the bloody hell didn't you say something about it?"

Hugh was silent for a moment, a muscle jumping along his jawbone. "What makes you so certain I simply wasn't thinking about it?"

"How much is it?"

"Somewhere in the neighborhood of thirty thousand pounds."

Sebastian whistled. "You were thinking about it," he said, and after a moment, Hugh nodded.

Sebastian drew up and turned to face him. "Is there anything else? Anything at all that you haven't told me?"

"No. I swear."

Sebastian studied his friend's shuttered white face and wished he could believe him. "I hope to God you're telling me the truth. When was the last time you saw Farnsworth?"

Hugh stared out over the misty sweep of his fields. "I don't know. It's been a long time. I generally tried to avoid the man as much as possible."

"Why?"

Hugh looked at him. "What do you mean, why? Because whenever I saw him, I wanted to smash his face in and choke the life out of the bloody bastard. Why the hell do you think?"

Sebastian found himself giving his friend a crooked smile. "If anyone else asks you that question, I suggest you come up with a less incriminating answer."

Hugh ran a shaky hand down over his face. "It looks bad, doesn't it? You haven't found anything—anything at all—that might explain what happened to him?"

"I'm not sure. It would help if I could talk to Tess. How is she?"

Hugh huffed a soft laugh. "Angry at you."

"Still?"

"Yes. Mainly I think because she's . . . afraid."

It was a telling admission. "Afraid you're going to be unjustly charged with Farnsworth's murder? Or afraid because she's not convinced that you didn't do it?"

Hugh sucked in a deep breath, then let it out in a harsh sigh. "Both."

They found Lady Tess seated beside the fire in the house's small parlor, an embroidery frame lying forgotten on her lap, her gaze fixed in an abstracted way on the flickering flames on the hearth.

At the sight of Sebastian, she stiffened, but Hugh went to crouch down beside her and take both her hands in his. He spoke to her in low, urgent tones that Sebastian tried hard not to listen to. Her hands trembled in Hugh's; then she nodded and looked over at Sebastian.

"What is it?" she said, her voice rough. "What do you need from me?"

Sebastian went to stand on the far side of the fire, his hat dangling from the fingers of one hand. "Do you know if Lord Preston maintained rooms somewhere? Secret rooms where he either kept a mistress or . . ." Sebastian searched for a gentler way to express it and finally settled on "took women?"

She stared at him blankly. "No. I mean, I'm not saying he didn't. But if he did, I didn't know about it."

"Who would be likely to know?"

She thought about it a moment. "His valet, surely. But beyond that I can't think of anyone. Most of his friends and colleagues were in the Society for the Suppression of Vice, and that's not the sort of thing he would have been likely to share with them, now, is it?"

"Probably not. What about the chapel off Swallow Street where he was found? Do you know if he had any connection to it—either to the chapel or to the house that once stood there?"

"No. I'd never heard of the place until this happened."

"Did Lord Preston fence?"

Her brows drew together in a puzzled frown. "No. Preston was never what you might call a sporting man. His idea of exercise was his after-dinner walks." She threw a quick glance at Hugh, still crouching beside her. "Why do you ask?"

"Just looking for explanations."

Sebastian saw her hands twist within Hugh's. "What if there is no explanation? What if whoever did this is simply mad? You'd have to be mad to pose a body that way, wouldn't you?"

It was a possibility that had occurred to Sebastian more than once, but he shook his head. "Farnsworth went to Swallow Street that night for some purpose. If we knew what that purpose was, it might help us figure out who killed him. You can't think of any reason—any reason at all—that might have taken him there?"

"No. None. But then, it's been six years since I had anything to do with him. He didn't even live in St. James's Square when we—when I—" She broke off, unwilling to finish the sentence.

"He didn't?"

She shook her head. "He bought the house after he won the lawsuit against Hugh. He couldn't have afforded it otherwise. Preston was never anywhere near as plump in the pocket as he liked to appear, and he isn't—wasn't—nearly as clever with investments as he liked to think he was, either. It's one of the reasons he and Hester went after Quinton-Thomas—because they needed the money. He'd have lost my dowry long ago if Father hadn't tied it up so tightly."

"Any chance he could have been in debt?"

"I suppose it's possible."

As far as Sebastian knew, no one had thought to look into Lord Preston's finances as a potential explanation for his murder. After all, he was a Farnsworth; he lived in an elegant, unusually large house in St. James's Square and devoted his time to furthering the aims of the Society for the Suppression of Vice and other worthy projects.

Aloud, he said, "Do you know if Lord Preston ever had anything to do with the tarot?"

"I know he hated anyone and everyone involved with that sort of thing. Fortune-tellers, astrologers, spiritualists—as far as he was concerned, they were all handmaidens and servants of Satan. The fires of Smithfield were stoked by men like Preston."

"What about you? Have you ever had an interest in the cards?"

"What the devil are you suggesting, Devlin?" swore Hugh, pushing to his feet.

Sebastian kept his gaze on Tess's pale face. "I ask because if you did, it might explain why someone posed Farnsworth's body that way—to make you look like the killer."

She shook her head. "I fooled around with it a bit before I was married—you know, attending séances, having my palm read, that sort of thing. But it was all for fun, and I wouldn't say I did it more than others. And after we were married, Preston made his opinions on the subject quite clear. I wouldn't have dared. As for now . . ." She gave a wry smile. "I don't exactly go to fashionable parties these days, do I?"

"Why do you think someone posed his body like that?"

She shrugged. "To mock him, perhaps? I remember the card, but I can't say I know what it's supposed to mean. Do you?"

"As far as I can tell, it can mean a variety of things. Treachery. Betrayal . . ."

"So perhaps he betrayed someone. Someone he should have known better than to cross. He was always so arrogant, Preston. He thought he was smarter than everyone else. And that can be a dangerous delusion to have, can't it?"

"Yes," said Sebastian. "Yes, it can."

Chapter 36

Later that afternoon, Sebastian paid a visit to the King's Theatre in the Haymarket, looking for a certain young violinist. Even with the opera closed for the season, he managed to find an aged carpenter who was able to give him the address of a cheap lodging house in Piccadilly. After drawing a blank there, Sebastian started making the rounds of public houses known to be the haunts of a group of radical reformers known as the Spenceans. But by the time he left the Cock in Soho, he was running out of options.

At some point in the last several hours the heavy clouds that had been pressing down on the rooftops all day had blown away, leaving the air fresh and the sky a clear periwinkle blue. Then the church bells of the city began to toll the hour, one mournful tone after another, until the low *bong*s drifted away into silence.

Sebastian found himself pausing, his head turning toward the west. And for reasons he couldn't quite have explained, he knew where Damion Pitcairn was.

Because the exclusive Mayfair church of St. George's, Hanover Square, was hemmed in on all four sides by streets, it had no churchyard. The parish was thus forced to inter its dead in completely separate, isolated burial grounds, the newest of which lay on the outskirts of the city, just off Uxbridge Road beyond the Tyburn Turnpike.

Reached through an archway beside a cluster of houses known as St. George's Row, the cemetery was unusually large, taking up all of what had once, within living memory, been a farmer's field. As he wove his way through the labyrinth of ivy-draped table tombs, weathering headstones, and weeping marble maidens, Sebastian could hear the haunting strains of a violin concerto drifting over the otherwise silent burial ground. The last time he'd heard this particular piece, its composer told him it wasn't finished yet.

It was surely finished now.

Following the music, Sebastian came to where the violinist stood before an elaborate marble tomb made in the style of a miniature Greek temple and inscribed on the pediment with the name MCINNIS. The musician was young, in his early twenties, built tall and slim, with tawny skin and a classic profile that always reminded Sebastian of the relief carvings of ancient pharaohs he'd seen half-buried in the sands of Egypt. The man had his eyes closed, his body moving with the fluid, supple grace of a born dancer or master swordsman. And so total was his absorption in his music, and so palpable his grief, that Sebastian regretted coming. He was turning away when the music ended and the man named Damion Pitcairn opened his eyes.

For a long moment they simply stared at each other, the younger man's chest jerking with the agitation of his breathing. Then he said, "How did you know where to find me?"

"A hunch. But I apologize for intruding. We can speak some other time."

"No." Damion lowered his violin. "Now is as good a time as any."

Sebastian glanced at the tomb, remembering the beautiful sixteen-year-old girl and her mother who now lay there. "Do you come here often?"

"Not often, no." Damion crouched down to lay his violin and bow in the case at his feet. "Why did you want to talk to me?"

The first time Sebastian had seen Damion Pitcairn, he'd been taking part in a fencing exhibition staged at Carlton House for the entertainment of the Prince Regent, for in addition to being a talented musician and composer, the young man was brilliant at swordplay. If Damion had been white, he'd have had a promising future ahead of him. But as the son of a Scottish plantation owner and an enslaved woman of Ethiopian and Arab ancestry, his options would forever be limited.

Sebastian found himself hesitating. "I wanted to ask if you still hold fencing lessons in the courtyard of those old ruins in Swallow Street."

Damion's head fell back, his eyes narrowing as he stared up at Sebastian. "What are you thinking? That maybe I killed the bastard they found hanging upside down there?"

"No. But I was wondering if you'd ever seen him around the old house or its chapel. Or if you had any idea why he might have gone there the night he was killed."

Damion shook his head. "It's been so damned wet lately I haven't been there myself in months. I have a friend with a house near Fleet Street who's been letting me use his attic for lessons."

Sebastian watched the younger man fasten the straps of his case. "How do you know Farnsworth was a bastard? Did you ever tangle with him?"

"Me, personally? No. But I know people he's gone after. Good people. And he destroyed them." Damion pushed to his feet. "Why do you care who killed him? The world's a far better place without that rotter in it."

"You aren't the first person who's said that to me. Who do you know that Farnsworth went after?"

For a moment, Sebastian didn't think the man was going to answer. Then he readjusted his hold on his violin case and said, "Ever hear of Barnabas Price?"

"The man who used to print the *Poor Man's Weekly*?"

Pitcairn nodded. "That's right. He also used to publish things like Thomas Paine's *Rights of Man* and *Common Sense* in cheap editions that workingmen could afford. Farnsworth hated him. As far as his lordship was concerned, Price was Robespierre, Pontius Pilate, and Beelzebub all rolled into one. It took a while, but Farnsworth finally managed to have Barnabas arrested and convicted of blasphemy, libel, and sedition. Except that while Barnabas was in prison, his wife, Beth, kept publishing the paper. So then Farnsworth went after *her*."

He paused, his jaw hardening. "She was just twenty-three years old, brilliant, funny, kindhearted, and fiercely passionate about the need for reform and the ending of ancient privileges. She was also very pretty, so Farnsworth offered to make sure she didn't go to prison if she'd fuck him."

"Did she?"

"She spit in his face. So Farnsworth had the Society prosecute her. She died in Newgate of jail fever."

"When was this?

"That she died? Maybe a year ago."

"And Barnabas Price? Is he still in prison?"

Damion shook his head. "His sentence expired a couple of months ago. Last I heard, he was planning to emigrate to America."

"Did he actually go?"

"Why would he stay here?" Damion threw Sebastian a hard look. "What are you thinking now? That Price might have killed the man?" He jerked his chin toward the city that stretched out far to their east. "There must be hundreds of people out there who hated Lord Preston Farnsworth. Hundreds. Any one of them could have killed him."

"How many of them do you think are familiar with the tarot?"

Something flickered in the younger man's eyes, something quickly hidden by the downward sweep of his lashes. "That I don't know."

As the two men turned to walk toward the gate, Sebastian said, "Did Farnsworth do that often? Offer to keep women out of prison in exchange for sexual favors, I mean."

"It's the only instance I know the particulars of. But the man had a reputation on the streets."

"A reputation for what?"

"Abusing women. Hurting them. Not just hurting them, but humiliating them." Damion paused and turned to face him again. "You find that hard to believe?"

"No, not at all," said Sebastian. "Do you know if he kept rooms someplace? Someplace where he could take women?"

"I don't know, but it makes sense that he would, doesn't it? I mean, what was he going to do? Take them back to that grand house on St. James's Square that he shared with his sister?"

"Who would know? Can you think of anyone?"

"Me? No. And to be honest, I'm not sure I'd tell you even if I did."

"I don't intend to allow some innocent man to be hanged for this murder, if that's what you're afraid of."

For a long moment, Damion stared at him. Then, with a swordsman's uncanny ability to read an opponent, he said, "That's why you're doing this, isn't it? Because someone you know is a suspect."

"That's part of it, yes."

Sebastian thought he might ask about the other part, but he didn't.

Chapter 37

Saturday, 24 *August*

The inquest into the death of the man who had attacked Sebastian in Golden Square took place at nine o'clock the next morning in a small, stuffy room at the parish workhouse. His assailant had been identified as Joe Pots, a common thug well-known to the local authorities, and the inquest was a brief, perfunctory formality that attracted none of the popular interest that had swirled around Lord Preston's inquest.

The verdict exonerating Sebastian of any wrongdoing came swiftly.

Afterward, Lovejoy joined Sebastian at a nearby coffeehouse. The rain had started up again, and Lovejoy shivered as he wrapped his hands around his cup of hot chocolate. "The pressure from the Palace to indict someone for the murder of Lord Preston is becoming more insistent," he said. "I fear it won't be long before Sir Nathaniel makes an arrest."

Sebastian felt a heavy weight pressing on his chest. "So who is the Chief Magistrate planning to charge?"

Lovejoy cleared his throat and looked away.

"It's Major Chandler, is it?"

Lovejoy nodded. "Unless something changes soon. Sir Nathaniel has suspected him from the very beginning. And unfortunately, the Major is the only viable suspect anyone has been able to come up with."

"Because he has no alibi?"

"That and because he has a seemingly endless number of powerful incentives for murder."

"What about Lord Quinton-Thomas?"

"We've verified that his lordship was at his club until shortly before nine o'clock that evening, at which point he walked home and went to bed. We've confirmed that chronology of events with both his club and his servants."

Sebastian watched the steam rising from his hot coffee. "We've been assuming Lord Preston was killed shortly after he left his house at half past seven that evening, but we don't really know for certain, do we? He could have been killed much later—as late as the following morning. Especially if he kept rooms someplace."

"True." Lovejoy drew a deep breath that flared his nostrils. "There was initially some talk of blaming Lord Preston's murder on Half-Hanged Harry, but the surgeon's report as to the lethal nature of the gunshot wound to the scoundrel's chest would make any attempt to portray his subsequent hanging as a suicide ridiculous."

"When is Harry's inquest?"

"Half past twelve. Given the links between his death and Lord Preston's, I suspect it will be a similar circus."

"I think I'll pass on this one," said Sebastian, taking a cautious sip of his coffee. Fortunately, Bow Street had located some half a dozen men who'd seen and spoken to McGregor between nine and half past ten that night, in three or four different pubs, which eliminated the need for Sebastian himself to testify. "No luck finding anything about the 'secret rooms' Letitia Lamont talked about?"

"Not yet. Lord Preston's man of business says he knows nothing about them but concedes it's possible Farnsworth made the arrangements himself. In fact, he says his client did something similar in the past."

"Interesting."

"Indeed. His valet scoffs at the very idea of their existence. But if the rooms do exist, I find it doubtful the man wouldn't know, and at this point I'm not inclined to believe anything he says. I've set one of the lads to watching him. With any luck, he may very well lead us to them."

"Good idea. Word on the street is that Farnsworth liked to hurt women. Humiliate them. And that he wasn't above using the threat of criminal prosecution to extort sexual favors. That suggests he had someplace to take them."

"A week ago I would have been inclined to dismiss such allegations as nothing more than vicious rumors. But now . . ." He shook his head, his features strained as he stared out at the rain. "On top of everything else, we have another dead Frenchman."

"Another? Who is this one?"

"An eighty-year-old émigré who has been most vocal in his criticism of the behavior of the Bourbons since the Restoration. Found dead in his bed this morning by his valet. Sir Nathaniel has decided the man obviously died in his sleep of old age, so there will be no autopsy."

"More pressure from the Palace?"

"I fear so. According to the man's valet, his master was worried about a possible threat from the Bourbons to someone he knew, a woman named Angélique." He gave the name its French pronunciation. "But we've no idea who she is."

"Angélique?" said Sebastian more sharply than he had intended.

Lovejoy looked up. "You know who she is?"

"It's an unusual name," said Sebastian, and left it at that.

There had been a time when Sebastian could have gone to a certain Irish actress for any badly needed information about the Bourbons and their various allies and enemies. But it had now been over a year since Kat Boleyn left London for the Continent; last he'd heard, she was in Vienna. And so, as Lovejoy hurried off to Half-Hanged Harry's inquest, Sebastian turned his steps toward Golden Square.

Madame Blanchette was paused at a street stall, inspecting a pile of tarnished brass and silver candlesticks, when Sebastian walked up to her.

"Monsieur le vicomte," she said, glancing at him sideways. "We meet again—although I can't imagine what you think I might know about this troublesome dead nobleman of yours that I haven't told you already."

"So tell me about the assassin the Bourbons have sent here to London to kill those they don't like," he said in French.

"Ah. *Lui.*" She kept her gaze on the jumbled pile of metal before her. "Unfortunately, when a royal family believe themselves anointed by God, it's an easy step from there to the conviction that anyone who dares to criticize their dynasty is criticizing God."

"And therefore can be killed without compunction?"

"When you flatter yourself that you're doing God's work, that does follow naturally, does it not?" She studied a delicate, beautifully made candlestick black with age and neglect. "McClellan is this man's most important target, but he has others."

"Such as an eighty-year-old émigré who didn't actually die of old age in his sleep last night?"

She nodded. "There is also a woman. But I believe he doesn't know exactly who she is."

"You mean Angélique?"

Madame Blanchette looked up at him sharply. "What do you know of Angélique?"

"Nothing beyond her name and the fact that Lord Preston was also interested in her. Do you know where she is?"

"Me? No." She asked the stallholder in English for the candlestick's price, haggled with her a moment, then nodded. Returning to French, she said to Sebastian, "What is it you want from me?"

"The assassin's name. Where to find him."

She was silent for so long, slowly counting out her money and handing it to the woman, that he didn't think she was going to answer him. She tucked the candlestick into her string bag, then said, "He calls himself Noël Cartier, although it is not, of course, his real name. As to where you might find him . . . the Bourbons have always been fond of Grillon's and Grenier's Hotels. But someone with your quarry's disinclination to attract attention might prefer someplace quieter. Robinson's, perhaps?"

He touched his hand to his hat. "Thank you."

He would have turned away, but she put out a hand, stopping him. "You are worried about the Maréchal?"

"Not only about McClellan."

Her eyes narrowed as she searched his face. "You will meet him someday," she said softly. "But the time is not yet right."

He felt his breath catch, so that it was with difficulty that he managed to keep his voice light as he said, "'Someday' as in 'some future date'? Or did you mean to imply it won't happen until after we are both dead?"

But at that she only laughed.

Chapter 38

Robinson's Hotel lay on the eastern, less fashionable side of Jermyn Street, near a section that was scheduled to be demolished when the Regent's New Street plowed through here to create what was envisioned as a grand circle on Piccadilly. A four-story building with a new stuccoed front, the hotel boasted a wide central doorway and an iron-railed balcony that stretched across the long windows of its second story.

Dressed once again in a collection of shabby clothes culled from the secondhand stalls of Rosemary Lane, Sebastian lounged with his shoulders propped against the doorway of a shuttered apothecary's across from the hotel. He had a wide-brimmed, floppy hat pulled low over his eyes and the stem of an unlit clay pipe clenched between his back teeth. An elderly jarvey dozed on the seat of a hackney drawn up near one end of the street; a second hackney waited nearby, pointed in the opposite direction.

Cupping the bowl of his pipe in one hand, Sebastian shifted his position. He had watched the man who called himself Noël Cartier enter the hotel some forty-five minutes earlier. It was another half hour before the man walked out again.

He paid no attention to the scruffy workman loitering across the street.

Sebastian watched the Frenchman hail a hackney; heard his instructions to the driver. The man was still climbing up into his carriage when Sebastian signaled the elderly jarvey, who was not as asleep as he appeared.

They followed the Frenchman up to Piccadilly, where he turned eastward before threading over to the Haymarket, then south to the Strand. Heading east again, they had almost reached Somerset Place when the Frenchman's hackney drew up.

"Wait here," Sebastian told his jarvey and hopped down.

Blending easily into the medley of costermongers, shopkeepers, actors, musicians, prostitutes, and thieves who populated the area around the theaters and Covent Garden Market, Sebastian trailed his quarry up Catherine Street. He thought the Frenchman might be headed to Drury Lane, but at Russell Street the man turned left, then immediately swung right again onto Bow Street.

"Bloody hell," whispered Sebastian as he watched the Frenchman cross the street toward the public office.

A man Sebastian recognized was standing in front of the steps of the Bow Street Public Office: a plump, ordinary-looking man with thinning gray hair, rounded shoulders, and a short neck. Officially, John Stafford was Bow Street's chief clerk, a man known and admired for his understanding of criminal law and his skill at framing indictments. But Stafford was far more powerful and important than that simple description might imply. It was Stafford who directed the Home Office's domestic spies, who recruited its legion of informants and agents provocateurs, and who worked closely with Sidmouth and Jarvis to mastermind the destruction of the various reform movements that threatened to undermine the dominance of the aristocracy.

As Sebastian watched, the Frenchman walked right up to the Bow Street clerk. The two spoke for a moment; then Stafford nodded and they crossed the street together to disappear into the Bear.

"My lord!" yelped Jarvis's clerk, jumping up from behind his desk as Sebastian strode past him toward the inner sanctum of the Carlton House apartments provided by the Prince Regent for his powerful cousin's exclusive use. "You can't— Not again!"

Sebastian flung open the door.

Jarvis looked up from where he sat reading dispatches in a comfortable chair beside the empty hearth. For a long moment, he stared at Sebastian. Then he turned to his anxiously hovering underling. "Close the door behind you when you leave," he told the clerk. Deliberately laying aside his papers, Jarvis laced his fingers together, tilted his head back against his chair, and said in a weary tone, "You're looking decidedly martial this afternoon. What is it now?"

"The French assassin," said Sebastian. "The one who calls himself Noël Cartier. I just watched him meet with John Stafford."

Something flickered behind the wintry gray eyes that were so much like Hero's. "And this surprises you? No, not surprises; angers you. How very . . . fatiguing."

"What does Cartier have to do with the murder of Lord Preston Farnsworth?"

"What makes you think he has anything to do with it?"

"Angélique."

Jarvis frowned. "Angélique?"

"Don't pretend you don't know who she is."

Moving slowly, Jarvis reached into a pocket and withdrew an

enameled gold snuffbox. He flicked open the lid with one finger, then said, "I understand you've developed an interest in a certain French priest, one Father Ambrose de Sancerre."

Sebastian knew a flicker of surprise. "What is he to you?"

"I assume you're aware that, despite being nobly born, he was an ardent revolutionary?"

"At one time—as were many others, including the French King's own ill-fated cousin Philippe d'Orléans. That changed when the Revolution changed."

"For some. But not for others." Jarvis lifted a pinch of snuff to one nostril and sniffed. "How much do you know about Angélique?"

"Only that Farnsworth was interested in her—as is your assassin."

Jarvis's lips tightened in a rare betrayal of annoyance. "He is not my assassin."

"Right. He's employed by your friends, and you're more than happy to help him when necessary."

Jarvis closed the snuffbox with a snap. "That's the way these things work. Surely you're not so naive as to think otherwise?"

"Who is Angélique?" Sebastian said again, tightening his jaw.

Jarvis tucked the snuffbox back into his pocket. "At one time she was a French nun, one of the many thousands driven out into the world when their convents were closed by the revolutionaries. Except that, rather than being lost and traumatized as were so many such innocents, Angélique embraced the Revolution with a rare fervor. Eventually, of course, she was forced to flee France for Spain. That's where she and the priest, Father Ambrose, became lovers."

Sebastian was careful to keep his reaction off his face. "So why exactly do the Bourbons want to kill her? Because she supported their removal twenty-five years ago?"

Jarvis braced his hands on the arms of his chair and rose to his feet. "You don't know what you're interfering in here."

"Oh? So tell me. What does this Angélique have to do with Farnsworth's murder?"

"I fail to understand what makes you think she has anything to do with it."

The two men stared at each other.

Sebastian said, "There is some connection. I may not know what it is yet, but I will." He turned toward the door.

"You're overreaching," said Jarvis. "You know that, don't you? And if you think your marriage to my daughter will protect you, you're wrong."

Sebastian paused at the door to look back at him. "I know what you're capable of."

Jarvis snorted and picked up his dispatches. "You flatter yourself."

Chapter 39

Sebastian found the small cobbled court with its row of stone horse troughs empty. His knock on the old arched wooden door in the corner went unanswered.

Returning to Deadman's Place, he found a toothless, aged Irishwoman selling lace from a battered tin tray on a nearby corner and asked if she knew where he might find the priest. She screwed up her face with thought, then said, "Ye might be tryin' the Cross Bones. Saw him headed that way a while ago, and I didna see him come back."

"And where precisely is this Cross Bones?"

She jerked her chin toward a nearby mean lane. "'Tis down there."

Sebastian assumed he was looking for a public house of that name. But as he rounded the lane's long, sweeping curve, he could see in the distance a wretched open space rank with overgrown weeds and surrounded by a low wall topped with broken glass. Within the wall, the bulging earth rose some three to four feet above the level of the pavement; an open trench ran along one side of the enclosure, and amongst the raw earth thrown up at its side Sebastian could see a jumble of dirt-stained long bones, vertebrae, ribs, and skulls.

The French priest stood in the center of the crude, overflowing burial ground, his head bowed, his eyes closed, his lips moving in silent prayer as his fingers shifted over the beads of his rosary. And it occurred to Sebastian as he paused in the graveyard's open gateway that he seemed to be making it a habit of intruding on such private moments.

Then Father Ambrose tightened his fist around the rosary and opened his eyes.

"Monsieur le vicomte," he said. "Looking for me, were you?"

Sebastian nodded, his gaze drifting around the bone-strewn wasteland. "What is this place?"

"This? They call it the Cross Bones burial ground. For centuries, it's been the final resting place of those whom the good citizens of Southwark have rejected." He swept his arm through the air in a wide arc that took in not only the crude graveyard but also the crowded streets and alleyways that stretched beyond it to the river. "There was a time when almost everything you see here belonged to the Bishops of Winchester." He nodded to a distant church tower. "I'm told their palace was there, beside what is now St. Saviour's."

Sebastian had heard of the once-grand palace of the Bishops of Winchester, with its private wharf, stables, brewhouse, tennis courts—even its own prison, the notorious Clink. In those days Southwark had been outside the control of London, so the various forms of entertainment that were forbidden in the city were set up here—everything from theaters such as Shakespeare's Globe and gaming houses to whorehouses. And all of those establishments, including the whorehouses, were licensed by the bishops, who collected a tidy sum in fees from such lucrative dens of sin. The bishops also owned the buildings along the river that the brothels used, which meant the houses paid the bishops rent, too. Eventually, the brothels came to be called "the Stews" because that was the name of the bishops' nearby fishponds. And because so much of what they earned made its way into His Excellency's coffers, people took to calling the prostitutes who worked in those wretched establishments "Winchester Geese."

The priest tucked his rosary into a pocket of his worn robes. "You know about the Winchester Geese?"

"Yes."

The priest nodded. "Despite the fact that their work helped make the bishops rich, when the women died, those fine holy men in their grand palace refused to allow prostitutes to be buried on consecrated ground. So the women's bodies were dumped here." He paused, his gaze drifting to the open trench. "Now the parish uses it for their poor hole."

"It's still unconsecrated?"

"Officially. Most of the area's poorer French refugees and Irish immigrants end up here, so I come once a week to pray for them—for them, and for the Winchester Geese of long ago."

Sebastian studied the priest's weathered face, the deeply incised lines of his forehead and cheeks, the thick gray eyebrows and blobby broken nose. "Tell me about Angélique."

A flare of surprise flickered in those kindly soft brown eyes. Surprise and something else that might have been alarm. "Angélique? What do you know of Angélique?"

"Very little. Virtually all I know is that Lord Preston was obsessed with finding her. That he saw her as a threat to society." *And that you were once lovers,* but he didn't say that. Yet.

"And what makes you think I can help you?"

"I'm told you were once an ardent revolutionary."

The smile lines beside the priest's eyes deepened. "I don't know if I'd go so far as to say that, but I certainly believed France needed to change." That hint of a smile faded. "Unfortunately, things got out of hand, as they often do."

"Yes," Sebastian agreed. Then he said it again. "Tell me about Angélique."

"There is not much to tell. At one time she was a nun at a convent in Liège. Then the Revolution came." The priest let out his breath in a long, painful sigh. "It was much like what happened when your King Henry VIII went after church property here in England two hundred and fifty years before. The monasteries were seized and pillaged, irreplaceable manuscripts and works of art destroyed, and tens of thousands of cloistered men and women cast penniless out into the world."

He fell silent, a sad, faraway expression creeping over his features. Sebastian waited, and after a moment the priest continued. "By that time Angélique's mother and father were dead, but she managed to make her way to her brother, Jean-Pierre. He was in Paris as a delegate, first to the Estates-General, then to the National Convention."

"He was a revolutionary?"

The priest shrugged. "He was a Girondin. At first the Girondins favored a constitutional monarchy, but after the attempted flight of the King, they became republicans. Angélique shared many of her brother's beliefs and worked with him." He paused. "Even when the Revolution grew increasingly darker and more violent, she kept hoping that in the end good would triumph. But the day came when she could no longer make excuses for the horror of what was happening, and she turned away from it—as did her brother. When Robespierre moved against the Girondins, Jean-Pierre was arrested and guillotined, but Angélique managed to flee France."

"For Spain?"

"Yes."

"Is that where you were lovers?"

Father Ambrose sucked in a deep breath. "Who told you that?"

"Jarvis."

"Ah."

"Is it true?"

"It is." He paused, his eyes narrowing as if he were looking into the distant past. "At that point we were two very . . . troubled souls. We took comfort in each other. Gave each other a reason to keep living. And eventually helped each other find a way back to our vows."

"That's when you came here?"

"Yes."

"Why do the Bourbons want to kill her?"

"That is because of Marie-Thérèse." His lip curled. "It's the Most High, Most Potent and Excellent Princess Marie-Thérèse who wants her dead."

Sebastian was only too familiar with Marie-Thérèse, the sole surviving child of the ill-fated Louis XVI and his wife, Marie Antoinette. As such, she was the niece of the current, childless King of France; she was also the wife of his nephew and eventual heir, which meant that someday she, in turn, would be Queen of France . . .

If the Bourbons lasted that long.

Sebastian said, "She wants Angélique dead because her brother was a regicide and she supported him?"

"Ostensibly. But in reality?" Father Ambrose shook his head. "It's because of something Angélique knows."

"Something about Marie-Thérèse?"

The priest nodded. "You see, in the convent, Angélique was a nursing sister. And there were times when Marie-Thérèse was held prisoner in the Temple that Angélique was asked to . . . to tend to her."

"Ah," said Sebastian. Marie-Thérèse had always vehemently denied the persistent rumors of rape and secret childbirth in her Temple prison. But Sebastian had never believed that the men who treated her younger brother, the little Dauphin, so cruelly would have been any kinder to his beautiful sister. And that meant the unknown French nun was the custodian of a very dangerous secret indeed.

He said, "Where is Angélique now?"

The priest gave him a long, steady look. "At this moment? I have no idea."

Sebastian swallowed a spurt of annoyance. "You do realize that she is in danger?"

"Yes."

"So tell me this: How did Farnsworth come to know about her?"

"Lord Preston worked closely with the Home Office for years, helping to destroy those the government considered Radicals."

"And Angélique is a Radical?"

Father Ambrose huffed a soft laugh. "Well, she does still believe in the need for reform. But I doubt those such as Farnsworth and your Lord Jarvis know the reality of why Marie-Thérèse wants Angélique dead. They simply assume she was and is a dangerous revolutionary."

"'A threat to society,'" said Sebastian.

"Yes."

Sebastian again let his gaze drift around that mournful burial ground, to the carelessly unearthed skulls with their bared, grinning teeth and vacant, staring eyes. "You need to tell me where I can find her."

"I told you, I don't know where she is at this moment."

"At this *precise* moment."

Father Ambrose shrugged and said nothing.

And Sebastian knew he would get nothing further from the priest.

Chapter 40

Sebastian returned to Brook Street to find Hero out on an interview and his friend Hugh Chandler pacing up and down in the library. The Major's face was ashen, his breeches, boots, and coat liberally splashed with mud, and he still held his riding crop gripped in one hand.

"I'm damned sorry for making myself at home like this," he said without preamble when Sebastian walked in the library door. "But I had to see you."

Sebastian closed the door behind him. "What is it, Hugh?"

Tossing the crop onto a nearby table, Hugh went to stand at the windows overlooking the street, his fists opening and closing at his sides. "I've just had a visit from that bloody Bow Street Chief Magistrate, Sir Nathaniel Conant. He . . . he's discovered I wasn't exactly honest about something."

Sebastian walked over to pour a healthy measure of brandy into two glasses, then handed one to his friend. "Such as?"

Hugh took the brandy and downed half of it in one long gulp.

"When I said I couldn't remember the last time I'd seen Farnsworth. That wasn't true. I had a run-in with him just a couple of days before he died."

"A run-in about what?"

Hugh brought up a hand to rub his eyes. "The Thursday before he was killed, someone took a shot at Tess when she was out riding. It spooked her gelding, and if she weren't such a good horsewoman, she might have been thrown. That would have been troubling enough, but then, when she got home and was changing, she found a bullet hole in the sleeve of her riding habit, here." He touched his upper left arm. "It so happened that just as the shot was fired, she wheeled her horse to say something to her groom. If she hadn't, the bullet would have struck her in the chest and killed her. Old Squire Adams—he's our local Justice of the Peace—tried to shrug it off. Said she was damned lucky, but I was daft to be thinking it was deliberate. That it must have been some fool out hunting."

"You didn't think so?"

Hugh looked at him. "Hunting what? At this time of year?"

"A poacher, perhaps?"

"You really believe that, Devlin?"

Rather than answer, Sebastian said, "You're suggesting Lord Preston was trying to kill her?"

"Himself? Probably not. But I could sure as hell see him hiring someone to do it."

"Farnsworth could have divorced Tess anytime these last six years. Why the hell would he try to kill her now?"

"Because he wants to remarry."

"You know that for a fact?"

"No. But there were . . . rumors."

"It's not as if it would have been hard for him to still obtain a divorce. Tess has been living with you openly."

"Yes. But divorces are bloody expensive."

Sebastian wasn't going to argue with that. Divorces were ruinously expensive, and a frank discussion between Lovejoy and Farnsworth's man of business had revealed that Lord Preston was not as plump in the pocket as he'd liked people to believe. "Please tell me you didn't confront the man and accuse him of trying to murder his estranged wife."

Hugh nodded grimly. "Not only that, but I told him if anything happened to Tess again, I'd kill him."

"Bloody hell, Hugh! How did Sir Nathaniel find out about it?"

"Someone must have overheard me—either that, or Farnsworth told someone about it. I tried denying it, except Sir Nathaniel had already talked to the Squire and Tess's groom, and I doubt if there's anyone in my household who didn't know I'd gone off to London that afternoon in a rage."

Sebastian fixed his friend with a long, cold stare. "Well, I can certainly see why you tried to keep this information from Bow Street. But why the bloody hell didn't you tell me?"

Hugh's chest jerked on a deeply indrawn breath. "I guess because I was afraid it would make you think I actually did kill the bastard. I mean, it's just one more reason for me to have murdered him when I already had more than enough reasons. Plus—"

He broke off.

"Plus—what?" said Sebastian.

Hugh looked awkwardly away. "I guess you don't know about the relationship between Farnsworth and your sister?" There was no mistaking his implication.

"Amanda?"

Hugh simply stared back at him.

"You can't be serious. If he wanted to remarry, why the bloody hell would Farnsworth choose a widow in her forties when he could have his pick of any number of young heiresses only too eager to bear the heirs of the next Duke of Eversfield?"

Hugh shook his head. "Lord Preston was incapable of fathering children and he knew it. As for an heiress . . . Well, your brother-in-law left Lady Wilcox a wealthy woman. Perhaps wealthier than you realize. And they . . ."

"They what?"

"They'd have been well suited, wouldn't you say?"

Sebastian wasn't going to argue against that. "When did Sir Nathaniel confront you about this?"

"This afternoon. Why?"

"Because I heard this morning that he's on the verge of having you arrested. Probably Monday, if I had to guess."

Hugh drained his brandy and set the glass aside with an unsteady hand. After a moment, he said, "Do you have any idea—any idea at all—who did actually kill the man?"

"Not really. But if there is anything else you haven't told me yet—anything at all—"

"No. I swear."

"What about Tess? What is she holding back?"

"Nothing! She's at as much of a loss as I am when it comes to explaining what happened to him. I mean, everyone knows Farnsworth had a long list of enemies, but I can't see any of them deciding to hang him upside down in an abandoned chapel off Swallow Street. It makes no sense. Whoever did it must be mad."

"Either that," said Sebastian, draining his own brandy glass, "or crazy like a fox."

"This doesn't look good for Hugh, does it?" said Hero, later, when Sebastian told her of the visit from his friend. She had returned from her interview to find him sitting in one of the armchairs before the nursery fire and reading a picture book about a bunny rabbit to Miss Guinevere St. Cyr.

"Frankly, I'm not sure it could look any worse," he said as Guinevere wiggled from his lap and tottered over to her mother's outstretched arms. "Unless perhaps Bow Street finds someone who saw him actually stringing Farnsworth up by his heel."

Hero gave the baby a kiss, then sank into the chair on the far side of the fire, still holding Guinevere's hands in hers as the baby swayed back and forth on unsteady legs. "You think Hugh actually did it?"

"No, I don't. Not because I believe Hugh incapable of killing, because I know he is. But to then pose his victim hanging upside down in a way that deliberately echoes a tarot card? Why would he do that?"

"Why would anyone do it?"

"You have a point there."

Guinevere babbled a string of nonsense, and Hero hoisted the baby up onto her lap. "Do you think Hugh could be right? That Lord Preston was planning to marry Amanda?"

"Honestly? As ridiculous as I found the idea at first, the more I think about it, the less incredible I find it. Hugh is right: They would have suited. Amanda is every bit as arrogant, haughty, nasty, and devious as Lord Preston. And I keep remembering how upset she was when she came to see me—far more than could be explained by mere friendship."

Hero started to say something, then hesitated.

"What?" said Sebastian, watching her.

She rested her chin atop the baby's head. "Has anyone looked into who will inherit the house on St. James's Square now that Lord Preston is dead?"

"Not to my knowledge. I assumed he would leave it to his sister. Why?"

"If Lord Preston had married a young, weak-willed bride just out of the schoolroom, Lady Hester would no doubt have been able to control the poor girl shamelessly. But Hester could never have dominated Amanda, and she never could have borne continuing to live in that house once she was no longer its mistress."

"What are you suggesting? That Lady Hester killed her own brother so that she wouldn't be forced to move from their nice big house into smaller quarters?"

"Why not? She's a tall woman—taller even than her brother—so I think she would be capable of doing it, physically. And I wouldn't put cold-blooded murder past her. Would you?"

Sebastian thought about it. "No. But why would she pose her brother like *Le Pendu?*"

"To cast suspicion onto the gypsies and cartomancers, perhaps? She knew her brother was going after them. She even made it a point to mention it to me."

"Yes, except she still keeps insisting Hugh must be the killer."

"Well, it's what everyone would expect her to do, isn't it?"

Sebastian closed the book he still held, half-forgotten, in his hands and set it aside. "I think I need to have another talk with Lord Preston's brother."

Chapter 41

That night, Sebastian prowled the exclusive gentlemen's clubs of St. James's Street, looking for Archibald Farnsworth, the current Duke of Eversfield.

The evening was cool and misty, the damp air heavy with the scents of roasting meat, spilled ale, and the hot oil from the dim, sputtering streetlamps above. Normally at this time of year, the city's wealthy and titled retreated to their summer estates. But the wretched weather had driven many members of the Upper Ten Thousand back to Town in search of amusement, and the street was crowded with clusters of well-dressed young men laughing and singing and ogling the perfumed, high-priced barques of frailty who eyed them speculatively. When he drew a blank at White's, Brooks's, and two other discreet establishments, Sebastian continued up to Piccadilly, where he found Lord Preston's congenial older brother playing macao in the cardroom of Watier's.

The opulently furnished room was thick with tobacco smoke and crowded with hushed onlookers, for the play at Watier's was notoriously deep, and it had been only a few months since a disastrous run of bad luck at macao had forced the great Beau Brummell himself to flee England to escape his creditors. Propping his shoulders against a nearby wall, Sebastian crossed his arms at his chest and settled in to watch. The Duke was in a rollicking mood, laughingly self-deprecatingly and readily attributing his consistently enormous wins to Lady Luck. But it didn't take Sebastian long to realize that the Duke was a shrewd, formidable player who was neither as blithe nor as drunk as he chose to appear.

When the Duke drew a natural 9—which meant he received triple the amount of his bet—the other punters groaned, while Eversfield threw up his hands. "What can I say? I keep doing my damnedest to lose, but the cards won't let me." He leaned back in his chair with an exaggerated grimace. "And my back keeps reminding me I'm no longer as young as I used to be. If you gentlemen will excuse me?"

He collected his winnings, then walked up to Sebastian and said, "I take it you wanted to see me?"

"Is there someplace we could talk?"

The Duke nodded. "A walk might help clear my head."

The two men collected their greatcoats, then walked down the club's short flight of front steps into the wet, coal smoke–scented night. As they turned toward the park, Eversfield said, "Sir Nathaniel Conant tells me they're about to arrest the man who killed my brother."

"So I've heard," said Sebastian.

Something in his voice brought the Duke's eyebrows together in a frown. "I take it you don't agree with Bow Street's conclusions?"

"I don't, actually."

The Duke nodded. "To be honest, I have my own reservations. I've known Hugh Chandler since he was a young lad—his grandfather's estate touched ours at one point, you know. And while there's no doubt war can change a man, there are surely limits. I mean, I could see Hugh calling Preston out and blowing a hole through his head. But bashing in his skull with a club and hanging him upside down like a side of beef? Nah. I don't buy it."

"I'm told your brother was thinking about getting married again. Do you know anything about that?"

The Duke coughed in embarrassment and looked away. "Well, yes—although I only learned of it because I happened to see Preston one day when he'd just found out how much it would cost to shepherd a bill of divorce through Parliament. Shockingly expensive, you know, and Preston always did sail too close to the wind. Threw him into a rage."

"When was this?"

"That he was ranting on about it? Some weeks ago now. Don't recall exactly."

"Do you know whom he was planning to marry?"

The Duke's eyes bulged. "Well, er, um, as to that, I'm sure I couldn't say."

"By which I gather we're talking about Lady Amanda Wilcox?"

"Well, as it happens, er, yes." The Duke gave an awkward laugh. "I was a bit reluctant to mention it, her being your sister and all." He threw Sebastian a quick, searching look. "Surely you're not thinking that might have something to do with what happened to Preston, are you?"

"Just trying to clarify a few things. Do you know if your brother kept rooms someplace in London?"

"You mean someplace he could take women without Hester being around? I wouldn't be surprised, but I can't tell you where. His valet might know."

"If he does, he's keeping your brother's secret."

Eversfield was silent for a moment, his jaw going slack as they paused to watch a swirling white mist rise from the dark waters of the long reservoir in Green Park. "We buried him today, you know—well, at least for now. Eventually, I'd like to take him up to settle him permanently in the crypt of our old parish church, where the Farnsworths have been laid to rest these last four hundred years or more. It's so odd . . . He's buried, and yet somehow I still can't believe this has happened—can't understand *why* it happened." He glanced over at Sebastian. "I loved my brother. I even admired some of the work he was doing, although I'll admit I found all that nonsense with the Society for the Suppression of Vice downright asinine. But I don't think I realized how much I didn't *know* him until now that he's dead."

That's probably a good thing, Sebastian thought. Aloud, he said, "Did Lord Preston talk to you much about his work with the Society?"

"Nah. He knew my opinions on the subject. I'll never understand why a certain sort feel the need to be so damned busy about other people's business. What makes them think they have a right to go around interfering in how other people choose to live their lives—telling complete strangers what they can and can't do when it doesn't have a bloody thing to do with them? I mean, don't they have anything better to do?"

"Evidently nothing that appeals to them as much," said Sebastian. "Have you been able to think of anything—anything at all—that might explain what happened to your brother?"

"No. I've tried and tried, but I can't come up with anything. Not a blessed thing."

The man's voice cracked when he said it, and so bleak was his expression that Sebastian didn't have the heart to question him further. Shifting the conversation to the ever-fruitful topic of the summer's strange weather, Sebastian turned their steps back toward the club and kept up a flow of small talk until he parted with the Duke in front of Watier's.

Sunday, 25 August

Early the next morning, Lady Amanda Wilcox was standing in the entry hall of her house in St. James's Square, easing on a pair of fine black kid gloves, when her butler opened the front door to Sebastian. She wore a long-sleeved gown of silver Merino crepe trimmed around the hem and up the front with a cable of black silk crepe; a silk-trimmed black cloak lay over the chair beside her.

"Whatever it is," she said, barely glancing over at her brother, "I don't have time to discuss it with you at the moment." Turning to the mirror over the hall table, she thoughtfully studied her reflection before adjusting the tilt of her high-crowned hat. "I'm on my way to St. George's, and I have no intention of being so rude as to arrive late for Mr. Carmichael's sermon."

"We can have this conversation here in the hall, before your servants, if you wish. But I suspect you'd prefer to hear what I have to say in private."

Amanda froze with one hand still on the brim of her hat, for she knew him well enough to know that he would not hesitate to say something outrageous in front of her butler. Her nostrils quivering with indignation, she stalked over to the library door, threw it open, and waited for him to enter. Then she followed him into the chilly, disused room and slammed the door behind them.

"Say what you've come to say and then get out."

He turned to face her. "You didn't tell me Lord Preston had asked you to marry him."

She raised her chin. "Why should I? It's none of your affair."

"It didn't occur to you that it might have something to do with his death?"

"And what precisely do you mean to imply by that question?"

"I'm not implying anything. But since you were obviously closer to the man than I'd realized, I thought you might have some insights that could help explain what happened to him."

"You are the only person in all of London who insists on continuing to believe that the identity of Preston's killer is some strange, impenetrable unknown. There is no mystery, no need for all this puzzlement and earnest search for answers that will never be found because they don't exist. Major Hugh Chandler murdered his lover's husband, and if you weren't so willfully blinded by your friendship with the man, you would realize it."

Sebastian kept his gaze on Amanda's face. "I'm told Lord Preston balked at the cost of getting a bill of divorce through Parliament."

"And what precisely are you implying?"

"Someone tried to have Lady Tess killed, and I think it more than likely that person was Lord Preston. Murder is considerably cheaper than divorce."

He watched something flare behind Amanda's vivid blue eyes, something that was neither disbelief nor hurt. Something it took him a moment to identify for what it was: anger, mixed with a hint of consternation.

"My God," he whispered, his breath backing up painfully in his chest as he stared at this tall, icy woman who was his sister. "You knew. You knew he had decided to have her killed."

Amanda stared back at him. "I don't have the slightest idea what you're talking about."

He found himself wondering, oddly, why this revelation surprised him. Hadn't there been a time not so long ago when Amanda looked forward to watching him hang for a crime she knew he hadn't committed?

And then he wondered whose idea the scheme had been: Preston's, or hers?

He said, "I wonder if you realize how lucky you are. Men who murder one wife frequently go on to murder another. And Lord Preston had expensive habits; he'd have run through your money very quickly."

"Don't be ridiculous. Preston was Eversfield's heir."

"Well, there is that. I suppose a man who's willing to kill his wife could also decide to remove his elder brother and hasten the inheritance. Fancied yourself as a duchess, did you?"

She glanced pointedly at the ornate clock on the mantelpiece, angry color riding high on her cheeks. "It's past time for this ridiculous conversation to end. My carriage is waiting."

"In a moment. Lord Preston Farnsworth maintained a set of rooms someplace in London. Do you know where they are?"

He could tell by the quick parting of her lips that this, at least, was news to her. "Rooms? What are you talking about? Why would Preston keep rooms when he had a lovely house right here on the square?"

"Because he liked to pick up whores, and he could hardly take them back to a house he shared with his sister."

He'd made the phraseology deliberately crude to shock her into honesty, and it had its intended effect. For a long moment she glared at him, too outraged to speak. Then she said, "You are beyond despicable. You're making that up simply to hurt me. My God, I can't believe even you would stoop so low."

"Are you saying you actually didn't know he kept rooms?"

She walked over to jerk open the library door. "We're finished here. I can't think what Jensen was about, opening the door to you like that. Rest assured that if you come again, you will be denied entry."

"I think I've learned enough," he said, nodding to Jensen as the butler hastened to open the front door. "Do give my best to Bayard. I haven't seen him around lately. In the country on a repairing lease, is he?"

Amanda tightened her jaw and said nothing. Her only surviving son, Bayard, had inherited the barony upon the death of his father, the previous Lord Wilcox, five years before. Still only in his twenties and worryingly unstable and erratic in his behavior, Bayard had thus far been more than happy to have his mother continue managing the London house, his estates, and even his finances. But Sebastian had sometimes found himself wondering how much longer Bayard would be content to allow that state of affairs to continue, and what Amanda would do if he decided to bring it to an end.

Now he knew.

Sebastian was walking back toward his carriage, his thoughts in an unpleasant place, when he became aware of one of Lovejoy's constables hurrying toward him.

"Lord Devlin! I say, Lord Devlin," called the man.

Sebastian paused and turned toward him.

"I'm glad I caught you," said the constable, breathing hard as he drew up. "I've a message from Sir Henry."

"What is it?"

"They've found Lord Preston's rooms, sir. In Saville Street. And just wait till you see them!"

Chapter 42

Saville Street was a short, exclusive enclave consisting of a single row of dignified eighteenth-century stone-dressed brick houses, generally either three or four stories tall plus basements and attics. There were no houses on the western side of the street, only the high garden walls and imposing rear gates of another stretch of houses that faced west onto Old Burlington Street.

The houses here tended to be occupied by aging dowagers, generals, admirals, physicians, and members of Parliament. Only one of the houses, Number 19, near the northern end of the street, had a tailor's establishment on the ground floor, with each of the other three floors let independently as suites.

The rooms rented by Lord Preston Farnsworth lay on the first floor, up a grandly sweeping open-well staircase with twisted balusters and heavy, imposing newel-posts kept nicely polished. As he climbed the stairs, Sebastian could see Sir Henry Lovejoy standing on the landing above, deep in conversation with a thin, well-dressed man who looked to be in his early thirties. The man nodded in response to something Lovejoy said, then turned to mount the stairs to the second floor.

"How did you manage to find this place?" Sebastian asked as Lovejoy walked over to meet him.

"One of my lads followed Lord Preston's valet when he left St. James's Square this morning. Seems the reason the man pretended ignorance of the rooms' existence is because he saw an opportunity to make a tidy sum by quietly selling the contents on the sly."

"Charming fellow."

The suite consisted of two rooms: a spacious front parlor that overlooked the street and a slightly smaller bedroom behind it. Sebastian paused at the entrance to the parlor, his gaze taking in the room's plaster frieze of cavorting, naked nymphs, the green marble fireplace with fluted pilasters, the thick Turkey carpet, the comfortably padded sofa and armchairs covered in a fine green and champagne striped silk. "He spared no expense, did he?"

Lovejoy sniffed. "Apparently not."

A small, plump man in his forties with thinning dark hair, a pasty complexion, and forgettable features sat at one end of the silk-covered sofa, his arms crossed at his chest, a bored, faintly supercilious expression on his face.

"The valet," said Lovejoy. "Leonard Dudley is his name. He says he was with Lord Preston some fifteen years, and that before he hired this place Farnsworth had rooms in Jermyn Street. Seems he gave them up and shifted here six or eight months ago."

The valet cast them a quick look, then glanced fastidiously away.

Sebastian said, "What else have you managed to get out of him?"

"Very little, I'm afraid. He claims Farnsworth used the rooms for 'quiet contemplation.' He also denies he had any intention of selling the place's contents and says he kept Farnsworth's secret out of respect for his dead master's privacy." What might have been a hint of amusement narrowed the magistrate's eyes. "You're more than welcome to try your hand at him if you wish."

The valet looked up, his face wooden as Sebastian strolled over to him. "So tell me this," said Sebastian. "When was Lord Preston last here?"

The valet kept his expression blank, his eyes blinking rapidly. "That I can't say," he said in a prim, high-pitched voice.

His lips curling into a hard smile that showed his teeth, Sebastian rested one hand on the sofa's arm and leaned down until his face was even with that of the gentleman's gentleman. "I think maybe you could if you tried. If not, a night or two in Coldbath Fields Prison might help loosen your tongue. I understand the old chums up there like valets." He lowered his voice. "If you know what I mean?"

The valet edged away from him, his Adam's apple bobbing up and down as he swallowed hard. "Of course, I know that Lord Preston was here several days before he died—maybe that Wednesday?" His voice rose even higher. "But I didn't always know when he came."

"Could he have left St. James's Square last Saturday, walking, and then taken a hackney here?"

The valet nodded his head vigorously up and down. "He did that sometimes, particularly on Saturday nights. Then he would send me up to put things to rights a day or two later."

Sebastian and Lovejoy exchanged glances.

"And it didn't occur to you that this information might be helpful to us in understanding what happened to him?" snapped Lovejoy.

The valet looked from Sebastian to the magistrate and back again.

Sebastian said, "Where did Farnsworth get the women he brought here? And don't even think of denying that that's what he used these rooms for."

The valet's nose twitched. "Different places. The abbesses were always careful to take good care of him, but he also enjoyed picking up women from the street and bringing them here."

"What else?"

"Nothing! There isn't anything else I can tell you! I swear."

"If you think very hard," said Sebastian, pushing away from the sofa, "I suspect you might come up with more. So do try."

The valet was still nodding vigorously when Sebastian turned away.

"We can start checking with the jarveys who work the area around St. James's Square," said Lovejoy. "Hopefully, we can find one who remembers bringing Lord Preston here that night."

"Have you searched the rooms yet?"

"Not yet. Sir Nathaniel said he wanted to see the place before we started tearing it apart."

"Perhaps this will convince him to broaden his personal list of suspects," said Sebastian, going to stand in the doorway to the other room.

"Perhaps," said Lovejoy, although he sounded doubtful.

This second room was dominated by the wide silk-hung bed that stood along the near wall, its embroidered dark blue counterpane half-buried beneath a jumble of clothes the valet had obviously been sorting in preparation for selling them to secondhand clothing dealers. The bedstead was of elegantly carved mahogany, the room's two bureaus and a small round table with two chairs were exquisitely inlaid French pieces, and a vast array of pictures arranged in towering rows covered the dark blue silk-hung walls. Some were heavily framed oils, some delicate watercolors, others deliberately crude prints. All were erotic.

"Quite a collection," said Sebastian, wandering over to study a massive oil painting of Leda being raped by a swan.

Lovejoy cleared his throat uncomfortably. "Indeed. We've spoken to the owner of the establishment downstairs. He says he doesn't know if his lordship came last Saturday. He rarely saw Farnsworth and had the impression he mainly used the rooms at night. The gentleman who lives on the second floor—a Mr. Bingley—says basically the same thing. The third floor is currently vacant."

Sebastian moved on to a print of a naked Daphne dancing before an equally naked Apollo. "Makes sense that he would come mainly at night, given what he used the rooms for."

Lovejoy nodded gravely. "The house itself is owned by the widow of an Admiral Munstead. We're trying to contact the solicitor who handles her affairs to verify everything, but I doubt he'll be able to tell us much."

"Probably not." Sebastian let his gaze rove over the carved wooden pipe left lying casually on the inlaid table, the man's brush and comb arranged neatly atop one of the bureaus. Farnsworth might have brought women to these rooms, but there was no sign that one had ever actually lived here. And that suggested that rather than keeping a mistress, Farnsworth had chosen to satisfy his sexual desires with a long string of women he either picked up from the streets or arranged to hire through brothels. "It would be interesting to talk to some of the women he brought here. There must have been dozens of them."

Lovejoy sighed. "Undoubtedly. And yet I'll be surprised if we can find even one who'll be willing to admit it."

"Not now that he's been murdered," agreed Sebastian, going to stand at one of the room's two tall rear windows. Someone—presumably the valet—had opened the heavy curtains to flood the space with light. The back of the house overlooked a small, well-tended garden. Beyond that stretched the rear gardens of a row of houses that faced north onto New Burlington Street, while to the right ran a long, low series of brick buildings he realized must be Burlington Mews. And directly to the east lay the swath of destruction that marked the path of what would someday become the Regent's New Street.

"Well," said Sebastian after a long moment, "at least we now understand what Farnsworth was doing up here that night."

Leaving Lovejoy to await the arrival of Sir Nathaniel, Sebastian walked out of Number 19 Saville Street and turned right. Only one house separated Number 19 from the behemoth that stood at the corner of New Burlington Street. Turning right again, he walked past just six more houses before reaching the ruins of what had once been Swallow Street.

For a long time Sebastian stood on the corner of that ghostly, windblown street. Overhead, the clouds were gathering again; he could smell the coming rain, smell the dust from the nearby demolished buildings and the dankness of old wet stone. If he were to turn right once more and walk several hundred feet he would be directly opposite the crumbling stone archway that led to that ancient Tudor courtyard and its death-haunted ruin of a chapel.

"So why the bloody hell did you come *here*, to Swallow Street, that night?" Sebastian said aloud, as if the wraith of Lord Preston

Farnsworth himself stood silently beside him. "Why leave your warm secret rooms, your bottles of French brandy and erotic pictures, perhaps even the willing woman you'd hired for the night, to venture into this dark, deserted wasteland and get your head bashed in?"

Why, why, why?

Chapter 43

Charles, Lord Jarvis, settled back in one of the comfortable chairs beside his library fire, his elbows propped on the chair's padded arms as he studied the man who stood before him. "Lord Preston's funeral was yesterday, was it not?"

Sir Nathaniel Conant, Chief Magistrate of Bow Street Public Office, executed a neat bow. "It was, yes, my lord. Sir Henry and I both attended, naturally. Although, interestingly, I noticed that Lord Devlin did not."

"And this surprises you?" The magistrate started to answer, but Jarvis raised a hand, cutting him off. "You realize it has been over a week since the man was bludgeoned to death?"

The magistrate blanched noticeably. "Yes, my lord. But we anticipate having someone remanded into custody tomorrow."

"The war hero?"

"Yes, my lord. But we do not expect any difficulties. Public opinion has moved decidedly against him as the particulars of his affair with the dead man's wife have become better known. Conduct unbecoming an officer and a gentleman and all that."

Reaching for his snuffbox, Jarvis flicked open the sapphire-studded lid with one finger, then raised a delicate pinch to his nostrils. "And the other matter?"

"Cartier tells us he has received information that should enable him to deal with the woman. It seems she has resumed her vocation and is once again using her religious name, hence the difficulty locating her."

"So she's here as a nun?"

"Yes, my lord," said Sir Nathaniel, opening and closing his hands nervously.

But Jarvis simply laughed.

Chapter 44

"Perhaps Lord Preston *didn't* go to the chapel that night," said Hero, later, as she and Sebastian walked along the swollen gray waters of the Serpentine in Hyde Park. "At least, not willingly. The killer—or killers—could have confronted him in his rooms, dragged him down the stairs, and manhandled him around the corner. Not as early as seven that evening, of course, but later—much later, when no one was awake to hear."

They were taking advantage of a break in the weather to get the children out in the fresh air, with Sebastian carrying Miss Guinevere on his shoulders and the two boys running back and forth on the path ahead of them. Sebastian's eyes narrowed as he watched Simon pause, his gaze following the hopping progress of a fat toad toward the water's edge. "Perhaps. Or the killer could have been waiting for Farnsworth outside the house—someone who knew his habit of going there on Saturday nights. If the man stuck a pistol in Farnsworth's side, there'd have been no need to manhandle him. I suspect he'd have gone quietly enough."

"*Simon,*" called Hero. "Don't even think about getting any closer to the edge of that lake." To Sebastian, she said, "Except that if the killer had a pistol, why bash in Farnsworth's head with a cudgel? Why not simply shoot him?"

"Perhaps our killer was afraid someone might hear."

"He shot Half-Hanged Harry," said Hero.

"True. But Harry might not have been as quietly cooperative as an arrogant, overconfident duke's son."

She was silent for a moment, watching Sebastian as he lowered the now squirming baby from his shoulders to his arms. "I can think of another scenario."

He looked over at her. "What?"

"We know Farnsworth enjoyed hurting and humiliating women. What if he frightened the woman he'd picked up that night so badly that she ran away from him? Or perhaps she'd been supplied by a brothel. Many of their women are either trapped or tricked into a life they never wanted; she might have seen an opportunity to run away and taken it. He chases after her, following her around the corner into Swallow Street. She sees the entrance to the courtyard and ducks into it, not realizing it's a dead end, and finds herself trapped in the chapel. Desperate to defend herself, she grabs a hunk of wood, hits him with it, and kills him."

"And then strings him upside down and carefully poses him in the posture of *Le Pendu*? Why would she do that?"

"Why would anyone do that?"

He shifted his hold on the still-squirming baby. "To mock him, perhaps. Or to shame him. Or . . ." He paused. "Or to send us a message."

She lifted Guinevere from his arms and balanced the baby on one hip. "What message?"

"Think about this: If whoever killed Lord Preston had taken his watch and purse and simply left him lying in those ruins with his head bashed in, everyone would have assumed it was the work of footpads. It's the sort of thing the Bourbons' assassin has been doing, and so far it's worked just fine for him. Of course, the murder of a duke's brother would have caused far more of a sensation than the death of a few random Frenchmen. The editors of all the newspapers would have written countless articles bemoaning the supposed rise of crime in the city. But then Bow Street could have rounded up a batch of prominent thieves and hanged them with much solemn pontificating on the wages of sin, and that would have been that. Instead, by posing Farnsworth in such a shocking, sensational posture, his killer has forced us all to focus on Lord Preston's life—to look into who might have wanted him dead and why. And what we're finding has been quite illuminating, to say the least."

"Because we're looking at it from a different angle," said Hero. "Wasn't that one of the card's meanings?" She fell silent for a moment, her arms tightening unconsciously around the baby. "I can't see a simple, frightened whore running away in terror having the presence of mind to come up with something like that."

"No," said Sebastian, one hand flashing out to grab Simon before the little boy tumbled into the lake. "Neither can I."

They arrived back at Brook Street to find Sebastian's tiger impatiently awaiting him.

"There y'are, gov'nor!" said Tom, leaping up from the chair where he'd been perched with his crossed ankles swinging restlessly back and forth. "I still ain't found that blasted Jamie Gallagher, but wait till ye hear *this*!"

Sebastian sent for hot tea and biscuits for Tom, then took the lad into the library and poured himself a glass of wine.

"Start at the very beginning," said Sebastian, wise by now to the ways of his tiger.

Tom sucked in a deep breath and nodded. "Well, ye see, I been lookin' for 'im all over St. Giles and I ain't stirred up a whisker of anybody who's ever heard of the lad. So I got t' thinkin' 'bout how there's plenty o' Irish on the *other* side of the river, and that jist because this Jamie's been hangin' around Swallow Street and Great Marlborough Street don't mean 'e's necessarily from anywhere around there, if'n ye get me drift? So I took meself off t' Southwark, and what d' ye think? Turns out 'e's been on the streets down there ever since 'is da died a couple o' years back. They say 'e usually hangs around Naked Boy Court, but ain't nobody seen 'im this last week or so."

Sebastian took a long, slow sip of his wine. "And where exactly is this Naked Boy Court?"

"Off Deadman's Place. But 'ere's the really interestin' part: Seems 'e used t' have a sister called Jenny. After their da died, Jenny took up with some costermonger. From what I hear, 'e was a real looker, but also somethin' of a rotter. Left 'er with a babe, on account o' which she ended up in the Bridewell. And then, jist as soon as she got out, she disappeared."

The boy paused dramatically, his face alight with excitement.

"And?" prompted Sebastian.

"At first folks thought she musta jist took off. But then, a few days later, some wherrymen fished her body outta the Thames. Everybody said she musta killed herself on account o' the shame of all that'd happened. But Jamie, 'e was convinced she'd been murdered. And get this: Word is he swears Lord Preston Farnsworth is the one musta done it!"

Sebastian froze with his wineglass raised halfway to his lips. "What made him come to this conclusion?"

"That I never could find out. But it makes ye think, don't it?"

"Yes," said Sebastian, setting aside his wine. "Yes, it certainly does."

Father Ambrose was eating a plate of sausage and eggs in an old half-timbered, low-ceilinged tavern near the wharves when Sebastian came to stand on the far side of his table.

"Monsieur le vicomte," said the priest, setting down his fork and swallowing hard. "I wasn't expecting to see you again so soon."

Sebastian curled his hands around the edge of the heavy old table and leaned into it. "I've spent the better part of the past week looking for a boy named Jamie Gallagher. Something like fourteen or fifteen years old. Small for his age. Blue eyes. Black hair. Very bright. The assumption at first was that he was probably from around St. Giles because he's the one who found Lord Preston hanging in Swallow Street, and I saw him later in Great Marlborough Street. Except now I discover he's actually from Southwark, and if you try to tell me that you don't know him, I'm sorry, but I won't believe you, Father."

The priest finished chewing another mouthful of sausage and swallowed again. "No, I won't deny it."

"Why the bloody hell didn't you tell me you knew the boy who'd found Lord Preston?"

"I know many people."

"Don't play games with me, Father. I want to know about Jenny Gallagher."

At her name, the Frenchman's eyes widened. Then he set down his fork again with a clatter and pushed heavily to his feet. "Very well; I can tell you some—but not quite all—of what I know."

They turned toward the river, past the burned-out ruins of old brick warehouses, gray rotting docks, and charred remnants of mean tenements. A cold wind was kicking white spume off the tops of the turgid waves out on the Thames and ruffling the feathers of the sea gulls keening overhead. This was a part of Southwark that had once been the site of the sprawling great palace of the Bishops of Winchester, and reminders of it were everywhere, from the place-names like Clink Street and Winchester Yard to the ancient, fire-blackened stone walls of the bishops' Great Hall and various other parts of the vast medieval complex that had recently been revealed by a massive fire that had swept through there.

"She was a lovely child, little Jenny Gallagher," said the priest, his gaze on the broken remnants of the hall's great rose window rising high above them. "Bright, cheerful, always laughing—one of those people who seem to grab life with both hands and drink of it with an infectious delight." He smiled for a moment as if at the memory. Then the smile faded. "After Liam Gallagher—their father—died, she took up with a young costermonger named O'Malley. A handsome devil, no doubt, but a man with a dark, dark soul. He used to hit her, and when he found out she had his babe growing in her belly, he beat her dreadfully, probably in the hopes that she might lose it. That's when she finally left him. But the parish goes after the fathers of illegitimate babes, you know, to force them to pay support, so after the child was born, O'Malley threatened to kill it. She knew him well enough to be afraid he'd actually do it, so she abandoned the little boy on the altar up at St. George's."

"Why there?"

The priest shrugged. "St. George's is a wealthy parish. She thought if the child had any chance of surviving, it would be there. But she was seen leaving the church by a charwoman, and the rector had her hauled up before the magistrates. She was sentenced to six months in the Bridewell."

"The rector being Mr. Carmichael?"

"Yes."

"What happened to the little boy?"

"He went into the Bridewell with her, of course. Except they're not exactly known for being overly generous with food, are they? Jenny's milk dried up, and the child died." The priest paused, his gaze on the crumbling stones of the palace's old cellars. "When she was let out at the beginning of summer, she came to see me. Between what she'd been through with O'Malley, those months in the Bridewell, and losing her babe, she was a changed woman—somber, desolate. So when the wherrymen pulled her body out of the river a few days later, most people assumed she'd killed herself. But she hadn't."

"How can you be so certain?"

"I heard her confession. Obviously, I can't go into detail, but . . . let's just say she wasn't planning to kill herself."

"Perhaps something happened that changed her mind."

"I suppose anything's possible, but "—he paused—"the thing is, you see, there've been an extraordinary number of young women pulled from the Thames over the last two or three years. Some from Southwark, some from London or Westminster. The authorities assume they've killed themselves, so the postmortems are typically cursory. The lucky ones are buried in their local poor hole, while the unlucky ones end up at the crossroads with a stake through their hearts."

Sebastian stared out over the churning, white-topped waters of the river, toward the worn stone piers of London Bridge. He was thinking about the decomposing corpse of a young woman he'd seen lying on the stained granite slab in Paul Gibson's dank outbuilding. "When exactly did she die?"

"It must have been late June, or something like that."

"And what made Jamie think Lord Preston had anything to do with it?"

The French priest met Sebastian's hard gaze and held it. "I can't tell you that."

Sebastian tried hard to swallow his frustration. "Had she been raped?"

"What?" The question seemed to puzzle him. "No; nothing like that. What makes you ask?"

"Something I learned this morning."

"You can't . . . surely you can't be thinking that *Jamie* killed Lord Preston? He's a boy!"

"Boys can kill. Can and do."

The priest sucked in a quick breath. "Does Bow Street know?"

"What I've discovered about Jamie? No."

"But you will tell them?"

"Eventually," said Sebastian, "although not just yet. If you can come up with any explanation besides chance as to how a boy who suspected Lord Preston of murdering his sister somehow ended up being the one to stumble upon the man's dead body, I'd like to hear it."

But Father Ambrose simply turned to stare out over the scorched ruins of the once-grand palace of the Bishops of Winchester, his eyes narrowed and his features troubled.

Chapter 45

Sir Windle Barr was in the rear garden of his elegant house on Oxford Street, shaking his head over a row of yellowing, sickly-looking rosebushes, when his butler showed Sebastian out to the Chief Magistrate.

"Please accept my apologies for disturbing you on a Sunday," said Sebastian, pausing at the edge of the bluestone terrace.

"Just look at this black spot, will you?" said Barr, throwing up his hands in disgust. He was dressed in old buckskin breeches and a coat so worn that he might almost have been mistaken for one of his own gardeners. "This bloody rain has already killed a lovely pink China I bought last year, and these three damasks have barely a dozen leaves left between them—if that." He drew a deep breath and let his hands fall, his mobile mouth tightening into a wry smile. "But I don't suppose you've come here today to discuss the woes of my roses." He set to work yanking off his heavy rose gauntlets as he turned to mount the steps toward Sebastian. "How may I help you, my lord?"

"I'm wondering what you can tell me about a young woman who was pulled dead from the Thames last June. Gallagher was her name; Jenny Gallagher."

Sir Windle paused at the top of the steps, his bushy gray brows drawing together in a thoughtful frown. "Gallagher? Hmm. Gallagher . . ."

"Young; quite pretty. She'd only recently been released from the Tothill Fields Bridewell."

"Ah, yes; I remember her now." The magistrate shook his head sadly. "Tragic case, that one. Gave her six months in the Bridewell for trying to abandon a babe she'd just birthed out of wedlock. The child died while she was in there—doubtless smothered by its own unnatural mother. And then, once she'd been let out, what does the fool girl do but go and throw herself into the embrace of Old Father Thames." He heaved a heavy sigh. "Frailty, I fear thy name truly is woman."

"How do you know she threw herself in the river? Did someone see her jump?"

"Unfortunately, no. When someone sees them, they can occasionally be saved in time."

"So if no one saw her jump, it's possible she was pushed—or thrown into the river already dead."

"Murdered, you mean? Nah. We're always finding young women who've drowned themselves."

"How often?"

"What do you mean?"

"How often are dead young women pulled from the Thames?"

The heavy gray brows came together again. "Not certain I could say. I suppose we might have six or eight of them brought into the Mount Street deadhouse every year. It's the designated destination for bodies pulled from this part of the river, you know, but I couldn't tell you how many are found in the river as a whole. The ones found farther east and west are taken elsewhere."

"The inquest ruled that Jenny's death was a suicide?"

"It did, yes, but she was fortunate. The vicar, Mr. Carmichael, was able to convince the coroner she was of unsound mind when she took her life, so she wasn't dumped naked at the crossroads with a stake through her heart. Her family were allowed to bury her."

"How kind of him. Was a postmortem ordered?"

"Oh, yes. We aren't as hasty about such things as some are, you know. The surgeon said her lungs were full of water; there was no doubt that she'd drowned." He heaved another sigh. "From time immemorial, women have been killing themselves when they find themselves in trouble. It's sad, but understandable."

"Except that Jenny wasn't 'in trouble.' She'd already birthed her babe."

"And, as I said, in all likelihood killed it when they were in the Bridewell. I've seen cases of women who jumped into the river with their newborn babes in their arms." He looked away, blinking. "Those are the ones that really rip you apart."

The magistrate fell silent for a moment, then brought his gaze back to Sebastian. "Look, I know the families of some of these young women like to think their daughters and sisters didn't kill themselves, particularly when they consider themselves good Christians. They convince themselves that someone must have murdered their little girl. But it's just wishful thinking; that's all." His eyes narrowed. "What's your interest in some dead Irish trollop, anyway? I thought you were looking into what happened to Lord Preston."

Sebastian nodded. "Did you know Lord Preston kept rooms in Saville Street?"

"No, but I can't say I'm surprised. Preston was a decent, morally upright man, but he was no monk. With his sister living with him like that, what else was he supposed to do after his wife ran off and left him?"

"He could have divorced his wife and remarried." *Or eliminated her another way,* thought Sebastian, although he didn't say it.

Sir Windle huffed what might have been a low laugh. "Just because a man likes a woman in his bed now and then doesn't mean he wants to find himself leg-shackled to one for life. Can you blame him, after what happened with Lady Tess?"

"Perhaps not," said Sebastian.

Sir Windle brought up one hand to rub thoughtfully at the skin above his left eyebrow. "Saville Street, you say? That's right around the corner from the chapel on Swallow Street, isn't it?"

"Yes."

The magistrate turned to stare out over his waterlogged garden and said softly, "Well, I'll be damned."

Heading next to Tower Hill, Sebastian found Paul Gibson seated at his kitchen table, his hands wrapped around a thick, half-eaten sandwich piled high with roast beef.

"Have a seat," said the surgeon around a mouthful of sandwich. "Didn't expect you to get here this fast."

"What do you mean?" said Sebastian, sliding onto the opposite bench.

Gibson looked puzzled. "I sent you a message maybe half an hour ago. You didn't get it?"

"No. I was thinking about that Quaker you were telling me about, the one who asked you to try to identify the body of a young woman he'd found washed up on his property down by Rotherhithe. You said he'd found two other such young women in the last couple of years?"

"That's right. What makes you interested in him?"

"I'm not interested in him. But I'm told that an unusual number of young women have been pulled from the Thames in the last year or two. Do you know anything about that?"

Gibson stared at him a moment, then swallowed hard. "You're thinking they might have been murdered?"

"I am, actually."

Gibson set his sandwich down on his plate. "I've seen maybe two or three myself—not counting the one from the other day." He was silent a moment, then pushed the plate away. "I remember one in particular . . . Maddie was her name. She was a tiny thing, little more than a child, really. Alexi had delivered the girl's baby maybe six months before. The girl's mother was a widow with five other children, and Alexi thought the girl was helping feed the family by working the streets."

"And then the girl was fished out of the Thames?"

Gibson nodded. "There was no doubt in my mind she'd drowned, but she had bruises on her wrists and arms. I pointed them out, of course." He gave a low huff of something that was not amusement. "I remember Sir Nathaniel saying they were immaterial, that she'd probably acquired them in the pursuit of her 'profession.' Either that or she must have hit a pier of whatever bridge or dock she'd thrown herself off. Then he warned me that if I made too much of it at the inquest, they were liable to refuse to allow her to be given a proper burial."

"And dump her at the crossroads naked, with a stake through her heart instead?"

"Yes."

Sebastian went to stand at the mullioned casement window overlooking the garden with its rain-soaked roses, honeysuckle, and dark, dark secrets. It was a moment before he said, "Why did you send me a message, anyway?"

"Ah. That was on account of the body Bow Street sent me this morning. It's a woman, not exactly young, but not old, either. So far she's unidentified."

"And what makes you think I'd be interested?"

Gibson leaned back to swing his truncated left leg awkwardly over the bench, then his right leg, before pushing up. "Come, and I'll show you."

It was raining again, soft drops that pattered on the leaves and battered blossoms around them as they followed the wet, winding path toward the old stone outbuilding at the base of the garden. The door of the building stood open, so that Sebastian could see the still, sheet-covered body lying on the granite slab within.

"Recognize her?" said Gibson, going to flip the sheet back from the woman's face and bare shoulders.

She looked to be somewhere in her late thirties or early forties, with stylishly cropped fair hair and a thin, not unattractive face. The thick, ugly bruise encircling her slim white neck left little doubt as to how she had died.

"No," said Sebastian, one hand coming up to rest against the doorframe beside him. "Where was she found?"

"A night soil man came upon her body dumped in the middle of the Strand early this morning. He thought at first she'd simply collapsed."

Sebastian's gaze shifted to the woman's pink velvet spencer, fine muslin gown, and delicate underthings piled up on a nearby shelf, along with a pair of half boots in a soft pink kid. "Nice clothes."

"Oh, yes," said Gibson, going to pluck something from the enameled basin resting beside the clothes. "They're all new."

"So what made you send for me?"

Gibson held out a thin piece of card stock. "This."

Sebastian found himself staring at a small rectangular card with a familiar green, white, and red patterned back. Reaching out, he took the card and turned it over to reveal the image of a sobbing, fair-haired woman in a red dress and lace-trimmed shawl who sat huddled on the ground, her head bowed, her face buried in her hands. Before her loomed the large, naked figure of a man, his penis erect and prominent. He held one hand stretched out over the woman's head as if he were a puppeteer controlling a web of invisible strings that held her in his thrall. Except of course he was not really a man, for his fingers were like claws, his legs ended in hooves, and horns grew from the top of his head.

And below the image, in bold black letters, was printed XV: IL DIAVOLO.

The Devil.

Chapter 46

By the time he left Gibson's surgery, the drizzle had turned into a downpour, and Sebastian found his tiger walking the chestnuts up and down Tower Hill to keep them warm.

"This blasted weather," said Sebastian, leaping up to take the reins as the boy scrambled back to his perch. Except then, rather than driving off, Sebastian sat for a moment, his gaze fixed unseeingly on the looming, soot-stained ancient battlements of the Tower of London.

"What is it, gov'nor?" asked Tom, watching him.

Sebastian gathered the reins. "I think I need to pay a visit to Seven Dials."

Tom stared at him. *"Seven Dials?"*

Sebastian smiled and gave his horses the office to start. "Seven Dials."

Lying at the heart of St. Giles's notorious warren of narrow, filthy streets, mean, dilapidated courts, and noisome, urine-drenched alleyways, the area known as Seven Dials took its name from an elaborate sundial that once stood where seven streets converged together to form a star. It was a wretched, dangerous place crowded with impoverished Irish immigrants, formerly enslaved Africans, mutilated beggars, thieves, pickpockets, whores, and murderers. But because of the potent symbolism of the streets' layout, the area was also popular with various practitioners of the occult arts, from astrologers and alchemists to cartomancers and mesmerizers. And none of them observed the laws against Sunday trading so fiercely protected by the Society for the Suppression of Vice.

Buttoning his greatcoat against the cold drizzle that was still falling, Sebastian started on Little Earl Street and methodically set about going into one eerie, dimly lit shop after the other.

"I'm looking for a tarot deck," he told the young dark-haired woman he found reading a massive leather-bound tome behind the first shop's strangely carved wooden counter. Bunches of musty dried herbs dangled from heavy overhead beams, and everything from ancient copper bowls and yellowing parchment rolls to dirt-stained, grinning skulls filled the surrounding shelves, so that the place looked and smelled like a cross between a centuries-old tea emporium and half-robbed tomb.

A sly smile spread across the woman's face as she set aside her heavy book. She was quite pretty, and she obviously both knew it and was accustomed to using it. "We have many different decks, *monsieur.*"

"The one I'm looking for was produced in 1813 or 1814 by the Milanese press of Ferdinando Gumppenberg from a set of engravings by Giorgio Bassano. Do you have it?"

"Bien sûr," she said smoothly, reaching beneath the counter to come up with a deck she laid face up on the scarred wooden surface between them. "Here it is."

The top card, the ace of *Denari*, or coins, bore a neat inscription that read *Regia Fabbrica di Milano. Fabbricatore Gumppenberg.* A twenty-five centesimi tax stamp from the vanished Napoleonic-era "Kingdom of Italy" was prominently displayed below that. But when Sebastian picked up the deck and fanned it open, he found himself looking at a succession of exquisitely rendered neoclassical figures, and when he turned the deck over, the pattern of dots and dashes on the back was a geometric swirl of blues and yellows.

"This isn't it," he said, handing the cards back to her. "The deck I'm looking for is by an artist named Giorgio Bassano. The figures are in Renaissance dress, and the pattern on the back of the cards is green, white, and red."

The woman—a Creole from Louisiana, he'd decided—tapped one long fingernail on the top card. "These are the work of Bassano."

"Perhaps. But it's not the right deck."

"There is no other by Bassano." She picked up the cards to fan them open again, turning them toward him. "The images are very beautiful, yes?"

"Yes. But it's still not the right deck."

She shrugged and reached for her book.

He tried another shop, then another, his tall, well-dressed figure attracting more attention than he would have liked in the dirty, crowded, decaying streets. Some of the shopkeepers he spoke to tried to pass off a different deck as the one he was looking for; others swore that such a deck didn't exist. But finally, in a bizarre little shop crowded with incense sticks, Chinese jade carvings, delicate prisms, strange concoctions in dark bottles, and small, deadly-looking packets of mysterious potions, he found an aged, white-haired woman in a traditionally embroidered Palestinian gown such as he'd seen years before in Gaza, who listened carefully to his description, then said in a clear, rarefied accent that wouldn't have been out of place in a lecture hall in Cambridge or Oxford, "I have heard of this deck, but you won't find one for sale anywhere in England. In Italy, perhaps. But even there you might have difficulty finding one."

"Why?"

She pursed her lips and shrugged. "You can thank the Austrians for that."

"The Austrians?"

"Well, them and a bad choice of colors for the pattern on the deck's back."

"I don't understand."

"Ever hear of the *Bandiera d'Italia*?"

"No."

"It was the war flag of the Lombard Legion of Milan, back in the days of the Cispadane Republic. Green, white, and red, it was. And what does Gumppenberg do but put those colors on the back of his new tarot deck: green, white, and red. Then he runs his first printing in May of 1814, just days before an Austrian army under Field Marshal Heinrich von Bellegarde drives the French out of Milan. Von Bellegarde takes one look at the green, white, and red pattern on the back of Gumppenberg's new tarot deck, decides it must be some defiant reference to the Italian Republic's tricolor flag, and orders not only the finished decks but all the uncut sheets and even the plates themselves destroyed." She whispered something he couldn't quite catch under her breath, then said more clearly, "Barbarians."

"But there are some Bassano decks in England."

"I know of two. Before the Austrians took over, Gumppenberg managed to send one of the decks off to a cartomancer in Golden Square and another to that nasty Turkish astrologer over by Cross Lane. But I can guarantee you, neither will sell you their deck."

"What nasty Turkish astrologer over by Cross Lane?"

She stared at him for a long moment, then said, "There is only one."

The astrologer's name was Rasim Ataman, and he cast his charts from the ground floor of a dilapidated seventeenth-century building just off Cross Lane.

Pushing open a warped, weather-swollen door, Sebastian found himself in a cramped, oak-paneled room dimly lit by a single branch of flickering candles that sent eerie waves of light and shadow dancing over soaring walls hung with everything from smoke-darkened Russian icons and medieval Spanish *santos* to strange, colorful Chinese mandalas and a large, beautiful diagram of the relationship between body parts and the signs of the zodiac. In a series of cases across the back, everything from a bain-marie, astrolabes of varying antiquity, and a kerotakis jostled for space with various mineral specimens, a small Roman statue of the god Mercury, and row after row of ancient and modern volumes, their spines bearing titles in German, Italian, Greek, Latin, Arabic, and languages Sebastian couldn't even identify.

Beside the cases, at a dark, heavy desk half-buried beneath piles of rolled parchments and more books, sat a man dressed in the kind of faded, slightly worn silk and woolen robes that might once have belonged to Nostradamus or Jabir ibn Hayyan. He was younger than Sebastian had expected him to be—much younger, probably no more than thirty-five or thirty-six, a handsome man with thick black hair, long-lashed green eyes, and high, prominent cheekbones.

"Found your way here, did you?" said the man in lightly accented English, leaning back in his chair. "Took you long enough."

Sebastian pushed the warped door closed behind him with some difficulty. "I beg your pardon?"

"There can't be that many tall, well-dressed gentlemen brave enough to walk the streets of St. Giles." The man set aside the pen he'd been holding, but stayed seated. "I understand you're looking to buy a copy of Bassano's Renaissance tarot."

Sebastian used the back of one gloved fist to wipe the rain from his face. "Word travels fast around here."

"You are rather conspicuous." The man studied Sebastian in silence a moment, then folded his hands and rested them together on his desktop. "I draw up natal charts, you know. I don't sell tarot cards."

"So you still have the Bassano deck?"

"Of course I still have it."

"Are you quite certain?" Reaching into his coat, Sebastian drew Gibson's green, white, and red–backed card from his pocket and held it up so that the devil seemed to dance in the shimmering candlelight. "Because this was found on the body of a murdered woman someone dumped in the middle of the Strand early this morning. I assume you recognize it?"

Ataman stared at the card in silence for a long moment before saying, "I wonder, do you know what it means?"

"Not really."

"It stands for temptation, addiction, excess, vice . . ." The astrologer paused, then added, "And evil," in a vaguely sinister way that rolled the final word slowly off his tongue.

Sebastian said, "Another card from the same deck, the Tower, was left on the body of a man found hanging in Swallow Street six days ago."

Something flared in the astrologer's dark green eyes, but his expression remained stoic and unreadable. "I had nothing to do with either of those deaths."

"No? Then let me see your deck."

Sebastian thought for a moment the man meant to refuse. But

the astrologer was no fool; as a foreigner, his position was precarious, and he knew it. A muscle jumped along his clenched jaw. He said, "Wait here," then stood up and disappeared through a curtain at the rear of the room.

He was gone long enough for Sebastian to begin to wonder if the man had decided to try to flee the country when Ataman came back. "Look at them if you like," he said, tossing a familiar green, white, and red-backed deck amidst the clutter of papers, books, and scrolls on his desk. "They're all there."

Wordlessly, Sebastian picked up the deck and went through it, card by card.

Ataman stood woodenly, watching him. "You see?" he said when Sebastian had finished. "Not a card missing. I have nothing to do with these killings. Do you understand that? Nothing."

Sebastian held up the Bassano Devil card he'd brought with him. "So where did this come from?"

"I have no idea."

"No? How did you come to have this deck, anyway? I'm told most of them were destroyed by the Austrians over two years ago."

The man shrugged. "I knew Bassano's work. He did a neoclassical deck for Gumppenberg five—no, six years ago now—that I admire. So when I heard Gumppenberg had commissioned another set of engravings from him, I wrote and reserved a deck. He sent me one from the first printing."

"Is that sort of arrangement common?"

"Common? I don't know if I'd say it's common. But it is done, yes."

"Who else is likely to have ordered one of these decks from Gumppenberg?"

"How would I know?"

"I think you might."

Ataman reached for the deck, only instead of picking it up, he pushed the pile of cards toward Sebastian. "You still want it? Fifty pounds and it's yours."

"I thought it wasn't for sale."

"It wasn't. It's a beautiful, rare deck, but I don't need this trouble." *From you or from Bow Street.* The words didn't need to be said to be understood. He gave the deck another shove. "Take it."

Sebastian counted out fifty pounds. It was a steep price, but Ataman was right: The deck was both beautiful and rare, and Sebastian had no desire to take advantage of a man far from home, a stranger in a hostile land.

He tucked the deck into an inner pocket of his greatcoat as he turned, and had almost reached the door when Ataman said, "The hour of your birth: Do you know it?"

Sebastian looked back at him. "No," he lied.

A strange, unexpected smile of genuine amusement curled the astrologer's lips. "I think you do. But it doesn't matter; I can find out."

Half an hour later, Sebastian arrived back at Brook Street to find Hero out on one of her interviews and a note from Paul Gibson awaiting him.

Bow Street has identified the woman found strangled in the Strand as an abbess who was released from the Tothill Fields Bridewell just yesterday morning. Does the name Letitia Lamont mean anything to you?

Chapter 47

Sebastian stood for a time beside his library fire, thoughtfully fingering his friend's message. Then he tossed the note aside and went to where he had left Rasim Ataman's Bassano tarot deck resting on his desk.

Turning the cards over one at a time in his hands, he selected three images that he laid face up in a row on his desktop.

A hanging man.

A collapsing tower.

A naked devil.

Then, setting aside the Bassano deck, he retrieved his original Marseille-style cards from the desk's bottom drawer, found its version of the hanging man, and laid it beside the Bassano card. Because the Marseille-style deck was French, the card was labeled *LE PENDU*, the Hanged Man, rather than *IL TRADITORE*, the Traitor, like the Bassano card. But that wasn't the only difference.

"Well, hell," said Sebastian softly.

He was aware of the sounds of Hero coming in from her most

recent interview, heard her speaking to Morey in the entry hall, then looked up as she paused in the doorway to the library, her arms crossed at her chest with her hands cupping her elbows to hold them close against the sides of her somber gray carriage dress. "Is what I'm hearing true?" she said. "That Letitia Lamont has been found dead?"

He nodded. "She was released from the Bridewell yesterday morning. She then bought herself some grand new clothes, had her hair cut in a smart new crop, and somehow managed to get herself strangled, all in less than twenty-four hours."

"How bizarre." Reaching up, Hero untied the ribbons of her hat and tossed it aside. "But surely her death can't have anything to do with what happened to Lord Preston. A woman like that must have had many enemies. Dangerous enemies."

"No doubt. Except whoever killed her wanted to make certain we knew it was his handiwork." Sebastian held up the Devil card from the Bassano deck. "He left one of these in her pocket. It's from the same deck as the card that was left on Half-Hanged Harry."

"Dear God," whispered Hero, pushing away from the doorframe to come take the card and stare down at it thoughtfully. "What a horrible image." She looked up. "What does it mean? Do you know?"

"According to the vaguely unsettling astrologer who sold me this deck, the card stands for temptation, addiction, excess, vice, and, basically, evil."

Hero set the card back on the desktop. "I must say, that does sound appropriate for Letitia."

"It does, indeed. But here's the interesting thing." Sebastian reached for the Hanged Man from the Marseille deck and held it up. "Lord Preston was posed exactly like this: suspended by his left foot, with his arms tied behind his back. His killer even bent his right leg and tied that foot behind his left knee in order to precisely echo the posture of the man in the card." He picked up *Il Traditore* from the new deck. "Here's the same card from the Bassano deck."

"They are quite different, aren't they?" said Hero, taking both cards to hold them up side by side. "Not only is the man in the Italian card hanging from his right foot instead of his left, but his hands are dangling down over his head, not tied at all. And his other leg is swinging sideways rather than bent back to his knee."

Sebastian nodded. "It reminds me of the Renaissance-era red chalk sketch Mr. Carmichael showed me the other day."

She looked up, her lips parting on a quick breath. "Surely we couldn't be dealing with two different—" She broke off, as if unwilling to put the inevitable conclusion into words.

"Two different killers?" he said, finishing for her. "I suppose it's possible, although I find it hard to believe. But it does rather beg an important question." He tapped the image of the hanged man from the Marseille deck. "If Lord Preston's killer deliberately posed his victim's body in the exact posture used in the style of decks typical of southern France, why did he then leave cards from the Bassano deck when he killed Harry McGregor and Letitia Lamont?"

"Perhaps he simply decided to use that deck."

"Perhaps." Sebastian began to gather the scattered cards together, putting them back in order. "Except that most of the Bassano decks printed by Gumppenberg were destroyed by the Austrians when they overran Milan. I'm told the only other deck in England besides this one is in the hands of a cartomancer who lives in Golden Square."

"Madame Blanchette," said Hero softly. "But there must be another deck. She still has her deck's Tower card. You saw it."

"Yes."

"So where did the killer get *his* deck?"

"Presumably, he also ordered one in advance from Gumppenberg. What I can't understand is why he's leaving us a trail of cards from a deck so rare that he must surely know it could potentially lead us back to him."

"Perhaps he knows enough about the tarot to be aware of the various cards' meanings but not enough to realize that the deck he's using is dangerously rare."

"But if that's the case," said Sebastian, looking up to meet her worried gaze, "then how does he come to have such a rare deck?"

Chapter 48

Monday, 26 August

"The unfortunate truth is that, every year, a certain number of young women choose to drown themselves in the Thames," said Sir Henry Lovejoy the following morning as he and Sebastian walked along the terrace of Somerset House overlooking the broad, wind-whipped expanse of the river. "Almost inevitably it's because they've found themselves with child. They've been dismissed by their employers, abandoned by the father of their unborn babe, and rejected by their own families. They're ashamed, alone, frightened, and in despair, so that for far too many, death seems the only option." He glanced over at Sebastian. "What makes you ask?"

"Something I heard the other day," said Sebastian, unwilling as yet to expose Jamie Gallagher to the merciless and often fatal scrutiny of Bow Street. "How many women a year are we talking about?"

"It's difficult to say precisely, given that many such bodies either sink or are swept out to sea. The Royal Humane Society—the former Society for the Recovery of Persons Apparently Drowned—are the ones who keep the records on such things. Generally, in any given year there are something like a hundred and fifty corpses pulled from the river. Of those, perhaps seventy-five are the result of accidents, twenty-five are considered suicides, and the rest are classified as 'found dead.'"

"And how many of those are young women?"

The magistrate frowned thoughtfully. "Of the known suicides, perhaps sixteen or eighteen, although it may be more. I know the numbers have risen lately, presumably because of our current economic woes. But when it comes to those classified as 'found dead,' many of the bodies are in such an advanced stage of decomposition when recovered that determining the deceased's identity or even age can be difficult, and frankly, the authorities often don't bother."

"So postmortems aren't always performed?"

"Where there is some question as to how the individual died, they are, yes. Although when the individual is obviously a foreigner, or in the case of known suicides, the examinations can sometimes be rather cursory. The ratepayers object." He paused, then said, "These questions are not idle, are they?"

"Not exactly. But at the moment it's all speculation."

Lovejoy nodded as he stared out over the churning expanse of the river, a dull pewter now as it reflected the heavy gray clouds overhead. "Incidentally, we've discovered the origins of the note Lord Preston received that night shortly before dinner. It actually came from Bow Street—from John Stafford, to be exact. He was relaying some information from Sidmouth. From the sound of things, it had nothing at all to do with the man's death."

Sebastian looked over at him. "Is Sir Nathaniel still determined to arrest Major Chandler?"

"I fear so."

"And why precisely is the Major supposed to have killed Letitia Lamont?"

"That isn't entirely clear. Half-Hanged Harry is believed to have seen the two men together that night, which provides the motive for his killing. But given that the abbess was still in the Bridewell at the time, the assumption is that she must somehow have known . . . something." Lovejoy paused at the edge of the terrace to watch a sea gull take flight from the low wall beside them, its feathers ruffled by the growing wind as it rose into the sky. "The truth is, the Palace wants the fears of the populace quieted *now*. Our times are so . . . disturbed. Another ex-soldier and a former sailor were found starved to death in the streets this morning. There is a growing fear in certain quarters that London may soon see an outbreak of the sort of 'Bread or Blood' riots that shook East Anglia several months ago. The harvests are failing, and people are desperate. They're also dangerously angry—at the shopkeepers, whom they blame for the high price of food; at their current or former employers, because of falling wages and vanishing employment opportunities; and at the government for failing to do more to help those in need. Yet Liverpool remains determined to continue slashing expenses in order to bring down the unprecedented level of government debt."

"At least we aren't seeing the massive floods that are sweeping Switzerland and the Netherlands," said Sebastian. Then added, "Yet."

Lovejoy was silent for a moment, his face bleak as he glanced up at the gray sky above. "It's strange—is it not?—how as a species we like to think that, however messy human affairs may be, the earth itself will always be there, always the same: orderly, stable, eternal, reliable. But it's not, is it? *Something* has gone terribly wrong with our world. And simply because we don't understand what it is doesn't mean it isn't real."

"According to a natural scientist named Lancelot Plimsoll, the strange disruptions we've been seeing—the altered patterns of rain and drought, the unseasonable temperatures—are being caused by a massive volcano that erupted near Java last year and spewed vast clouds of volcanic dust and ash into the air."

"I hadn't heard that explanation. It seems rather fanciful, though, doesn't it? Volcanoes have been exploding since the dawn of history, and they've never done this."

"I gather this was a spectacularly large explosion."

"Indeed. And what does your Mr. Plimsoll think will happen next? Will this be our lives from here on out? Will it get worse and kill us all? Or will things eventually go back to normal?"

"That he doesn't know."

Lovejoy drew a deep breath and let it out slowly as they watched the strengthening wind lift a frothy spume from the tops of the choppy waves beside them. "I've heard that some are blaming lightning rods, saying they prevent the earth from releasing heat back into the atmosphere. Others suggest the internal temperature of the earth is cooling, causing a lack of circulation in the electrical fluid that moves between earth and the heavens."

"And don't forget the malevolence of witches. I understand the Americans have become particularly fond of that explanation."

"It sounds about as good a reason as any," said Lovejoy, and smiled.

Chapter 49

The former soldier's once-grand red jacket hung in tatters on his thin frame. His straight flaxen hair was long and unkempt, his young-old face gray with chronic ill health, his empty right pants leg knotted below the knee. But his eyes were bright with intelligence, and when he spoke, his accent was that of a gentleman.

"Why in the name of all that's holy would you want to write an article about former soldiers and sailors?" he asked Hero when she explained to him her reason for conducting her current series of interviews.

"Because people need to know about the hardships our veterans are facing," she said, looking up from writing *Sgt. Alexander Watson* on a new page in her notebook.

"You think they don't know already? All they need do is look around."

"Some people find it easy to close their eyes."

He was sitting on a low stone wall bordering Artillery Place. Lying to the south of St. James's Park, this was a humble part of

London, filled with charity schools, almshouses, institutions such as Westminster Hospital and Emmanuel Hospital, and St. Margaret's overcrowded churchyard. Its proximity to various Army barracks and armories—and the Bridewell—meant that it was also the haunt of a number of former soldiers.

"Nice luxury to have, I suppose," he said, turning his head to stare off across the nearby irregularly shaped square to where an underfed man in the ragged green coat of a rifleman had his head bowed as he stood in earnest conversation with a quietly sobbing woman. The woman held a babe cradled in her arms; another child who looked to be perhaps five clutched at her mother's shabby skirts.

Hero studied Sergeant Alexander Watson's sun-darkened, half-averted face. "How old were you when you enlisted?"

"Sixteen," he said, still watching the impoverished family. "As a lad I was always army mad, but when you're the eighth of eight sons born to a Nottinghamshire vicar, there's no way your father can afford to buy you a commission. He was planning to apprentice me to an apothecary, but that wasn't the life I thought I wanted. So I ran off and enlisted. I had this idea that I'd be able to wrangle a commission somehow." He huffed a soft, humorless laugh. "Obviously, that never happened."

"Which regiment were you with?"

"The 59th Foot, 2nd battalion. We were with the lot that had the stuffing kicked out of us in Spain back in '08 and '09, then rotted our guts out in the Walcheren Campaign before being sent back to the Peninsula in 1812."

"You went over the Pyrenees with Wellington?"

Watson grimaced as he shifted the stump of his right leg, then nodded. "We did. After that they sent us to Ireland, before quickly shipping us back to the Continent again—Belgium this time—when Boney decided to try for a rematch."

"You were wounded at Waterloo?"

A ghost of a smile tightened the fan lines beside the man's soft blue eyes. "Noooo," he said, drawing out the vowel as he shifted his leg again. "The 59th didn't make it to Waterloo in time. My leg got smashed on the way home. They loaded eight hundred of us on two transports—three hundred on the *Seahorse* and five hundred on the *Lord Melville*. Then they sailed us into a howling gale off the coast of Ireland."

Hero felt her breath back up in her throat, for she knew where he was going with this. "Which ship were you on?"

"The *Seahorse*. They saved a little over a hundred from the *Melville* that night, but only twenty-four of us made it off the *Seahorse*. I was the only one out of my mess that made it. There was another transport went down in the same storm with a different regiment—I don't recall which one. But altogether there were nearly a thousand British soldiers lost that night, and the French didn't need to fire a shot."

"Do you have a pension?"

Again that crinkling of the eyes that suggested a smile. "I do, yes, ma'am. I suppose it's one of the advantages of having received a gentleman's education—you know to get your letters of commendation, make sure your papers are in order, and how to lay your case before the worthy Commissioners of Chelsea Hospital. I get five pence a day, delivered quarterly." He nodded to the ragged, barefoot little boy sweeping the nearby crossing for a stout, middle-aged woman in black bombazine and a feathered hat who stood waiting on the corner, her arms crossed at her ample bosom. "It's more than he makes, I'll grant you that. But a man could hardly support a wife and family on it, so it's a good thing I don't have either one, isn't it?"

Five pence a day worked out to about seven pounds a year,

which was less than a quarter of what Hero paid her housemaids—in addition to providing them with room and board.

"I was down in Chelsea for a while," he was saying, "trying to help some of the other lads get their pensions out of the board. But it was so infuriating it started getting to me, so I thought it best I come away for a bit. There was this one lad I knew—no arm, coughing up blood—threw himself in the Thames when the Commissioners denied his pension. They told him pensions are only for good soldiers, and he'd been flogged once. The way they act, you'd think they wish the lot of us had just died over there rather than coming home to be a burden on the government. They say they can't help us any more than what they do because the country's so deeply in debt. Except why are we in debt? Because they spent hundreds of millions of pounds they didn't have just to put old King Louis back on his throne!"

Watson nodded to the ragged family, now crossing the square toward the Blue Coat School. "You think *they* care who's sitting on the throne of France? What they care about is finding work, and feeding their children, and keeping a roof over their heads, and maybe getting someone to teach their little ones how to read and write so they don't grow up as ignorant and poor as their fathers and grandfathers before them. Seems to me that's the kind of thing their government should be caring about, too."

Hero found her grip on her pencil tightening. He wasn't the first veteran she'd heard voice such thoughts. The endless war against France might have dampened popular enthusiasm for the revolutionary philosophies of the eighteenth century, but it hadn't extinguished them. And the increasing woes of the postwar years were giving the ideas of the Radicals a new impetus. It was one of the government's greatest fears, she knew—that educated, reform-minded men like Alexander Watson would join up with the poor of the working class and give coherent, reasoned voice to their grievances.

She said, "Have you ever thought of getting into politics?"

He laughed and spread his arms wide. "And how would a man like me go about doing that?"

"Have you considered going back to Nottinghamshire?"

His arms fell to his sides as he drew a deep, shaky breath. "I did go back, actually—right after I first finished wrangling with the Chelsea Commissioners and passed the board. But . . ." His expression grew wistful. "Everything's different up there now. It's not the same place I left twelve years ago. So many people I once knew are dead, and the ones that are still alive . . . well, they've changed. I suppose the truth is, I've changed, too; I'm not the same person I used to be." He turned his head to stare out over the square again, to where Hero's coachman was watering his horses at a rustic pump. "It just won't leave me, you know. The war, I mean. I'll see a hedgerow and my heart'll start pumping. I'll think, *Who's hiding behind that?* Or I'll hear a loud bang and jump half out of my skin. People up there thought I was crazy—I know because I heard them whispering about me. So, after a couple of months, I left and came back down here again—well, to Chelsea. I'll probably go back there in another day or two. Somebody's got to help those lads. So many of them haven't the faintest notion how things work or what they need to do."

He was silent for a moment, watching a small, lithe man in an eye patch and the worn uniform of a hussar turn down Brewers Row. "This morning, when I was up by the barracks, I heard some officers complaining about how hard their lives are, trying to live on half pay. I'd like to see them try to get by on five pence a day—or nothing at all, which is what most veterans get. But do you know how much the government has given Wellington? The better part of three-quarters of a million pounds! Four hundred thousand pounds for being a duke, plus another two hundred thousand for I forget what. And then when Parliament voted to award eight hundred thousand pounds to the Peninsular War survivors, what do they do but turn around and give fifty thousand of that to Wellington, too. Know how much men like me got out of it? Somewhere between two and six pounds—if we were lucky. Just think how many starving veterans and their families the government could have helped with Wellington's three-quarters of a million pounds. What man needs three-quarters of a million pounds? How could he even think about taking it, knowing how the rest of us are suffering? It's like we were bleeding and dying just to make him and his lot rich. Who was it that said the comfort of the rich depends upon an abundant supply of the poor?"

"I believe that was Voltaire," said Hero.

"So it was. Back before the Revolution, he tried to warn the French government about where letting their people starve was going to take them, but they didn't listen to him, did they? All those years we spent fighting the French, I guess the one thing it did do was unify the people of this country, didn't it? Enemies are good for that. But now the French king is back on his throne and it's the people here who are starving." He gave a faint, disgusted shake of his head. "You know what else Voltaire said? He said, 'If this is the best of all possible worlds, then what must the others be like?'"

Hero was surprised into letting out a choked laugh. "*Candide*, right?"

He nodded. Then his smile faded away into something bleak. "Lately, I've been wondering, if I could go back in time to my sixteen-year-old self, would I do it all again? Become a soldier, I mean."

"Do you think you would?"

"I don't know. If I hadn't joined the Army—if I'd stayed in Nottinghamshire and become an apothecary—I know I'd always have regretted it. I mean, I wouldn't have had any idea what soldiering was really like, now, would I? I'd probably have imagined myself performing all sorts of grand heroics, getting showered with endless honors and all that nonsense. I wouldn't know about the muddy graves that will forever haunt my dreams, or what it's like to try to hold your friend's guts in while he dies, or what a village smells like when every living thing in it—every single thing—has been killed by one of our artillery barrages. It must be a nice feeling, to be able to look back on your life in satisfaction and say, Yes, I made the right decisions. I like the way my life turned out; this is the life I wanted to live." He paused. "But that wouldn't have been me."

"'All's for the best in this best of all possible worlds,'" Hero quoted softly.

And this time, he was the one who laughed.

It was when Hero was crossing the open, dusty square that she saw him again—the small, lithe man in the worn dark blue jacket and gray overalls of a hussar. He was coming back from Brewers Row, walking swiftly toward her. Except this time he wasn't wearing an eye patch.

It might not mean anything, of course. The eye patch could be a ruse he donned for begging and removed when it wasn't needed. The worthies of the Society for the Suppression of Vice were always accusing beggars of such subterfuges. It was a harmless enough deception. And yet Hero found herself hastening her step toward her carriage as her hand crept into the opening of her reticule to close around the handle of her small muff gun.

Then the man broke into a run.

She saw the gleam of the knife in his hand; saw the determined slant of his thin lips and her footman's frightened face as he started toward her in alarm.

There was no time to draw the small brass-mounted pistol from her reticule. He was four feet away when she thumbed back the flintlock's hammer and brought up the reticule to fire through the silk.

She saw dark red blood spurt from the hussar's black neckcloth as the bullet tore through his throat. Saw him falter; saw his eyes widen with shock and fear. He was young, she realized with a stab of regret; surely no more than eighteen or twenty, with bright green eyes and sun-streaked fair hair and a thin, fading scar that curved around the side of his face. She saw his knees buckle, his body swaying.

Then his face tilted up toward the sky as his legs crumpled and his eyes rolled back in his head.

Chapter 50

"I wasn't aiming for his throat," she told Devlin as they stood with Sir Henry Lovejoy beside the young man's sprawled body. A wind had gusted up, bunching the gray clouds overhead and sending a torn sheet of worn newsprint tumbling across the dusty paving. "I was aiming for his chest." It bothered her that she'd come so close to missing him. And yet . . . "Perhaps if I'd hit him in the chest, he might have lived."

"I'm just thankful you stopped him," said Devlin, his voice rough.

"Have you ever seen the man before, Lady Devlin?" asked Sir Henry.

"No. Never," said Hero.

Devlin hunkered down beside the would-be assassin, his eyes narrowing as he studied the dead man's blood-splattered features. "I wonder if he actually was a hussar."

"Do you recognize the regiment?" said Sir Henry.

Devlin nodded. "It's the 25th."

Oh, no, thought Hero.

The magistrate's lips tightened into a thin line. "That's Major Chandler's regiment, is it not?"

Devlin pushed to his feet. "It is, yes."

Sir Henry tucked his chin back against his neck. "Easy enough for someone to have purchased the uniform from one of the secondhand stalls, I suppose."

"Yes." Devlin kept his gaze on the dead man's sun-darkened features. "Although that looks like a scar from a saber slash along his jawline."

Sir Henry's eyes narrowed as he bent to inspect the man's face. "Yes, I see it now." He glanced up at Hero. "Can you think of a reason someone would want to kill you, Lady Devlin?"

"I can't, no. I'm writing an article on the hardships faced by all the sailors and soldiers being discharged, but surely no one could object to that."

Straightening, Sir Henry let his gaze rove over the crowd of curious onlookers being held back by constables. "It might help if we knew who he was. Hopefully, someone in the neighborhood will be able to identify him."

"Let us hope," said Hero. "But if not, I would like to see that he is properly buried."

She was aware of two frown lines forming between Devlin's eyes as he quietly studied her.

"I'm all right," she told him.

And then she said it again, as if by doing so she could somehow convince herself and him. "I'm all right."

That afternoon, Sebastian drove with Hero out into the open countryside, far beyond the last dirty, wretched, straggling outskirts of London. A stiff breeze from out of the south had blown away most of the clouds, leaving the sky a rare, freshly scrubbed blue and drenching the rolling green hills with rich sunlight. On the far side of a clear, gurgling stream, they left Tom with the curricle and went for a walk along the quiet, winding lane.

"It's lovely out here," she said, smiling faintly as she twirled her parasol and drew the clean air of the country deep into her lungs.

"Yes," he said.

She glanced over at him. "I really am all right, you know."

"I know."

"It isn't as if he's the first man I've killed."

"No."

Adjusting the tilt of her sunshade, she paused to look out over a herd of brown cows grazing contentedly in the sun-soaked, wind-ruffled grass of the hillside below them. "It's just that he was so very young. I keep thinking that somewhere out there is a mother who has been waiting desperately for her son to come home from the wars. A mother, or perhaps a sweetheart. And now . . . he'll never come."

"The choice was his."

"Yes."

They stood side by side for a time, watching a hawk soaring high overhead, the sun warm on its wide, outstretched wings. Devlin said, "There may be no one waiting, you know. No mother. No sweetheart."

She looked over at him. "In its own way, that's desperately sad, too, isn't it?"

"Yes."

She turned to face him, her lips parting on a deeply indrawn breath as she searched the oh-so-familiar features of his face—the lean cheeks; the fierce, deeply set yellow eyes; the strong, square chin. "Does it never bother you? When you've killed someone, I mean. Or does one grow accustomed to it after killing so many during the wars?"

He took her hand and, holding it between both of his, raised her fingers to his lips. "It bothers me," he said, then added, "afterward," in a way that made her wonder exactly what he meant, although it didn't feel right for her to ask.

"I'll admit some deaths are more disturbing than others, but I don't think it ever gets easy—or at least it shouldn't as long as we retain a sense of our shared humanity. And that's something I never want to lose. It's what separates us from the monsters, isn't it?"

"You think someone hired him?"

"I think it's likely, yes. And his death is on that person's head. Not yours."

"I wish I could believe that. Truly believe it, in my heart of hearts."

"Believe it," he said. Then he wrapped his arms around her, drew her close, and held her.

Simply held her.

They arrived back at Brook Street to find a dilapidated carriage drawn by two horses pulled up before the house and Lady Tess Farnsworth turning away from the front door to descend the steps.

At the sight of them, her hand tightened around the iron railing at her side. "Oh, thank goodness you've come," she said, taking the steps in a rush as Sebastian swung Hero down from the curricle's high seat.

"What is it?" said Hero, stepping forward to grasp Tess's trembling hands. "What has happened?"

"It's Hugh! *Oh, my God,* they've taken Hugh."

"Who?" said Sebastian, steadying Tess as her knees began to buckle beneath her. "Who has taken him?"

"Sir Nathaniel! Bow Street! He's being remanded into custody for the murder of Preston and those two other people we'd never even heard of before all this started." She sucked in a deep breath, her voice becoming a torn whisper. "I don't know what to do. It's all my fault—all of it. This never, ever would have happened if I hadn't left Preston. God help me, what have I done to him?"

She looked up at Sebastian with pleading, tear-filled eyes. "*What have I done?*"

Chapter 51

Sebastian reached Bow Street to find Sir Henry Lovejoy standing on the pavement before the public office's front steps, one hand on the open door of a hackney carriage drawn up before him.

"Ah, Lord Devlin," he said, closing the carriage's door again and dismissing its jarvey. "I was just on my way to Brook Street to see you. I take it you've heard?"

"About Major Chandler? Yes, just now. Have they taken him up to Coldbath Fields? Or is he already at the Old Bailey?"

"What? Oh, so you haven't heard, then, have you?"

Sebastian shook his head. "Heard what?"

"Sir Nathaniel has ordered the Major released. Some French priest turned himself in and confessed to Lord Preston's murder. At first we were inclined to dismiss his claims, but he knew several important details that were never made public."

Sebastian stared at him. "Are you talking about Father Ambrose?"

Lovejoy put up a hand to grab his hat as a sudden gust of wind whistling up the narrow street threatened to carry it away. "Yes. You know him?"

It was some time before Sebastian was able to arrange to speak to Father Ambrose alone, in a small room tucked away behind the Bow Street Public Office's central staircase.

The oak-paneled chamber was sparsely furnished, with an aged barley twist table and four chairs in the center and a row of worn, dusty cabinets lined up along the back wall. The French priest sat in one of the straight-backed wooden chairs, his shoulders hunched and his clasped hands resting on the table before him. He looked up, his face expressionless, when Sebastian entered the room.

"Lord Devlin," he said, his accent unusually pronounced. "I owe you an apology. From the beginning, I should have told you the truth. I never intended for anyone else to suffer for what I did."

"That's why you turned yourself in?"

Father Ambrose nodded. "As soon as I heard that major was to be charged." He brought up one hand to swipe a spread thumb and fingers down over his thick, graying beard. "I did not intend to kill him, you know—Lord Preston, I mean. It was an accident."

"You 'accidently' bashed in his brains, did you? And then you 'accidently' hanged him upside down in a careful imitation of *Le Pendu?*"

"I see I must explain."

Sebastian pulled out the chair opposite him and sat. "Please do."

The priest sucked in a deep breath. "You know Farnsworth kept rooms in Saville Street?"

"Yes, although I only discovered that recently. How the hell did you know about it?"

He gave a very Gallic shrug, as if it were immaterial. "So you see, I was in the area that night—"

"Why?"

"What do you mean, why?"

"What were you doing up by Saville Street?"

"I was walking. I . . . like to walk."

"Quite far, evidently. And you just happened to walk up Saville Steet?"

"No, Glasshouse Street. I was walking on Glasshouse Street. But Lord Preston, he must have seen me, because when I turned up Swallow Street, he followed me."

"You're saying *he* followed *you*?"

"Yes."

"Why? Why would he follow you?"

"Because I had just that morning accused him of murdering a number of impoverished young women he considered 'morally deficient.'"

Sebastian studied the Frenchman's lined, aged face. "So that confrontation you told me about—the one in the Strand; it wasn't actually about a boy who had died in Newgate?"

The priest tilted his head to pull awkwardly at one earlobe. "No, it was about Cian Donahue. Or at least, that's how it began. Then I lost my temper and moved on to the young women."

Sebastian shook his head. "I still don't understand why he would follow you later that evening in Swallow Street."

"I'm getting to that. The thing is, you see, I didn't realize he was following me. I mean, I could hear a man's footsteps behind me, but I didn't bother to glance back and see who it was. Why should I? Look at me; no thief in his right mind would see me and think I had anything worth stealing."

"So precisely how did the two of you end up in the chapel?"

"Ah. Well, it was raining, you see? Not hard at first. But then it began to come down harder, so I ducked into the chapel to wait it out."

"And Farnsworth came in after you?"

The priest looked Sebastian straight in the eye and said, "Yes. As I said, it was raining quite hard by then. He was carrying that walking stick of his—you know the one? The one with the short sword hidden in it? He told me he was going to shut me up once and for all; then he pulled the blade and came at me. I grabbed one of the chunks of wood scattered about the chapel floor and hit him with it, just here—" The priest pointed to the right side of his head. "Above the ear. I'll admit I swung hard—I wanted to stop him. But I wasn't trying to kill him. Only then, when he staggered back, he stumbled over some rubble and fell."

"And hit the back of his head?"

The Frenchman nodded.

"And Half-Hanged Harry and Letitia Lamont? Why did you kill them?"

"I did not kill them. I had nothing to do with either of their deaths."

"So who did kill them?"

"I don't know."

Sebastian pushed up from his chair and went to stand in the open doorway. One of Lovejoy's constables was waiting just outside the room, but the man was picking his teeth in uninterested abstraction, his vacant gaze fixed on nothing. It was a moment before Sebastian turned back to where the priest still sat at the table, calmly watching him.

"No one is going to believe you," Sebastian said. "You know that, don't you?"

"Of course they will believe me. The Palace wants someone to hang for this murder, as quickly as possible." The old priest spread his arms wide. "And here I am."

Sebastian shook his head and switched to French. "Who are you trying to protect?"

Father Ambrose stared up at him with wide, solemn eyes, his arms dropping to his sides again as he answered in the same language, "I don't know what you're talking about."

Sebastian wanted to grab the priest by the front of his worn black habit, haul him up out of that chair, and shake him. Instead, he said, "Something made you—you and Jamie Gallagher both—suspect Farnsworth of killing not only Jamie's sister but any number of other women as well. What the devil was it?"

"That I can't tell you."

Sebastian slammed his fist down on the tabletop between them. "Why the bloody hell not?"

"It was told to me in confidence."

Sebastian took a deep breath and forced himself to say more calmly, "The first time I spoke to you, you could have said something about the growing number of young women being fished out of the Thames. You could have told me you thought they weren't all suicides, that some of them were being murdered. You could even have told me that 'someone' suspected Lord Preston was involved in their deaths. So why didn't you?"

"Because I was a coward. I was hoping you'd hear about what was happening to the young women some other way. I was afraid that if I were to tell you about my suspicions—if I were to be the first to mention the dead women—it might somehow lead to Bow Street realizing that I was the one who had killed Farnsworth."

"You? Or Jamie?"

"Me!"

Sebastian shook his head. "You say Farnsworth attacked you with a blade from his walking stick. But there was no walking stick in that chapel."

"No. I took it with me and threw it in the Thames."

"Why?"

"I don't know."

"You don't know," said Sebastian, making no effort to keep the incredulity out of his voice. "You want me to believe you were afraid of being caught, and yet you took the time to hang Farnsworth upside down? Why? If you'd taken his purse and watch and left him lying where he'd fallen, everyone would have assumed he'd been killed by footpads."

"But I didn't want his death to be dismissed as the work of footpads! I *wanted* the authorities to look at his life and discover what he had been doing."

"Why? He was dead. Even if what you suspect is true—that he was murdering impoverished young women and making their deaths look like suicides—you ended that by killing him."

Father Ambrose glanced toward the open doorway, then leaned forward and lowered his voice even more, although they were still speaking French. "Except that Lord Preston wasn't killing those women alone."

Sebastian held himself very still. "You know that for certain?"

The priest hesitated a moment, then nodded.

"And let me guess: You can't tell me how you know that, either."

Father Ambrose stared back at him with wide, earnest eyes.

"Bloody hell," swore Sebastian, flattening his hands on the tabletop and leaning into them. "These other men—do you know who they are?"

"No. All I know is that there were three of them, including

Farnsworth." He hesitated, then said, "There is what looks like an old sarcophagus in the ruins of the palace of the Bishops of Winchester, in a small courtyard near the river. The men would fill it with water, hold the heads of the women they wanted to kill under until they were dead, then throw their bodies in the river. That way, if the bodies were found, a postmortem would show that the women had drowned. Any superficial bruises could be easily explained away."

By saying the women must have jumped off a bridge or dock and hit something as they fell, thought Sebastian. Aloud, he said, "Someone saw them?"

The priest leaned back in his chair. "I can't tell you that."

"No, of course not. And yet you claim not to know the identities of these two other men."

"If I knew, I would tell you. Believe me."

"Believe you?" Sebastian pushed away from the table. "Why the bloody hell should I believe a bloody thing you say?"

The priest drew a deep breath. "I have thought about the death of Harry McGregor, and I think it's possible he saw Farnsworth and the others murdering one of those young women. That's why he was killed."

"And Letitia Lamont? She was in the Bridewell until after Farnsworth was dead. Why would someone kill her?"

"That I don't know."

Sebastian fixed him with a hard stare. "How does a priest become so familiar with the tarot?"

The Frenchman shrugged. "Someone I was close to once used the cards. The images have always fascinated me. They are very"—he paused as if searching for the right word—"evocative, yes?"

"They are indeed. So how do you explain the tarot cards this other, 'unknown' killer left with McGregor and Lamont?"

"I can only assume it's an attempt to make all three deaths look like the work of the same killer."

"If so, it's been very effective." Sebastian paused. "Tell me this: Why the hell did you send Jamie to me?"

An expression of chagrin flashed across the priest's face, then was gone. "I didn't send him; that was something he decided to do on his own initiative. I was . . . very upset with him for doing it."

"How did he even know that Farnsworth was dead?"

"What do you mean?"

"Obviously, the boy didn't just 'happen' to duck into the chapel that afternoon to get out of the rain the way he claimed. So how did he know Lord Preston was dangling upside down in Swallow Street? You'll never convince me you told him."

The priest drew a quick breath, then another.

"Didn't think of that, did you?" said Sebastian.

Father Ambrose licked his lips. "He . . . he overheard me telling someone else about it. Someone I can't name and—and someone Jamie does not know. I was concerned because the body hadn't been discovered yet. And so Jamie, he decided to go tell you."

"You know, Father, you're a very accomplished liar for a man of God."

The priest shrugged again.

Sebastian blew out a long, frustrated breath. "I can't help you if you're not honest with me."

The Frenchman leaned forward. "You want to help me, my lord? Truly? Then find the men who were working with Lord Preston Farnsworth to kill those young, impoverished women. I'm an old man; what happens to me at this point is not important. But the women those men killed were young—some little more than children. They should have had their entire lives ahead of them. Instead, no one even knows they were murdered. They're completely forgotten, their families ashamed of them, their bodies dumped in unmarked graves or swept out to sea. You need to find out who besides Farnsworth has been killing these women, and you need to stop them. Please. Before they can kill again."

Chapter 52

That night, Sebastian sat beside the bedroom fire, a glass of brandy cupped in one hand, his gaze on the dancing flames before him.

"Do you think any of what Father Ambrose told you is true?" said Hero, coming to stand behind his chair and loop her arms around his neck.

He tipped back his head so that he could look up at her, one hand coming up to rest over hers. "Some of it, undoubtedly. The question is what? And how much?"

She was silent for a moment, her gaze, like his, on the fire. "Is it possible Jamie killed Lord Preston?"

"I was wondering that myself, at first. If Father Ambrose knew—or suspected—that Jamie was the killer, I can see the priest turning himself in, both to save the boy and to keep an innocent man like Hugh from hanging for a murder he didn't commit. The problem with that scenario is that I can't see a fourteen-year-old street rat like Jamie being calculating enough—or knowing enough about the tarot—to hang Farnsworth up like *Le Pendu*."

"I hadn't considered that."

Sebastian took a slow sip of his brandy. "I think Father Ambrose actually did kill Farnsworth. And it was probably deliberate, too."

"Why deliberate?"

"Because Gibson told me that if Farnsworth was hit from the front, his killer is in all likelihood left-handed, but if he was hit from behind, then I'm looking for someone right-handed." Sebastian took another drink. "The first time I met him, Father Ambrose was gardening. And he was working with his right hand."

"That's disturbing." She rested her chin on the top of his head. "If Father Ambrose is actually that ruthless and brutal, then it's possible he also killed Half-Hanged Harry—*if* he thought Harry had seen him with Farnsworth. But what possible reason could a French priest from Southwark have to kill Letitia Lamont?"

"No reason I can think of. Which makes me suspect that Harry and Letitia were both killed by someone else. Someone in possession of an exceedingly rare tarot deck."

"And this 'someone' left the tarot cards to make everyone think their deaths were the work of whoever murdered Lord Preston?"

"It would be a clever thing to do, wouldn't it? Particularly if one had a solid alibi for the night Lord Preston was killed."

She eased the brandy from Sebastian's grasp, took a sip, then handed it back to him. "And this ancient burned-out courtyard with its water-filled stone sarcophagus? You think it truly exists?"

"I don't know, but I intend to find out." Setting aside his drink, he tightened his hand on Hero's to pull her around and take her in his arms. "Can I interest you in some early-morning exploration?"

Tuesday, 27 August

The next morning dawned cool but calm and clear, with a fine mist that hung over the unnaturally still waters of the river and drifted through the gaping doorways and empty windows of the ancient, fire-blackened palace walls.

"I didn't realize so much of it was still here," said Hero as they picked their way through the ruins. "Just hidden away behind the dilapidated warehouses and tenements that were built in and around it over the centuries. Forgotten."

"Like the Winchester Geese buried in Cross Bones," said Devlin.

"Or young women deemed by Lord Preston and his friends to be too dangerously 'immoral' to be allowed to live." She was silent for a moment, her head falling back as she stared up at the broken remnants of the Great Hall's once-magnificent rose window. "I keep thinking: If what Father Ambrose told you is true, how could it all have come about? I mean, how do three people decide to commit murder together? Were they just sitting around one evening, drinking their good French brandy, digesting the lovely dinner they'd eaten at their club, and grumbling about the way the loose, morally deficient women of the lower orders were driving up the parish poor rates? And then one of them—Farnsworth or perhaps one of his confederates—up and says"—she lowered her voice in a brutal imitation of Farnsworth's tone—"*What we ought to do is just kill the little whores. Kill them, toss their bodies in the river, and save ourselves the cost of dealing with both the hussies and their useless spawn.*" She let her voice come back to normal. "And the other two, they raise their glasses and go, *Hear! Hear! Capital idea, old fellow?*"

Sebastian looked over at her and smiled. "Probably something like that, yes."

"God help us," said Hero, taking his hand as they climbed over the broken remnant of a brick wall.

They were in what might once have been a large workroom of some sort. The roof was now open to the sky, its ancient beams blackened and collapsed. Clambering over piles of rubble, they made their way to a gaping doorway that opened onto a small courtyard. And then Hero paused, her breath leaving her chest in a rush. "Oh, no. There it is."

An ancient sandstone coffin some five and a half feet long and perhaps three feet high stood against the courtyard's far wall. Looking as if it might date back to the twelfth or thirteenth century, it bore on its long side a large incised Greek cross surrounded by sheaths of palm fronds. At some point—perhaps during the time when Oliver Cromwell had gifted the bishops' palace to his cronies—the sarcophagus had been dug up, the bones of its original occupant unceremoniously dumped out, and the stone coffin moved here to serve as a trough for watering animals or processing wool. The large hole in the center of the base that had once allowed the fluids from the decaying body to drain away had been sealed tight and a smaller hole drilled at one end. That hole was now fitted with what looked like a very new cork, still in place, so that the recent rains had filled the crudely chiseled stone interior nearly to its brim.

"Somehow," said Hero, "I didn't think it would really be here."

"Neither did I." He let his gaze rove around the courtyard. Its high brick walls were largely intact, and someone at some point had cleared the space of rubble and debris. An archway tucked away in a corner of the western wall opened to a short lane, also cleared, that led back to Clink Street.

"That's how they did it," he said. "It's a perfect setup. With everything around here burned, this place must be deserted at night. All they'd need do is drive a carriage or closed cart down that lane, drag their victims in here, hold their heads underwater until they quit struggling, then haul the bodies out onto what's left of the old dock and dump them in the Thames. It would be appallingly easy."

Hero went to stand in the broken archway, one hand coming up to rest against the stone coping as the breeze off the river lifted the curls around her face and ruffled the modest plumes in her hat. "How many? I wonder. How many women have they killed?"

"I suspect we'll never know."

"Will they keep doing it, do you think, with Farnsworth now dead?"

"Why not? Not here, perhaps. But there must be other places that would serve their purpose almost as well."

"I wonder how they set about identifying the women they wanted to kill."

"If I had my guess, I'd say through the Society for the Suppression of Vice."

"Or the courts."

"Or the courts," he agreed.

She turned to face him again, her hand falling back to her side, her features solemn. "We must stop them."

"Yes. But first we need to identify precisely who 'they' are."

She gave a faint shake of her head. "How?"

"I think I know where we can start."

Chapter 53

Mr. Crispin Carmichael was in the vestry of his church, all the doors of the long line of cupboards before him thrown open and a frown forming a fine line across his high forehead as he stared at them. At Sebastian's entry he closed one of the cupboard doors, then turned to greet him with a polite smile.

"Good morning, Lord Devlin," he said as the rectory's housekeeper curtsied and hurried away. "Forgive me for receiving you here, but I've made it a practice to personally inspect the vestments on the second and fourth Tuesday of every month. The one time I delegated the task to a deacon, he missed a serious infestation of moths from what I believe is the Tineidae family. They had wreaked havoc by the time I discovered them. Absolute havoc."

"Thank you for agreeing to see me," said Sebastian, his gaze drifting over the endless stacks of precious silks and fine wools. "I wanted to ask you about Jenny Gallagher."

Mr. Carmichael turned to close another door, then paused, his fingertips coming up together to touch his lips as if in prayer.

"Jenny Gallagher? The name is unfamiliar. Is she one of my parishioners? Has something happened to the poor woman?"

"It has, unfortunately. One of the church's charwomen caught her leaving her newborn son on the altar steps. You had her hauled before the magistrates, who convicted her of child abandonment and sentenced her to six months in the Bridewell."

"Ah, yes; I recall the incident now. Such a sad, sad case. I believe she later smothered the poor child."

"Or he died when his underfed mother's milk dried up."

"Perhaps."

"Do you know what happened to her?"

"Presumably, she was released. Let's see . . . sometime late last spring, it must have been. If you're looking for her, I suggest you direct your inquiries to Covent Garden or the Haymarket. That's where her kind inevitably end up, I'm afraid."

"As it happens, she's dead. She was pulled out of the Thames in June."

"Killed herself, did she? How terribly sad." He heaved a great sigh. "The burden of guilt over the murder of her child must have been too great for her to bear."

"Actually, it appears more than likely that she herself was murdered."

"Oh, surely not." Mr. Carmichael gave a prim, condescending smile. "Such women throw themselves in the Thames all the time, I'm afraid."

"You know of others?"

The smile was gone. "Not from this parish, fortunately."

"You don't have any idea who might have killed her?"

"Me? Good heavens, no. How could I? Jenny, you say her name was? I barely remember her."

And yet you set in motion the chain of events that ended her life, thought

Sebastian. Aloud, he said, "Do you know if Lord Preston carried a walking stick with a blade concealed in its shaft?"

"He did, yes. It's a clever thing. I believe he purchased it years ago when he was in Paris as quite a young man—back in 'eighty-eight or early 'eighty-nine, it must have been."

"Did he typically carry it when he went for his evening walks?"

"Always. He was most concerned about the dreadful level of crime in the city, you know; he carried it everywhere."

"That makes sense," said Sebastian, who had also sent a note asking Lovejoy to confirm the point with Farnsworth's valet. "I'm told Lord Preston was particularly disturbed by the number of what he called 'immoral women' in the city. Is that true?"

"Oh, yes. We've been concerned about the deleterious impact of such women on society for years."

"Are there other members of the Society for the Suppression of Vice who shared Lord Preston's emphasis on the conduct of these women?" He'd almost said *Lord Preston's obsession*, but changed it just in time.

"Doesn't every decent, right-thinking man worry about such things?" said Mr. Carmichael. "It's how it all starts, you know—with lust-filled, incorrigible women luring innocent young men into a life of vice and crime."

"Yes, of course," said Sebastian. Reaching into his coat, he drew out the Tower and the Devil cards from Bassano's deck. "Are you by chance familiar with these?"

Mr. Carmichael's lips flattened into a thin, tight line of distaste as he reached gingerly to take the Devil. "It's Satan, of course. How utterly abhorrent." He looked up. "But what has any of this to do with the death of Lord Preston?"

"That card was left on the body of a woman named Letitia

Lamont. She had been released from the Tothill Fields Bridewell just hours before she was killed."

"And you think her death is somehow related to what happened to Lord Preston? Simply because this card was found on her? Bit fanciful of an idea, isn't it?"

"Is it? How familiar are you with the palace of the Bishops of Winchester?"

Mr. Carmichael handed him back the card. "You mean the ruins of that section of Southwark that burned several years ago? There's not much left of it anymore, is there?"

"Not much," Sebastian agreed, tucking the cards away. "Someone was saying they thought Lord Preston might have been coming to see you the night he was killed. Is that possible?"

It was a lie, of course, but considerably less confrontational than asking the churchman bluntly, *Where were you that night?*

The vicar looked puzzled. "I can't imagine he would have been coming here. I was meeting with some of the leading members of our vestry that evening."

"And Lord Preston would have been aware of that?"

"Oh, yes; in fact, we'd discussed several items I was intending to present. I don't know who suggested such an idea to you, but they must surely have been mistaken."

"And you can't think where Lord Preston might have been going that night?"

"No." The vicar's eyes drifted sideways to the still-open cupboards. "If there is nothing else, my lord, I do need to finish this task. I am scheduled to visit Lady Simpton this afternoon to offer my condolences on the recent death of her father."

"Yes, of course. Thank you for agreeing to see me."

"Anytime," said the vicar, turning back to the stacks of silk and fine woolen garments, the cost of which would have kept his poorest parishioners fed through many a brutal winter. "Anytime."

"So, what do you think?" Hero said later, looking up from where she sat beside the drawing room fire, Miss Guinevere asleep in her arms. "Could the good vicar of St. George's be one of the men who has been helping Lord Preston cleanse the city of wayward young women?"

Sebastian poured himself a glass of burgundy and came to stand beside her. "I certainly see it as a possibility. But that could just be because I don't like coldly ambitious prelates."

"He certainly is that."

Sebastian took a slow sip of his wine. "Sir Henry tells me that, according to his valet, Lord Preston was indeed carrying his walking stick when he went out that evening. And it did contain a concealed blade."

"And the man didn't think to say something about it before? It—" She broke off as the sound of someone knocking loudly on the front door reverberated through the house. "Expecting anyone?"

"No."

He heard the murmur of a boy's familiar voice, followed by Morey's curt reply. Then the majordomo climbed the stairs to pause with a bow at the door of the drawing room and say, "The lad who came to see you last week is here again, my lord. With a young female."

Sebastian and Hero exchanged quick glances. Then Hero rose carefully with the sleeping babe in her arms while Sebastian said to Morey, "Show them up right away."

Chapter 54

Jamie Gallagher came in clutching his tattered cap in both hands, his face pale, his eyes bleak. The "young female" who slid into the room behind him was unknown to Sebastian, but from the looks of things she was still a girl, probably no more than fourteen or fifteen. Small and slightly built, she had even features, a light scattering of cinnamon freckles across her upturned nose, and thick, flaming red hair she wore tucked up under a plain bonnet. Her modest brown stuff gown was old but clean and made high at the neck with a round collar.

"I come t' tell ye I'm the one who did it," announced Jamie, his features stark and tense as he drew up just inside the doorway. "I'm the one killed Farnsworth, not Father Ambrose. I've tried tellin' Bow Street, but they ain't listenin' to me. They think I'm just sayin' it t' try to save Father, but ye gotta believe me because it's the truth. And if ye can't help me get them t' believe it, I don't know what I'm gonna do because they're gonna hang Father for sure—hang him for somethin' I done!"

Sebastian glanced at Hero, who was just coming back down the stairs from handing Guinevere to Claire.

"Please, come in and have a seat," she said, drawing the reluctant pair over to the fire, where they perched uncomfortably side by side at the edge of the sofa. "How about some nice hot tea?"

"Oh, no, ma'am," stammered Jamie. "We wouldn't want to be troublin' ye."

"It's no trouble at all," Hero said with a smile and quietly left the room again.

Sebastian rested one arm along the mantel and took a slow sip of his wine. "You're going to need to tell me exactly what happened that night—the night you say you killed Farnsworth. From the very beginning."

Jamie leaned forward, his hands now clenched tightly together between his knees. "Well, I was up near Swallow Street, ye see, and—"

"Why?" said Sebastian, interrupting him.

Jamie stared up at him, his lips parting and his eyes going wide. "What do ye mean, *why*?"

"Why were you up there?"

The boy cast a nervous sideways glance at the girl beside him. "Sure then, but I just was, that's all." He obviously wasn't as smooth a liar as Father Ambrose. "Lord Preston had rooms up there, ye see. On Saville Street."

"So I have discovered. But how do you know that?"

The boy shrugged. "Just know it, I do. Anyways, I come face-to-face with him, ye see, sorta accidental-like, and he recognized me."

"He recognized you? From when?"

Jamie shifted uncomfortably. "I reckon it was from when I'd lit into him earlier about what he done t' Jenny."

"I don't believe I've heard about this confrontation. When did it occur?"

"A few days before, or thereabouts. Anyways, I guess he thought maybe I was gonna start in on him again because he got all red in the face and started in t' shoutin' at me, sayin' as how he was gonna call the constables on me. So I ran."

"You ran up Swallow Street?"

"Yes, sir. Only, he ran after me. He's hollerin', *Stop! Thief!* which weren't nothin' but a lie because I ain't stole nothin' from him. But me, I'm thinking there ain't no way anybody's gonna be takin' the word of somebody like me against the likes of him. I can see there's these three men standin' a ways farther up the street, and I know if I run up there, they're gonna grab me for sure. So when I spot that old archway, I'm thinkin' there'll be a passage through to King Street or somethin'. 'Course, I see real quick-like that it was a right stupid thing for me to 've done, on account of there weren't no way out. So there I am, trapped in this courtyard with Farnsworth comin' in after me. Only thing I can think t' do is duck into the chapel. I can see there's light comin' through a hole in the back wall and I'm thinkin' maybe I can squeeze through that. But it's kinda high up, and I'm still tryin' to climb that pile of rubble to get to it when he comes in after me."

Sebastian was aware of Hero sliding back into the room to take up a position just inside the door. "So what did you do?"

Jamie scrubbed one hand down over his face. "Well, I tried kickin' him away from me, but he just grabs me leg and drags me down, swearing at me somethin' awful and sayin' how he's gonna be shuttin' me up once and for all. So I kick him again, real good this time, and make a run for it. But I ain't even made it to the door when he grabs me by the arm and swings me around so's I go flying. I try to catch meself, but I can't, and I land smack on me back on the floor. Knocked the wind outta me, it did. So I'm layin' there, tryin' to catch me breath, and Farnsworth, he's smiling, 'cause he knows he's got me now. He brings up that fancy walking stick of his—ye know the one he always used to carry? And I realize it's got one of them little catches on the handle that ye push and it releases a blade."

Jamie fell silent, his head bowed. The girl beside him reached out to take his hand, and he held on to her tightly. It was a moment before he managed to force himself to go on.

"I was that scared, I was—so scared I could hardly move. Then I started scrabblin' around, trying to get up, and I whacks me hand against this big hunk of wood that's layin' there. So I grab it, and when Farnsworth comes at me with that knife, I hit him—just here." Jamie paused to lift his left hand to his head. Except instead of pointing to the left side of his head he reached across his face to touch above his right ear.

"And then what happened?" said Sebastian. There was no doubt in his mind that this part of the boy's tale, at least, was true.

Jamie squeezed his eyes shut and drew a deep, shuddering breath. "Me, I'm thinkin' he's gonna be comin' at me again fer sure. Only, when he staggered back, I guess he tripped over some of the stuff that's scattered all around there." The boy swallowed hard. "There was this big piece of stone there, ye see, and he hit the back of his head on it when he fell. It made the most awful sound, like somebody crackin' open a big ripe melon or somethin'. And then he just lay there."

"What did you do?"

The boy rubbed his eyes with a splayed thumb and forefinger. "I dropped that piece of wood so's I could grab that fancy little blade of his, and the walkin' stick it'd come out of, too. All I could think of was gettin' them away from him so's he couldn't come at me with 'em again. But then I took a better look at him, and I knew then he wasn't gonna be comin' at me again, that he was dead. So I ran."

"Still holding the walking stick and dagger?"

The boy nodded. "Yes, sir. And I grabbed that big chunk o' rock he fell on, too."

"Why?"

"I don't know why. I didn't even realize I still had 'em 'til I'd nearly reached the Strand. Threw them all in the river on my way over the bridge."

"And then you went to Father Ambrose?"

Jamie nodded again. "I'd worked myself up into something of a state by the time I got there, so it took Father a while to get out of me what'd happened. And then Father, he says to me that maybe I'm wrong, that for all we know, Lord Preston could've just got up and walked away by then, or maybe he's layin' there hurt. I kept sayin', *No, he's dead.* But Father, he says, *There's nothin' for it, Jamie; we're going to need to go and see. If he's hurt, he may need help.*"

Jamie paused, his head bowed, his chest heaving with the agitation of his breathing.

"Except Farnsworth was dead?" Sebastian said quietly.

Jamie nodded, his head still bowed, his gaze on the carpet at his feet. "Yes, sir. I says to Father, *What am I gonna do?* And Father, he says, *Let me think for a moment.*" Jamie swallowed hard. "Me, I'm just wantin' to get away from there as fast as I can. But Father, he says somebody might've seen Farnsworth chasing me—maybe those three men, or maybe somebody else. That scared me so much I thought maybe I was just gonna curl up and die right then and there. But Father, he says he's got this idea that's not only gonna make people think there's no way a boy like me could've had anything to do with killin' Farnsworth, but it's gonna be so strange that it'll get Bow Street t' lookin' in another direction entirely."

"'To view things from a different perspective,'" quoted Hero quietly.

Jamie looked up at her and nodded. "Yes, ma'am. That's exactly what he said. He said if we could get Bow Street to take a look at Farnsworth's life while they were trying t' figure out who killed him, then maybe they'd find out he'd been murderin' all those women—*and* find out who's been doin' it with him."

Sebastian drained the last of his wine, then stood for a moment simply holding the empty glass. He couldn't shake the feeling that something was being left out of this tale—something important. But the boy's story fit together far better than he'd expected it to. He said, "How did you and Father Ambrose know Farnsworth was killing young women?"

Jamie stared up at him, his jaw set hard, his nostrils flaring wide on a quickly indrawn breath.

Then the girl beside him cleared her throat and said in a hushed, broken voice, "I told them."

Chapter 55

She said her name was Bridget Daniels, and that she was fifteen years old. Her parents were dead, and she had been on her own for more than three years.

"After m' mother and da died," she told them, her head bowed and her hands twisting together in her lap, "I tried tattin' lace for a while. But I was never any good at it. So then I took t' sellin' apples in the streets. And when I couldn't make a go of that, I, well . . ." She shrugged one shoulder. "You know."

She had been fourteen when she gave birth to a premature baby girl who took one gasping breath and then died.

"I hadn't told nobody. Truth is, I didn't know what was happenin' to me for the longest time, and once I figured it out, I was too scared to say anything. But I was lucky because when the baby come, the landlady heard me screamin' and come up to see what was wrong. So she was there when my baby was born, and when they tried to accuse me of murderin' my own babe, she could tell them she saw my little girl die—that she was just too tiny to live. But they still hauled me up before the magistrates and sent me off t' the Bridewell for six months for concealin' a pregnancy. I didn't even know that was something they did."

She fell silent, a single tear rolling down her cheek before she brushed it away with a fist.

"When were you released?" Hero asked gently.

"Last month. Father Ambrose, he'd come to see me while I was in there, and then he tried to help me when I got out, to keep me from goin' back on the streets. But I . . . I just didn't think I *deserved* better, if you know what I mean? It was only a few nights later, when I was working the Haymarket, that this tall, skinny nob with blond hair comes up t' me. He's dressed all somber-like, in black, but I can tell his clothes are real fine. So me, I'm thinkin' he's gonna want to take me to the back room of a coffeehouse, like they do. But he says no, he likes doing it in alleys—says he thinks it's excitin'." She pulled a face. "Some nobs are like that, you know. So I think I know where he's takin' me. But as soon as we get around the corner, he wraps an arm around my waist and clamps his hand down on my mouth and starts dragging me toward this old carriage I can see sitting there in the shadows, like it's waitin' for us. So I bit his hand and was about to scream when he cuffs me on the side of the head so hard everything goes kinda black. When I come to, I'm in that carriage with a rag tied tight over my mouth, and we're pullin' into this dark lane."

"Do you know where you were?" asked Sebastian.

The girl nodded. "Yes, sir. We was down by the river, where all those warehouses and tenements burned a while back. As soon as we stop, this other cove gets off the box. At first I'm thinkin' he must be the coachman, but he weren't dressed like any coachman I ever seen."

"What did he look like?"

"He was a lot older than the first cove, gray-haired and kinda stout, but he had a kerchief tied over his nose and mouth so's all I could see was his eyes. I tried fightin' them, but they dragged me outta the carriage and through this archway into a queer old courtyard where I can see this *third* cove waitin' for us. He's standing beside some stone coffin-lookin' thing—sorta like you see in old churches, you know? And me, I'm trying to hang back, but they drag me across the courtyard. I can see that stone coffin-lookin' thing is full of water, and then I realize the cove standin' next to it is Lord Preston."

"How did you come to know him?"

She sniffed. "He was the bugger behind gettin' me sent to the Bridewell."

Sebastian was beginning to realize there was a pattern here. "But you didn't recognize either of the other two men?"

"No, sir."

"So then what happened?" asked Hero.

"Lord Preston, he takes the gag out of my mouth. I managed to scratch the side of his face while he was doin' it, but then he wraps his hand around the back of my neck and shoves my head under the water."

She drew a deep, shaky breath. "I fought like the bejesus. At one point I even managed to get my head out of the water long enough to grab a quick breath. But then that older bugger, he comes up to help, and together he and Lord Preston shove me back down under the water and hold me there."

She stared at the fire for a long moment, as if she were seeing again the moonlight dancing eerily through the churning water, feeling the strength of their hands on her body, hearing the disembodied, cultured voices of the men who were killing her. Then she swallowed and said, "I'd figured out by then that it weren't no use me tryin' to fight 'em. So I made myself go all limp and tried just holdin' my breath, hoping maybe they'd think I was dead and let me up. Then I guess I musta sorta blacked out or somethin', because the next thing I know, I can feel the breeze off the river against my wet face, and I can hear them laughing. They're *laughing*—laughing about how they've rid the world of another 'useless bloody whore,' and makin' fun of Lord Preston on account of how I'd scratched his face. One of them—I think it was the old bugger—he says, 'You need to watch those Irish wenches; they'll claw your eyes out if you give them a chance. Remember the last one—what was her name?' And the skinny cove, he says, 'Gallagher.' Then the first one laughs and says, 'That's right; Jenny Gallagher.' Then all three of 'em laugh again and Lord Preston says, 'It's difficult to keep them straight at this point.'"

She fell silent again, watching her fingers pluck at the worn cloth of her gown where it draped across her knees. "By then I could hear the rush of the river, and their footsteps started sounding hollow-like, and I knew they were takin' me out onto that abandoned old dock there. One of 'em takes me by the shoulders while the other has my feet, and Lord Preston, he goes, 'Heave-ho,' and they kinda swing me back before letting me fly forward again and letting go."

She looked up, her face pinched, her soft blue eyes haunted. "I managed to suck in a big gulp of air right before I went under. I wanted t' scream, but I knew I couldn't, so it was like I was screaming in my head—if you know what I mean? It was all I could do t' keep from clawing my way back up to the air, but I knew I couldn't let 'em see I was still alive. So I just let the river take me—take me away from them. When I couldn't hold my breath any longer, I had t' come up. But I was careful to only work at keepin' my head above water—I didn't dare try to swim at first 'cause I was afraid they'd see me. I can swim a little," she said proudly. "I grew up in Kent, and there was this old millpond near our cottage. But it weren't nothin' like tryin' to swim in that river. I thought I was gonna drown for sure. To tell the truth, I don't know how I managed t' make it to the riverbank. But then, when I hauled myself out and looked back, those men, they weren't even out on the dock anymore. I guess it didn't make no difference to them where my body went."

She fell silent again, her head bowed, her breath coming hard and fast.

Hero said quietly, "What did you do then?"

Bridget looked up. "At first, I was too scared t' do anything, ma'am, 'cept lay there coughing and cryin' and tryin' t' breathe. But I was wet through, and so cold I thought I might die if I didn't get movin'. I thought about goin' back to the room I was sharin' with some other girls, but then I realized I couldn't do that. I mean, those men knew I'd seen their faces—well, Lord Preston's and that other cove's. If they ever figured out I was still alive, they'd kill me—kill me for sure next time."

There was no point, Sebastian knew, in asking the girl why she hadn't gone to the authorities; who would have believed her? He said, "Where did you go?"

"To Father Ambrose. I knew he wouldn't tell nobody. But when he heard what those men had said about Jenny Gallagher, he said it would be a kindness if I could bring myself to let her brother know what had really happened to her. At first I didn't want to, but Father, he has a way of makin' you do things you really don't want t' do because he makes you see it's what's right. So, in the end, I did."

She glanced over at Jamie. "Father made him promise he wouldn't tell nobody. But Jamie, he said we couldn't just let Lord Preston and his friends go on killin' people, that we needed to stop 'em. And Father, he said Jamie was right. Only, I told Jamie he could accuse Lord Preston of killin' his sister all he wanted, but he couldn't say nothin' that'd let those men guess that one of the women they thought they'd killed was still alive."

"And you've been with Father Ambrose ever since?"

"Oh, no, sir. With Sister Anne Marie," she said. Then she sucked in a quick breath, her cheeks flaming with color as Jamie shot her a warning look.

"Ah," said Hero, glossing over that telling exchange. "I know Sister Anne Marie. She is very kind."

Bridget and Jamie stared at her. Jamie said, "You know her, ma'am?"

"Yes. She—" Hero broke off, a strange expression darkening her eyes. Then she changed what she'd been about to say to "She's a very interesting person" and left it at that.

"So who is this Sister Anne Marie?" Sebastian asked after they'd sent Bridget and Jamie off to the kitchens for something to eat.

Hero went to stand at the window, her gaze on a tinker in the street below. "She's a French nun who works with the poor. Mainly Irish and French Catholics, but anyone, really."

"A French nun?" repeated Sebastian.

Hero turned to look at him. "I know what you're thinking, but surely she can't be the woman they call Angélique. That was my first thought, too, but there must be hundreds of French nuns in this country, if not more. They're not visible because they're not allowed to wear their habits, but they're here, and Father Ambrose must surely know many of them."

"Anne Marie could be her religious name—the name she adopted when she took her vows—while Angélique is her birth name or a name she chose to use during the revolutionary years. How old is this Sister Anne Marie?"

"It's hard to say, really. Forty-five? Perhaps more. She's a very striking woman; she must have been beautiful when she was younger. But she's so gentle and good, I can't see her as a violent revolutionary."

"I don't think Angélique was a violent revolutionary. She was a nursing sister, and then she supported her brother's efforts to push through some desperately needed reforms. But the Bourbons had prevented reforms for so long that once the changes started, they lost control of everything and it turned into the stuff of nightmares."

"But how in the world does Angélique—whether she is Sister Anne Marie or not—fit into any of this?"

"That I can't begin to fathom. But Jamie obviously didn't want Bridget mentioning her."

Hero was silent for a moment. "From the sound of things, the 'stout old cove' is probably Sir Windle Barr, don't you think? Unless it's the Chief Magistrate of Bow Street himself."

"Sir Nathaniel Conant?" Sebastian considered this. "Yes, I can see that, too. Or even the clerk, John Stafford. The trouble is, there must be any number of affluent, stout older gentlemen in London who share Lord Preston's attitudes toward 'the frail sisterhood.'"

"But how many of them do you think Lord Preston was friendly with? So friendly that they would be comfortable killing together?"

"You have a point there."

"And the 'tall, skinny cove' is Mr. Crispin Carmichael?"

"I think it very likely," said Sebastian thoughtfully. "We need to find a way for Bridget to see him—without being seen herself."

Hero glanced at the clock. "It's Tuesday, isn't it?"

"Yes. Why?"

"I have an idea."

Chapter 56

One of Mr. Crispin Carmichael's many vanities was his singing voice. Having been blessed by his Creator with a clear, rich tenor, he made it a point to delight his parishioners every Tuesday and Sunday with evensong.

Arriving early, Hero ushered her charge into their pew and then slid in beside her. Given the short time available, it hadn't been easy to find a plain but respectable light blue gown that Hero was able to quickly adjust to fit Bridget's small frame. As much of the girl's flaming red hair as possible was tucked up under a modest, unassuming hat, and a short, dense veil hid her features. Bridget knew they thought she might see the "tall, skinny cove" at church, but they had been careful not to suggest that it was the vicar himself who was of interest.

"I ain't never been in a place like this before," whispered Bridget, her head turning this way and that as she watched Mayfair's residents file in. The church was filling rapidly, for the strange, inexplicable weather had begun driving more and more of even the most jaded members of the ton to seek comfort in their religion. "Everybody's so grand you'd think they was goin' to a ball or somethin'."

"Well, it's certainly a place to see and be seen," said Hero with a smile.

"Where's this cove you want me t' take a look at?"

"Just keep watching. And remember: If you do see him, don't say or do anything that might call attention to you."

"No, ma'am."

The girl watched intently as the choir trooped in to settle with much clearing of throats and rustling of music sheets. Then Mr. Crispin Carmichael himself arrived with a grand flourish, trailing silk, gold embroidery, and ostentatious holiness.

"Gor," breathed Bridget, watching the Reverend take his place. "Is he the English pope or somethin'?"

"No. He's simply the rector of this church."

"Oh. Well, he sure is grand, ain't he?"

Because of the veil, it was impossible for Hero to see the girl's face. But as Bridget watched the service in rapt fascination it became more and more obvious to Hero that the girl did not recognize the vicar of St. George's.

Afterward, as they joined the stream of parishioners leaving the church, Hero leaned in close to Bridget to say, "Did you see anyone—anyone at all—who resembled the man from that night?"

"No, ma'am."

"The Reverend is quite tall and thin," Hero said casually.

"Yes, ma'am. But he don't look nothin' like that cove. And he's *really* tall."

Hero looked at her. "The skinny man wasn't *really* tall?"

"Well, he was way taller than me, that's fer sure. And he was taller than the old bugger, too. But he weren't much taller than Lord Preston. He weren't even as tall as you are, ma'am."

"Oh," said Hero, radically readjusting her mental image of the man.

"His voice was different, too," Bridget was saying. "Sorta husky, but in a funny way, like he was trying to sound different from what he normally did."

"Perhaps he was deliberately—"

"Ma'am!" said Bridget with a gasp, grabbing Hero's arm.

"What? What is it?"

"That's him," Bridget whispered, her fingers digging into Hero's elbow. "There! In that black bombazine. I mean, I know it ain't a *him*, it's a her. But it's still *him*, I swear. And you see that cove she's talkin' to? I think he might be the old bugger! I know I didn't see his face, but he was all round-shouldered and dumpy-lookin', just like that."

Hero forced herself to turn casually and smile as she followed the direction of Bridget's gaze. And there was Sir Windle Barr, deep in earnest conversation with Lady Hester Farnsworth.

Chapter 57

"The problem is, we can't prove any of it," said Sebastian, later. "No jury is going to take the word of someone like Bridget Daniels over that of such worthies as Sir Windle Barr and Lady Hester Farnsworth—even if Bridget were willing to testify, which she is not."

"Can you blame her?" said Hero.

"No." He went to stand at the library window, his fingers drumming on the sill. Dusk was falling, bringing with it a mist that crept up from the river to curl through the darkening streets and wrap around the flickering oil lamps.

"Watching him," said Hero, "it's telling that Barr went out of his way to attend evensong tonight and speak to Lady Hester. You already suggested to him that Jenny Gallagher might have been killed. And if he's heard from Bow Street that there's talk several of the young women found in the Thames might not have been suicides—and I suspect he has at this point—then he may be getting nervous. Or Lady Hester is."

Sebastian turned to look at her. "I wonder if we can make them more nervous."

"Why? What do you think they'll do?"

"I'm not sure. But it might be interesting to find out."

Sir Windle Barr was seated beside his drawing room fire, a glass of brandy cradled in one hand and a heavy leather-bound book open on his knee, when Sebastian was shown in.

"Lord Devlin," he said, setting the book aside as he pushed to his feet. "This is an unexpected pleasure. Come in, come in; may I offer you some brandy?"

"Yes, please," said Sebastian. "My apologies for intruding on you at home at this hour, but I won't keep you long. I wanted your opinion of some information that has recently come my way."

"Of course; only too glad to help," said the magistrate, going to pour another brandy. He handed Sebastian the glass, then resumed his own seat, saying, "Sit down, please, and tell me what you've discovered."

"It's something that may help explain what happened to Lord Preston. It seems there is a belief in certain quarters that three men have been preying on London's lower-class women. Killing them. Now, I don't for a moment think that Lord Preston was actually doing anything of the sort, but there does appear to be increasing evidence that several women have been murdered and their bodies thrown in the Thames. So it's possible that Lord Preston was killed because someone thought he was one of those responsible. We're hearing that of these three individuals, one was approximately Lord Preston's size, one is described as tall and thin, and the other is older and rather stout. All three are believed to be gently born, although there is some suggestion that the taller man may in fact be a woman in disguise."

Barr sucked in a deep breath, his hand clenching around his brandy glass. Then he visibly relaxed and laughed out loud. "Good heavens. Wherever did you hear this nonsense?"

"Unfortunately, I'm not at liberty to say. But we do believe it is reliable."

"Indeed?" Barr drained his brandy. "And what does Bow Street have to say about this?"

"They're the ones who suggested I speak to you," said Sebastian, silently apologizing to the absent Sir Henry for the blatant lie. "You see, it's believed that all three individuals involved are residents of Mayfair."

"Oh, surely not." Barr pushed to his feet and walked over to where the brandy carafe stood on a side table. He poured himself another drink, then turned back to Sebastian. "What I'm about to tell you is in the strictest confidence, you understand?"

"Of course."

Barr settled in his chair again. "As it happens, I have been looking into a few things myself since our conversation the other day. It's my belief that if someone has indeed been murdering these soiled doves—and that's still an *if*, of course—then the killers are in all likelihood French republicans who've fled the Restoration of the Bourbon monarchy and are now here, working in alliance with our English Radicals. Their ultimate objective may be to use these murders to stir up the English poor, discredit the government, and eventually overthrow the British monarchy and our entire way of life."

"Oh?" Sebastian took a slow sip of his brandy. "What makes you think this?"

Barr leaned forward and dropped his voice as if imparting a secret. "There is one woman in particular—a Frenchwoman—whom we've been hearing about. It seems her brother was a regicide, and she herself actively supported him in his murderous campaign before coming to England. We've recently learned that she's here in London posing as a simple nun, and she has now been identified—just this evening, in fact."

Sebastian had to work hard to keep his reaction off his face. "Do you mean Angélique?"

Barr relaxed back in his chair. "Ah, that's right; I remember you were asking about her yourself a few days ago."

"And you say you've identified her?"

"Not me personally. But we work closely with representatives of the French Crown in these sorts of things, and they have proven themselves to be quite effective in cleaning up the remnants of their revolution who've sought to cause problems over here. Ironically, it turns out she's someone Preston long ago identified as a threat to our stability."

"Do you know her name?"

"I do, although of course I'm not at liberty to divulge it. But I have every confidence that she'll be taken care of soon." Barr's lips pulled back from his teeth in a hard smile as he glanced at the neoclassical clock on the mantel. "Quite soon."

Chapter 58

"You need to tell me where I can find Angélique," said Sebastian, leaning over the crude table where Father Ambrose sat with his hands folded together before him, the features of his face composed in a calm, untroubled expression. "Now."

They were in a cold, dank room deep in the bowels of Newgate Prison, with a single torch flickering on the wall and a turnkey with his arms crossed at his brawny chest waiting outside. The past twenty-four hours had taken a toll on the aged French priest. His clothes were torn, his lip split, his swollen left eye a deep purple. But his dignity and strength of purpose remained undiminished, and for a moment Sebastian didn't think the old man was going to answer him.

Then Father Ambrose sucked in a deep, ragged breath and said, "You truly believe she is in danger?"

"She is. But even if she weren't, do you seriously think I would betray her?"

The priest swiped a hand down over his tangled beard but remained silent.

"She's Sister Anne Marie, isn't she?"

Father Ambrose stared at him. "How did you know?"

"That doesn't matter now. What I don't understand is how she fits into all of this."

"Lord Preston hated her."

"Why? How did he even know about her?"

"He didn't, exactly. He hated Sister Anne Marie because of the work she does here now, helping poor women and children, but he didn't realize she's Angélique. That night—the night he was killed—she had Bridget with her. Bridget and Jamie, both. They were walking down Glasshouse Street when Farnsworth passed on his way to his rooms in Saville Street, and he saw them."

"He recognized Bridget?"

"He did, yes. He shouted at his hackney driver to pull up, then got out and came after them. He told Sister Anne Marie she was the devil's handmaiden, and then he grabbed Bridget's arm and started to drag her back toward his carriage. That's why Jamie kicked him. Bridget managed to pull away and run, so Farnsworth turned on Jamie."

"And chased the boy up Swallow Street?"

"Yes."

"You should have told me."

"I couldn't. The secrets were not mine to reveal."

Sebastian blew out a long, frustrated breath. "Tell me where I can find her. Now. Don't you understand? It could already be too late."

The priest drew a deep breath, then said, "She has a room in the house just to the north of the Catholic chapel."

"You mean the one behind Golden Square?"

"Yes."

The Catholic Bishop of London occupied two adjoining houses on Golden Square and had, at some point in recent years, built a small chapel in the houses' backyard so that it faced onto Warwick Street. There had been a time not so long ago when the British monarchy had subjected Catholic priests and nuns to hideous tortures and executions. But with the coming of the French Revolution, the British government found itself allied with the Catholics of France against the dangerous forces of republicanism and modernity. A Roman Catholic Relief Act was passed in 1791, repealing the penal laws that prohibited the saying of Mass and relaxing some of the strictures against Catholic priests and nuns, many of whom found refuge from the Revolution in the houses around Golden Square.

Rapping at the door of the rooming house to the north of the chapel, Sebastian waited impatiently. Then he pounded harder. And harder. He'd about decided no one was going to answer when the door opened and a woman's head appeared around the panels. *"Bonsoir, monsieur. Puis-je vous aider?"*

"Bonsoir," said Sebastian with a bow. "I'm looking for Sister Anne Marie."

The woman smiled and opened the door wider. Average in height, she was what the French call *d'un certain âge,* her hair just beginning to be touched by gray and her waist to thicken. *"Je suis désolée, monsieur,* but she is not here. She left a short while ago."

"Do you have any idea where she went?"

"Oh, *oui, monsieur.* A woman came, you see, asking for her help. It seems some tiny orphan has taken to hiding in the ruins of an old palace on the other side of the river. A girl, not much more than five or six, who speaks only French. The woman was hoping Sister could coax the child to come out so that they can help her."

"Thank you," said Sebastian. He was turning away when he felt a sudden frisson of alarm and stopped. "This woman—what did she look like?"

"She was about my age, monsieur, but tall and thin. Quite tall, with blond hair and—"

But Sebastian was already running for his curricle.

Chapter 59

The fog was thicker closer to the Thames, a ghostly white swirl that hovered low over the water and clung to the ancient brick chimney tops of the tumbledown houses of Southwark.

Leaving his horses with Tom near St. Saviour's, Sebastian slipped quietly into the mist-shrouded, burned-out ruins of the once-grand palace of the Bishops of Winchester. The palace—and the remnants of the mean tenements and warehouses that had been built in and around it over the centuries—sprawled along the river on both sides of Clink Street and stretched far back toward Borough Market. He had assumed at first that Barr and Lady Hester meant to kill Angélique the same way they had killed so many of the city's young, impoverished women: by holding her head underwater in that small, grim courtyard and then throwing her body in the Thames. But the more he thought about it, the more convinced he became that Barr, or Lady Hester, or whoever's idea this was wouldn't want the French nun's death to echo those earlier killings.

Although the fact they'd chosen to kill Angélique here, in the palace ruins, showed a distinct lack of imagination.

Desperately hoping he wasn't too late, Sebastian had to force himself to work his way slowly and cautiously through the piles of debris, the broken walls, the scattered stones, bricks, and charred lengths of ancient wood, lest a careless footfall betray his presence. With each step he listened intently, cursing the fog and the way it deadened all sound and obscured everything more than five feet before him. Then, for a brief moment, the mist eddied and he caught the dim glow of lantern light through the broken tracery of the Great Hall's ancient rose window.

Shifting closer, he heard a woman's voice, her words still carrying the inflections of her native France. "I don't understand," she said with admirable calm. "Why would you wish to kill me?"

"It would have been better if you'd brought the little redheaded harlot with you," said Sir Windle Barr, sounding almost bored. "But I don't suppose she'll be too hard to find with you out of the way."

Wishing like hell that he'd had time to swing by Brook Street for a pistol, Sebastian eased his knife from the sheath in his boot and crept along the hall's broken wall to where he could see three long, narrow shadows cast across the surrounding rubble by the light from the horn lantern someone had set atop a flat stone.

Dressed in a plain black gown with a high white collar that echoed the age-old habit of her order, Angélique stood with her head held high, her hands clasped before her as she stared at the round-shouldered, rather dumpy man some ten feet before her, the muzzle of his single-barreled flintlock pistol pointed unwaveringly at her. Lady Hester hovered off to one side, her palms cupping her elbows to draw them close to her sides, her face a tense mask.

"Ironically," Barr was saying as Sebastian eased closer, "the Frenchman who told me about the girl didn't even realize my interest in her. I considered simply letting him take care of you, but I trusted Hester here to induce you to bring the girl, too."

"I tell you, the girl wasn't there," hissed Lady Hester, her voice unnaturally high and tight.

"It's a pity," said Barr, pulling back the hammer of his flintlock.

"No!" shouted Sebastian, pushing to his feet and breaking into a run just as Barr swung the pistol toward Lady Hester and fired.

She let out a sharp cry, crumpling slowly. But the magistrate was already moving, his jaw tight with determination as he yanked a braided leather garrote from his pocket and leapt to loop the cord around the Frenchwoman's neck.

"We appear to be at a bit of an impasse," said Barr, drawing the garrote tight as he swung Angélique around, her hands coming up helplessly to her throat as he held her before him like a shield.

Sebastian drew up. "Let her go," he said.

"I think not." A hard smile curled the magistrate's lips. "If I let her go, that knife of yours will end up in my belly."

Sebastian shook his head. "No. But I can promise you this: If you kill her, I will kill you. Without hesitation."

The magistrate made a *tsk*ing sound. "What to do, what to do? Ah, I know. She can come with me—very slowly and carefully, do you hear, my dear?" He stooped to place his lips inches from the French nun's ear. "We shall back cautiously away from the decidedly lethal Lord Devlin here, to where my carriage awaits me at the end of Clink Street. Understand?"

The Frenchwoman's eyes met Sebastian's. He was reminded that this was a woman who had lived through some of the worst horrors of the French Revolution; who had tended a princess brutalized by her captors and then watched her own brother die beneath the blade of the guillotine before escaping over the Pyrenees to exile. For one telling moment, she held Sebastian's gaze. Then, letting her hands fall, she reached down and back, grabbed Barr by his testicles, and squeezed as hard as she could.

Sir Windle's eyes widened, his mouth sagging open and his breath leaving his chest in a pained *oof* as Angélique wrenched away from his hold and Sebastian stepped forward to drive his knife deep under the man's ribs with an expert upward thrust.

The garrote fluttering from his fingers, Sir Windle took one step, two, then collapsed. Sebastian watched him fall, watched his hands grope feebly toward the handle of the knife still embedded in his chest, then spasm and slide away.

Carefully crouching down beside the dying man, Sebastian slid an arm beneath Barr's shoulders and lifted his head.

"Stupid bitch," said Barr, looking up at him with pain-filled, stricken eyes. "How bad is it?"

Sebastian glanced down at the dark red blood pulsing out from around the knife still buried in the man's chest. "Bad."

Barr nodded and coughed up blood. "Thought so." His voice was broken, breathy; his tongue crept out to lick his dry lips. "Made a tactical error, didn't I? Telling you the Frenchman had found Angélique, I mean. Didn't think you knew who . . . who she was."

Sebastian shook his head. "Why shoot Lady Hester?"

"She was becoming . . . a threat. Too . . . frightened. Saying and doing stupid things. Telling you about Lamont. I thought . . . thought the nun would be easy enough to strangle. But Hester, she's a big woman. . . . Knew I had to . . . shoot her, kill her first. Was going to make it look like . . ." His face spasmed, his eyes beginning to roll back in his head.

Sebastian had to fight the urge to shake the man. "Why the bloody hell did you try to kill my wife?"

Barr drew a painful gasp. "Didn't. Guess you have another

enemy . . . someone you don't know about, hmm?" The ghost of a smile touched his bloody lips. Then he sucked in a rattling breath, and another. And as Sebastian watched, the light went out of his eyes and his chest stilled.

Sebastian lowered the man to the ground, surprised to see that his hands were smeared with the dead man's blood. He tried to feel something, but he was dead inside. And he found himself wondering if this was what the war had done to him and to so many others like him—made him dead inside at the time of a kill, so that he didn't feel whatever it was a person was supposed to feel when they took a life. So that the haunting shadows of endless torment came only afterward, in the darkest hours of the night. He was suddenly, almost painfully aware of the mist cool and damp against his face, of the stench of burnt black powder still hanging in the air and the distant slosh of the river against its bank. But inside, he was dead.

Wiping his hands on his breeches, he pushed to his feet and went to where Angélique now knelt beside Lady Hester, one of the woman's limp hands in her own.

"She's dead," said the Frenchwoman without looking up at him.

"Good."

Angélique—or Sister Anne Marie, he supposed he should think to call her—carefully lowered Lady Hester's hand and then settled back on her heels, her palms pressed flat against her thighs. "It would have been better if she could have had time to confess her sins and make her peace with God."

Sebastian hunkered down beside the dead woman. Barr's bullet had caught her square in the chest; she must have died almost instantly. "She wouldn't have," he said. "Confessed her sins, I mean."

"You can't know that."

Sebastian looked over at Sister Anne Marie. It was the first time he had taken a really good look at this woman who had for so long been only a name. She was built small and fine boned, with clear blue eyes, delicate, aristocratic features, and smooth skin. To see her, one might think her as young as thirty, except that having heard something of her history he knew she must be at least forty-five, if not more. "Perhaps not," he said. "Are you all right?"

"Yes." She touched one hand to her crushed high collar, then let it fall. "I am sorry you had to kill that man. For his sake, and for yours."

"It isn't—" Sebastian started to say, then broke off, his head turning as he caught the soft whisper of shoe leather rubbing against stone and the click of a hammer being carefully eased back.

"Get down!" he shouted, throwing himself at the Frenchwoman, knocking her flat. He felt the rush of a bullet passing his cheek, heard the rifle shot echo around the burned-out shell of the old medieval hall.

"Are you hit?" he said hoarsely.

"No, but—"

"Stay down!" he shouted, and pushed to his feet to take off at a run.

With no way of knowing if the shooter was alone, had a second weapon, or was standing his ground and calmly reloading, Sebastian ran in a zigzag, cursing the drifting fog as he raced down the length of the ruined hall.

He could hear the sound of running feet as the shooter fled. For a moment, the French assassin's lean, familiar figure appeared silhouetted against the mist as he darted through a jagged opening in one of the long, broken walls, his rifle still gripped in one hand. Then he was swallowed by the fog.

Sebastian tore after him. He could hear Cartier's stumbling progress across a rubble-strewn courtyard; saw him trip and catch himself as they raced, one after the other, through the ruins of a warehouse. Sebastian's leg was already howling with pain; under normal conditions the Frenchman would have been able to outpace him. But the night was dark and the ancient palace grounds dangerously littered with debris, forcing him to slow, while Sebastian had the night vision of a wolf.

He narrowed the distance between them to fifteen feet. Ten. Then the Frenchman caught his foot on something lurking unseen in the rank weeds and went sprawling, the rifle flying from his hands as he fell.

He came up fast, a dagger held in his fist as he crouched low and smiled. "Pity you left your knife in Barr's gut."

"Think that gives you an advantage, do you?" said Sebastian, snatching up a charred length of wood from the rubble at his feet.

Both breathing heavily, the two men circled each other warily, sizing each other up. Then the Frenchman lunged, his blade aimed at Sebastian's chest. Sebastian sidestepped nimbly, putting all his weight behind the blow as he swung his makeshift club at the assassin's head. He felt the impact reverberate up his arms to shudder his body, heard the *thwunk* of wood striking flesh and bone.

And the snap of something vital as the man's neck broke.

His head bowed, Sebastian was sitting on his rump in the rank weeds beside the man he had just killed, his arms propped on his bent knees as he waited for his heart to quit pounding and his breath to quiet, when he became aware of the woman who had once been known as Angélique walking toward him through the swirling mist.

"You are unhurt?" she said, her hands fisting in the black cloth of her gown as she drew up some feet away.

He looked up at her. "Yes."

She stared down at the dead man beside him. "I don't understand. Who is he?"

"You know Marie-Thérèse wants you dead?"

She met his gaze and said quietly, "I know."

He nodded to the Frenchman's motionless, blood-streaked face. "Since he's been operating in England, Monsieur Cartier here has been careful to make his killings look more natural—or at least easily explainable. But he's been finding it difficult to catch you alone, so I suppose he decided that, under the circumstances, one more body with a bullet in it wouldn't make a great deal of a difference." Sebastian paused, then said more gently, "They will send someone else, you know."

"Yes."

"You could leave. Emigrate to New Orleans, perhaps. They speak French there."

"No. My work is here." She hesitated a moment. Then she knelt in the rubble beside him, crossed herself, and bowed her head to pray for the man who had died trying to kill her.

And for the soul of the man who had killed him.

Chapter 60

"This is going to be . . . complicated," said Sir Henry Lovejoy sometime later, his hands braced on his knees as he leaned over to stare at Lady Hester's pale, waxen face and then twisted around to gaze at the nearby bloody sprawl of Sir Windle Barr. The dead Frenchman lay out of sight, beyond the Great Hall's shattered west wall.

"Yes," said Sebastian.

Lovejoy straightened to look at him. "Whatever were you doing here at this time of night?"

"I was told someone I needed to talk to was here."

"They set you up?"

"Not exactly."

The magistrate frowned. "I think you need to explain."

Wednesday, 28 August

Shortly before dawn, Sebastian awoke to the distant sound of barking dogs.

The bed beside him was cold. Turning his head, he could see Hero wrapped in a blanket and standing by the bedroom window, her gaze fixed straight ahead. In the light from the dying fire on the hearth he caught a faint glimmer of wetness left on her cheek by a single tear.

"Can't sleep?" he asked softly, going to her.

She rested her head against his, her back snuggling into his chest, her hands coming up to rest on his arms as he slid them around her waist to hold her close. "I keep thinking about those poor young women . . . how desperate and terrified they must have been. What a cruel, brutal way to kill." She fell silent for a moment, her chest rising and falling with her soft breathing. "They enjoyed it, didn't they? Lord Preston, Sir Windle, and Lady Hester, I mean. They *enjoyed* killing those women. Frightening them. Hurting them."

"I think so, yes."

She cradled one of his hands between both of hers and brought it up to press her lips to his palm. "I could have lost you last night."

"No," he said, and she chuckled softly at his arrogance.

She kept her gaze on the mist-swirled darkness beyond the window. "If Barr was telling the truth when he said he hadn't sent anyone to try to kill me, do you think it's possible Lady Hester is the one who was behind what happened the other day in Brewers Green?"

Sebastian considered this. "I suppose it's possible. But why would she go after you rather than me? She can't have been a very good judge of character if she imagined an attack on my wife would somehow cause me to stop looking into her brother's activities."

"There have been times in the past—mainly when I was conducting my interviews, although at other times, too—when I have felt as if someone were watching me. I've never said anything about it because I assumed I was mistaken—that I was simply being fanciful. But now . . . now I wonder."

He tightened his arms around her, holding her close. "You're the least fanciful person I know."

That made her smile. "Perhaps. Or perhaps I simply keep my worst flights of fancy to myself."

Late that afternoon, Sebastian walked with Sir Henry Lovejoy along Whitehall toward Charing Cross. The day had dawned cool but clear, with only a faint, pleasant breeze blowing from out of the south.

"I had an awkward interview with Lord Jarvis this morning," said the magistrate, his features carefully schooled into an unreadable mask.

"Oh?" said Sebastian. He himself had considered paying a visit on his father-in-law, then decided it would be better to wait until he felt less inclined to smash the big man's face in. "And?"

"To be frank, I had the impression he was more disturbed by the Frenchman's killing than by the deaths of Sir Windle and Lady Hester."

"That I can believe."

"Unfortunately, I suspect the Bourbons will simply send someone else."

"Yes."

Lovejoy sighed. "Incidentally, Lady Hester's abigail tells us that Lady Hester did indeed possess several suits of male clothing she would occasionally don to disguise herself when leaving the house with her brother late at night. We've also begun searching Sir Windle's home and office—discreetly, of course. So far the only thing we've found is this." Reaching into a pocket, he drew forth a deck of cards with familiar green, white, and red-patterned backs. "According to one of his colleagues, Sir Windle took them from a cartomancer he arrested last spring."

"And then used them to throw the blame for his own murders onto whoever had killed Lord Preston. He obviously didn't realize how rare they are."

"Indeed." Lovejoy tucked the cards away. "Needless to say, the Palace has decreed that the public must never be allowed to know that the chief magistrate of one of our most prestigious public offices has been murdering young women in concert with a duke's brother and sister."

"So how does the Palace intend to explain that illustrious trio's deaths? By blaming the Frenchman? How very convenient."

"It is, isn't it? Of course, rather than being acknowledged as a tool of the Bourbons, Monsieur Cartier will be recast as a rabid republican."

"Of course. And Father Ambrose?"

"Will be released, hopefully by tomorrow."

"Good," said Sebastian. He was silent for a moment, his gaze on the bedraggled mess the weather had wrought on the Privy Garden beside them. "I wonder how many women they killed."

Lovejoy shook his head. "I don't see how we'll ever know. How ironic that it may be Lord Preston's sensational death that finally convinces Parliament to create the centralized police force he always wanted."

Something about the way the magistrate said it caught Sebastian by surprise. "It's what you've always wanted, too, isn't it?"

Lovejoy looked vaguely troubled. "It is, yes . . . in principle. Except I must admit to having serious misgivings about the direction these more recent proposals are taking. I'm all in favor of replacing the current parish-based system of aged night watchmen with a central force of fit, healthy men. I'd also like to see the establishment of a criminal investigative division—something along the lines of what Vidocq has created in Paris." The suggestion of a smile tugged at his lips. "Although I realize it's something of a heresy to suggest that we use the French as a model. And unfortunately, that's not what they're talking about. Basically, they want to use their new police force to change the way the poor of this country live, outlawing everything from costermongers and Punch and Judy shows to street musicians and ballad singers. They have this idea that if they empower a phalanx of men in uniform to watch people—meaning poor people, of course—and arrest them for any and every minor moral infraction, then major crime will simply disappear."

"You don't agree?"

"No, I don't. I can't believe that allowing hardworking men to drink on Sundays or a blind man to earn money by playing his flute on a street corner is going to somehow lead to them deciding to break into other people's houses to steal their silver."

"Well, it's definitely easier to arrest couples for kissing in dark corners than to chase down thieves who've looted a warehouse when you weren't looking."

Lovejoy sighed. "That it is. And as if all that weren't bad enough, they're also talking about taking away magistrates' investigative responsibilities and turning the office into something strictly judicial."

"So who would be investigating murders and thefts?"

"The assumption is that putting uniformed police on the streets and arresting people for the least little infraction will lead to such crimes magically disappearing."

"And this idea came from a man who was quietly murdering any number of young women he'd arrogantly decided didn't have the right to live."

"Telling, I suppose," said Lovejoy, his gaze drawn to the fading old houses and offices clustered around a nearby ancient courtyard known as Scotland Yard. "Have you by chance seen Major Chandler?"

"This morning, yes." Hugh and Lady Tess had both come to thank Sebastian and, in Lady Tess's case, to apologize. "He and Lady Tess are looking into buying a house in Italy. They plan to live there once the legalities surrounding the reversion of her dowry are completed."

"Wise. I suspect many will continue to believe them guilty no matter what the official verdict is." He paused. "The one thing I still don't understand is why Barr killed Letitia Lamont."

"I can only think that she must somehow have suspected what he and Lord Preston were doing and was unwise enough to say something to him after her release from the Bridewell."

"Yes, that makes sense. But why go after Lady Devlin?"

"I don't think Barr was behind that."

Lovejoy drew up and swung to face him. "Then who was?"

Sebastian met his friend's troubled gaze and shook his head. "I wish I knew."

Friday, 30 August

On a gloriously warm, sunny afternoon two days later, Sebastian was descending the front steps toward his waiting curricle when he noticed Father Ambrose walking toward him, with Jamie reluctantly trailing a pace or two behind.

"We've come to thank you for all that you've done," said the priest, pausing at the base of the steps. "To thank you, and to apologize for our failure at times to be as honest with you as we might have been." He nudged the boy beside him. "Isn't that right, Jamie?"

The boy hung his head and nodded. "Yes, sir. I'm ever so sorry, sir."

"Please, won't you come in?" said Sebastian. "Have some tea, perhaps? Or would you prefer a glass of wine?"

The French priest shook his head. "No. Thank you, but we don't want to keep you." He squinted up at the blue sky above. "It's a rare fine day, yes?"

"Yes," said Sebastian. "Rare, indeed."

"Perhaps the rumors of our earth's impending doom are exaggerated?"

Sebastian gave a soft laugh. "Hopefully. Are you quite certain you won't come in?"

"No, we must be going." Man and boy started to turn away; then the priest stopped, his hand coming up to his forehead. "Ah, I almost forgot: Have you heard anything more about the Maréchal McClellan?"

Sebastian felt an ache deep within his chest. "No. Why?"

The priest nodded, as if he had expected as much. "It's my understanding he has gone to Egypt."

"Egypt?"

Father Ambrose nodded again. "The pasha there, Muhammed Ali, is intent on modernizing his army and is looking to the veterans of our recent wars to assist him in that aim. By not joining Napoléon on his disastrous return from Elba, the Maréchal managed to preserve his reputation intact. I'm told the pasha is delighted to have him."

Sebastian felt a rush of relief that caught him by surprise. "You know, you never did tell me how you happen to hear these things."

But the French priest simply rested his forefinger beside his nose and winked.

Author's Note

Known as the Year Without a Summer, 1816 was a time of bizarre weather abnormalities. The floods, crop failures, riots, strikes, mutinies, and widespread apocalyptic fears described here were real, as were the concerns that rising prices and increasing starvation might provoke a new wave of revolutions across Europe. One of the things that makes this period so fascinating is that, at the time, people knew little about their planet and could not begin to understand what was happening. That the sun was dying and the end of the world was upon them seemed a very real possibility and engendered a pervasive sense of terror.

The theory Lancelot Plimsoll comes up with here to explain the strange weather is fundamentally correct, although to my knowledge no one at the time advanced it. By 1816, London was aware of the eruption of Mt. Tambora in what was then called the Dutch East Indies (at the time it was temporarily under British rule as a result of the recent war but would soon be given back as part of the Liverpool government's budget slashing). Yet no one seems to have connected that distant, massive volcanic explosion to the deadly worldwide climate shifts that followed—or to the brilliantly colored sunsets immortalized by painters like William Turner. It was only in the early twentieth century that an American meteorologist named William Humphreys first suggested that volcanic dust and ash could cool the climate, and it wasn't until the nuclear weapons tests of the 1950s—which also drove fine dust up into the stratosphere—that the idea gained much credence. Computer simulations, plus monitoring of the eruption of Mount St. Helens in 1980, led to the theory's general acceptance. Since then, studies have linked a number of turning points in history to climate disruptions caused by volcanic activity, including the mysterious Bronze Age Collapse in the Mediterranean. Mt. Tambora is believed by many to be the largest known volcanic eruption in the last 2,000 years (although some say it was the second largest); it was ten times more powerful than Krakatoa and a hundred times more powerful than Mount St. Helens.

The loss of life caused by the eruptions of Mt. Tambora, its tsunami, and the starvation and disease that followed are difficult to tally. It is estimated that something like 90,000 people died in the Dutch East Indies alone. Disruption of the monsoon season caused extensive crop failures and starvation in various parts of Asia and is believed to have contributed to the massive cholera outbreak there. British soldiers then carried the disease around the world, killing hundreds of thousands and introducing cholera to Britain. Floods and widespread starvation in Europe killed an estimated 200,000 more and contributed to the continuing political unrest. Another 60,000 starved to death in British-occupied Ireland. Africa, the Middle East, and Latin American also suffered. The massive crop failures in the United States spurred tens of thousands to leave their farms along the Eastern Seaboard and push west. And on the shores of Lake Geneva, a group of literarily inclined friends took shelter in their rented villa from the ominous, endless rains and entertained themselves by writing some rather dark stories and poems. One of them, Mary Shelley, penned *Frankenstein*; Lord Byron composed his poem "Darkness"; while the young novelist John Polidori was inspired to later write *The Vampyre* (which in time led to Bram Stoker's *Dracula*).

For more on how the world reacted to this period of dramatic climate disruption, see *The Year Without Summer* by William K. Klingaman and Nicholas P. Klingaman.

The character Lancelot Plimsoll was loosely—*very* loosely—inspired by William Smith, an Oxfordshire blacksmith's son turned surveyor, canal builder, and mapmaker. It was Smith who first realized that the deep layers of mineral deposits he could see in mine shafts—and the fossil records they contained—formed a consistent, predictable pattern that could be traced across Britain and beyond. His observations and analysis enabled him to single-handedly produce, in 1815, the first true geological map of Great Britain (or of any country, for that matter); his work on fossils and their evolution helped lay the foundations for Charles Darwin's later discoveries. Simon Winchester's *The Map That Changed the World* is a fascinating look at both Smith and the ignorance and prejudices of his time that he struggled against.

For the devastating economic and social repercussions of Britain's rapid demobilization after Waterloo, see Evan Wilson's *The Horrible Peace: British Veterans and the End of the Napoleonic Wars.* Daniel Philip Resnick's *The White Terror and the Political Reaction after Waterloo* is a good source for events in France in the aftermath of the second Bourbon Restoration.

The Society for the Suppression of Vice really did exist and it was, if anything, even more obnoxious than portrayed here. Like

Sir Nathaniel Conant, who was indeed a member of the Proclamation Society that preceded it, the Society believed that crime could all be traced back to the evil influences of loose women, drinking, swearing, and failure to observe the Sabbath. Sir Nathaniel earned his knighthood and the plum position of Chief Magistrate at Bow Street by cooperating with the Regent's nasty investigation into his wife, during which a variety of individuals were bribed into testifying that Princess Caroline had given birth to one of the orphans she adopted.

Both Sir Nathaniel and Robert Peel (who at the time of this book was off driving up the death toll in Ireland and beefing up his résumé by serving as Chief Secretary there) had long agitated for the creation of a centralized London police force. The Metropolitan Police Force they envisioned finally came into being in 1829. As Lovejoy feared, its focus was on policing the manners of the lower classes; much of what characterized life on the streets in Regency England was outlawed, helping usher in the dour, repressive days of the Victorian Era. Ironically, the Met initially lacked a detective force to solve actual crimes, an omission that wasn't remedied for a surprising number of years. And as Lovejoy also feared, magistrates' age-old investigative responsibilities were completely taken away, thus turning the office into something strictly judicial.

The journalist Barnabas Price is fictional, but he was loosely inspired by Richard Carlisle, a Radical journalist targeted by the Society for the Suppression of Vice. Outraged by the economic hardships of 1816, Carlisle became increasingly interested in politics and published several different Radical newspapers. Both his wife and his sister went to prison for continuing to print his paper while he was in prison. He died in extreme poverty.

The powerful twelfth-century Bishop of Winchester who originally built the opulent palace on the south bank of the Thames was the brother of King Stephen. Because the area (long known as the Liberty of the Clink) was outside the jurisdiction of both London and the county of Surrey, various activities forbidden within the jurisdiction of the city—such as theater—flourished there. This was the site of William Shakespeare's Globe, bear baiting, gaming hells, and whorehouses. Shakespeare mentions the Winchester Geese in *King Lear.*

The crude Cross Bones burial ground Sebastian visits still exists. There was an attempt to build on the land several years ago, but an energetic outcry by activists managed to save it.

Winchester Palace was turned into a prison for Royalists during the Commonwealth and sold to a developer. Although returned to the bishops after the Restoration, it was found to have seriously deteriorated and was eventually sold to a different property developer. Rather than being torn down, the palace was broken up into a warren of tenements and warehouses. When a fire swept through the area in 1814, it exposed many of the palace's old walls. The palace then stood in ruins for several years until eventually much of what was left was torn down. Today, little more than the west wall of the palace's grand twelfth-century Great Hall with its enormous rose window (added slightly later) survives.

The German printer Ferdinando Gumppenberg arrived in Milan from Munich in 1809, bringing with him the German tradition of commissioning decks from various illustrators and engravers. Some of his tarot decks and playing cards were simple stencil-colored woodcuts, but others were printed from exquisite copper engravings. He is probably best known for the "Della Rocca" tarot (commissioned from the artist Della Rocca and sometimes also called the "Tarocco Sopraffino"), as well as a famous neoclassical deck from 1810 and the "Corona Ferrea" deck, which used images from the history of the Lombard Iron Crown. Some of his decks have not survived, and I have taken the liberty here of imaginatively re-creating one by an artist "Giorgio Bassano."

The Italian tricolor flag was first officially established in the short-lived Cispadane Republic in 1797; Napoléon then made Milan the capital of his Kingdom of Italy. When the Austrians seized Milan in May of 1814, it was placed under the governance of Field Marshal Heinrich von Bellegarde before being annexed back into the Habsburg Empire as a province after the Congress of Vienna.

The memento mori carried here by Lord Preston Farnsworth was inspired by a similar watch now in the Louvre. It dates to the seventeenth century and was made by Genevan watchmaker Jean Rousseau—ancestor of the troubled philosophe Jean-Jacques Rousseau. Mary, Queen of Scots, is said to have carried a similar piece.

The marital and legal entanglements of Lady Charlotte Cadogan (daughter of the Earl of Cadogan), her husband Henry Wellesley (brother of the Duke of Wellington), Lord Paget (son of the Earl of Uxbridge), and Lady Caroline Villiers (daughter of the Earl of Jersey) provide a good illustration of British law at that time. Only Parliament could grant a divorce, and passing an act through Parliament was expensive. In England, a man could obtain a divorce on the grounds of his wife's adultery, but a woman could not. So while Wellesley was able to divorce Lady Charlotte, Paget could not divorce his own wife (since she had not committed adultery), and as a woman she was not legally able to divorce him for adultery. However, when Caroline fell in love with one of Paget's friends and wanted to marry him, the Pagets found a work-around by moving to Scotland. Under Scottish law, a woman could sue her husband for divorce for adultery. So the Pagets arranged for him to be "caught" in bed with a "whore" (actually her ladyship in disguise); she then divorced him and married the Duke of Argyll, which left Paget free to marry Charlotte. Between his two wives, Paget had eighteen children.

In 1818, when a lovely organization called the Society for the Suppression of Mendicity was formed, the reformed Paget (by that point a war hero and a marquis) became one of its vice presidents. This society would round up beggars and investigate them to see if they were truly impoverished or a part of the "undeserving poor." The undeserving were sent to prison.

There was no 25th Regiment of Hussars or Light Dragoons in the Napoleonic Wars, which is why I chose to have that be Sebastian's regiment.

What is now Savile Row was in Sebastian's time called Saville Street. The expression "crazy like a fox" is not recorded until later in the nineteenth century, but it sounds like something Sebastian might have said. And, finally, the 20,000 pounds Hugh Chandler was forced to pay would be the equivalent of more than 2,600,000 pounds today.